12 SF[...] 3

The General

The General

A Novel

STEPHEN LONGSTREET

*America is a country which has grown
by the leap of one hero past another.*
—NORMAN MAILER

W. H. ALLEN · London
A division of Howard & Wyndham Ltd
1975

First British edition, 1975

Printed and bound in Great Britain by
The Garden City Press Limited, Letchworth, Hertfordshire SG6 1JS
for the publishers, W. H. Allen & Co. Ltd,
44 Hill Street, London W1X 8LB

ISBN 0 491 01853 3

This book is dedicated

to

Edward T. Chase

Who saw merit in the work

and assisted strongly

This novel is wholly a work of fiction and its people are not to be taken as portraits of anyone living or dead. In a few places where actual people from the past appear, they do so under their true names. Chapters 12 and 13 contain some material I acquired while working with its author on the as yet unpublished Memoirs of W. W. Windstaff.

Book One

It was the saying of Bion, that though the boys
throw stones at frogs in sport, yet the frogs do
not die in sport but in earnest.

—PLUTARCH

(From Simon Copperwood's notebooks)

Chapter 1

MORNING,
An old man

Asleep. Something kindly and defenseless about a face that when awake is always guarded and a façade.

Someone enters to wake him.

The old coot, the intruder thought—the feisty old coot sure looked a hell of a lot younger asleep—no shame in living, not afraid to laugh—asleep, a hell of a lot younger than his years. Sleeping there in the mustard and lilac-colored light that snuck in past the pleated bedroom drapes. Yes, he sure did sleep deep, thought Master Sergeant Jake (for Jacob) Waitley (for the great-grandfather who took the name of the man who bought him in Charleston for six hundred dollars as a ricefield hand).

Well, old man, don't fight time, it's a lost battle.

Jake Waitley held steady the silver tray with the two-ounce shot glass of bourbon, held it to one side, and with his free hand pulled back a drape so the sunlight came in, cruel, bone-white, to make the sleeping man twitch, creasing his face. Jake looked down on the weathered features again as they settled back in sleep. Handsome dog still, sure, worn down maybe, but all his own teeth and a lot of hair left, salt-and-pepper maybe, the neck wattled some—not a turkey buzzard's neck yet. But he was old, oh he *was* old, not young like the newborn flies on the back porch. The sergeant gave a snorting chuckle, not loud. The tray was steady, balanced on the outspread black hand, the three fingers of Jim Beam bourbon amber-yellow with highlights. Just one more of the million morning-trays he'd brought the sleeper, like he were King Nebuchadnezzar in that there Babylonia.

"General." The sergeant in overwashed, starched Army garb smiled as he bent low to repeat it louder, closer to the scarred left ear. "General."

He was a big man, the sergeant, middle-aged, a mahogany-

[3]

colored Negro—he hated the new word "black"—pockmarked or battle-scarred cheeks, it was hard to tell which. Regular features, with a long, thin, aristocratic Sephardic Jew nose (some said), a thin slit of a mouth, eyes dark-blue, a thatch of white hair clipped short. A thirty-years-in-the-Army man—a "lifer" the term was. The sleeper scowled as the contour of dreams became erased—he clicked his teeth, seemed to be muttering a curse as the black sergeant slapped the back of his free hand across the sleeper's naked shoulder, almost a karate blow.

"General, open them eyes."

The sleeper's mouth moved under the triangle of neat mustache, a pampered growth, just a bit too long; the mouth made some angry twitches, aggravated, yet procrastinating, resisting awakening. The breath snorted in protest from a nose once, or more times than once, broken, but resurrected by surgeons, still handsome for all its battered condition. No ordinary nose, the sergeant felt, big, yes, a bit oversized. . . . Sure no ordinary blower, thought Jake Waitley, stepping back, the bourbon glass on the silver tray setting up a rolling motion of its contents. . . . Querulous, but he's coming round. The eyelids of the sleeper fluttered. Jake made as much noise as possible, shooting back the rest of the drapes, banging a chair against a baseboard. He'll chew my ass out for sure. The strong Virginia sunlight poured in. Jake always thought of Virginia sunlight as made for the cocksmen fox hunters, and the red oaks sooted with Washington's smog as having a special color—gin with a touch of Angostura bitters.

The sunlight caught the awakening general rolling around a bit, making fistlike gestures with his hands, kicking some of his toes against the light, silk-trimmed brown blanket that covered the long lean body.

"Jake, you noisy bastard," said a voice deep in the general's throat. The sunlight made sharper the details of the large—too large—but neat bedroom, the antique early American furnishings polished like a prize horse at a show, the carvings on the teak headboard of the bed showing various fruit and wheat and corn, cut deep into the wood a long time ago. Old blue Delft china on the fireplace, polished brass lamp bases, leather-bound books, their spines saddle-soaped.

The general shivered, as if remembering some tenacious, mean bit of dream. His eyes opened, closed, opened again in a wary manner, then moved into an unfocused stare. Hazel-brown eyes flecked with gold when they were at last ordered to stay open. The hard-muscled yet sensual mouth under the mustache fluttered, the throat cleared itself of something that sounded like pebbles rattling on a brook bottom and turned into a roar.

"You dog robber, I told you never to touch me when I sleep. Had an aunt used to wake me sticking her thumb in an ear." The voice was friendly, casual, amused, only a thin edge of annoyance. "Never take away a man's sleep. Only time he feels at home in his skin."

"This is *der Tag*, sir," said the sergeant grinning, offering the tray. "Here you are, sir, to cut the morning slimes."

It was an old line, once amusing, now part of a ritual.

They were wary of each other; the general felt Jake knew too much, much too much of the soft underbelly that was covered by the armor the general had built for himself over the years. And Jake knew his job was easy pickings, no use rubbing the old coot the wrong way.

The general's hand fumbled at the night table for a heavy, butter-gold watch and chain, a watch resting by some books, a flashlight, several loose-leaf notebooks holding irregular sheets, some showing looping hens' tracks of a bold but hard to read handwriting.

"Hell—it *that* late?"

The hand, brown-spotted, heavy-veined, seeming older than the face already taking on its role for the day—the hand reached for the tot of whisky. He knocked it back into his throat with one pleasured gesture, swallowed, sucked on his teeth, and said softly in an irrelevant aside, "Christamighty. That's good whisky." Jake grinned. When the old coot he goes to talking cheerful on waking—look out.

In the full light the general looked his age. He was sixty-eight. He glanced up at Jake Waitley and saw the grin on the big Negro's face and said, *"Der Tag,* eh?"

My birthday, thought the general; look at the grinning bastard. He knows I'd kick his ass after all the years we've been together if he said "Happy Birthday, sir." No sense of culmination and peace, just a mess of unsorted memories. Hell. *Der Tag*. Got to get hold of myself and face up to something today. Goethe said it as *Dichtung und Wahrheit*—fiction and truth—the old Heinie knew.

"General, we gotta hurry."

The general laughed. He had a good barking laugh when happy, a delight in the savory aspects of living. Yes, he thought stretching; *der Tag*, right on him like a punch in the nose. He sat up in the bed, enjoying the good bourbon aftertaste. "Jake, they can't start any ceremony without us. We've got them by short hair there."

He stretched again his long, thin yet still muscled arms and looked out the nearest window. Expensive Virginia country landscape with good care of the trees—costly as brain surgery —too-green grass. But goddamn it, look at how close the newly widened highway is to the old house. The mystery is why I stay on. In the end you come down to what that addled Joan of Arc in pants, Charlie de Gaulle, said to you one day just before he kicked out NATO: "There can be no power without mystery. There must always be a 'something' which others cannot altogether fathom, which puzzles them, stirs them, and rivets their attention. . . ."

It doesn't go as the old Greeks had it that that which a man most loves shall in the end destroy him. No, no, not *this* morning, no digging in the deposits of the past or remembering the dead. Damn it—how many people I've known, and all dead, or senile, or behind a high wall. Give yourself sufficient introspection and you'll remember every corpse, every fresh kill, every mistake in battle. Better take my shower. Not let Jake dent my legend of infallibility . . . just whistle the old tune and try and remember the words when I was DCSPER—Deputy Chief of Staff for Personnel—trying for action on D-Day with the MOS.

> No retreat, no retreat
> They must conquer or die
> Who have no retreat retreat . . .

From the *Beggar's Opera*, yes, I saw it with that English girl,

[6]

Shivaun, breasts like a fat lady's knees, and we had come out humming the tune and gone to bed at the Claridge, two nights before D-Day, while her husband—that Navy patrician, with a nose like a sleeping reptile. . . . Yes, he suspected that I had been bedding his wife—a liaison Shivaun had called it. And the poor bastard gone down in the Channel with a part of his portable harbor, gone down in a storm. And Shivaun? Lord, the geography of that marvelous body. Went back, she did, to those Irish acres in Mayo in the Far West. Casual sex, unlike light conversation, is not a waste of time. Now? And he? Here he was on *der Tag*—in his house near this highway pointing the fat cats to the Senate, to the Pentagon, Joint Staff of the Army General Staff, and the lobbyists, all with heavy breakfasts, going to their dirty trade. Wish I were hungry, wish I had an appetite like when I got to CUMUSMACV—Vietnam, and chewed out all the chickenshit colonels fresh from command and General Staff College at Leavenworth.

Look now at Alexandria, Virginia, outside my window, creeping to enfold this old wreck of a house. Out there the new rows of trashy ranch-type boxes, trashy but costly developments for the higher placed Civil Service hotshots or loafers, ulcer boys or goofoffs, sweaty bureaucrats and the permanent political hjngers-on. I don't, (ah, me!) love the human race this morning.

"My father-in-law," the general said to Jake Waitley, "inherited it—this was his house once. He gave it to my wife. He always said the country was going to hell in a hack. Know what a hack is, sergeant?"

"You tell me again, general. Now git out of the bed. Captain Wystan is getting the medals out of the bank vault."

"Screw the medals. I'm not wearing them. Medals—wore my set here the night my father-in-law gave us this house, when I married the last Mrs. Copperwood. I was the new son-in-law; the house was already old. I was only a low-rank two-star then. I felt one believes in the necessity of what one does, or its usefulness."

"I was a fiddle-footed recruit then, sir. Rather eat Army pork chops than have a hundred dollars."

The sergeant casually let one thick thumbnail, shaped like a tiny turtle-shell, tap on the bottom of the silver tray. "The TV people, the Pentagon brass are all busting out for you. The

[7]

White House first, for the presenting of the presentation. Can't keep *him* waiting."

"Him!" The general sat up, anger made a brisk circulation of his bloodstream. He sat up in introspective silence for a moment; he slept naked. As he handed back the empty shot glass, he looked up at Jake Waitley, looked with that hooded eagle's stare. His field inspection stare, 20 below. Jake Waitley had a sassy, lippy streak and mostly it amused him. But not this morning.

The sergeant went to turn on the shower in the blue-tiled bathroom opening off the bedroom's west wall. The general, with a quickening perception of the bright day, put on his worn Kabuki actor's robe that he preferred to the newer robes in his wardrobe, gifts from women mostly—affection and nostalgia. His horn-rimmed glasses lay by the books with which he fought nightly insommnia. A stray, stained volume of Pepys' *Journal* picked up in the ruins of Hamburg, the fourth volume of Gibbon's *Decline and Fall of the Roman Empire*, one of Stendhal's volumes on Rome, also Gray's 1836 *Manual of the Botany of the Northern United States*.

The Army—how did it stand today? he thought as he committed the morning indecencies in the bathroom. A bit costive. Prostate touchy. All the perceptions and changes taking place. But how do you climb over the bland harmonizers at the desks, and the obsolete combat leaders in the war colleges who still teach 1939 tank battles on the Polish plains? The best men are the colonels who never make general. So, so what will happen today? The final throw of the dice for four-star General Simon Bolivar Copperwood—a little more activity, *or* decrepitude and death. Four stars to five, to be General of the Armies, or slowly not so slowly fade away. Dismissed.

The general dropped the robe as the sergeant came in with fresh towels, and he began to recite to himself Psalm 91, which he had been forced to learn as a boy. "You shall not fear the terrors that come by night; nor the arrow that flies by day; nor the evils prepared in the shadows; nor the demon that destroys in the noonday sun. . . ."

Well, in the noonday, he'd face the chowderhead. As always anticipation of some crisis made him horny. He smiled. Sex is, after all, the closest thing to religion—the complete and total saturation of self in a mystery. . . .

He stepped into the shower.

The general saw himself in the full-length bathroom mirror, just a glimpse as it fogged up. Lean gut, flat belly, hairy as an ape, good legs for all the silver fuzz on the barrel chest and around the genitalia. Still well hung. Margerie had put in that mirror to parade in front of it.

But Holy Joseph and Mary—he was getting shorter. Was six-three back at the Point as a plebe in 1916, and now the medical-major quack at Walter Reed said I'm only six-one-*and*-a-half now. ("It's natural, General Copperwood, just natural as one ages that the cartilage between our vertebrae shrinks a bit, you see. We lose our height. Your heart is good, a bit fast, but strong. It's not a young heart we have there, is it, general? Let's remember that.")

Our. We. It takes a lot of medicine to make even a bad doctor.

The popinjay going to retire me today at the honoring ceremony? Was the C-in-C going to grandstand, give the Judas smile and then zap me in the East Room? Pinning some fancy bronze and colored ribbons on me, that smile turned on full voltage. Then the cold-fish handshake. And? *Yes* or *no? In* or *out?* Do I get the fifth star, General of the Armies, *or*, Well done, old soldier, go out to grass. As Pliny put it: "There is nothing certain but uncertainty."

It was enough to make one with deliberate intent get out the Colt .45 from the old chest of drawers and blow a Hemingway through my head. Today, maybe, maybe, he'd *have* to add that star. The press, certain newspapers, the proper corporation heads of the defense industry who contributed; they were pressing, passing the word, dialing the right numbers. But there were all the antagonists, depreciators—those who wanted a blindfolded nation.

It isn't as if I haven't earned it. Look at my body, the ugly scars of field medics and boozy surgeons. Search attitude-reports, my files in the subcellars of the Pentagon. Not that they don't have a lot against me. Those times, those things when you make enemies. The last three boarders in the White House had pro-

[9]

moted a lot of crap artists, fancy stumblebums to big commands; but held off that last star for me.

They can't just kiss me off. There are only a few real soldiers left for high place. There had always been a shortage of monomaniac military genius. Since the Civil War. Omar Bradley, of course, a little monkey of a great talent in the field and over the maps, a fistful of real madmen of splendid abilities, men like Mac and Patton, maybe me even better. At sixty-eight I can't be modest. So I'm as addled as old Pearl-Handled himself. But now the Kingdom of Heaven is defended by missile sites. And nobody could have the super sixteen-jewel superego of old Mac chewing his corncob pipe stem with the fervor of a crackpot martyr. No more Lees or Grants, Jacksons, even Shermans in my day.

"A big breakfast, Jake. A steak."

Chapter 2

"CUT off the phone, Jake," said the general, tingling from toweling and still damp from his shower.

"The whole thing is still top secret, sir."

"No phone, no reporters. No White House publicity."

The sergeant took the best English tunic off its hanger, a damn miracle of Bond Street cutting and stitching. "No Sam Browne belts since the twenties, Jake. Last ones I saw were when they busted General Mitchell at his court-martial over that air power hubahuba. Poor Mitch—never kissed ass at TECOM or MUCOM. No boots, Jake. Mitch loved his boots. We all did. Jesus, in 1918 I went into the Belleau Woods and Saint-Mihiel fighting wearing spurs and owned a sword like a goddamn Crusader before Acre." He was unaware he was thinking out loud.

"Class in them days in the Army, general." Jake adjusted the jacket's shoulders, put one dark hand up the general's back under the tunic, and pulled the shirt taut. "Mules, too, gone.

Good company, Missouri Army mules, mean but human."

"You may be right about the mules at that." The general stepped into his shoes, inspected them, moved toward the kitchen and breakfast corner of the old house, floorboards creaking. Captain Marcus Wystan was sipping coffee at the scarred, overwaxed table found by the general's wife in a New England barn; a rare antique now. The captain was in a crisp uniform, tighter than the general's. He looked in his late twenties, was blond, ironic of expression, seemed always at jocose ease. Handsome but too lean, his mouth dropped to the left and he was a bit walleyed, which spoiled his looks for some people. His left eye wandered at times, and in rough weather tears fell from it. Captain Marcus Wystan came from a South Carolina tobacco family; a popular brand of cigarettes a generation back had been named after the Wystan racing stables and breeding farm. The general liked Marcus but not his upper-class family background—"People who lack nothing and lose everything."

The captain stood up as the general came in, keeping the coffee cup in his hand. His voice was clear, yet had a lazy burr to it which fooled people who didn't know his high IQ or the clarity of his perception of the Army pecking order, its protocol, its covetousness.

"No sweat, general, they can't start without us."

"Without my body, anyway. 'Anatomy is destiny.' "

"Freud?"

"Freud, captain. Sergeant, bring it on."

The general enjoyed the combination dining corner, country kitchen. He preferred it to the formal Adams Federal Period dining room with the six original Chippendale chairs and a dozen replicas, the doubtful Gilbert Stuart of a Major Casslin, a spinet once kept in tune. The house's original rafters were low overhead in the breakfast corner, a row of Rowlandson prints of the Napoleonic Wars hung on the plastered west wall. Jake was busy at the stove; the sound and odor of cooking were pleasant. The captain took up a clipboard.

"Now, sir—" He spoke clearly; the general was getting a bit hard of hearing.

"Hold your water, Marc. Let me get some tea into me."

"Great day, general, happy day."

"You know the house rules, Marc. No sagacious greetings, no goddamn six-story cake. No happy happies."

"Talking about the presentation at noon."

The general took tea very hot—no sugar, cream, or lemon. "What do you think, captain? Heads or tails?"

"Frankly, sir?"

"Frankly."

"Very frankly?"

Captain Wystan drum-tapped his fingers on the table edge. "General, you should have kissed ass more. The President resents how you acted to two other Presidents; they were his friends."

The general began to cut into the steak, smiling, chewing with vigor. He was very proud of his teeth; true, the back ones with a lot of inlays, but *all* there.

"Don't bother reading me the order of the day, captain. No press meeting after the circus unless there is a no. I'll open fire then."

"I typed up your speech if it's a no—the way you dictated it."

"You better had." He waved a knife blade with which he had dipped up some salt—an old habit from a tour of duty at a Chinese station.

"Jake, set down the eggs and grits."

The general, slashing with his fork began to break up the eggs Jake had set before him. "Whatever is to happen I want my desk and files cleaned out at the Pent. *Everything* I can claim."

The captain decided against another cup of coffee. "Cleaned the files out two days ago. Everything boxed in plain containers."

"Where to? Don't want some meth-freak Maoist or some newsmagazine to find anything."

The captain whispered, "Private storage near Baltimore." He tapped his chest, looked to see if Jake were listening. "Give you the receipts for your safe."

"You hold them, Marc. In some bank vault. I might get raided. Jake, get the pigskin briefcase."

The general watched the sergeant leave the room. "He's pretty trustworthy. File cabinet and safe B-2?"

"Emptied it. Took out its contents in grocery bags, A&P bags."

"That easy, huh? Damn rotten security."

The general wiped his lips slowly and took a Monte Cristo cigar from the sergeant and rotated it in his mouth as the sergeant held a burning match to the tobacco. It was a careful ritual, the solemnity of an old habit of inhaling, rotating the tobacco, flame held just the right distance from the end of the cigar. As a satisfied grunt from the general signaled the tobacco was properly lit, Jake shook out the match. "We got five hundred left of the Havana extra-claro stuff, that's all."

"I'll be dead before I'll smoke Perfecto Gracias. Marc, the age of the fine cigar is over—the Hoyo de Monterrey, Upmann, Rafael Gonzales—like loving beautiful, polite women. Well, we'll take the Bentley this morning, gentlemen."

Behind the general's back the sergeant made a grimace at the captain, some kind of signal. Captain Wystan said, "Might rain, general. Just waxed the Bent."

"Let it rain forty days, forty goddamn nights, you're not delivering me to the White House in any Army Lincoln. The Bentley."

"The Bentley, sergeant." The captain suspected a lot about the general, but nô senile dementia. Just a sentimentalist with a hard shell—alive and vulnerable inside.

"Silver-star plates screwed one on each front fender, and two flags over the hood. Captain, you and the sergeant up front. Let's go down shiny and bushy-tailed, *all* flags flying."

"You're not going down, general."

"Keep thinking that, Marc. There are times I don't give a fiddler's fuck if I am. But if it *is* down—I'd be better off in Arlington already than pitied by berserk paranoids in office. Yes, an honorary firing squad in volley-firing position, scared pigeons wheeling in a good blue sky, survivors envying me. But I'll probably die of a winter bronchitis unlike my Uncle Brewster and my brother Craig."

"You've got twenty years yet, sir."

The general rose, clamped on his heavy ornate cap. " 'The best is yet to come?' That horse's ass Robert Browning wrote that, eh?"

"Yes, sir, I suppose he did."

"Always thought his poetry was a crapout; exaggerated Victorian corn. As for Arlington, remember my memo, Marc. No place within sight of the Boston Irish holy plots ground— those lace-curtain mackerel snappers. Once in London I almost kicked their old man down the stairs of the National Union Club. I told him a few truths." The general looked at the glowing end of his cigar with pleasure. "He had repeated his persistent remark to the Limeys there that night—that the Germans couldn't be beaten by any power on earth. So bury me at safe distance or I'll come up out of the ground and fly around the Capitol with my bat wings."

"Was the old man ambassador then to the Court of St. James's?"

The general laughed. "That's why I got passed up for promotion that year. Let's roll."

"Right, sir."

"Go by way of the Rock Creek Cemetery."

The captain shrugged at this sure sign of inner disquiet settling on the general. "The sweet, soft side" he had once written in his journal.

In the blue-black, overpolished Bentley, the last of the cigar beginning to taste off, the general sat back, eyes half closed, feeling the palpitations of the heart—as always before a battle. Better think of Margerie. He hadn't thought, really thought deeply about Margerie for a long, long time. Now here he was, going to visit her grave before facing what could be the end of his active life; some omniscient pattern that had failed to shape up. He'd have Captain Wystan pick up some flowers. Yellow roses, the kind she liked, Baroness von Kristonhoff's.

Later he sat on a stone bench in the Rock Creek's silent acres of burials, looking at Saint-Gaudens' statue, where Henry Adams had buried his wife, also after suicide; Margerie's grave just in sight, to the east. He wondered why people called the green bronze of the seated woman, "Grief," her head hidden in folds of drapery. Why Grief? There were moments like this when all his purpose in life slackened, when the futility of all human endeavor seemed a pain. So many gestures that fail to find motion.

What had Margerie said when they parted for the last time?

"To be too strong at times is often to be always condemned to be strong. . . ."

Margerie dancing at the cotillion at the Waldorf to "The Teddy Bear's Picnic," he in all his glory . . . all those good times, too short times, lusty times. Dust.

> Good-bye to flattery's fawning face,
> To grandeur with his wise grimace,
> To upstart wealth's averted eye,
> To supple office, low and high . . .

Good-bye. . . .

A rising wind moving over the graves did not ruffle the metal drapes of the statue. Yes, the general decided, it *was* grief, sure as shooting, that the statue expressed. He rose with a snap of his fingers, looked off toward where the Bentley waited on a deserted bluestone road. He didn't fit in. Nothing did any more. And he had a moment's vision again of the Kingdom of Heaven defended by missile sites. That thought delighted him. He must remember *that*; tell it at the Army Club. Handsome, adjusting his military jacket and his face to its public façade as he stood up, onward now to meet the C-in-C. To know which it was to be. Yes. No.

He felt as vulnerable, as wondering as he had always been. And always he had hidden it from the world, never exposed "the vein of pity and feeling in yourself," Margerie had said. He couldn't pray for favors any more as he had at six years of age at bedtime in the big run-down Copperwood mansion in Silver Bend, the kid earnestly asking for a Flexible Flyer sled that steered. He, tall as a pump handle then, on his knees in his nightshirt. "Gentle Jesus, meek and mild, listen to a little child."

Chapter 3

THE best place to find the splendid Montana rattlesnakes —big ones—Simon Copperwood knew already as a boy, was along the old mine workings, the talus slopes of Tobacco Root Mountain by the pyrite rock discards, out among the horsemint and yellow vetch grass. When he was eight, going on nine, he had his own six-foot oak stick with the solid V fork at the end of it. Made for him by Charlie Rockefeller, who claimed to be a Sioux. Charlie served the Copperwoods in a lazy, goof-off manner; served as handyman, coachman, chauffeur, to Brewster and Dolly Copperwood. Even if the Copperwoods had run out of money, mines, cattle, and railroad bonds. Charlie was bowlegged, bull-chested; maybe yes, maybe not, a full-blooded Sioux. His family name came, he said, after the time Sitting Bull of the Hunkpapa Sioux brought the tribe back from exile in Canada —sometime in the 1870's—to settle at Standing Rock Reservation. Charlie's grandfather, Long Nose, picked a last name for the family for the Indian agent from a can of kerosene: ROCKEFELLER OIL CO.

Charlie was top waddy in the snake hunts. Simon's older brother, Craig, was fat and given to puffy moans when he tripped over the rocks among the tamarisk and Jimsonweed. But he had a good eye for a flat stone that could hold a rattler under it.

The trick was to flush your snake out in the open, then prong him with your V stick just behind the head. And press. While he rattled and thrashed around, Charlie Rockefeller would put a .22 slug through his head, best of all, between the predator's omniscient eyes.

Charlie was a marvelous skinner, peeling off the rattler's beautiful rough skin, all pebbly and jewel-spotted, before you could recite the first verse of "Casey Jones." A good long rattler's skin brought a dollar. Real good money in Silver Bow County, Montana. But first you nailed the skins scales down to a board, scraped them clean, salted them, exposed them to sun for a week for a proper tanning. The firm in St. Louis that bought the rattler skins—Louis Cohen and J. J. O'Hara—made them into hatbands and belts and sold them as genuine Indian craft. It was a dangerous way of earning, but Simon and Craig made their spending money by it. Sharing, of course, with Charlie, who rarely got paid his wages in full, twenty dollars a month, things being promising but vague with the Copperwood fortunes. Uncle Brewster used to say, "Remember, boys, it's *always* morning someplace in the world."

Simon, already growing out of his clothes, loved the rattler hunts, and had no fear of the big snakes which cooled themselves among the kinnikinnick berries where the vesper sparrows came to feed.

They had started, that day of Simon's first rattler hunt, as the dawn came up lacquered with dull pink, and with a smudge on the horizon where some rancher had let a fire get out of hand among the harvest stubble. It was a good day, Simon felt, after his breakfast of liver pudding, onion and sage, bread and honey, coffee half-filled with condensed milk. He walked with his V stick held tight, glad of a hot sun after the dark and inanimate night. The Montana land delighted him; it had morning dimension and substance, and he was a hunter at last. Charlie carried the gunnysack over one shoulder, had the rusty .22 stuck in his belt, and a chaw of tobacco in one cheek like a most monstrous toothache. He also had a pint of local moon in an old Dr. Glover's Family Medicine bottle.

"Now, you tads just don't git yourself bit. Them king rattlers, I seen one once kill a bull, they'r so full of spite. They got gumption."

"I need ten dollars," said Craig. "Want a gold watch chain?"

"I want to keep my first skin," said Simon.

"Whatever the devil for?" asked Craig, wearing one of Uncle Brewster's golf caps. Craig was the only young male, aged thirteen, in Silver Bend who said *devil* when he meant *hell*. He said *bulldust* when he meant *horseshit*. Craig had a head for figures, (Senator Ott at the bank said, "This Craig Copperwood, he'll do well. But the one to watch is that young snot Simon. He'll talk sassy to anyone. And no matter what his age. I wouldn't trust Simon with a fdmale dog, young as he is, the way he hoots at the women and girls when he's in back of that old Pierce-Arrow the Copperwoods still own.")

"Every skin is a dollar," said Craig, stopping to mop his face.

"I want it for a belt." Simon went to lifting a flat rock and

[17]

stepped back. No snake. Charlie, not given to palaver when on the hunt, moved off to the left, lunged down his V stick, and the boys ran up to see a marvelous diamondback thrashing about, his head held firmly unmoving by the heavy V of the stick.

Charlie smiled. "Ought to git two dollars fer this one. Big enough to make a jockstrap fer Jack Johnson, the Telon Sioux Injun World Champion. Si, you catch holt of my stick here *and* keep pressin'."

"Jack Johnson is no Indian—he's a darky."

Simon leaned on the stick, held the dark-eyed head of the reptile pressed into the earth, felt the tail brush his high-laced logger's shoes. Charlie aimed the .22 at the gemmed top of the snake's head, a head it seemed to Simon set with colored rubies and emeralds.

"Sheet, Si, Johnson ain't no nigger."

The shot sounded and echoed up the canyon, and the snake's body seemed to slow down a bit but not stop moving.

"You're as full of crap as a whale," Simon said.

Charlie took the insult silently. He got out his skinning knife. "He'll not die, this here snake, till sunset. You can't kill a snake by blowing his head off."

"Bulldust," said Craig, fanning himself with his cap. "It's just reflexes. He's dead enough."

Charlie slit down the white stomach of overlapping scales, cut round the fragments that were left of the head, pulled the skin off with a shout—rattlers and all.

"You don't know nothin' Craig, no more than Si here," said Charlie. "See, I undressed the critter and he's still movin'. Ain't he, Si?"

"Why not send Jack Johnson the skin?"

"Watch out I don't kick you into the middle of next week, Si."

Charlie was irked. He put the skin away in his gunnysack, took out the pint of shine—local untaxed whisky. He took a pull and offered Craig the bottle after wiping the neck with a shirt sleeve. Craig shook his head: "No." Simon held out a hand.

"You wait till yer pecker has hair around its neck 'fore you drink boiled whisky. You git delirium tremens at yer age."

They got two more rattlers in spite of Charlie's growing instability of temperament from the whisky. Simon got his first one among the blue-cedar berries and ragwort flowers, cornered his snake in a rocky, dried-out gully. He had heard the warning rattle, then saw the muscled, coiled shape of the snake. And Charlie cried out, "Keep him followerin' you with his eyes and keep him recoiling to foller you. Now just don't pick him up by his ears."

"Snakes have no ears."

"Push, Si! Now. Git 'em!"

It was good. Lunge and push, a quick drive of the V stick down on the rolling neck thick as a wrist, a shape like one long muscle. He pressed. Charlie stood to one side after taking a sip of the bottle, stood silent. Craig hoped the Indian was alert in case Simon had misjudged and he had to shoot fast. Charlie stood lost in introspection.

"How it feel, Si? Fairly raise yer hair on top of yer haid, don't it?"

"It's mine, it's mine!" He dared to look around at the purple dolomite mountains, the sage and dust. He leaned on the stick.

Charlie took out his plug of Old Mail Pouch, bit off a fresh chunk, pushed it into place, got it shaped right and chawed. Simon stood still, the stick in both hands, firm, pressing. The Indian half-breed bastard was trying to spook him, hope he'd get rabbity and crybaby. Maybe even get him to admit the darky Johnson was a Sioux.

Craig waved his cap. "Kill it, Charlie, *kill* it!"

"Why, shore." Charlie broke open the revolver, spun the cylinder, dropped out the empty cartridge shells. "Gotta reload. Now, where I put them rimfires? Hold tight, Si."

Simon looked away toward a dusty clump of piebald maples where a gray fox barked. The land seemed dimensionless, indifferent. He'd not give that Indian sonofabitch any word to hurry up. His palms sweated, the fingers slipped a bit down the peeled-oak stock. Simon steadied himself, felt the perspiration pour down his armpits into the old tartan shirt. The moment transcended reason. The ecstasy, exhilaration were gone. He felt the world unprincipled.

Craig was beginning to weep. "What you waiting for, Charlie? He's getting loose, the rattler. Look at him thrash about!"

Charlie found two shells and inserted them slowly into the .22—tested the heft of the gun. Simon felt his throat dry out, his red-gold, long hair float into his eyes, the sweat slide onto his nose. He felt a quiver in his arms; the damn snake was active as ever, trying to pull his own life free from the V. Well, Simon thought, I'm just a kid, but I don't yell uncle for a no-good half-breed prick like Charlie Rockefeller. I'm not begging for him to shoot until he's ready. He's getting back at me for what I said. I'll stand firm here like that old four-power Fresno field machine rusting in the barn. No, *no*, I'm not asking, not begging . . . Charlie smells like mule musk and Craig looks like he's wet his pants . . . the sun is boiling, the snake's getting stronger . . . I'm getting not weaker . . . *just* tired. Some place there was a woodfire among the loblolly pine above them and the drumming, like ruffled grouse, or was it his blood in his ears? Or maybe an ivory-billed woodpecker in that old dead tree. . . . Simon's knees gave way—only his pressing on the stick kept him up.

Charlie spit amber chewing tobacco juice, smiled. Craig tried to grab the pistol. "You wait until Uncle Brewster hears about this!"

Charlie just brushed Craig aside, took another swallow of the shine. "Aw, Si's a strong boy, ain't ya, Si? He don't ask Charlie fer help, does he?"

Simon closed his eyes, infused with ardent hate of the Indian, felt that death was the redbugs running on his arms and the ants climbing up his shoes, and as he began to pass out, it was bull bats bellowing around twilight by the old barn. He fell forward, remembering still to press down on the stick as he fell; fell toward a toad-strangler of a storm coming up, the thunder close. Or maybe it was a shot. . . . Then it was all black for him.

He came alive, the sun's incandescence full in his face; found himself lying on some slabs of shale, the dead snake, its head all reddish mush, by his feet. Charlie was bending over him, sopping him with a dirty handkerchief wet with whisky. Craig was just staring down, sobbing, blubbering up his too full lips, spewing spit and air and words that weren't clear from between them.

Simon looked up at the Indian face. "Am I bit?"

"No, you were spunky, you held 'im."

Simon sighed with no sense yet of reality. He was only eight years old and was tired. He had always suspected that death was something on another planet—the moon perhaps—and happened to people one never met. But, it had been clear there for a moment, death was everyplace. Simon shivered. He knew he could always face it, and always fear it.

Simon moved his head. By the tattered riding boot of Charlie's left foot lay the rusty pistol. Simon's hand reached for it casually, then grabbed it. He lifted his arm, his finger oily on the trigger. His scrotum tightened; he had a mean thought, a desire to even the score.

Charlie stepped back, his coffee-colored face turned darker instead of white. "Careful with that there pistol. It's a hogleg with a loose trigger."

"I'm going to kill you, you dirty sonofabitch of a no-good half-breed." It sounded clear and firm, but he wished his voice had changed and become more like Craig's.

Charlie stepped back and held his hands palms forward in front of his chest, his soiled yellow and red shirt. "No, kid, I was just fer funnin'. Wasn't I, Craig?"

Craig said nothing, his eyes on stems, his mouth a wet O. He knew Simon was belligerent, but nobody shot Indians any more except for a lynching now and then.

Simon raised himself on one elbow and pulled the trigger. Charlie jumped sideways just before the slug left the gun barrel. He tripped on a scrub oak root and began to fall, moving his arms wildly as if hoping to fly. Simon pressed the trigger again. It clicked but there was no fire. Charlie had loaded only two shells.

Spinning in the dust, Charlie rolled over, then stood up and dusted his elbows. He took out his knife from its belt pouch. His voice was dead level and low. "Si, I better skin your snake for you."

Simon nodded, scared.

Charlie did a good fast job, not looking up at the boy watching him, the harmless pistol in his hand. When Charlie had peeled the skin off, he held it up—a good, wide, long rattler's special —the sun catching the colors and the markings. "It's yer first one, Si, and among the Sioux if it's a boy's first hunt and if he was

[21]

good at it—brave that is—that makes him a man. Nobody has the right to say he ain't no man. That's the truth. There is *this* done." He bent and dipped up a drop of snake blood, touched Simon's cheek. *"Nadowersiv Tinneh."*

Simon stood up and threw down the pistol. "It's a pretty good-sized snake." Charlie gave a tight screechy laugh, a sound of mislaid composure. "Bigger than an elephant's pecker, ain't it?"

There was no more snake hunting that day. There was some sense of ceremony among them as they walked back across the ridges slowly, each with his own thoughts.

The Copperwood brothers' code was that neither would snitch on Charlie Rockefeller. And he never reported their misdemeanors. Even the dreadful moment of Simon's snake hunt was among the three of them. As for a conciliating gesture, it was hard to come by. Simon was stubborn "as a mule refusing to be baptised" as Uncle Brewster put it. "When he raises up a grievance, he holds onto it."

At supper, after Aunt Dolly had made him wash his face, Simon sat in a silence that seemed to him to hint of a discovery of something deep. Yet he ate well of the rooster, whose raucous and insistent death cries he had heard that day before from the chicken-yard area at the hands of Bo Hue, the Chinese cook. Simon had two big helpings of dried apple and raisin pie, and went to his room. It was a long narrow room with a badly stuffed Arctic owl, the old Winchester Yellow Boy with its trigger action missing, that once belonged to Old Arnie, his grandfather; the rows of Oliver Optic books, Burton's and Stanley's volumes on Africa, Doré illustrated classics; a calfskin rug, a brass bed, two cane-bottomed chairs, and a table with one short leg. Craig had painted the table red for him. Several moths: giant Skull Eyes, Brown Rover's, Hairy Harry's (local names) were pinned to drying boards. A large volume of Henry Ward Beecher's sermons was used as a press for collecting ferns and leaves: sumac, shagbark, hawthorn, honey locust. Two brass oil lamps with red glass shades hung from the leak-stained ceiling.

Simon lay down on the narrow bed with its cast-iron decor of roses, hands clasped over his filled stomach. . . . Maybe I am a

[22]

man, he thought—now maybe I will get fuzz around my cock.
Maybe being scared doesn't have to ever show. Next week I'll go
after eagles besides rattlers again. I didn't get scare-boogered. I
wasn't rabbity, didn't cry.

Charlie never tried to get back at him or test Simon
Copperwood's bravery again. They caught many rattlers among
the burdock and staghorn bush, made enough spending money
shipping the skins to St. Louis to buy steel spring-traps and run a
winter line for weasel and fox pelts. Once they found a fresh
wolf's paw in a trap and the chicken-head bait gone. Charlie
disappointed Simon—he had no woodsman's skill, no Indian
lore, didn't know cougar spoor from bearshit. Simon got books
by Dan Beard and Ernest Thompson Seton and early Boy Scout
manuals. He made snowshoes and designed a tepee. They got
wild-bee honey from sorghum trees. They fished for steelheads,
cooked them in a spider skillet with strips of bacon, and ate out in
the open. And by the time Simon showed signs of the fuzz in the
proper place and entered Silver Bow County High School, they
were talking bawdy. Drinking bottled beer from Dutch Haber's
saloon and whorehouse, and feeling itchy and randy.

Young as he was, Simon knew he had more wonder and awe of
the world outside than Craig, realized the inherent limitations of
Silver Bow, had more awareness of the world. To Charlie the
brothers seemed soft-shelled cooters; yet Si, he had some kernel
of some special secret, whereas Craig thought of money and
compound interest and land values.

Craig graduated from high school and went to buying a pair of
silver-rimmed glasses he didn't need. They hung on his too small
nose with a spring clamp. Craig took to tapp
eeeis fingers together when he talked of his job in the bank.
Charlie just talked about whisky and women, fur prices, and a
man with six fingers on his right hand and a kerosene lamp his
aunt owned with a blue glass shade with "nakit" girls dancing on
it. Charlie also talked about Chicago, where he had ridden with
Buffalo Bill's Wild West Show. "It's a big bastid of a place, like all
cities, millions of blocks of used terlet paper and horse apples."

Simon wanted to clear up many things; like the big decaying
house, the way it was. He heard talk that the Copperwood
mansion had once been a hungdinger—out there among the

spruce and black alders and the buck coons and mine tailings. That's the way it was according to the old-timers and the loafers at the railroad depot at Silver Bend. All them Venetian glass chandeliers General Grant and Lillian Russell once stood under. Gold leaf and sandalwood in the ballroom. Velvet portieres and looped draperies the hired girls called "dust catchers." And, the loafers told Simon, "A real Methodist parlor organ with tall silver pipes done from the Copperwood silver ore out of their own mines." That was "when they had millions, gold pisspots." But it was all before Simon's time, even his brother Craig's time. Like the talk of twelve servants when evening dress was *de rigueur* at the Copperwoods', and governors, two of them drunk, of six states, came to a Copperwood party. And old Arnie got shaved in the Koch patent barber chair by a "nigrah" in a white jacket, a barber from Trinidad with a British accent. Even a maid hired from the Winfield Scott Hotel, Virginia City, to do the ladies' hair. The maid insisted there were books in French, and proved it by showing a copy of Pierre Louys' *Chansons de Bilitis* she had toted off as something to remember one of the big parties at the Copperwood mansion. Simon wasn't sure that any of it was true. Dolly and Brewster didn't like to talk of how it had once been.

To Simon the old house was a place where you had to walk with care over certain rotted-out floorboards, and when it rained the walls sometimes grew green and yellow mold, and you could hear the water dripping someplace in the walls, moving down toward the empty wine cellar to float an empty bottle that once held, according to Uncle Brewster, rare wine or brandy.

Simon, at the window looking up at Taurus and the Pleiades in the night skies, wondered what had happened to all the glory. All the money.

Chapter 4

IF the Copperwoods had little else left, they had lots of family history. Silver Bend, Montana, never claimed to be much of a town, but Simon soon learned that it used to boast of the Copperwoods as they *were* in the last part of the 19th century. Back a couple of generations, when silver was really paying off, and old Arnie Copperwood—he ·was "Old Arnie" at thirty to the natives—he was importing whores from Denver from Mattie Silk's fancy cathouse, and the Tobacco Root mines were running full blast, and he was building the big Copperwood place out of redstone and imported hardwood lumber, marble; with cast-iron pillars and Italian statues of real rosy-streaked marble. Even sporting a racing stable with Copperwood colors of silver and blue at Denver, Bay Meadows, New Orleans, Chicago. He owned the trotter, Fancy Lady, that broke the two-minute mile at Saratoga. And then Old Arnie, *really* old, he died, sitting with his bare feet in a pan of hot water and mustard powder. Having come home feverish after spending two days in a freezing duck blind on the Beaverhead River.

That's the way Simon Copperwood heard of his grandfather when he was a boy growing up in the huge rundown house, the copper and slate roofs leaking, the layers of wallpaper peeling off "Like an onion," his Aunt Dolly saying. "The goddamn termites are standing on each others' shoulders to hold the miserable place together." There were no silver mines any more, the lodes were all played out, and the racehorses all gone, except for Fancy Lady—stuffed and leaking sawdust out in the coach-house. A coachhouse of old carriages, buckboards, and their first autocar. Folks said, "Well, those feisty bastards, the Copperwoods,. they've sure had their comeuppance now. Too bad there are so few of them left to poor-mouth. Time they learned their lesson."

Uncle Brewster just said, "The hell with time, Simon. Commit yourself to history. Not that this mean town knows anything of history."

In 1912, Simon Copperwood, reading of all the rich folk who went down on the *Titanic,* didn't think the Copperwoods were poor-mouthing at all. "Maybe bareass poor," he told Craig, "keeping the big wreck of a house going by raising some farm horses, and the war talk in Europe would be good for horse sales, if the war comes."

It came. "The Great War" the papers called it in 1914, and every night Simon a,d Craig would move pins with colored heads around on a *Review of Reviews* magazine map, and learn new names of places where a couple of million men were strangling and dying in the mud. It was true the war in Europe was good for the horse market. A million horses and mules were dying on the Western Front alone, and the Russians had agents in Montana and Wyoming buying horses for the war.

There was a short time of inherent hope when it looked as if the Copperwoods would be "riding in new silk again," as Aunt Dolly put it. "Diamonds in our ears and Brew smoking dollar Havanas again. No more cornmeal mush and cabbage with side pork."

Aunt Dolly wasn't a Copperwood. She had married Brewster, the nephew of Old Arnie, his only surviving relative. Dolly Tremain was a missionary, from Yunnanfu—someplace in China. That was before she met Brewster in Chicago at a temperance conference at the Palmer House. He came to her room one night to deliver some booklets against the Demon Rum. Brewster was a reformed alcoholic then—two months on the wagon. Almost. He had been suffering for drink, his mind dissolving. . . . He grabbed Dolly, shucked his pants down, and, as she admitted later, had her virginity in a hurry. She was amazed at the pleasure of it all. Delighted. Next morning as Brewster sat—a lapsed crusader—sipping Old Kentucky bourbon in the Palmer House bar, it was clear to him nondrinkers were sexual beasts. He decided the only thing to do was marry Dolly Tremain. A gentleman from Silver Bend, Montana, didn't take a missionary virgin's maidenhead without doing the right thing. Years later Simon decided Brewster lacked sense. Brewster actually had no interest in sex, or in "screwin' 'round" as it was called back home. He had been a devotee of alcohol since the age of nine. He had joined the Temperance League that year when the last mine closed, hoping to cure himself and make a fresh fortune. But as he soon began to take a pint of whisky after a hard day's meeting with the Anti-Saloon people, his efforts, Dolly assured him, were doomed to failure anyway. Her missionary soul felt there was good to be done on Brewster.

As a captain in the 32d Infantry of Volunteers, Brewster had fallen deeper into drink in Cuba in the Spanish-American War, beginning with the native rum. He hated Teddy Roosevelt from then on, and also hated a song, "A Hot Time in the Old Town." Simon used to play it on the gramophone until Brewster broke the record.

They were a fine couple, Mr. and Mrs. Brewster Copperwood; made a successful marriage. Dolly learned to drink, but rarely beyond moderation, and to smoke little black cigars. She developed a sensuality beyond Brewster's interest in sexual matters. Brewster Copperwood, on a pint of bourbon a day, often stayed sober for three months at a time, usually terminating with a three-day bat, a period in which he stayed in his room, locked in, and one could hear the bottles breaking as he tossed them empty out of the second-story window onto the red brick drive, in a paranoid ferocity ending in weeping and loud lamenting.

They were mother and father in a casual, easy way to Simon and Craig Copperwood, orphans. Their father, Arnold Copperwood, only son of Old Arnie, had grown up in Paris, where his mother had gone after Old Arnie told her she was "a puke-making, frigid bitch," and after she had found out he had two whores stashed away at the Original Indian Head Hotel. So she fled to Paris with Arnold, their son, and raised him much too carefully. Arnold knew Henry James and Jimmie Whistler, John L. Sullivan, and for some time, he knew intimately a grand courtesan, Cora Pearl, who kept him broke, even on the good allowance Old Arnie coughed up. Arnold married a Boston heiress, Constance Abbott Strange, but her income came from Chicago trolley lines, and the Great Fire ruined her family, who lost their faith in the durability of investments. Simon always remembered the glaring lithograph of the Great Chicago Fire in the Copperwood Land Company office in the Copperwood Block on Main Street, Silver Bend. . . . Arnold began his life in Silver Bend, trying to revive the silver mines, and after Old Arnie grew old, he made an effort to get better mares for the horse ranch, as he hoped to sell a well-formed carriage and buggy horse. "A fading hope," Brewster said, "in the days Geronimo and King Edward became old men, and the autocar began to stink up the country."

Arnold, as Brewster remembered it, brought his weeping and pregnant bride to the old horror of the Copperwood mansion, examined the fine teak and walnut paneling, the painted tin bathtub set on brass lions' heads, a toilet paneled in golden oak with a chain to flush with the roar of Niagara. The huge, thundering kitchen stoves frightened Constance. The kitchen was ruled by Chen Oboy, a tall, laughing Chinese, father of Bo Hue Oboy, the later cook. Chen showed her how to glaze the biscuits by sucking up a mouthful of milk and spraying it on the dough before slipping it into the oven. "Best, missy, when you got no flont teef."

Old Arnie didn't welcome his son Arnold back with any fattened yearling, only speaking ill of his late wife, Arnold's mother, buried in Père Lachaise, Paris' best graveyard, near Oscar Wilde—referring to her as "a puke-making, frigid bitch." That remark, repeated three times, was the cause of Arnold knocking down his father, who was two hundred and fifty pounds and had once been as strong as a beerwagon horse. But Arnold knocked him down the grand staircase covered with turkey-red carpeting, Old Arnie yelling, "I didn't kick *my* father past any first landing." Arnold's lessons with John L. Sullivan proved that skill over mere brawn was the thing.

Old Arnie, in some incredible rapture, respected anyone who could knock him down. He was a mean, lecherous man, a man not at all the noble empire builder, the splendid pioneer the local newspapers wrote of on his death. The family came originally from Hull, England, Brewster wrote in a small book he printed in 1928. Then they settled in Upper New York State, always managing to make money, in timber, railroad ties, buffalo hides, village and town waterworks, river steamboats. They came West after the Mexican War, states *The Copperwoods—A Family*, "when Old Arnie was Young Arnie." The town talk—*not* in the book —was that he elbowed the original discoverer out of the Tobacco Root copper and silver holdings, and being a trained engineer of sorts, invented a process with Spencer Penrose to smelt low-grade Guggenheim tailings. One day he had enough millions of dollars piled up in a San Francisco bank to look around him and say, "I'm rich enough. It's time I had me some fun." He had lots of sense "but no sensibilities," folk said of Old Arnie—but he lived high, fed high, spent.

Then silver and copper fell, and other better smelter processes came along, even if Old Arnie gave money to get William Jennings Bryan to run for the Presidency a couple of times as a Free Silver man, in the hopes silver would replace gold as the country's prime metal.

When Old Arnie died with his feet in a pan of hot water, there was little hope of the Copperwood millions—spent at the Everleigh Club, at Canfield's Saratoga, and on the wheels at Monte Carlo—ever being replenished. Old Arnie had ruined himself with his last millions in stock deals, drilling of dry wells —dusters—in Texas, with wildcatters spudding in near Spindletop, just missing getting a share of boom times in Beaumont's big gushers. The heightened perceptions of Old Arnie's youth failed in the end.

Arnold and Constance Copperwood produced two sons; in 1895, Craig Arnold, who was a fat body and stayed fat all his life, and in 1898, Simon Bolivar, so named because Arnold Copperwood had invested in a scheme that year to set up rubber plantations along the Amazon. And the best-known name to Arnold and Connie of any heroic South American was Bolivar.

Simon, a blond, beautiful baby, flourished; the Copperwood rubber plantations didn't. The Brazilian politicians they bribed were overthrown—several even shot—the rubber gatherers killed by Indians. The little rubber produced was not profitable because of the graft and payoffs to new officials and Brazilian customs agents. All that remained in the end was the name Simon Bolivar Copperwood.

After Old Arnie's death, Arnold came to Copperwood Mansion and joined his Uncle Brewster in drink. Connie went East to visit relatives and rarely ever came back to Silver Bend except to sell some furniture to antique dealers. Those rare times she came to Silver Bend the whole town would be down to the depot when the Grand Divide Transcontinental RR car, attached to the B.A. & P. Cheyenne Express came in behind the big Baldwin 8-6-6 engine, pumping black smoke into the robin's-egg-blue sky, the driving wheels spinning, the bell clanging, and then in a blast of Westinghouse airbrakes sliding up to the depot platform, spitting steam, dogs yelping, crated chickens going insane. The feeders at table in the dining car—usually the Delmonte or Maxim, sat looking down on the wool-hat yokels, ranchhands and station loafers, while darkies in white jackets stood around behind the car windows with silver bread-trays and steaming tureens of Fred Harvey's best $1.75 eight-course meal.

Down onto the platform would step Connie Copperwood, as Simon remembered his mother, in high-buttoned shoes, feathered hat, some new smart cut to her coat. He remembered, too, her pale, worried face, showing the strain of this return for money. Behind her would come Netta Kelly, mama's maid ("hired girl" the town folk said), cursing the porter for losing some hatbox or bit of luggage. "Oh, curse the nagger lout of a black divil!"

Arnold, sober, flanked by Simon and Craig, both wearing flat caps, he himself carefully shaved, bits of toilet paper covering the cuts on cheek and neck from a nervously held long razor —would move forward dragging a boy by each hand, herding the two before him. Simon always hated the long black stockings they wore; the tight kneepants, Norfolk corduroy jackets, or mackintoshes if was late fall with the fields all cold stubble, the horse herds down from the slopes of Tobacco Root Mountain.

The overly effusive welcome and conversation never varied much.

"How are you, Connie?"

"I'm feeling better. Baden-Baden helped."

"Hello, Ma," Craig said.

"They look peaked."

"They eat enough."

"Baby, you're growing too fast." This to Simon, held at arm's length.

Simon would press his face to his mother's jet-buttoned or braid-decorated jacket, and smell. French rice powder, failed dress shields, a suggestion of a Fred Harvey lunch on her breath, and something he might have identified as a House of Booth martini; but the town boys of Silver Bend knew nothing of the martini or gin. It was a community loyal to bourbon and rye whisky, and unlike Connie, the women drank Lydia Pinkham, 30 percent alcohol.

The return of his mother, to Simon's dismay, didn't last long. "I'm too involved in a nervous condition to take you back with me to Marienbad." Except for warnings against overdoing self-abuse, which term the brothers did not connect with handling of the genitalia or the groping of schoolgirls at the William Cody School. They thought self-abuse meant nose-picking and biting one's fingernails and smelling the gook between one's toes.

Arnold and Connie were both dead when Simon was ten. Killed, oddly enough, because Arnold had two practical ideas that might have renewed some of the solid cash in the Copperwood ledgers and put cases of Dom Pérignon back on ice.

Arnold began to believe in the autocar, or the automobile, as it was beginning to be called, and also in the crazy crates, the flying machines the Wright brothers were sending up to flutter, as Brewster put it "in the air like a duck with a hernia." He had also arranged to set up the Ford Agency for tin lizzies (the flivver, the Model T) in Silver Bow County, covering Dillon, Twin Bridge, Laurin, Arnstead. He put money into a factory to build an aeroplane, or flying machine, in the barn of August Ormsbee, a local inventor who filched Wright designs and was sure he could produce an aeroplane to win the U.S. Army contract as the successful bidder for a scout plane. Simon fell in love with the Army manuals August had, learned insignia, rank, decorations.

To win the Army contract a machine had to fly thirty-five miles an hour and sustain itself in the air for one hundred miles.

The whole family, Arnold, Connie, Brewster, Dolly, Craig, and Simon, drove out to Ormsbee's meadow in the Pierce-Arrow, driven by Charlie Rockefeller—all to view the first flight of the finished model. It was roaring its twin propellers, driven by a set of crossed bicycle chains of the first Ormsbee-Copperwood flying machine, the 8-horsepower motor vibrating loudly. There was room on the airship only for Connie and Arnold, in goggles and white linen car dusters, besides August Ormsbee, his cap on backward and larger goggles on his eyes, gloved hands on rudder, wing-warp controls. The plane took off with a wobble and a wriggle of its rear end and swooped, then rose to two hundred feet, Simon running along shouting below it. Simon always thought he heard his mother scream, but that seemed not too unlikely in a dive from five hundred feet. The machine didn't crumble or lose a wing, it just gracelessly aimed itself for the ground and kept to its purpose. It hit with a fearful crash and a smashing down of cottonwood saplings and blueberry bush, driving some dairy cows to near-paranoid collapse. Brewster and Dolly, in shock, weeping, drank up the bottles of Grands-Echézeaux brought for celebration.

The funeral in Shoshone Hill Cemetery was simple, and everyone who could make it was there. Brewster sober, Dolly in tight black, black sunshade, black veil, weeping, holding on to Simon and Craig, they in black ties, black flat caps. Dolly loved all the Copperwoods, and told Simon on the ride back to the old house in the big car, "I should have stayed in missionary work. I had a feel for it, you know, to knock Christ and the Bible into their heads, to get the natives to stop crapping into the streams they drank from, and buggery with the goats. Jesus needed me, and I was flesh. I've brought the Copperwoods bad luck." She had had, Simon knew, nearly a whole bottle herself.

Brewster, watching the neck of Charlie Rockefeller, handyman and chauffeur, just said, "We needed you more, Dolly dear. Didn't we, lads?" The boys nodded.

Charlie, the full-blooded Sioux (well, nearly full-blooded), said, "Godamighty, I don't know how they separated everybody into the right coffins. I sure don't know. They was all so—"

Dolly said, "You shut up your goddamn half-breed trap and just drive."

Simon, who was trying to escape the consciousness that death ends all, was thinking the same thing as to *who*, reassembled, was buried more or less in *what* casket. He put his head out the car window and quickly got rid of six slices of French toast, three fried eggs, a ham steak, and two cups of coffee-and-milk. . . . He was a child in the first perilous zone of his life, in the ache and pain of being, and without complacency about recent events.

The consciousness he retained most about his parents was the luck of being named by them Simon Bolivar Copperwood, a name he wrote in those Army manuals. The "Simon Bolivar," he often felt, helped get him his appointment to West Point. In time he glossed over the truth that it was rather more Mollie Ott and Senator Ott who led him to West Point. "Simon has inherited," Dolly said, "Old Arnie's hedonism."

Brewster added, "A born cocksman."

Chapter 5

"SIMON," Uncle Brewster would say, "live like a cork," when he celebrated some holiday or event important to him, and so ran beyond his quota of a quart and a half a day. "Float."

A strange life and yet a free one for a boy who was curious and not shriveled up by the town's narrow ideas. He found the local school numbing and backward, its teachers little better than simple country girls trying to teach the unteachable young of the Silver Bend country with 1870 maps, and oleander growing in nail kegs. The big bookcases in the dark Copperwood parlor yielded trash and literature and Simon read Methodist bishops' sermons, reports on the watershed studies of Montana, the novels of forgotten writers about castles and Balkan kingdoms and swordplay. Some books he could not understand, and this made him aware of his deficiencies in education. Dolly didn't encourage too much reading. "Base ideas and corruption come from books, you can bet on that. They'll knock your mind out colder than mackerel, Si, those writers."

She had matured into a sparkling, full-bosomed beauty, far from her missionary past. "Craftiness and guile in books. Better help me feed the turkeys."

Dolly was proud of her turkeys, strutting white ones, full of dignity and then going into panic. And so stupid. But Dolly treated her turkeys like royalty. Come some holiday, she'd thin the flock, get Charlie Rockefeller to chop off gobbler heads for Bo Hue to pluck the birds and present them as a series of baked items from the oven. Turkey carcasses brown and stuffed with chestnuts and canned oysters, cornbread and sage.

To Simon, Dolly seemed to float through the old house, its vast echoing hallways of teak and mahogany and hickory, its grand staircase, treads loose in spots, the tapestries often hanging in rags, showing Greek rapes, royal hunts. There was a stuffed bear, a moose head which had to be tossed outside onto a bonfire, as it decayed and broke from its setting high over the redstone fireplace. The staind-glass windows were often repaired by bits of tin and board, and the plumbing thumped, made indecent noises, sprung leaks, and failed. So Simon saw strange continents on the ceilings, whole oceans and clouds and strange monsters as water seeped through the walls while he lay sick with tonsilitis. More and more of the plumbing failed, and was either repaired poorly by Charlie or whole sections were disconnected. One winter two great brass hot water cylinders inside one of the stoves threatened to explode. The hot water always ran rusty when it ran at all, rushing out like pulsebeats. But Simon and Craig had to have a bath twice a week and were given warning by Dolly not to play with themselves. "You'll snap them *off* and you'll grow old regretting it."

Dolly had no fears for Craig's future. He was fat, careful, sly, obliging, always interested in costs of things, in unpaid taxes, payments overdue; all items Brewster usually ignored. Simon worried Dolly. She sensed in him some disembodied presence, as a carryover from her missionary readings. She felt a brooding in him at times that seemed to hint at a secret. Yet he was loud and wild and played hard and lived in a buoyant excitement. Still, he would often sink into a black leather armchair, deep as an abyss, and just stare at the piñon and mesa-oak logs burning in the red-boulder fireplace, a fireplace into which Old Arnie had set some samples of gold quartz. Simon would then appear to be full of a subtle perception and could explain to Craig with piercing clarity information on the speed of light, or how to make a whip from a bull's pizzle, or from Army manuals draw a field howitzer. Craig would say, "You scatterbrain, you move around like a turtle on roller skates." At which remark or one like it, Simon would launch himself like a runaway train at his brother, head-first, butting, kicking, fighting with hard fists until he was pulled

[34]

off, and Craig would nurse a cut lip or cheek. "The little bastard. I just oughta bust his damn jaw." And he'd kick Simon's rump.

But this grew harder to accomplish as Simon grew taller and taller, tougher too, thinner. When he rose from a chair and stretched, the crunch of joints would be heard. "He'll be a big um," Charlie Rockefeller said. "Mean, too. Got the jaw of a beaver." Simon would shadow-box with the battered marble garden statues offering him only stumps of arms, he taking the stances of Gentleman Jim Corbett, or the heavy crouch of Jess Willard. But often he caused Dolly trouble by stating he was Jack Johnson, now in exile in Europe, fleeing a Mann Act conviction. Dolly, who was usually free of prejudice, didn't think it right for the darkies to admire white women. "I mean it isn't as if their own high yellows are not attractive."

"Let kind go to kind," said Uncle Brewster, who didn't care one way or another about sex. He had none of that kind of drive left at all, and had never, he admitted, had hardly any at all. "Just four legs in a bed—ha!" he told Simon, sitting on the big side porch, Brewster sobering up after a reunion of the Spanish-American War vets at the Odd Fellows Hall.

"And fear not the unexpected in life, my boy. For instance, I've just been in jail overnight. Coming home from the reunion, walking, as I felt the need of some air to refresh me, I felt the need to pass water. The liquids in a man's body they move downward, and when they're below the waterline as it is—know what I mean? They want freedom. It being two o'clock in the morning, the night dark, no one stirring in Silver Bend, I unbuttoned, take out an old friend, and stand at the curb. And I proceed. Along comes Rodger Tooter Perls, town constable, and he asks me what I'm doing. I say, 'Taking a leak, Rog,' and he takes me down to the hoosegow and says, 'The charge is indecent exposure.' "

"Just for taking a leak, Uncle Brewster?"

"That's a fact. So this morning I appeared before Judge Ben Wilkinson, he had a headache himself, I could see that. He was with me in the Army in Tampa, in ninety-eight. Was at the reunion, too. Well, he looks at me like I was a total stranger, some bindlestiff off a freight car. 'Sergeant Copperwood,' he says, 'I mean, Mr. Copperwood, you can plead public nuisance, which is

[35]

a five-dollar fine.' 'Or?' I ask. 'Or,' he says, 'you plead not guilty, if this hooter Perls insists on it being indecent exposure, and then it's gotta be a public trial.' "

"What happened?" asked Simon.

"Perls, he didn't dare go against Judge Wilkinson, seeing as how Rog Perls needs support in the coming election; so I paid the five dollars as a public nuisance, and the judge says to me, 'You have to understand, Mr. Copperwood, the only creature who has the legal right to pass his water in our streets is a horse. Come into chambers for a drink.' Which we did, drank *auf Bruderschaft*. He had some fine applejack, taken in a raid on a still."

Uncle Brewster sighed, his face the color of roast beef, as he held his head. "So you want some important advice for success in this life, you study the habits of our society. Always end a fight laughing, arm in arm. Holding a grudge is bad." Brewster said it with dry solemnity hidden in a cough, and uncle and nephew sat and watched some lizards skating figure eights among the gray-stone paths.

Simon went out to the kitchen with its spur-marked linoleum to get a slice of bread and apple butter dusted in cinnamon powder from Bo Hue. Bread in hand, Simon retreated under the main staircase into a closet smelling of forgotten overshoes, unwashed woolen mittens, and mice litter. There he slowly ate his bread and apple butter, and luxuriated in fine dreams of glory, mixed with images of Mollie Ott's thighs and piggy-pink lacy drawers when she bent over to take a drink from the bubble fountain at school. They had had some rustic love play together with red-faced laughter, and he grew horny by her odor of lilac bath powder, girl body-sweat, and the tuna sandwiches she sometimes ate at lunch from a red metal box. Thinking like this often gave Simon a glow. Even if Craig claimed Mollie was sort of *his* girl.

Craig, already an apprentice bank teller at Senator Ott's bank, wearing cylindrical detachable cuffs, a high, starched collar, and with two kinds of pencils and a gold fountain pen in his lapel pocket.

Craig sniffed the spray of myrtle in his lapel buttonhole, looked down at his well-kept nails.

"You humping that married woman whose husband is freight agent at the depot, Craig? Always asking for you as a teller at the bank?"

Craig just slammed the door. Simon thought of tawny mountains with blue distances backing them up, and as he tried to scratch his shoulder blades, he already knew that life can be lived in exquisite episodes. Also that the quickness of perception he had was something special with himself, and he took pride in it.

Chapter 6

THE Copperwood horses didn't share in the boom the Great War of 1914 brought on, as the oldest, spurred European generals kept insisting to their governments that the saber and the cavalry charge were the only means to end trench warfare. The Copperwood herds roaming the brush and grass of the valley of Tobacco Root Mountain seemed to suffer not merely from the native ticks, horseflies, and worms, but from the rupture of flexor tendons, rare intestinal parasites, quarter cracks, ossicles of the ankles, inflammation of the cannon bones. Even when in 1915 it appeared the Copperwood stock had overcome most of its illnesses, its reputation remained damaged. The remarks of other horse breeders ranching nearby did the Copperwood herds no good. They gossiped to Italian, French, and English officers acting as horse buyers, hinting that the Copperwood stallions had inherited bog spavin, whirl bone, distended hock joints; that the mares threw foals given to navicular bone erosion. And the biggest lie of all was that many had arthritis of the joint capsules and paralysis of the laryngeal air passages if ridden at too steady a gallop.

Brewster, Dolly, and an ancient veterinarian, Doc Cougar, whose actual specialty was mules, worked on the ills of the

Copperwood horses with ice, linament, and medical pills handled by Simon and Craig, pills big as gold balls that had to be blown down the creatures' throats through a glass tube. Simon administered painkillers like Butazolidin. He never forgot the time when the herds seemed in good health in 1914 and a Don Cossack general, Mikhail Petrovitch Nekasoff, appeared in Silver Bend to buy five hundred horses for the Siberian Mounted Rifles. Colic ran through the Copperwood animals, fluids had to be drained from an epidemic of arthritic knees. At the end of 1916 the herds had been auctioned off for dog food. The sale barely met the cost of the feed bills and Doc Cougar's fees.

Simon was a great reader of the Sherlock Holmes stories, the Tarzan books, Jules Verne. He was the only serious reader in the family. Although there were tattered volumes of bound magazines in which he found *Leaders and Battles of the Civil War*, marvelous woodcuts of explorers' adventures in Africa, Dr. Kane's expeditions, Admiral Perry's Arctic explorations. To the town people the Copperwoods were a strange, ingrown family; Brewster, a sphinx with no riddle, drinking modestly but steadily, and Dolly, remembering her days as a Methodist missionary living in virgin austerity among the rice Christians on the Yellow River.

Nights, when he should have been asleep, Simon was going after raccoons and other varmints along the creeks with a bull's-eye lantern; he would sometimes catch a glimpse of Dolly in her long yellow dressing gown going along to the coachhouse where Charlie Rockefeller lived in the former tack room. It was no secret that her husband, Brewster, hadn't inherited any of the Copperwood sensuality, and Dolly was getting her quota of sexual satisfaction with the Indian stud. ("Sensible people," Brewster once said while deep in drink, "reach sensible conclusions.")

Dolly wasn't proud about it, or ashamed either, and during the day she treated Charlie—sex was his only sorcery over her—like a chauffeur and handyman. Once she knocked him across the porch when he pinched her mellow-melon of a shapely rump while she was watering the elkhorn ferns in the hanging redwood boxes. "You try *that* again, Charlie, and I'll run you off the place with an oak two-by-four soaked in neat's-foot oil."

Charlie scowled and left. He was in the Silver Bend pokey the next day, jugged for wrecking the lunchroom down at the depot, for tossing a bowl of "red"—the town's best chili—through the glass panel of the player piano, he giving out war cries all the time. It took six men to club him down and get him behind bars. Next morning Simon drove the buckboard to the town's jail and paid the three-dollar fine. On the way back Charlie sat by Simon's side, smelling of hoosegow blanket and unwashed Sioux, and bursting with grievance, indiscretion, and humiliation.

"It's not good, Si, I know it. But I'm not goin' to be nobody's pet humper. Hell, might just as well stand in the winder, a stud fer sale. Don't get me wrong, Si. But my grandpappy was a war chief. . . . Well, I'm gonna enlist in the cavalry. There's a war comin'. I'm goin' to count coups, take scalps."

"You better not talk loud that way about Aunt Dolly. Besides, you're no Sioux. You're a breed from up the White Sulphur Spring country."

Charlie looked tragic, scratched an armpit. "Listen, Si, that's all bullshit about me not bein' a Sioux. My granny was Crazy Horse's sister, and her son what was killed in Billy the Goat's saloon in Dallas he was my pappy and a reservation hostile. . . . Even if he, well, got me by a railroad station waitress in Kansas City."

"Crazy Horse was some damn fine Indian." They drove on, both seeing in the sterile landscape ghosts of raiding parties, old tribal villages.

"I gotta feather of Crazy Horse's headdress someplace, I'll give you when I pull tracks. I'm no goddamn stud stallion, just on call after dark. You take my advice, Si boy, you git outta here yerself. Ain't no place fer a smart boy what's readin' all the time and actin' out battles in the potato garden. Oh, I been watching you with that sword and old cap of your Uncle Brewster's. You stay around here you'll be like the rest. The hoss herds are nuttin. Yer brother Craig, he's fat and workin' in the bank. And come the time soon Dolly she'll go after you. You're still chicken? Still have yer cherry, I bet."

Simon whipped up the old gray roan horse. "Don't bet on it, Charlie. I been spending some time at Mrs. Bancrum's cathouse with the hookers."

"I mean beaver pie you don't have to pay fer."

Truth was Simon did enjoy Mrs. Bancrum's whores, but he also groped, at the high school dances, various giggly girls in cotton drawers, their big feet in dancing slippers with two straps across white stockings. Still, at fifteen, he hadn't actually penetrated unpaid for and respectful female flesh. So it was Mrs. Bancrum's, to mix with ranchhands, loggers, gandy dancers, bindlestiffs.

Craig didn't go to Mrs. Bancrum's—he was wearing garter armbands and a blue-green eyeshade as a full-time teller in the Miners and Drovers Bank of Silver Bend. Even accepting a cigar from the bank's founder and president, Senator Julius Ott. Senator Ott was what the muckrakers called "a railroad Senator," owned by the Huntingtons, Hills, Harrimans. But a popular figure in Washington and always sure of reelection. "For Julius Ott," Brewster said, "is a warmhearted man."

The politician told Craig when the Senator put him in the bank: "Every man should get his share of the good things. I like to share, I like to see Americans living easy and good."

Uncle Brewster said: "You know, he really hates to foreclose on a mortgage; he's carrying fifty thousand dollars of notes he hasn't foreclosed. Including a lot of ours." Craig, smelling of barbershop chypre and lavender, just said, "He's keen. Said to me, 'Nobody will get rich picking up dimes *I've* dropped.'"

The Miners and Drovers Bank managed to make a good return for its stockholders, perhaps by the fact that it cheerfully advertised itself as not hardhearted or greedy. Yet, Brewster pointed out, it somehow ended up with fine ranchlands, mineral rights, and the notes *were*, after all, in the end foreclosed and bankruptcies took place. Craig said, "Senator Ott usually pays a busted family's railroad fare to their next of kin, buys drinks for bankrupts at the Pioneer Bar, and finds jobs for girls whose folks go off without them—positions as chambermaids in farmers' hotels as far east as Cleveland."

Simon said, "I bet he doesn't even pinch them."

"You have a low mind, Simon. Many a bum the Senator has set

[40]

up as a night watchman, or if too far gone, got him into the post offices or old soldiers' homes. Mollie understands what keeps a bank popular."

Mollie Ott was the Senator's only child. He was a widower who feared women as harpies, and worse, when used as sumptuous diversions. As Craig put it, "He'd rather play a good hand of poker than take Theda Bara to bed."

Simon said, "You'd rather marry Mollie."

Craig adjusted his pearl-pinned cravat. "I respect her—she'll be splendid when fully mature."

Mollie was fifteen; to Simon mature enough—he, too, was fifteen. So he came loping up the Ott bluestone drive toward the Rhine River *Schloss* the Senator had built; fitted it inside with deer antlers on the walls, steel engravings after Sir Edwin Landseer, California, mission furniture and stained-glass lighting fixtures over oil lamps. The town was talking of building a gas plant, and the bank would float the bond issue for the Silver Bend Utilities—but so far oil and candles lit the country.

Simon, not fearing Craig as a rival, put a copy of *The Adventures of Sherlock Holmes* under one sleeve of his Norfolk jacket, and visited Mollie Ott. No holes in his black stockings, his short pants held up at the knees by the thick rubber bands cut by Charlie from an old Michelin inner tube. He wore a gray cap Dolly had brought him from San Francisco, where she had spent a fine two weeks at a Chinese Missionary conference with Rufus B. Dillington, president of the B.A. & P. Railroad—a good time with satisfaction and impunity. The Copperwoods after that never paid for railroad tickets, for Dolly had a family pass good on all Western lines.

Mollie Ott was in the back garden in what she called a gazebo. It was made of sawed, narrow timbers, covered with gourd and morning-glory vines and infested by spiders, a wasp's nest, and wood beetles. Mollie didn't mind any of this desecration; she liked to sit in the old porch-glider exiled there and rock herself back and forth imagining she was a film actress like Norma Talmadge, Clara Kimball Young, or Pearl White, menaced by rape, torture, and evil Oriental predators; hedonistic fiends panting in heat, who showed a lot of teeth and were always

[41]

grabbing hold of some actress with extreme tenacity and wrestling her back and forth. Tearing a bit of her clothes off before some long-chinned American broke in and clobbered the rapist to the floor, the girl swooning with relief and adulation in the hero's arms.

At fifteen Mollie never knew for sure what came next. The film ended there. But she wondered and slept rolling around in agitation in her big bed. She knew nothing of human sexual behavior, and thought the physical business was reserved for dogs, horses, roosters mauling hens, and Indians. The Senator wanted her raised, as he put it, "pure." He had hoped she would never marry, but just keep house for him; be a credit to the Otts' position in the state and his holdings in banks, railroads, oil land, and stocks. If she had to marry to produce heirs—well, there was Craig Copperwood down at the bank. Very serious about money.

"What," asked Simon, greeting Mollie on the swing, "are you doing in the goddamn spider's nest?"

"Come in and swing me, Simon."

"There's a wasp nest, too."

"Let's get a broom and stir it up. Buzz! Buzz!"

"You crazy, Mollie? Your face would get all swollen up. It's a jim-dandy of a pretty face. Kerist, you damn well know it is."

"I don't cotton to boys that talk profanity. Talk d-i-r-t-y."

"That's not dirty. S-c-r-e-w, now, *that's* dirty."

Shocked, Mollie sucked in on her postnasal drip and put one patent-leather shoe on the worn plank floor of the gazebo. "What?"

Simon was loaded with worldly wisdom. He was rather amazed to discover Mollie had no true idea what the word meant—just that it was a forbidden thing, some sort of horror—had actually never heard it fully defined. But then Simon remembered that winters Mollie went to a convent school near Butte, even if the Otts were Full-Dip Baptists and knew the Pope was a Jew.

While he sensed Mollie was perhaps being fattened for Craig, Simon invited her that afternoon to the old Starkweather boathouse to read Sherlock Holmes. Senator Ott did not approve of modern fiction for young girls. Simon had spent several sticky, clutching afternoons in the old boathouse on Partner's Lake behind the failed apple orchard. The Starkweathers were too old to use it anymore, so it was deserted. Simon had kissed Mollie's breasts while she cried out, "Oh, oh, that's something nice!" Had bitten her knees below the piggy-pink drawers, kissed her thighs, but had been robbed of complete victory by the intricacy of Mollie's undergarments. As he opened the Conan Doyle volume, he was happy to see she seemed to be wearing a sort of wraparound, and her rather large breasts were free of any harnessing.

Penetration Day, he decided as they sat in the boathouse, facing the drying lake bed and its fringe of beech and maple. They sat on an old wicker sofa whose calico upholstering gave off gray dust and obscene stuffing. He had gotten past the first page of *The Adventure of the Red Headed League* and was kissing her, and Mollie was kissing back. He explored his tongue between her small white teeth and she responded with a happy moan and the kicking off of her patent-leather shoes with the rhinestone buckles. For one moment Simon thought of Craig's holdings, or rights, to the body of Mollie Ott. But the moment passed—Craig didn't even listen to a Bert Williams record of "I Ain't Got No Satisfaction." There was just a shift under Mollie's wraparound, and he got one splendid breast out, tested it in his palm for weight, resiliency, and warmth. He wondered if Mollie was really only fifteen, and popped the goody into his mouth. Mollie let out a war whoop of joy. Simon didn't desist. He sank down, buried his head in her belly, ending in a demand he "Stop-it-or-I'll-scream." He hiked up the wrap and slip and got one hand on the goal. The pudenda still retained some girlish baby fat, was pliable as the Gulf Coast oysters he once ate on a trip to New Orleans with Uncle Brewster. He thought of a picture of Venus Callipyge in Madame Bancrum's parlor.

"What are you doing? My gawd, my gawd, Simon! *What?*"

"What you think I was doing?"

"Oh! What are you doing now?"

"I'm tickling. Tick, tick, *tickle!*"

"My gawd! *Gawd!*"

"Grand, isn't it?"

"What's that you're doin'?"

Mollie's head rolled about on the dirty cushions and she bit her lower lip.

"What you up to, Simon?"

"Show you something."

"Oh, that? Our collie has *that*."

"Just let me run the show."

"Aren't we too young for it?"

"Indians, Charlie says, do it at nine."

"What are you doing now? Tell me, tell me!"

"A game."

"A game? It's dirty."

"Does it feel dirty?"

"I don't know—I'm all sweat. I'm . . . *oh!*"

She stiffened, sighed, cried out, and rolled around. "You mustn't. You just mustn't. Craig—we're almost engaged and you're his brother."

"You feel good, don't you?"

That gave her thought. "But isn't it a sin?"

"Not yet. It's a sin only if done now without love."

(He had heard Aunt Dolly say something like that.)

Mollie said, "I never figured it—"

"Hell, it's the greatest invention since ice cream sodas."

That's how Mollie Ott started Simon Bolivar Copperwood out of town on his way to West Point. (They had to bury the stained slip under an old apple tree.)

He knew he did not love Mollie, not the way he loved the image of the ideal girl he had created out of his reading, and from dreaming. There was, some place, a perfect girl; witty-wise, slim, and desirable. He was not so foolish as to think she would be perfect in all ways. But she would be as near perfect as a human being could be. She would combine the pleasures he and Mollie took in each other's bodies with something a sensitive, not-yet-worldly boy would think of as ideal.

He was never to grow fully out of this romantic concept, and it made him a good, understanding man with all kinds of female types. Only, the boy, as he became a man, had less and less hope of finding the full dream. Few men in his long life ever knew this side of Simon. For he was a little ashamed of it; like being caught reading comic strips or enjoying a child's complicated toy.

Chapter 7

CRAIG COPPERWOOD, apprentice bank teller, regarded Senator Julius Ott as an honest man, so far as a banker could be honest. A man shaped like a Kodiak bear, and a United States Senator who loved his country and his office, and admired and served the men called empire builders by some, and robber barons by others. For whom he gratefully did favors. Craig knew the Senator, his future father-in-law, was devoted to Mollie. A bit stern, perhaps. Yet it seemed he went in great fear of his hefty female child—near sixteen now—whom he held fondly and gingerly to his paunch for a birthday kiss, or on Christmas morning. In public he appeared with Mollie at his side, as on election night, when he won his Senate seat again.

Julius Ott never confessed to Craig how much he feared his daughter as a female. He avoided thinking of those mysterious menstrual lunar events, her smell of damp, healthy girl, the sight of her enlarging breasts; all set up panic in Julius Ott. He feared women, was ill at ease with them unless making tepid jests, mistrusted them as he would Old Nick's tail and cloven foot. He felt it was unfair for nature to turn his darling child into one of those abrasive hostesses inseminated by Republican husbands. He had only a vague memory of his own indifferent contact with his bride on their wedding night in a three-dollar Billings hotel room. Sally-Jane Nordland, she had been. It was like falling prey to a giant, slobbering starfish, not the wispy little wife he had expected. Biting, howling, and so demanding of his body. Near dawn, smiling—"Julie, a lot of bitch in us Nordland girls." Luckily Sally-Jane had died. Sal is what he called her. Dead a year after Mollie appeared; a sudden fever, a sickroom smell and covered bedpans in the house. Remote acquaintances shaking his hand. "You lost a princess there." A neat burial just below the Copperwood plots in the already well-filled cemetery. Old Asa Quackenbush, Sally-Jane's favorite minister, read from the Book of Proverbs:

> Her house is the way of Sheol,
> Going down to the chamber of death . . .

It was Senator Julius Ott's housekeeper, Maud Hightower, who brought the bad news one morning as he sat over his well-browned cornbeef hash with two eggs on top, his lamb steak, his hot cornbread, the pint cup of coffee. She brought him the information that he was within range of becoming a grandfather. Maud was twenty-six, coal black, showed very large white teeth, had cured herself of shuffling, jettisoned an Alabama Negro accent, and was planning to become a schoolteacher.

The Senator broke an egg yolk with a silver fork.

"She hasn't, Mollie hasn't, if you pardon me, Senator, had the flag for three months, as the saying is. She's been catting up her breakfast regularly every morning now."

"What the hell are you talking about, Maudie?" These asinine niggers—once you educate them they're always maneuvering to impress you.

"A pregnant girl. That's what I'm talking about."

The Senator let cornbread crumbs fall down over his jug-shaped jaw and stared at the black girl, her arms folded under her apron, her features poker-faced.

"You just shut your mouth. *My* baby!"

"Don't come on hostile, Senator. She don't know it yet. But I know the signs. My sisters down in Droodville were always pregnant—four pregnancies in three years—and we hardly knew whom to blame. *Whom* to call their father."

Maud prided herself on the use of *who* and *whom*. Her last mail-order teacher's course had marked her "proficient in grammar." She was sorry for the Senator. A good man—he didn't trifle with a black girl.

The Senator slowly wiped his chin, felt the lump of cornbeef hash rise like a tennis ball in his throat.

"Who, Maudie, could have tampered with her, her innocence? Craig?"

Maud laughed. "That capon?"

"Who?"

"Simon Bolivar Copperwood, that's the 'who.' They have been larking and frolicking down by the old Starkweather boathouse. Very frisky. And she came back seven, eight months ago without her slip. Never gave a reasonable explanation of what had happened to the garment."

"That long?"

"Been going on since, too."

The Senator held up his coffee cup automatically and Maud filled it. He forgot to lower his arm for at least ten seconds. He had the expression of a too simple man, morally proper, trapped in the momentum of some nightmarish disaster. He reviewed some shameful sensations about his personal morality; not sexual, but political dealings not really dishonest (opportunistic, perhaps). He shook and shivered and spattered coffee all over his white linen suit.

"Maudie, get Brewster Copperwood on the phone."

After a walk in the hills, Simon had had a morning of insipid idleness, a desertion of will, a lack of desire to read Rider Haggard, build a clipper ship model. He simply sat with the coach dog, Walter, on the side porch, not even wanting to open the copy of *Under Two Flags* he had traded for a clasp knife with Mr. Ludlow, the high school gym teacher, who insisted all basketball players wear jockstraps and wash their feet and pray before a game.

Bo Hue came out banging the screen door and said, "They want you inside chop chop—shake yo' ass." Simon wandered into the parlor and was surprised to find Mollie there, her father the Senator, Brewster and Dolly, all seated around the fumed-oak, round dining table. A Last Supper, Simon thought, short a few guests. So grave, no coffee, tea, or cakes set out for company.

"Götterdämmerung!" said Uncle Brewster, not smiling.

[47]

Mollie looking pleased, the Senator impressive, a bit red-faced. His voice seemed to come out of a pocket. "The young swine."

Dolly was adjusting her high-piled yellow hair with a slow-moving hand. Brewster looked as if he would like a drink after setting the theme for the meeting.

It was Dolly who spoke first. "Simon, dear, you've done an unrestrained, evil thing."

"Thing?" said the Senator. "He's—"

Brewster waved a hand. "Natural for a boy, I suppose, Senator, but just not infra dig in our present morality, I agree." He hoped he had the Latin of it right. "Still, there is a moral social commitment. I at first thought you meant Craig."

The Senator cried out at Simon across the table, added with a hand gesture: "You sonofabitch—pardon me, Mollie, Mrs. B—but I could pistol you down and never regret it! A man's innocent child. Girl child."

Mollie just sat in a scent of myrtle toilet water, almost a smile on her face. She looked a bit plump, and she would be, Simon figured, a large, fat woman in ten years. But she was rosy and healthy-looking and not gross like some of Mrs. Bancrum's hookers. (Yes, he should have left this for Craig.)

Simon tried to keep a stony countenance, but he was frightened. He looked about him at the framed Remington prints from *Collier's*, the elk horns, a Chinese teak and mother-of-pearl screen in bad repair, the Victorian high-backed sofa with red plush upholstery. . . . Speech, voices sounded highly staccato. The parlor, one of two in the mansion, was large and smelled of imprisoned air, the decaying William Morris wallpaper. Simon had a sudden idea what the meeting was about. It wasn't just the meetings in the boathouse. Mollie was, was—oh, hell—a *baby!* At sixteen a *father!*

He tested his vocal chords. "I'm no sonofabitch. My mother and father were married."

Brewster sucked on his teeth, denoting a thirst. "So might you be soon. How old is he, Dolly?"

"Just over sixteen. No reason to rush into matrimony."

[48]

"I'll be damned first," said the Senator. "I'll be—be—" He made some helpless gestures with his arms.

Mollie said briskly, "It wasn't my idea coming here. . . . Hello, Si."

"Hello, Mollie." He had to hand it to her. It was her old man who was blubbering, not Mollie.

Dolly rubbed her fingers briskly together. "It's, I suppose, the only proper Christian thing to do. Think of the unborn child, Senator. I mean the coming infant. You are not going to be pigheaded about this, well, simple, very natural act of mating. 'Go, ye, and multiply and—' "

"It's not *your* tampered-with daughter. I wouldn't yell either if Mollie were a boy."

Brewster nodded. "Now, Julius, that's not our attitude at all. Happens in Silver Bend very often. If we had more sports activities, some vigorous outdoor outlets, you know, for these young studs. . . ."

Mollie said, "I want to get married. Si said he'd—"

Simon scuffed a shoe on the blue rug. "Not actually, I mean —like—" He gave up. "Like married."

The Senator shivered. "At just over sixteen! A wedding! You can't keep anything like this out of Washington gossip. A Senator's daughter knocked up—married, a shotgun wedding, a bastard baby in four, five months after the wedding." He gave way to tears, chest-tearing sobs.

"So that's what really worries you, Senator. It's your career!" Dolly scowled. "That's it, you selfish hog. Bullragging these two young lovers."

"Madam," said Julius Ott, recovering, making a screechy sound. "Respect my office. How do you think I feel having my child debauched by this hoodlum. Has he no honor for his *own* family. After all, she and Craig. . . ."

Brewster went to the Tudor chest, took out a decanter of whisky, and from a shelf took down some crystal glasses.

"Yes, of course, Julius, we too, expected it to be Craig. I mean—hints of a long engagement."

"His own brother," said the Senator, looking at Simon.

"I see your point, Julius." Brewster poured three glasses and handed one each to Dolly and the Senator. He swallowed his own quickly with a toss of his head and sighed. "I would think it best they get married. But I also see your situation. Oh, I see it clearly. Can't bark your shins in Washington. However, you have relatives? In San Francisco? Cleveland? New Orleans? Mollie can visit them for a few fertile months."

Dolly looked with approval at Brewster. "Solves everything."

"St. Louis?" asked the Senator. "Sister Clara."

"Too near," said Dolly.

"Solves *what?*" asked Mollie, rubbing her forehead.

Simon was standing hands stuck deep in his pants pockets, leaning against a golden-oak pillar. He was pale, feeling his heart pump. Still, he admired the way Uncle Brewster was handling things. The debility and lassitude of an alcoholic hid a lot of good thinking.

The Senator asked, "Boston?"

"Boston." Dolly nodded, sipping her drink. "You'll like Boston, Mollie. Shows, museums, sled rides—well, skip *those*. And summer there's sailing and clambakes. All kinds of really pungent seafoods cooked in seaweed, fat oysters and—"

"*Og,*" said Mollie, covering her mouth in panic, retching.

"Boston Common," hastily added Dolly. "Liberty Hall."

The Senator drank in sadness; his cheek moved in a facial tic. He held out his glass. Brewster nodded, refilled the glasses. "Boston then."

Dolly looked over at Simon standing in a perspiration of agony, held out her hand to him. He came over and took it, gripped it hard. "I don't," she said, "hold this event to be the end of the world. Sooner or later any normal two young people step into nature's little trap. Havelock Ellis wrote—never mind Ellis—Senator, it isn't the Dark Ages, it's 1916, the age of enlightenment—Woodrow Wilson, the Panama Canal, the time of science, art; well, progress." She was carried away, remembered some fragments of something uplifting in the *Literary Digest*. "Progress, yes. Mollie is too young to bear. So science can help her . . . in Boston. But that's all for later. Now what about Simon?" She patted his hand and smiled at him. "What about him?"

[50]

"Horsewhip him," said the Senator, "within an inch of his life."
He was not a deep-drinking man, but holding up his glass again:
"Flay the hide off him. Castrate him like a steer." He wept. "My
baby girl, my—"

Dolly firmly grasped Simon's free hand. "I was thinking of
West Point."

Simon felt his arms grow heavy, hands go damp in his aunt's
cool palm. He gave an involuntary frown, thought somehow
—why he didn't know—of Mollie's piggy-pink drawers at the
time of a certain game in the rowboat. They had been at it hot
and heavy, as the country expression was, *all* summer when they
met in the old Starkweather boathouse. . . . West Point.

"West Point!" shouted the Senator, then sat back in his chair
with a thud, his brow beginning to dampen, his fragile hold on
the reality of this domestic situation in danger.

"West Point," said Dolly. "You have an appointment you can
make to the military academy this spring."

The Senator became the politician, a wary one, the public
image. "A disgrace to the nation. It would be a blot on—you
realize the integrity and honor that exists at the Point?"

"Nuts," said Brewster, looking up from twirling his glass in his
fingers. "Pardon me, Mollie, Dolly."

"You're invading my public duties, my integrity." The Senator
was using his speech-making voice.

"Julius, five years ago you got that sleazy hog-butcher's son,
Hank Henshaw—that's the one, Henshaw—in as a cadet. And he
stole his mother's pearls before you appointed him and spent
two weeks in Nell Kimball's hustlers' house buying bubbly for
—never mind. They ran him out of the Point for stealing some
cadet fund, didn't they?"

"Never proved." The Senator waved off another drink, sat
back mopping his brow, cheeks, and jowels with a large yellow-
silk handkerchief. "Never proved . . . never—Oh, *my* God!" He
looked over at Mollie, and Simon was aware his heart was breaking. "I mean, darling—"

"I want to get married, Papa."

"Boston, Boston." He looked around desperately at the merciless Copperwoods, focused on Dolly patting Simon's wrist. She was smiling. Women, smelly monsters, thought Julius Ott—that Greek head in the Washington museum, hair all snakes—a true picture of them. Why on God's green earth were women made? Who needs them? Couldn't God have made babies—God, that is—out of cornmeal and yeast? He was drunk and aware of it.

The Senator took out his gold-rimmed pince-nez from a small metal case with a snap lid and put them on his nose. The glasses renewed his courage and gave a clear middle-distance vision. He still felt miserable, tragically besmirched, so very sad. He stared at Dolly and took inventory of himself. He had tried to lead a fairly honest and decent life. He was not a bad man. Had no great evil deeds in his past, planned none in the future—what he did for corporations was good for the USA, for Silver Bend. Now to send this young prick, this dangerous—most likely an IWW—young stud to West Point hurt his conscience. Yet, yet, he, Julius Ott, had at times enigmatic instincts, even unreasonable, that stung him at times like a horsefly. The boy was bright-looking, handsome, most likely I'd be doing the Army a favor getting them somebody like him. I could even some day be proud—once we get into the big war over there—when I read the sonofabitch has fallen in battle leading his men. He saw it with some final clarity. Yes, blown to bits. It made a nice picture. And Mollie free of the Copperwoods—even Craig, he's fired tomorrow—she married to some Chicago commodities commission merchant or a St. Louis beer family.

The Senator felt some dark dream hovering, not yet gone, smelling of booze, but hope of waking safe in his big bed. "There are standards and tests, not just an appointment. But if possible, perhaps, yes."

"I want to—" Mollie began.

The Senator lifted an arm—horrified at his instinct—as if to strike his daughter. "You young sl— shut up. You're lucky we're all up-to-date, tolerant people."

"Of course," said Brewster. "No moss growing on you, Julius."

"We'll be going now. You'll be on your way, Mollie, by Tuesday. On the Western Express with Maud for Chicago, and the Erie Flier to Boston. Your Aunt Binnie is going to throw a kinipchen fit. Oh, golly—I'm dizzy."

Simon looked at Mollie as she rose, fluffing down her organdy dress. He was almost in a state of euphoric stupor at all the machinations. He had followed the sequence of ideas around the table. It had given him a good look at how the adult world operated. The last he saw of Mollie was her being led off by her father, moving on her russet leather shoes with metal buttons, out of the room, the big blue bow over her behind seeming to flaunt itself with a wriggle, a final flick of her buttock muscles. He sincerely regretted what he had done—that day, anyway. And Craig would never forgive him. But there were other worlds and other things than country-town girls, and only Craig's future bothered him. It was clear he'd done his brother dirt. He would make up for it, do brave and wonderful things, and classy women—one of his dream girls—like those behind glass on the Cheyenne Express would admire him.

Simon never saw Mollie again. She married in a few years —Klaus Kissinger, a Kansas City importer of fairly good cigars. She settled in middle age as a very wealthy widow in Santa Barbara, California, and was often referred to as "a gracious patroness of the arts."

Even Craig benefited. He went over to the rival Silver Bend First National as full-time teller, was president at thirty, a millionaire four times before forty. But at the time Craig felt tragic, theatrically so. Simon, a week later, was filling out forms the Senator would submit for his appointment to West Point. Craig leaned against the door. "You rotten swine. If the Senator wasn't such a fair man, he'd have fired me with no recommendation."

"Well, you have the ass for a soft fall, Craig. Besides, you have a better job across the street. You really bring a lot of trade with you."

"You could of ruined me." Craig sat down and folded his plump arms. Outside from the front lawn came the *clop-clop* of the meeting of croquet balls. Charlie Rockefeller and Bo Hue played nearly every afternoon after lunch, betting packs of Piedmont cigarettes on the result. Craig bit at some loose flesh on one of his thumbs. He had fine, even teeth. "There's the matter of Mollie. I loved her, I mean decently, felt some day, some day we'd—together—"

[53]

"Yes, Craig, really—yes, it was true love—not the bank job. I had no real idea. It's not too late if you still—"

"No, no, the Senator is never going to let Mollie come back here. Sending her to Switzerland after Boston. Besides, it would come out—gossip—I've a career and—"

"I don't mean that you'd marry her just now."

Craig looked at his bank teller's long fingers, no fat there. "Would you marry her if you were in my position?"

Simon stared at the ink stains on his blotter made by Uncle Brewster's leaking Waterman fountain pen. "What do any of us know when we come right down to it? But I think I'd say no."

Craig screamed, "Outside of being very fine fun for you, Mollie's pretty dull. Frankly, you think she's stupid. Mollie, the only woman I'll ever love!"

"Stop acting."

Dolly came into the den and found the two brothers rolling on the floor, banging at each other with their fists, hair in disorder, Craig's left eye swelling, Simon with a bloody nose.

Craig began spitting out bits of a chipped tooth. Simon said, "I wish I could make it up to you."

"You—you—mucker."

Three months later, in the spring of 1916, Simon Bolivar Copperwood was a shaved-head plebe at the Point. He was neither homesick nor too remorseful. Did he really love Craig? He was missing Bo Hue's cooking, those garlic-studded stuffed veals, the marvelous hot breads, the way he did trout in some secret sauce no one dared ask the making of. . . . Woodrow Wilson was going to be reelected on the slogans: He kept us out of war, we're too proud to fight.

It was a time of nations marching. He could not spare the time to feel guilty for what he had done to Craig. He was just beginning to understand he could not like people like his brother. The careful, serious people whose idea was material success. Who saw everything as protecting one's class and one's income. Of being safe. Voting right, churching right, the right car in the right year. The right amount of children, on the right street.

Simon did not yet know what kind of world he was seeking. He knew he would have to appear hard, stern, hardworking. Whatever was behind his eyes, whatever thoughts came to his mind when not on duty, studying, these he kept to himself. He avoided certain kinds of classical music because it left him near tears; he was wary of great poetry with any glorious use of words; the whole world could explode in a golden bubble when a poem was just right. The sight of a green rain-damp hill and some old white houses, the purl of a stream over rocks, the march of clouds, all had to be limited experiences, or he would go off in directions away from what he now saw as his destiny, his path. The cadets who called him Wolf Trap, for his stern solid set of features, the crispness with which he talked, he was aware they did not know him at all. Good!

Book Two

And in the end the age was handed
The sort of shit that it demanded.

—ERNEST HEMINGWAY

(From Simon Copperwood's notebooks)

Chapter 8

As the young second lieutenant remembered it, the poet had not yet written it was "the cruelest month." It was late in April, 1918, that Marshal Ferdinand Foch, Allied Supreme Commander, looked at his map of the Ypres region and the positions of the five tattered British divisions there. He decided to move them south to merge with the Sixth French Army in the field. The general he put to command them—*à tort ou à raison*—was a proud and rather arrogant fellow, Denis Auguste Duchêne; superficially blown up with his own importance; he saw all battle ordered on the patterns set up *en joue* by Napoleon. He was under the already old Pétain, set in a casual animosity between them. The merged army held the sodden sector along the Chemin des Dames ridge. With casual conviviality the Americans were to be added to these forces.

General Pershing had placed Major S. T. Hubbard, of his Order of Battle section, at the HQ of the combined Allied forces, to keep his eyes open. With two shavetail second louies of eighteen, with only two years of West Point behind them. The staff also consisted of a major, who drank and was known in Paris at the Deux Magots and Lipps, a captain who was an expert with maps. Major Hubbard warned the dancing little French general Duchêne that von Ludendorff would be attacking in force maybe in May and would break through unless Duchêne moved on his own. And quickly, to knock the Boche out before he could gather his forces. The French general just shrugged in amusement. Major Hubbard said to one of his young aides, "The sonofabitch is going to get his ass kicked. He's got six knocked-out *poilu* divisions and the five beat-up Cockney units under what's-his-name, Copperwood?"

"General Sir Alexander Hamilton Gordon."

"Oh, my aching back. And the American second is stuck south of Verdun."

The young lieutenant said, "They call it a *bon secteur*, sir."

"They'll get over that when the cooties bite."

The general liked the young shavetail; clean-cut, no sport from the Pigalle bars, the Bal Musette, and the dives. Must be six feet three and still growing. Skinny, too thin, but hard-muscled. Close-cropped red-gold hair, always shaved, the uniform London-cut, good boots and spurs. One of Major Millhouse's boys.

"The Huns have fifty divisions up and are placing—so British Intelligence says—over three thousand guns in position. You speak French, Copperwood, what's the craphouse rumor here?"

"General Duchêne says it's just rotten intelligence."

"Go down to the second, take the intelligence files, and I'll write a private note to tell them it's coming. Frenchies are going to sit it out over their damn *hors-d'oeuvres* and let the Hun mass."

The lieutenant saluted, got his dispatch.

"And, Copperwood, have Lieutenant Holtzman go along and come back with a report of the Second Corps setup. Hear they have dugouts with electric lights and stoves, real beds. Goddamn it, it's a war, not an Elks' picnic."

"Yes, sir." There were no layers of subtleties in Major Hubbard—he laid it on the line.

The hall of the castle of the combined HQ had mud all over the Italian-marble floors, wood smoke from the Henri IV fireplaces smelling up the ancient frayed velvet drapes. A weary French sergeant sat at a field phone set on a Louis Cat table alongside a big board that held layers of maps marked up in red chalk. A dozen officers, English and French, stood around reading reports or gossiping in bored comradery. In the outer foyer by the drafty doors on a black bench were three bearded military police talking a Normandy patois, two company runners smoking fags and scratching. Also, a wide giant of an American lieutenant, too large for his uniform with the Rainbow Division patch, his neck too big for his tunic collar, his nose too large for the face, the pupils of his eyes a dark hazel, almost purple, the skin naturally dark, not weathered. He gave the appearance of a man consuming time too slowly, reading a copy of the London

Illustrated News, smoking a pipe. His legs were wrapped in puttees, not boots, his hobnail shoes caked with dried mud. He also, Lieutenant Copperwood noticed, needed a shave.

The big officer looked up and smiled. "Well, sport, a three-day pass in Paris?" The baseball-field nickname seemed out of place.

"Like hell. We're going down to the Second Corps with some dispatches. And you're coming back with a report on conditions." He handed the big man a paper.

"It's a Jewish holiday, I think. I'm dragtailed bushed. Been out on patrol with North Africans in what they call no-man's-land. I need soap, steam bath, sleep."

"Orders, Bruno."

Lieutenant Holtzman folded the magazine and looked out. April had passed, now the May day was rainy and gray. He looked at shattered trees, worn roads, a line of little Indochinese men driving trucks. The whole landscape seemed to be beating itself to nothing.

The two men put up coat collars and braved the day. The car pool gave them a mustard-painted Dodge with a canvas top, mica side-curtains, a fox-faced driver whose name was Jon Balbac and who said he was from Montmartre—*en tout cas* it was a rotten day. They started off, splashing up a lot of mud. Lieutenant Simon Copperwood tried to sleep. Bruno Holtzman did sleep as the Dodge bumped along the rutted roads. Three years of war had turned the roads into horrors of mixed horselitter, bones of dead mules, and perhaps worse. The stink of done-in animals, a sweetish reek all around them was, the driver said, dead horse—not Chateaubriand. Shattered buildings appeared as the rain struck the slopes with increased fury. Bundles of rags washed out along the ridges; dead men buried too shallow, some of them, the driver agreed, from two, three seasons of war gone by. "One gets used to it. It's the shelling you never get to like."

Simon winced at a flight of metallic thunder. It had been a dull war for him so far, had been office work and paperwork for the major. By them, the two second louies, shavetails, the lowest of the low. Mere West Point cadets hurried into uniform from their classes on the Hudson. There was a shortage of officers in the AEF, as the country prepared to blunder, work, talk big, and begin to send the first of a million men to France. All with songs, Simon felt, that begin with "Over There," "Zip Zip," and "K-K-K- Katy." Simon had seen shrapnel bursting in the dust, the cellars of Bouresches filled with dead men. Been stunned by a *Minenwerfer* shell that burst between him and Bruno one afternoon as they were inspecting the front lines, and once he had fed chaut-chaut clips fired in the direction of the enemy. A picture-book soldier, loaded as he was with Sam Browne belt, boots, spurs, sword packed away, gas mask, tin hat, grenades, a British swagger stick, canteen, and a short-barreled Luger he had bought off a company runner while swimming in the Marne at Croutte. Also, a dozen condoms, an Elgin watch, gift Bible, and a corkscrew. He had bought the Luger for a tin of Dukes Dunhill Mixture and a twenty-franc note.

As the Dodge slithered along, to the east a battery of 105's were firing. Simon would now tell the sound of the 77's, the 88's, by the *wozz* and *swish*, and when to duck. He had left a dugout just a week before, ten minutes before it was hit and nothing left but shreds of dog food. As he wrote his Uncle Brewster:

> There we were, at ease, eating captured *Kriegsbrod* fried in bacon grease, and drinking *Kaffee Ersatz* and a Vouvray wine, two British chaps and a French captain, talking of the good sound of the *soixante-quinze* firing over our heads. Then Bruno, my roommate at the Point, and I left them, still at chow, having a batsman cooking on a fire made of strips of 155mm gun high explosives, which makes a hot, smokeless fire for cooking—it's only dangerous in a shell. Well, we turned as we heard a Boche 88 come over and go slam bang right into the trench and the dugout, the whole frigging ridge. As Charlie used to say, the shit hit the fan. I had an impetuous minute. I wanted to scream.
>
> So far I'm still waiting for the real war in the sense of an American advance, a meeting of the enemy with the AEF. All we see of the Hun now is some dead body. On the wire maybe, been there six months, a year. The rats are horrible, big as jackrabbits, and I hate to think of them feeding. The cooties sure bite, and the French-

men smell like camels, and they move slowly but with a what-the-hell persistence.

The land is all chalk hills, mudholes smelling like Old Nick, wrecked villages, gruesome mazes of trenches carved out of old graves, rusted wire; such a mangled terrain. The part I saw was held by Chasseurs and a line division, and one day out with dispatches I got a glimpse of the towers of Rheims. I guess it was my first big thrill in France. Besides, I was drinking coffee-and-rum, and the English Tommies were asking for just a "fukkin' bon blighty in the arm." A mild wound to send them home. Pardon the bad word if Aunt Dolly reads this—the Cockneys are all about five feet tall and use it—that word—every *other* word. Believe it or not there are poppies growing in the wheat, and bits of the gray uniforms show of the *Feldwebel* who fell here last year.

We came across the big pond in a rotten old transport, a Cunarder brought back for war service, the *Saxonia*. Carried my division section from Dix, also Marines from Quantico. We left from Hoboken, and after a hell of a seasick trip—cold, coagulated, greasy food, air like a Chinese privy—we got to Brest, and for the doughboys onto those French freight cars. We officers got a *Bleu Train* car, not very clean, and we ended up in St. Aignan, which the AEF calls Saint Onion. It's no place for the finer sensibilities.

I'm now attached to a combined Allied HQ, can't write about it, or where and who. I carry a canteen of *eau de vie*, and don't duck any more when the Archies go off, big bursts of shellfire in the sky to keep off the raiding airplanes. Our Archies burst white, the Fritz ones black. Did get one ride in a Sopwith—refused a Spad and a Nieuport—damn canvas kites—and tossed my lunch. Flying has promise of a great future but—I have a feeling I shall die in battle. Soon. It's been like a hoodoo; death sticks to my mind with tireless persistence, making me feel dark and ornery. At eighteen it sure doesn't look so good to feel life is over, no future, no middle age or old age. And feisty as I am, a real Old Arnie Copperwood, there are a lot of women I want to love. Lots and lots of them. War is sure full of uncertainties but it's exciting, too. I guess feeling this adolescent and impetuous desire to do and be, I'm not as scared as I sometimes feel. And I keep up a fine façade—casual as a hired gunslinger in Tombstone. I'll send you, Uncle Brewster, a Mauser rifle and a *Gott-Mit-Uns* belt buckle for Dolly.   Love.

> Your nephew in peril,
> Simon, 2d Lt. USA.
> AEF
> (someplace in France)

As the bucking Dodge jolted his spine, Simon realized how far away the Point was from this battered world. Just three months ago he was there on the Hudson, a second-year man, no longer a callow jerk to be kicked around by any upperclassman, but enjoying marching to chow, arms swinging in cadence, looking forward to a weekend in Tarrytown, getting a sweet-smelling girl after the Army-Yale game. . . . West Point was a patch-up of images in his mind as he rode south in the muddy dirge of war. The Point as he first knew it as a raw Westerner—a gray, stone place on a river, of tight-nuts discipline, spit-and-polish, chapel. Taps on a lonely bugle. Good visits at the hotel run by the Department of the Army when the girls came up to the proms. Life in a dormitory. His had once been used by Southern cadets who died in battle, most of them, long ago in Confederate gray, and the windowsill in the room he shared with Bruno Holtzman had cut into it the name "J. E. B. Stuart." Had Stuart ever actually attended the Point? Or was it some kind of jest? The lights went out at eleven. Mornings were rushed; a hasty wash to open tacky eyes, awaken wobbly mind, then marching en masse across Thayer Road, cadet caps pulled low over eyes, big shiny bills on the caps, close-cropped scalps. View the houses of the officers, educators, sit in classrooms full of details to store in one's skull—mechanics, engineering, physics, history, languages, military arts, and, of course, English lit, at which somehow he was a cockeyed wizard expanded from his boyhood reading of just anything. Viewing, too, all the nameplates and the ranks of the teachers attached to the white frame houses of the educators and officers. He learned it was wise to take an officer's ugly daughter to a dance, out for a soda, give her a few feels; hope it helped the marks. Always a modest decorum, a sobriety of behavior; keep your hands above the blankets, plebe.

The first days at the Point were hell; the commanders gave it to them hard and straight as they faced them, raw material they would help form into the nation's muscle. The commanders glared down the refectory tables with iron stares. Morning light angled through the windows of Washington Hall, catching a corner of the mural, turning it bright. A noble, dishonest mural. Heroism and martyrdom, but no blood, no suffering. Gallantry and heroism, victory but no rotting bodies, no torn limbs, crushed faces. No stink.

The plain good food in Washington Hall under the heroic painting seemed to taste better after the first days, even if the upperclassmen braced you, sat you at meals ramrod stiff. Sadism was part of the course at the Point for the new men. All those great battles painted on the walls of the dining hall fascinated Simon, and he wondered, would new ones be there after the present war?

At the Point the Great War in progress in Europe was studied. Simon, with the second year cadets, listened to young Major Roger Millhouse (an authority on Baudelaire in his spare time) explain how easily it all began, that war—began like a ballet of toy figures in uniform, falling down in a row. There was the Dual Monarchy, a mixed-language nation called Austria-Hungary "made up of eight nations, seventeen countries, twenty parliamentary groups, twenty-seven parties." The name of the Bosnian town where the war fever incubated was remembered by Simon.

The lesson was that the leaders of the European nations were eager for warlike gestures, some earnestly hoping for battle, a short pageant of power. "Using the excuse of an assassination, the Austrians saw a chance to punish and grab off more of Serbia, and even when Serbia offered to meet *all* terms, the Austrians wanted war. The Russians came proudly to the aid of their Slavic brothers in Serbia. Russia was still medieval, autocratic. The Germans announced they must aid brother Austrians if the Great Slavic Bear moved; so the French gave notice they held to a treaty of aid to Russia. England stood firmly proud to its assistance alliance with France."

Major Millhouse also read them that remark of Sir Edward Grey, as he stood gloomily at his London window. "The lamps are going out all over Europe. We shall not see them lit again in our lifetime."

"In a crisis," added Major Millhouse, "the English, masters of a strong and splendid prose, never failed to come up with the proper sentence for the schoolbooks of the future."

The texts in military history showed that in 1914 all the nations had plans, all had long-studied charts, maps for victory. In the main it was to be a war of foot-slogging infantry, flanked by fine horsemen, with a great deal of artillery. Of the embryo air forces little was expected.

Would the United States get into it? Everyone at the Point hoped so. It is the prerogative of a soldier to desire battle. Or so the young officers seemed to hint. "Wars make quick promotions," said Major Millhouse. "Often *too* quickly."

Simon was lucky in a roommate. Bruno Holtzman was rather a madcap; the word "madcap" in 1916 was used for anyone who laughed deeply, had extra adrenalin flowing, and some sense of wit. Bruno was delighted with West Point. That he was a Jew and that that fact made things a bit sticky in the military world didn't bother him. "The Navy is meaner, Simon. Where the hell did you get a Heb name like that? The Navy, that's the anti-Semitic kettle of smells. Here among the ramrods and the marching *hauteur* I can take it, and as I'm on the boxing team I've split a few Baptist snozzles. Here I like my enemies."

"That's a Christian slogan."

Bruno, with jocular skill, excelled in physical sports. He played football as a halfback and got his nose bent sideways. He tried to pitch on the baseball team, but hardly controlled his curves, and was found too large for the crew, though he made a splendid cross-country runner. He was lazy as a student, and Simon had to punch him into the study of a subject in detail before an examination. He carried an 1810 coin as a talisman against misfortune.

Bruno disliked serious music, but he could handle a ragtime tune like "Maple Leaf Rag," or "Muskrat Ramble," playing the piano with ecstasy in the recreation center, and he knew songs, the new notes of whorehouse music, still spelled "jass," out of New Orleans' Storyville. Simon found Bruno was very good company, a great success with women, and he matched Simon's appetite for experiences. On holiday leave he and Simon would go to Boston, to the Old Howard burlesque theater, and they had the courage to talk two of the meaty shimmy dancers —rather worn-looking objects close-up—to join them in the Wharf Hotel for a night, where Bruno sang *"Heimweh nach Virginia,"* which he swore was the Kaiser's version of "Carry Me Back to Old Virginny."

During Easter Week the two were in New York City, invited to a house, designed by Stanford White, on upper Fifth Avenue. They danced the Bunny Hug, the Teddy Bear, the Castle Walk, swayed with society girls in hobble skirts, and took them to afternoon tea at the Ritz and for a hansom cab ride through Central Park, kissed them good-bye on a carved balustrade.

Simon made second base on the Point's baseball team and played the sax well and very fast, so soon everyone called him Sport Copperwood. He plucked a mandolin and sang Stephen Foster songs and cowboy laments.

> You done stole my Stetson hat
> I'm bound to take your life;
> He was a bad man
> That mean old Stagolee.

Bruno rescued him when he got drunk after an Army and Navy on a retired colonel's flask of brandy and was rolled by two sailors under the stands. He lost an elk's tooth that Charlie Rockefeller had given him on parting and which Simon had had set in a gold watch fob. He decided never to drink from offered flasks after a game.

Bruno's lazy, wild ways were always in danger of getting him sent down from the Point. He'd read his marks and cry, *"Das ist umglick!"* But his skill in handling drill teams equaled Simon's, as did his expertise in winning war games in extended camping exercises at Peekskill's outdoor camping season. Bruno starred in his ability to take apart and reassemble a Hotchkiss machine gun blindfolded. His instructors held to the hope he would make a splendid officer, able to handle men and tools. He envied Simon's ability with horses, his skill taking the hurdles. Bruno didn't read books for pleasure and was amused at Simon's talk of literature and how he managed somehow to find time for Balzac and Stendhal and the early P. J. Wodehouse, the last Sakis. In his second year he gloomed over the piled-up pathos of mortality in the Russians; Tolstoy, Chekhov, Gogol his favorites, not caring for Dostoievski or Pushkin. Bruno shrugged his shoulders. "The damn ink-slingers don't much know. Next time in New Haven on a beer bust let's get a copy of *Fanny Hill.*"

The two roommates puzzled their superiors; these two cadets were either headed for high places or for being kicked out in their third year. Bruno Holtzman lived a full physical life at the Point, enjoying the power of his limbs, the snap with which he marched on parade with the color guard, the vigor with which he ran cross-country. Simon trained down finer, with more grace. They both had moods—a disintegration of communication. Simon would wonder what made Bruno walk around as if in a trance for a day or two, scowling, not speaking. Give drill orders with a rasping bark: "In columns, four abreast!" or stand at artillery practice deaf from concussion of the shell bursts when they were using live ammunition. Simon was seriously studying French in hope of duty in the front lines when the war came to Americans. "Good French dinner, Bruno, costs seven francs, eighty centimes. That's a *bon* feast with wines, *comme il faut,* soup to nuts."

"I speak four languages, sport, and can't add or spell."

"Better bone up on your trig and physics."

That was Simon Copperwood and that was Bruno Holtzman—gay, wild, careless, but very able with men and women, built for laughter and endurance. Untested, very young. They entertained a New York Central train car full of passengers one day, both full of joy and a little too much alcohol, singing:

> I took my girl to a fancy ball,
> It was a social hop . . .

Bruno made his trombone gestures, Simon drummed on the back of the seat ahead.

> Then to the restaurant we went,
> The best one on the street,
> She said she wasn't hungry.
> And this is what she'd eat . . .

The conductor shook his head. Those damn hooched-up Pointers.

> A dozen raw, a plate of slaw,
> A chicken and a roast,

Outside the car windows the Hudson River banks seemed to be parading by.

> Some sparrow grass with apple sass,
> And softshell crabs on toast,

They finished the song at a fast clip.

> A big box stew with crackers too,
> Her hunger was immense.
> When she called for pie, I thought I'd die,
> For all I had was fifty cents.

At the West Point depot, Matthew Dodge, the station cop, held them in the baggage room and phoned Major Roger Millhouse, who came down and fed them hot coffee until their headaches began. The major was fond of them both—his best pupils. They never were bored during his lectures. In the major's class the next morning Simon and Bruno sat very still, repressing pain.

[69]

"The Great War is producing four major innovations in warfare, gentlemen, produced almost absentmindedly, from a sort of *mélange* of ideas that were around and available. They were the airplane, the machine gun, based on models fifty years old, chemical warfare, poison gas, the flamethrower, and the land tank, moving like a metal turtle on an endless belt, a road it laid in front and picked up behind itself. The planes are the only one that exceeded expectations. Leonardo da Vinci said, 'There shall be wings. If the accomplishment is not for me, for some other. . . .' "

The Great War—condensed, tidied away as time receded year upon year—was to take on the color of the last of the romantic wars. The Point watched with professional interest the realities of the trenches, millions living like moles.

The words of the songs were heard on marches along the Hudson: "There's a Long, Long Trail," "Smiles," "Pack Up Your Troubles in Your Old Kitbag." Beyond the parapets of the trenches that stretched and zigzagged from the Channel to the Swiss border came loud echoes of horror.

"It is the last war of gay uniforms, the white of the Hungarian Hussars, the polished brass helmets of the German General Staff, the Cossacks with chest armor of cartridge cases trotting by the Winter Palace where the Czar of all the Russias took their salutes and cries, the pale heir at his side. And overhead Igor Sikorsky's flying machine, the *Ilya Mourometz*, carrying sixteen passengers and a dog."

The major looked at the heavy silver English watch strapped to his wrist—the first wristwatch at the Point. "Dismissed, gentlemen."

As they marched to lunch Bruno Holtzman said to Simon, "The major is a romantic."

"Is that bad?"

"Oh, he sees clearly, but he colors it—'the polished brass helmets . . . the pale heir by his side.' Still, I suppose we'll be in the war by next year."

"Will we go? Or have to stay here and finish our four years? And is it so bad to feel so good the way a West Pointer does about war?"

Bruno rubbed his nose and smiled. "Not if we're training to be soldiers." And he recited:

> An evening red, and a morning gray,
> Will set the traveler on his way;
> But an evening gray, and a morning red,
> Will pour down rain on the soldier's head.

Chapter 9

As the Army Dodge bucked and dipped on the war-wrecked road, Simon thought again of those murals at the Point under which he ate his meals and was at first tormented by upperclassmen. Wellington and Napoleon at Waterloo with William the Conqueror at Hastings, Miltiades at Marathon, Gates at Saratoga, Arminius at the Teutoburger Forest, Cyrus at Babylon, Jeanne d'Arc at Orléans, Marlborough, Mohammed II, Alexander the Great, and others.

DUTY, HONOR, COUNTRY.

The staccato tap of heels marching to flannel hash. Those first days away from Silver Bend, Brewster, and Dolly. He heard one does not tarnish the Army image, and as he studied Article 92 of the Uniform Code of Military Justice, the lowly plebe came around to realizing the importance of obeying lawful regulations, and the evil of dereliction in the performance of duty. The cadet honor code didn't bother him too much after he had shaken a lot of Montana out of his system during the first year. Colonel McNeal of the chemistry department looked directly at him while reciting, "Quibbling, cheating, evasive statements, or recourse to technicalities will not be tolerated."

"Shape up, shape up," cried the jockstrap captain in the gym.

Simon fought down his pride so as not to be a nonconformist.

He thought himself self-disciplined; at first like an organism living in an alien element.

Major Roger Millhouse, teaching military psychology and leadership, gave it to the cadets straight. "The Army is more interested in the doer than the thinker. The Army is here to carry out the wishes of the political leaders of this country. The Army is *never* at fault, remember this. Mark that down in your notes—underline it. In time of trouble people turn on the military. Then we rationalize too much. We have different problems because of the frustrations, and anyone who has been in a war understands. I can understand it. But look, once you begin to break down, break down discipline and break down in general, it tears into a man's self-concept. I want you people here to grasp that, to look at it and understand it, to renew our integrity. . . ."

He was a bit of a dandy, Major Millhouse—after ten years as military aide in London, Paris, St. Petersburg. In private the major enjoyed having a group, four or five of the brightest cadets, to his bachelor quarters. On the walls Japanese prints, an icon from Crete, a Crusader's sword, the war shirt of a Hunkpapa Sioux chief. Major Millhouse would serve tea for the cadets, sip his scotch and soda.

Simon listened at these private talk sessions. Major Millhouse had his eye on him.

"Copperwood, are we *too* obsessed with appearance here, tidiness and care?"

"No, sir."

The major lit the authentic Tolstoy samovar in which he brewed the tea. "Shined shoes, skin haircuts, bracing, sadistic torture of plebes, partly sexual, all those niggling rules. . . . You survived our indignities. Good . . . oh, I liked your paper. Read it in Grant Hall this morning: 'Mormon Brigades in the Mexican War.' "

"I grew up knowing Mormons, sir. Their grandfathers were in it."

"You have a drive and a responsiveness. Very dangerous, Copperwood. Too much credulity, but precocity. You like the Point?"

"Yes, major. It is not Silver Bend." (And with that statement the Copperwood smile, the lowering of the head to one side.)

"Silver Bend, I gather—it isn't the world of deeper *Angst* and wider vision. It isn't the Point."

"It's just Silver Bend, sir."

"Not all cadets think we're an improvement on home. Correct, Holtzman? Please pass the cups."

Bruno lifted the tea tray. "A friend of mine left in his sophomore year. Was very methodical about it, talked to officers around for six months. We tried to dissuade him, Copperwood and myself, because he was a really good man, number one in aptitude. But it didn't work. He said, finally, that he had talked to the officers and decided that when he grew up he didn't want to be like them."

Major Millhouse laughed. "Not you, or you, Copperwood, you want to be like us?"

"I hope to make the Army a lifetime career. Well, I feel extensive horizons ahead."

The tea was gritty, poorly strained, but hot.

Later, in their shared room, with Holtzman plugging away at math, Simon said, "Bruno, I'm a bullshit artist. I meant what I said to the major, but I had to polish it up with Shinola. Be the eager beaver."

"Reticence and shyness get you no place in the Army. You don't fool the major, of course. He's all slick as silk and he's got his eye on you as command material. Me he sees as good solid bone, a line officer. Duty's child."

Bruno Holtzman was one of the few Jews that made the academy in those years. His father was a millionaire junk dealer in Rahway, New Jersey, who gave hefty sums of money to *both* political parties, planted trees in Palestine as a Zionist, and knew the ropes. Bruno at West Point was hard to provoke—he took the pressure from the bully martinets, mostly Southerners. He hoped, he told Simon, to become in time a four-star battle general. He planned to marry an English girl he courted in Newport. "Take her on our honeymoon to visit every major Civil War battlefield from Gettysburg south."

"What a romantic bastard you are, Bruno."

[73]

Bruno liked to repeat, "There aren't any heroes anymore. It's better that way. We're a service."

"A back-breaking service. Get some sleep."

Reveille was at 6:15 for a hard daily curriculum at West Point. Science requirements of three semesters of math, two of engineering, two of mechanics, two of chemistry, two of physics, two of electricity, two of engineering fundamentals, one of astronomy-astronautics, and one of world regional geography, four semesters of one foreign language. Simon picked two of military art, three of English, six of social science, and two of law, the core academic program. The department of tactics and the department of physical education supplied the crucial comments on aptitude.

Four days after the declaration of war by President Wilson and the Congress, and a new slogan, To Make the World Safe for Democracy, Major Roger Millhouse handed the class their second lieutenants' bars. "You're off to Fort Dix in three days and you'll be in France in six months. Be distrustful of extremes —avoid the fallacy of sentimentality. Keep your bowels open, your fly buttoned."

Simon said, "I hope we get there before it's over."

"Copperwood, you're still a healthy baboon. Be sure your men learn how to take care of their Springfield rifles properly, and good luck."

The major turned briskly away. Simon suspected the major always thought of himself as a Roman of the Aurelian period.

Before going off to Fort Dix, Simon went down to Blue Point, Long Island, to say good-bye to the married woman, Mrs. Tennel, with whom he had spent twenty gratifying nights of leave at the Astor Hotel and a month of the summer vacation in a Maine inn. Linda Tennel was seven years older than Simon. Her husband, Raymond, owned coal mines in Mauch Chunk, Pennsylvania, and was a feeble performer in bed, preferring to drive his Narragansett pacers in harness races, and to raise airdales and fox terriers. Linda Tennel, who laughed loudly, also wept often, her black hair loose, fan-spread on the hotel pillow. She talked of life and aging, quoted early Yeats, told Simon about the raccoons she kept in South Carolina where her husband had a showplace farm for his horses and dogs.

In the misty gray of a rainy morning, Linda came down to Hoboken to see Simon sail to war. How she found out the place and date, Simon never knew. He spent two hours with her in a frowsy, unmade bed over Kelsey's Hoboken Saloon, not daring to undress fully—the ship's siren might sound. They clutched each other, his mind half on B Company; the leggings didn't fit any of his company, blankets weren't rolled right. How can a man love properly under such conditions? And would he die or would he be torn up to become a basket case? She said she would *never* forget him, continued repeating—skirt off, blue-gray silk legs—that he was her last, last, very *last* true love, and nothing was left for her but Raymond Tennel's feeble grasp and her lovely splendor of soul. She gave out with Yeats:

> I have spread my dreams under your feet,
> Tread softly because you tread on my dreams.

So they washed up, shameless, side by side, at the basin and the pitcher of stale water, the half cake of suspect soap. The moment for both was tender-sad, bittersweet, and both suddenly wanted to part quickly and go their ways.

Simon never met Linda Tennel again. He never heard from her. There were so many young officers for matrons to ease life for. Not even a letter. In France, in hard moments, he often thought of how he had met Linda in the lobby of a theater during the intermission of the *Ziegfeld Follies of 1917*, picked her up boldly—a gracious smile, a direct offer—been taken to dinner, a late dinner at Delmonico's, heard the story of her arid marriage, her unhappiness, the hideous disaster of failed domestic copulation. And how this was the very first time she had let her emotions go so far as letting herself be taken to the Astor for a night of adultery. For Simon, Linda was a remarkable education, after whores, casual fornications. He thought of her on the blacked-out transport as it plowed the heaving Atlantic, a lookout in the crow's nest searching for U-boats, alongside a tin can of a four-stack destroyer bobbing like a flipped coin to their starboard. On the first French train, watching the damp land-scape sprouting hedgerows, he knew Linda had been the first true adult director of an adolescent's hopes—turning them into a refinement, a leisurely skill taken in a rising passion, to be played out in delicate, perhaps indecent detail, by Silver Bend standards.

When Simon heard the first guns, smelled his first dead war-horse, got a noseful of the shallow three-year-old graves, he knew that he would die always grateful to Linda Tennel, desper-ately romantic, trivial, yet passionate Linda, "Driven, darling, to duplicity with no pathetic assurance of happiness."

In spite of the battle reek, the jolting of the Dodge Army car, as Simon sat in the damp of the journey south to the 2d Division, he felt a sadness thinking of those Astor Hotel nights, followed by Linda leaving to catch a Long Island train and he going to the oyster bar at the Grand Central to await his train back to the Point. The hot stew, the two cups of strong coffee revived him into the reality of the time away from their wet bodies, shiny with rapport. Back to the business of passing the tests in HM 402, 401, 402; history of the military art; war from Herodotus to Hinden-burg, taking notes to the creaking, arthritic joints of Colonel Ambruster. "War is a fluid, *not* a solid."

Someplace in France, in the war, someplace nearby, they were firing 88's—the enemy was—and the Dodge skidded in the greasy mud, the dreadful mess of horse bones, liquid manure, bouncing over the sandbags that filled puddles. They drove past North African natives shivering in faded blue jackets as they filled shellholes. Stretcher bearers were in the roadway, sweating heavily as they carried shapes under stained gray blankets. Mats of camouflage covered airfield guns.

Simon said suddenly, "The real minority are the living in this goddamn country."

Bruno rubbed his aching rump. "We may not get to the Second Engineers, you mean?"

Simon laughed. "I was thinking of a marvelous Long Island woman I knew who typed my term paper: 'An Etymological History of the Military Terminology in *Tristam Shandy*."

Bruno tried to ignite his pipe with a lighter made of a machine gun cartridge. "My paper was 'Artillery Terminology Before 1600.' Didn't fool the major."

"Does the war make you excited, Bruno?"

"I could stand talking to a clean girl. I'm no longer engaged. It seems the shape of my grandmother's nose, my *baba*, got in the way."

"Maybe we'll get a three-day leave in Paris. I hear that—"

The driver spoke up as they skirted past a tank mired at a crossroads. "I could offer some good address in Paris for zig-a-zig. An aunt of mine runs a dress shop and a *maison de tolerance* on the rue de Fourcy. . . ."

Chapter 10

ON May 27 the great German bombardment began. Shells in a creeping barrage pounded the dark night all around Chemin des Dames for four hours. At 4 A.M. the German infantry came over, clots of moving squads, groups of massed men in field gray, bayonets gleaming under the flares, moving on a lope in their coal-scuttle helmets, following the mustard gas, the murderous shelling. The Allied 6th Army was mashed to ruins, the traverses of the trenches filled with dead, and broken men dying. Those who got their gas masks on often vomited into them and many choked to death.

The enemy, making *Toteninseln* of doomed companies, took *alles* in the center of Chemin des Dames. With chilling metallic tread they seized the undamaged bridges across the Aisne, moved on to the Vesle River. Their advance patrols were slaughtering companies in Fismes. It was clear the German drive was making for the Marne, a river that had kept them from Paris three years before. With a sickening apprehension reports read they were swarming around the railheads, the road hub of Soissons. In twenty hours the drive had taken twenty-two miles and was solidly set on the road to Paris. Life, death, to the defeated, seemed ruled by a drunken conjuror.

The American 2d Division lay in a quiet sector, General Harboard noted, at Gisors, forty miles northwest of Paris. The soldiers were gossiping of rumors the 26th Yankee Division had been blooded by the Hun at Seicheprey, near Saint-Mihiel —loose talk, discrepancies, tremors of actions foiled or aborted flood an army's rank and file.

Lieutenant Copperwood came into the barn with the half-torn-off roof, where Major General Omar Bundy, commanding the 2d, sat at an overturned pig-feeder tub talking to his senior officers humped over some fragments of maps. "We're going into battle. Thank God, there will be no more quiet sectors." No one felt this statement needed an answer.

Major Lester Haber, buckling his belt over his plump stomach, came toward Simon. His face was pale, almost a greenish cast, straining as in an attack of eructation. "Copperwood, we move up at daybreak. I don't know, I don't know how it's doing, this battle."

"We have Remières Woods, major, over a hundred Heinies dead."

"Last report it's not so good at Cantigny. The village yes, but—" Major Haber waved his gloved hand in a loose-fingered gesture and broke wind. "That pork last night bother you?"

"No, sir."

Simon saluted and went out to find his company. They were sprawled in some battered cellars, grousing, smoking, talking of women, wine, crap games, crops, and "that French talk about *élan vital*." In the mayor's cellar, Bruno Holtzman, with a three-day beard, his left arm bandaged from contact with a rusted shell fragment imbedded in a door, sat talking to Captain Saringetti, the little dark Italian from Mulberry Street, New York City, laughing and scratching vigorously under his tunic. Several bottles were at their feet.

Bruno grinned. *"Shicker ist der goy."*

The captain said, "Come in, Copperwood, come in. We go?"

"Daybreak. The major looks like he had the wind up."

"Dutch Haber? Les? He's a good peacetime officer. Great for policing the parade grounds in the National Guards. But he'll come through. Just a bit of a calamity howler."

Bruno began to fill his canteen with brandy from a bottle. "I'm going to die sober, but a nip before burial, eh? No Beluga caviar *au blinis*. Oh, well. This is like Hennessy Three Star."

The captain held out some tin cups. "A last booze all around and we'll try and get an hour's sleep. You Presbyterian, Copperwood?"

"My aunt says we're now Episcopalian."

They held the tin cups up. Bruno said, *"Lachaim."*

The captain sighed, crossed himself. "Where's the goddamn priest when you want him?"

Outside in the world of war the shelling was heavy. They could hear the rafters stir over their heads in the ruined house. The flames of the three burning candles shivered. Through gaps overhead could be seen the smoky blue-green of the changing sky.

With the first sliver of morning light the company moved, night still holding the village as they shuffled out, joined other companies in the May air, and moved toward where the sky burned, and the growl of shells, rapid rounds of fire lit up angry welts in the earth being fought over. Earth none of them wanted or gave a damn about.

Captain Saringetti was to the left with two companies. Simon and Bruno led their men side by side, up the cobbled road. "It's a big one," said Bruno. "A dog robber told me there's the Second Brigade, the whole Twenty-sixth and Twenty-eighth Infantry regiments in this show. What's the coordination?"

"The Heinie observation point by Cantigny. They want us to take it, that's all."

"Nom de Dieu. And I'm hungry as a bitch wolf."

The day brightened—took on color to show stretcher bearers with their Red Cross brassards. The flares and gun flashes grew paler. Water and ration parties kept going up to the front, cursing and wondering at the methodical shelling. Battalion runners passed, wary, bent over and cursing the ration parties under their loads. Simon moved his company up in the direction of the road northwest, his Luger in his hand. There was sustained rifle firing on his left, trench mortars going off, and one-pounders nearby. His ears buzzed and he wondered if his fear was visible to some shaggy *poilus* with their needle bayonets.

It was not himself that was scared; it was his goddamned body. It could betray him if he let it. God, was he so weak as to knuckle down and crap yellow like Major Haber? He felt his heart expanding, contracting, a bag of red liquid about to burst like a huge boil.

Shrapnel and HE were just ahead and the cry "Stretcher bearers!" came from a husky throat. No use looking at the bleeding lumps, some still stirring by the road. Simon led the company onto a wooden bridge where the 2d Engineers were moving heavy timbers to get trucks across. Debouching men, guns, horses, motor cars, all moved by several parallel roads toward battle.

"Pushoff time," yelled an engineer with a lug wrench in his hand. "You'll never come back, never."

Sergeant Chalky Welton yelled back, "You blue-balled monkeys!"

Simon said, "Spread the men out, sergeant."

They were moving slower now, among horse-drawn 75's, muddy soldiers with bandoliers and combat gear, gas masks, canteens, all becoming heavier. As they moved away from the 75's, Simon saw a hill of russet mud and rusted wire and a path ahead, and then came to some small camouflaged tanks, petrol-smelling, with mounted one-pounders, machine guns. Captain Saringetti lay there in a puddle of oily water beside an upturned Boche Maxim. Simon moved over and looked down at the captain as the tanks moved off. The back of the captain's head was gone, his eyes looking up. Bruno Holtzman turned away.

"Just like that. Something hit him."

"He was only about two hundred feet ahead of us." Simon looked around. Grenades and pyrotechnics were exploding close by. "Let's get off this hill." Private Conrad Seldes puked and Private Willie Wilson had a big damp stain spreading in the back of his pants. His file companions held their noses and laughed, and moved away from Willie. "Willie, he sure cut the mustard. *Phew!*"

From someplace in the brush a voice was crying out, "*Ach, Himmel. Hilf, hilf. Lieber Gott!*"

Bruno said to Sergeant Welton, "Go shut Fritz's yap."

To the left Senegalese and Moroccans with milk-chocolate faces were running forward.

"Hilf, hilf. Ban Brandighe!" There was a shot and the sergeant came back. "Poor Heinie bastard, half of him was gone, flattened out. A tank done it." Bruno Holtzman nodded.

They all went ahead, Simon wondering where regimental commander Major Haber was. They merged for a time with a company of automatic riflemen, and all were moving forward on the run, for now they were within range of something sinister up ahead, coiled, overwhelming danger. Hotchkiss guns were rattling away to the east. Overturned *camions* were scattered like children's toys among some battered poplars, and a platoon was rifling the trucks of hard bread and cases of goldfish. Opening salmon cans with their bayonets and feeding themselves over wet chins with grimy fingers. "The Twenty-sixth," said Bruno, glancing at shoulder patches, and they went on. The Boche had 77's up close; very close, by the bursts, Simon figured. He could identify the shells now by their sound—recurring concussions as they hit. It was methodical shelling, fastidiously planned for kilometers all along the sector. "The Paris-Metz road must be getting it heavy." The men had their bayonets fixed to their Springfields. Simon wondered was the rifle fire really deadly at 800 yards in battle range—as in practice.

"Lootenant," said Sergeant Chalky Welton, as the automatic riflemen ahead began firing their chaut-chauts, "what's the point we has to take?"

"Hill One forty-two. Be sure the men have bags of clips within reach." He felt shaky, but his voice was calm. There was even a passive exaltation.

"Battle sights," yelled the sergeant. "Fire at will."

In all directions, right and left, hundreds of men were moving forward.

The enemy Maxims were busy and Simon wondered if the Americans were facing raw recruits or a rumored battalion of *Sturmtruppen* and the Margrave of Brandenburg regiment. You couldn't tell, and the *Feldwebel* gray on top of the next rise was far off. Were there, were there, of course, young *Herr-Leutnants* over there, just like him in their first battle? Bet your ass.

Then he realized the enemy were rushing toward them. Hun boots, iron-pot heads, coming across a coppice, a deployment of Boche in strength. His gut contracted, his scrotum tightened (his genitalia seemed to want to hide in his body). Simon nearly did the Willie-poop in his pants. He ran forward waving his pistol, and the men followed until they came to a series of open cellars, shallow remains of stone foundations, and they all flopped in and down with a rattle and bang of gear. Simon got the men facing the oncoming attackers, who were still moving with terrible, almost mechanical steadiness. Only fifty meters away, or so he judged, and so little wire entanglements.

"Rapid fire, and then grenades when they get within range."

He was calmer now, felt a sort of spurious optimism. He didn't want to die, held a dim view of immortality—but if it had to be, he'd keep up a front—for all the total futility. He would face it. . . . What a lot of trash they fed you in books and poems about dying. . . . The noble Greeks in that mountain pass . . . with writers tossing metaphorical dead cats at each other about noble sacrifices . . . the Old Guard at Waterloo really crying *"merde!"* instead of the fiction: "The guard dies but never surrenders!"

Simon became aware of Sergeant Welton leaning on him—the pushy bastard—pouring out warm blood, smoky in the cool morning, pouring it on Simon's English tailor's uniform, the sergeant smiling and blowing blood bubbles. "Jesus, Jesus, kin you get me a drink or a priest, lootenant?" He fell away from Simon, and the rifle fire so heavy, the smell of the powder bursts so strong that Simon sneezed and expected Aunt Dolly to say, *"Gesundheit!"* The death of the flannel-mouthed sergeant, a notorious drunk, shook Simon.

The Boche came on again, unsteady now, falling away suddenly here and there as if giant hands came up from the earth to pull them down. Simon took up the sergeant's rifle, fed it shells and fired, kept firing. The enemy was coming in through the remains of an orchard, past the mushy remnants of a long-dead cow. Simon's company were tossing grenades. He liked the way they lobbed them overhand as if the grenades were baseballs they had been taught to throw. The Hun had grenades, too, things with handles the doughboys called potato-mashers. Several of these reached the cellar's outer bricks and blew on their eardrums. Then something flew in on them. Simon felt wet rags move past him as bodies thudded into cellar walls. Half his company were dead or screaming. He hoped the other cellars were stronger. He got hold of Corporal Kompinsky's arm and yelled, "Keep them firing. I'll see if we're to fall back."

"Aren't many guys left that can move."

Simon crawled into the next cellar. The air seemed to be dropping steel on him personally as he rolled down among Bruno and ten men in a root cellar. The whole area was smoky and splashed with patches of mustard gas in the hollows.

"Where's Major Haber?"

"Two cellars down. He's got a phone line and a crank telephone. Wha do you think, Simon?"

"We've got to pull out—unless they're sending up more men."

"We're sure up shit creek and no paddle."

"I'll see if we have orders to pull tracks."

Simon moved on to the next cellar, looked at his smoking coat sleeve where something hot had passed through. He felt of his own arm, searching for damage, tenderly, as if it were a great treasure. Discovered he was not hit, just a smarting burn above the elbow.

The third cellar held remains of wine barrels—once *vin blanc*—a three-story stone fireplace chimney that made it a splendid shelter from anything but the biggest HE or a Boche nine-inch shell. Jesus! Simon mopped his brow—the minutes pass like pickets on a fence. Major Haber, wrapped in a tan raincoat, was seated on two German waterproof sheets. Head down, legs spread, a huge, baggy crotch. He seemed asleep, but as Simon moved closer, in the light of two plumber's candles he saw the major was staring at the earthen floor. Two flummoxed sergeants and a whining corporal were staring at the major. A private sat chewing on his helmet strap and kept turning the handle of a field phone and saying, "Hello? *Hello?*" He shook his head. "She torn up someplace."

A sergeant said, "Keep tryin'."

"No dice. Somebody gotta go repair that wire line."

"It's your line, Nick."

"I gotta stay here."

"Why? If it's a dead line?"

Simon gave a half-salute at the figure on the waterproof sheets. "Major, I think we better pull back. Major, we've sustained real big losses." He looked around. "He hit?"

The major didn't move. He gave off a series of gentle moans.

"He's gone yella," someone said behind Simon.

"Got the wind up."

Simon pressed the major's right arm through the raincoat. "He ate something bad, that's all." He could feel the quiver of the major's muscles. A glob of spit was moving down from one corner of the major's mouth. The sonofabitch! Simon thought. He's paralyzed with fear. The men suspect, know. He said, "Major, any word from Brigade HQ?"

The man at the field phone had a cold. He sniffed. "Like I said, the line, it's been cut someplace."

"Before the wire was cut, any Brigade directions?"

"Just to proceed along with Plan Y. Take the hill with accompanying map reading number of—"

Simon leaned down, shook the major, taking hold of him by both hands. The face seemed to reflect a moment's intelligence, then the blank façade moved from him.

"That's who? That you, Copperwood?"

"Yes, sir. We can't hold. Attack waves throwing whole companies against us."

"Everyplace," said the major, eyes unfocused. "Fighting, dying. Bouresches, Vierzy, Fismettes." The major lowered his head and refused to speak—or couldn't—from then on.

Simon turned to face the dirty, unnerved men. "You, you, *you*, get wire, get back and trail the phone line-break, repair it."

"Nobody's et."

"Forget chow. Put your two automatic rifle men in front, sergeant. Get your men up at the openings and have your grenades ready."

"We ain't to pull out, sir?"

"Not until we hear from Brigade HQ." Simon laughed. "We may be winning the war out there!"

[84]

He left them, incoherent but nailed down, the major still sunk in stupor. Back in the cellar with Bruno—breathing as if air burned—he found that there things were holding, the Hun pulled back. But Bruno was lying on some straw, with a bloody thigh, very pale, teeth showing, smoking his pipe clinched hard on the stem, face very taut under the sallow cheeks.

"Look at that—clear through—a tunnel."

"Bruno, Haber is in a fit. He's a gone goose. It's us alone here."

"It's all yours, Simon B. I'm down on my rump with this thing. Bleeding bad. Have a belt tight around it to keep the gore in. What do you think?"

"I think tough tittie." He slapped Bruno's back. *"Very* tough tittie." He looked around, lowered his tin hat farther over his eyes. "Can't contact HQ. Line is cut."

"Pull us all back. The Krauts are going to try again."

"Bruno, no matter if it's the right thing to do. It goes on our record that we pulled two companies back without orders. I must be losing my mind, thinking of that. But—"

Bruno winced in pain. "Screw our records. We've held a long time. We have dead, wounded. Pull us back, sport."

"I'm having the phone line spliced." He turned to the men. "Keep your peckers up. Now set out your grenades, hold them till they're within smelling distance. Then toss. I'll get us all out of here."

Bruno watched silently, then saluted Simon with his pipe stem as Simon crouched for the run to his own company in the next cellar. He found the men of his company standing against the walls. Some were on the ground screaming, several were ominously silent, and very very dead. (The dead didn't look at all like those grand poses in Aunt Dolly's Bible with the illustrations by Doré.)

There was a sudden lull, a silence that made flesh crawl. Simon looked out between the stones of the foundation that remained. The gray lumps of dead Boche, with big buttocks up, were twenty feet away. Farther back more boot toes pointed up; the whole hill was potted by them, some kind of crazy planting of carrion. Eighty-eight's came over but there was no new attack. Twenty minutes later he saw the top of the hill fill up again with the enemy as if some giant were lifting them on the palm of his hands and tossing them forward.

"Here they comes again," said a little runty corporal, a Mexican-American, Jesus Cortez, from Los Angeles. "They comes a lot."

Simon said, "It's a ten-minute walk the way they come, slowly, before they start a lope, then a run, then a charge. Get your cartridge clips ready. How many grenades left? Count 'em."

He sat down, his back against the wall, legs rubbery, nerves rabbity. He fumbled for a Fatima cigarette, got it alight and smoked, inhaling deeply, exhaling plumes of smoke, watching the white smoke drift, break up. He had himself in tight rein-check again. . . . Let the time worm gnaw (as Major Millhouse used to say). Pull out? Wait a bit? Stay? That bastard of a yellow major, Bruno down, Captain Saringetti dead, half the companies down. Must pull myself up tight. Think of something else. Think of an afternoon far from here—after chapel on Sunday at the Point. Me, Major Millhouse, sitting on a green knoll, just us two—nothing in sight but green hills. He reading, translating that is, direct from the Greek, Plato.

"Let us imagine people living in a subterranean cave, with the entrance open to the light along the whole width of the cave. These people have been chained since childhood, with fetters on their legs and on their necks, so that they are compelled to remain in one spot, prevented from turning their heads and capable of seeing only what is directly before them. There is a fire burning at some distance above and behind them. Between the fire and the prisoners, and above them, a road has been built, with a low screen along it like the screen which the manipulators of puppets use to conceal themselves from the audience."

("Lieutenant, they're near.")

"Let us imagine then further. There are men moving behind the screen and carrying a great variety of objects which project above the screen; images of men and of animals, statues in stone and wood and various other materials.

"They are like ourselves. For do you believe that such prisoners would be able to see anything of themselves, or of one another, save the shadows thrown by the fire upon the wall of the cave that faced them? What would they be able to see of those objects projecting above the screen and carried by men who are hidden behind it? Would it not be the same?"

("Lootenant, a lot of 'em.")

"Then if those prisoners could talk, one to the other, do you not think they would name the objects that they saw on the wall, and discuss them, believing them to be real objects and only realities of existence? Then let us imagine that this cave prison has an echo from the wall that faces the prisoners. Would not the prisoners, when the bearers of images behind them spoke, hear the echo from the wall and credit the passing shadows with speaking? Would they even imagine any other explanation?

"Then to them, assuredly, Truth would be nothing save the echo of voices from a wall, and Reality naught but the shadows of the images."

(And now here. Oh, I'm in a great position. Lucky me.)

The methodical shelling had started again. He peered about him; the enemy was coming faster this time. Yes, like a dream you can't stop. He'd have just time to make trail if he now, *this* moment, fell back on whatever was behind him. Some deep, precipitous ravines there, and they had passed a battery of 105's, gunners behind their gun shields, piles of shells, voices calling "Range three hundred fifty," and the sound of officers' whistles all silver shivers. Some place to the west were the Chasseurs d'Alpine and the Colonials.

I'll stay, Simon decided. . . . Now, Simon, you dutiful dope, he said to himself, this dying business—*amour-propre*—should be fast. And with luck, dark and quick. Death is black for sure, and death is no memory, no pain, just infinite, tedious nothing. These men will die the way each man dies, all alone. It's all good and fine to stay—never mind any subterranean cave—a fine thing, and repeat to yourself the glory and gold-braid rules. For this is why you were trained, this is why you stand at the end of the tunnel. They sent you here to be just one item in a long roll call. Maybe they'll carve your name on some marble block at the Point, and some of the teacher's dogs will sport on the base. But that's all right.

("Every man stand. Rapid fire!")

To conk out and also to save the hash of that bastard Major

Haber. The gall is that in the report he'll get the credit for this last stand—all his—when we're all dead here. Uncle Brewster is so right; there is no irony like God's irony.

Rain came suddenly, in quick chopping sheets; long-buried dead were exposed in the mud. The Hotchkisses were rattling away. We owe ourselves, Simon decided, a natural pride that will not drop away.

A runner came crawling on his belly, dumped himself at Simon's feet, his mouth a gasping black hole showing crooked front teeth rimmed in gold. "Sir, we just can't find the break in that there phone line."

"Never mind. We'll pour on all the firepower we can."

"We're down, sir, to a third of the men able to hold a rifle."

"Pass the order along. Everyone who can, shoot to repel the attack."

He turned away, dropping the forgotten cigarette from his fingers. The advancing enemy were now all good target material, and his men were firing at them, looking up now and again at him—the young lieutenant, who looked back at unfed men, shivering men, boys really—boys who didn't want to show what they felt. That's the problem with war, he thought—*it's dangerous!* For them, Simon sensed, as for all the men now firing, ducking, falling in this war. Whatever it was that brought them here, how it all came about, didn't matter. The Army made no politics, just served those who made policy for this cave-living society.

Simon began to laugh and fire his rifle at the Germans, now beginning again to enter the stricken orchard. That dead cow must be very ripe, he thought, as the damn Heinies stomped through the mess. He found he had a tunic pocket full of dried prunes. Simon chewed prunes, spit out pits, and continued to fire.

All fear left him. There was no need to contemplate the future. No future, no fears. Why had the secret come so late?

Chapter 11

THE hospital at Châlons-sur-Marne had been a manor house of the Second Empire—warped parquet, dead furniture in dusty shrouds—and outside there were still shattered glass structures under which Jerusalem artichokes, pomegranates, and persimmons had once been grown. Lieutenant Simon Bolivar Copperwood, recovering from inhaling mustard gas —not much, just enough to make him puke much too often and not enjoy eating—lay in what had been the library, now just empty bookcases of inlaid wood with torn-off doors, no books left at all except for some out-of-date Michelin guidebooks.

There were six officers in low cots in the room; one usually weeping convulsively, a Frenchman; two Britishers who drank excessively of French cognac and smoked Ramon Allones cigars. One died silently during the night, his bandaged side turning turkey-red through the linen, and blood running down one arm in a steady drip. The other three were Americans who were soon to move to an American-run hospital. All were gas casualties, and only one was a bad case; he, with the head of a gray horse-skull, coughed in the night and retched. Eddie Walsh, a mild gas case, had a scraggy neck and a bold Adam's apple, and would sing on rising:

> Good-bye, Ma!
> Good-bye, Paw!
> Good-bye my mule,
> With your old hee-haw!

Simon Copperwood disliked jolly risers and wondered why people thought war nurses were always supposed to be beauties. "The Rose of No Man's Land," a popular song, was a tribute to them. At Châlons-sur-Marne the nurses were worn-down middle-aged nuns with sour expressions and aching feet. They had the sad stale smell of unselfish, yet defeated lives. The weeping Frenchman would often sing to himself: *"Viens, pou-poule"* and *"La Petite Tonkinoise."* Simon grew to hate all songs. His lungs ached, his throat burned.

The lisping rains washed the long windows that let in a view of the neglected garden. The grass was tall, the tree limbs mutilated by troops seeking firewood. Damp smoke curled and seeped from an old brick shed where the hospital laundry was done, and to one side on a slate walk bodies lay in waterproof sheets in the mornings. Waiting for a Gregoire wire-wheel ambulance to come and carry them off for burial. Simon, and Eddie Walsh, the singer of "Good-bye Maw, Good-bye, Pa," would bet on how many bodies would be carried out to wait for the Gregoire. The nearest guess won and the loser had to pay the ratty little sergeant from Alsace who wore a red kepi and swept up and emptied the *boîtes de nuit* and pushed the wheelchairs, for a bottle of a pretty bad brandy. Legs and arms didn't count in the betting; such items were a mixed bag of mere bulky packages.

And he never had no pappy, to tell him all he knowed.
Yes, he never had nobody, to point out the narrow road.
And he never had no childhood, playin' round the cabin door,
No, he never had no mammy, for to snatch him off the floor.

The morning that began with thunder was the one on which Simon lost for the third day in a row; he had bet six bodies and the singer, Eddie Walsh, had won with fifteen bundles—the actual count being seventeen. . . . The Austrian 88's had been very effective in making wounds up the line beyond Soissons on the Aisne River, and the hospital at Châlons-sur-Marne, as the Yankee singer said, "Got all that trade."

A very trim USA colonel came into the room, carrying a British officer's swagger stick. The uniform was American, but well-cut, clearly Bond Street, Simon thought, by its dashing styling and splendid whipcord material, tight brown boots, silver spurs. All suggested an exaltation of pride and taste.

"How's the *esprit de corps*, Copperwood?"

Simon opened his eyes wider, closed the gap in his pajama top. It was Major Roger Millhouse of West Point, only now Colonel Millhouse, by the gold insignia on the tabs.

"It's not bad, not good either. I want to get out of here, maj— colonel."

The colonel smiled, offered a gloved hand to shake.

"Yes, I got the chickenshit decor. On the staff with General Bullard, the Third Corps." He looked over to the other bed, took the salute from the Yankee singer.

"I suppose," said Simon, "the Point is empty."

"Of old stock, yes." Colonel Millhouse waved off the singer, who was trying to salute again from a reclining position in his bed. "But full of new broth. Can you walk, Copperwood?"

"Of course I can walk. I was *not* shot in the tail. I was gassed."

"Good to feel your Calvinistic ire. Let's walk." The colonel took an Army overcoat off a set of deer antlers serving as a rack and dropped it around Simon's shoulders, felt his arms, patted his back. The colonel was graying but more the Army dandy than ever.

"You've thinned out, Copperwood."

"The food here is mostly old cats, I think, sawdust brioches and monkey meat left over from the North African wars."

"I brought you some Dutch gin and Nouilly Prat."

The colonel led Simon through a one-time ballroom, past beds smelling of rotting limbs and bedpans, and into an oak-paneled room with a marble floor where a brushfire was burning in a cast-iron grate. A French medical officer saluted, a copy of *La Nouvelle Revue Française* in his hands. "Make yourself to home, *mon colonel.* You have any needs?"

"No, all is *comme il faut.*"

The French officer went out and Colonel Millhouse looked around the room.

"I have a grudge against Second Empire furnishings; it's such second-rate Balzac. But never mind. Sit down by the fire. I don't remember France so cold, nor so battered. Ah, well, I was a young man then studying military history and—never mind. You got your war, didn't you?"

[91]

They sat facing each other, Colonel Millhouse tapping his fingertips together like a steeple, a classroom habit Simon remembered.

"You're recommended for the Silver Star. You really did a gallant thing, you and the companies in those cellars, everyone holding on—the regiment."

Simon caught the burr on the word "regiment." A hint of ironic skepticism, a jocular lower tone.

"Lieutenant Holtzman, how's his wound?"

"Fleshy part of the thigh. Not serious. He's at Compiègne, maybe in Paris by now. I'm proud of my lads. Yes. Proud."

The colonel stood up and walked around the ornate carved table with its bronze eagle legs, tested the surface with a gloved hand (like a housewife for dust). They were well-fitting gloves, Simon saw, tight, tan gloves. "Yes. You sent in a good, crisp report of the action. Style of Caesar in Gaul. Some of it has been held up from—well, from official notice at HQ."

"Held up?"

"Oh, not the companies-in-action parts. Some personal comment."

"There were no personal comments, sir."

"Semipersonal. I don't mean there was rhetorical elegance."

The colonel looked out into the rainy, wrecked garden. A steady *drip-drip* fell across the glass where a broken gutter failed to do its runoff duty. "Major Haber is a nephew of Judge Amos Nelson Haber of the Virginia Supreme Court."

Some of the wounded in the ballroom began to sing in mocking tones to counteract Eddie Walsh's offerings.

> *Yankee Doodle, tiens-toi bien,*
> *Yankee Doodle dandy,*
> *Des pas, de l'air tu souviens*
> *Avec les girls sois poli! . . .*

Simon said, "Some of them aren't too fond of Americans, sir."

The colonel went to the door and shut it tightly. "You understand I'm here officially—not a friend—no old ties from the Point. Officially."

Il brilgue: les toves lubricilleux
Se gyrent en vrillam dans le guave,
Enmimes sont les gougebosqueux,
Et le momerade horsgrave.

Simon smiled as the colonel looked puzzled at the song. "Yes, they call it *'Le Jaseroque.'* "

The colonel laughed. "The Jabberwocky! From *Alice*. It's a goddamn crazy war. . . . About your report. It's your first big notice-report. Your whole career begins here. So—"

Simon set his jaw. Damn, he thought, damn the split halves of hypothetical self. Don't they know of the awareness of the human limits—do they have to put it on the line like this? He said, "I know my obligations—I also know the Army way, when to press for the responsibilities of duty—when to let the line go slack. But Major Haber!"

"Lester Haber is what is called a Good Joe. His record as a soldier is unblemished—oh, not brilliant. A willing workhorse of the National Guard—a West Point grad who went into private law practice. No demerits. Nothing to let us think he had anything on the day of battle but an attack of food poisoning that came over him in the heat of that battle."

Simon beat his fists together, sneezed, and blew his nose on some squares of cloth he carried in his pajama pocket. There were no delicate and subtle nuances in the official message.

"The gas, sir, it's hurt the mucous membrane of my nasal passages. . . . Major Haber funked it, colonel. He just folded with fear in front of some of his companies, left the regiment without a top senior officer in control. Our officer losses were very heavy."

Simon felt the situation ludicrous, absurd, the day depressing.

Colonel Millhouse turned from the window, came and sat down facing Simon, put a hand on a shoulder, and pressed gently on the pajama cloth—once, twice, three times, then patted the arm and leaned back, crossed his splendid boots. "Now, officially, I'm through here. Christ, boy, you don't know what it's like at HQ or the staff meetings of a corps. Protocol, rank, senior staff as jealous as catty women. All the top boys—off the record—outdated. Like walking through a cactus field bare. You

[93]

exist at HQ by picking your spot, *very* carefully picking your spot."

"But about that major—"

"I live by challenge and fulfillment. No wife, no dog. I have my favorites—unofficially. You, Bruno. Believe me, you two can be generals in thirty years. Who knows, you a five-star General of the Armies. Bruno, well, a Yid has to be pure gold to be taken for silver. You know I have no prejudices along those lines. . . . So, Simon Copperwood, don't dummy up on me. It's insulting to our relationship."

"Let me see. I'm going to get the top boys down on me *if* I persist in getting my report on Major Haber considered officially, maybe send him before a court-martial for—"

"Don't even repeat verbally the words 'court-martial.' Shall we say there will be an examination by a specialist, and retirement; thou good and faithful servant, Major Haber?"

Simon sat forward in the chair, felt a coughing spell come on. He held it back as he studied something in the smiling, handsome face opposite him. This was a strange officer; yes, all challenge and fulfillment. It was a grin Simon had seen in a version of the opera *Faust* that his Long Island lady, Linda Tennel, had insisted he take her to. Not Faust, but the fellow in the red rig with the feather in his cap had impressed him. Laconic, amusing, yet very direct. The colonel was hinting at *something*.

"I should, perhaps, insist on my report, in full, going upstairs?"

"Officially I didn't say that, Simon. I can't officially say that. Let us just take a classroom case, shall we? *If* a higher officer is vindicated in some strange, strong action, the lower-ranking officer will *not* fully get credit for his own gallant action in rallying decisive action. If, however, the lower rank gets full credit for the true events—even if a major were, well—" The colonel snapped two gloved fingers. *"De l'audace, encore de l'audace, et toujours de l'audace."*

"You advise I—"

"I *don't* advise. I only did an official duty. The rest"—he looked at his wristwatch—"I'm due at Epernay in two hours. Foch has met Haig at Mouchy, and we're trying to steal four

British reserve divisions to bolster our lines. Oh, as for you—you'll be ordered to a six-week tour of duty, to the airdrome at Fayolle. We've been shipping in our young USA fliers there, and they're dying at a miserable, murderous rate. You'll act as observer and report as to what can be done to lower our deaths there. File on field accidents, landings, and takeoffs."

"I'd rather like to get back into the line."

"You will. But first get over your lung problem completely. Mustard gas, phosgene, even with the respirators, is worse than the flamethrower, the 38cm gun. Lord, what a mess of mud and human meat, fine men's bodies out there. Not like the neat classroom lectures of massing movement and battle, is it?"

The colonel pulled off a glove and held out a firm, thin hand. "Well, good-bye, Simon."

They shook hands, looking each other in the eye as if searching each the other for reassurance. Colonel Millhouse set the swagger stick striking at a shiny boot and walked off. Simon heard him offer a parting answer to the French medical officer on a question of the progress of the war: *"L'arbre ne tombe pas du premier coup."**

On the way back to his bed Simon thought of the medal coming to him. Also of Major Lester Haber. He even thought back to the Trinitarian Christianity Roger Millhouse had advocated as a moral guide in his lectures at the Point. Simon had thoughts, gloomy ones, on Army caste, the conspirational drive for power.

The Yankee singer asked, "Want to bet two bottles on the number of deadies tomorrow?"

Simon said, "Shove them."

A week later, Simon in a fresh uniform, First Lieutenant Copperwood by a small promotion—a sustained masquerade, he felt—got a lift with a truck of an artillery battery of the 35th Division to a hospital chateau run by the 42d Rainbow Division, where Bruno Holtzman was convalescing. Bruno seated at a desk, a crutch at his elbow, was doing paperwork. Bruno looked

---

*The tree does not fall with the first blow.

[95]

pale but heavier, his hair cut even shorter, a bent pipe smoking in one corner of his mouth. Upon seeing Simon he hopped up, grabbed his crutch. The room was a large pantry done over as an office, with piles of yellow cartons ranged along the wall, some open and spilling their contents. A canary cheeped in a reed cage, scattering seeds, its black beady eyes set unwinking.

"Well, sport! The Silver Star!" Bruno flipped the decoration on Simon's tunic.

"You're due for one, too."

"Jaysus, Si, we really live through that hullabaloo up there?"

"That's what the reports say."

"Yes." Bruno sat down, and holding a kitchen match, with a thumbnail scratch he lit his pipe. Between puffs he said, "You nixed the windy major kaput, I hear. Set for a hearing. Well, he was no Greek hero clutching his courage in the orgy of battle, was he?"

"I just asked to have my *full* report sent up."

"Sure. You know who blew up over it? My new boss, MacArthur. Brigadier general, commands the Rainbow."

"Blew it in what way?"

"Oh, he's for you. Got angry that the staff tried to cover for the pooped-off major. Mac said he wants to meet you. You'll find Doug a specimen—he's only thirty-eight, an odd fish. All solid Army but *not* solid ivory. Know what I mean?"

"No time to meet him. I'm on my way to some airdrome. Just wanted to drop in, see if your Jew carcass was healing."

"How the lungs?"

"Doctors just nod and say I'll live."

"You're some pistol, Simon. Stay over. I've got two of the servant girls interested. Boney as sharecroppers' mules, but, you know—"

"The closer to the bone, the sweeter the meat. No, I was nearly down to a seamstress at the hospital. I want Paris, and something like a duchess, or say a stage star."

"Greedy bastard. It's Paris for us, hope to spit in your mess kit—soon as we arrange it."

"It's a contract."

Bruno made a tent of his fingers before his mouth. "Of course, you had to do it to the major. It bother you?"

"Someone pointed out a few of the facts of life and Army to me. The labyrinthine ways to success. I admit it all, Bruno. I'm greedy. If I live, I want rank. But I don't want it this way. I had just about decided to withdraw the report. And my hand was forced, in a way. No, I knuckle down to pressure. I don't like myself this morning."

"Some wise guy once said success is the talent to face the unavoidable openings."

They parted with the firm handshakes youth is addicted to, and some ribald remarks. There was a staff car to take Simon to the airdrome. The day was clear and the rains held off, the sky a child's crayon-blue. The driver of the car had a Kewpie doll attached to his dashboard. Simon hadn't seen a Kewpie doll since he and Mollie Ott one night, with swollen lips, tiptoed into her room and tried out some new discovery of sexual possibilities. Mollie had one of these Kewpie dolls on her dresser, pointed head, chubby cheeks, protruding stomach, and cute navel. Also there, Simon remembered, a big pink seashell lettered ATLANTIC CITY, N.J., a picture book with Maxfield Parrish painting in color, all too blue. How long ago that all seemed.

The car drove past a pile of shell casings dropped from the guns. 108TH FIELD ARTILLERY, the hand-painted sign read. He went by fields, mere rubbish dumps of rust, muck, bones; fields, if in range, still stirred by sullen explosions from distant cannon. The driver from Boston said, "Convoy sure took it hard [he pronounced it *hahd*] here two days ago. Kilt six medical corpsmen riding in a cah. Whole road just shell holes linked up from here on, held by the Gyrines of the Forty-ninth."

Simon wasn't interested in the landscape or the danger of more shelling. How did Bruno really see my action on letting the report on Major Haber go upstairs? You never knew with Jews. They were Scripture folk with that Old Testament morality in personal matters, always kept razor-sharp.

Chapter 12

Lieutenant Simon Bolivar Copperwood learned from the ground up, quickly, about the reality of air warfare. He found it easy to drop the lines of Rupert Brooke:

> Honour has come back,
> And Nobleness walks in our way again.
> And we have come into our heritage.

He felt a heritage of crashing cloth-and-wood, motor oil spurting over a broken body on some meadow scarred by plane wheels.

Assigned as liaison to the American fliers, brought in raw, half-trained, to get flying practice, Simon was based at the RAF field at Fayolle near the Oise River. The airdrome consisted merely of huts, tents, and hangars resting on mud. The shoddy construction of everything that housed men and planes left an indelible picture in Simon's mind.

Cubbyholes, sleeping quarters cluttered with maps, binoculars, dogs, a few cats, several monkeys shivering with cold. Smelly clothes, busted-up mementos of war. Shattered propellers, patches of enemy wing insignia cut from downed planes, parts of burned-out motors used as paperweights or ashtrays. On walls were group photographs of fliers, most of them dead, ugly pictures of dead enemy fliers, or friends mutilated by exploding dum-dums. Busted-up kids in charred death. A scattering of magazines, pipes, tobacco jars, yellow-bound novels, boxes of stomach pills. In all of this Simon settled in.

"Sorry, old chap," said the British ground major with the red pips on his collar. "It *is* rough."

"It's fine," said Simon. "Like camping out in Montana."

"Montana?" said the major. "Quite."

"USA."

"I expect so."

As a semipermanent field it had a tarmac cover tar and macadam rolled and pressed for a nearly smooth airstrip. Bomb craters would be quickly patched. Night lighting was poor —usually kerosene flares on oil barrels.

Three mechanics were assigned to each plane, responsible for its health, grooming, and mechanical being. Simon found these mechanics were filthy sights; oil-stained garments glossy with grease, hands ingrained with worked-in grime. Near the hangars were the buildings that housed the flying officers, and the mess halls. Each squadron had twenty to twenty-four pilots.

"You'll mess with us, of course, leftenant. Not top-hole, but fairly decent."

"Thank you, major."

"The whisky isn't bad. I say, leftenant, you *are* permitted to drink. I mean you *are* of age?"

"I drink, major. The fliers?"

"Not all on the base. Some are sixteen."

There were four squadrons at the airdrome and two squadrons at a time ate together. The enlisted men led a life of their own, the field having separate sleeping and eating quarters for telephone crews, mechanics, truck drivers, office personnel, and pilots' orderlies, called batmen in the British units.

It was gay enough at times. The young Americans tried to appear casual. They'd be flying with the British over the lines in a week, in Sopwiths and Spads. Music was obtainable on a stolen piano. But mostly the old hand-wound gramophone brought them "coon" songs, ragtime favorites, George M. Cohan, Chauncey Olcott, Al Jolson. The English preferred music hall entertainers.

Airfields and buildings were overrun by dogs, barking, mating, birthing litters. There were cats for ratting and mousing, and a goat. A stern commander of an airdrome could keep some kind of order and a surface cleanliness, but a slack one often had a roaring distress area on his hands.

Drink was the big problem. Whether legally or through connections, brandy, whisky, and cognac were available. Simon helped many drunken pilots to bed nights. All usually returned from leave in a very shaky condition. Light breakdowns were treated casually as "the shakes," unless violent or dangerous to limb or property.

Gambling was an outlet from the tension of being on patrol duty, flying over the front. Simon became an expert poker player. The Americans introduced crap shooting, but for those raised on whist and bridge or roulette at Monte, the rattling dice seemed vulgar.

"The Americans fly tomorrow, major?"

"Right. But not you, Copperwood. Orders. Paperwork, you know, is your task. Sorry."

"I would like to fly, major, as an observer."

"No. Officially. That would tear it. You're too valuable."

Simon figured he'd get up somehow in these muslin crates. He wasn't a flier, he wasn't a gunner, just an observer on the ground. But he'd always wonder about it if he didn't go up, how it was up there. An idea was forming in him that the air as a battlefield could be important in future wars. Some day, better, stronger, faster planes, superior weapons might, *could* decide ground combat, even wars. (He had been reading H.G. Wells.)

It wasn't at all as clear, as some writers many years later made it appear, that General Simon Copperwood came out of World War I, during a period of acrimonious controversy, with a fully formulated idea of victory through air power. Or that he in any way inspired Billy Mitchell, who was just then trying to get Pershing to permit a really vital AEF air force to swing in the sky. General Pershing, it was no secret, would not fly in one of those things. Never leave the ground. No, Simon had no fully rounded idea of what air power could become, not in those muddy, damp days at the secondary airfield at Fayolle. Not while drinking the major under the table with the major's prime stock of scotch and Jamison's Irish.

Simon met Billy Mitchell only twice; was impressed. Mitchell was a delightfully original character. Simon kept the leaflets Mitchell dropped to American troops from the U.S. planes. "Whenever a Boche plane is brought down in your sector, do not collect souvenirs from it; you may remove an article or marking

[100]

that would have given valuable information to us. If Boche aviators are not dead when they land, wait ten minutes before approaching within one hundred feet of the plane after they have left it; sometimes they start a time bomb. DO NOT TOUCH ANYTHING IN A BOCHE PLANE—they sometimes carry innocent-looking infernal machines. . . . Use us to the limit, show your panels, burn signal lights, wave a cloth; anything to tell us where you are and what you need. After reading this, pass it along to your buddy, and remember to show your signals."

Chapter 13

WHAT Simon wanted was to get into the air, fly with the young Americans. Their losses were heart-wrenching. But they were learning, the survivors. The best of them was Hike Harris, who spoke with a low-key irony, a quiet raillery. He had been a country-fair flier in the tall-corn belts, been jailed for taking rubes with marked cards at poker. Hike looked like a big hick; all he needed was bib overalls and a stray straw in his mouth to become a comic character with an exaggerated homeyness. But he had downed four German planes, and in his leather coat, a bit of scarf tied to his leather flying helmet, goggles in place, there was the impression of an oversized gristle-heeled folk hero.

"Hike, I'd like to go up with you some morning."

"Lootenant, maybe if I'm doing protection of some camera plane, I'll use you as ballast, huh?"

"You name the time. I can't say in my reports I've done my best if I've never been up."

"Nothing to it 'less you get seasick. The Sopwiths are bitches, just muslin and glue, the engine she spits oil, castor oil."

"Any time, Hike."

"Handle a Lewis gun?"

"Take it apart and put it together in the dark. Even a Vickers."

Hike pulled on his long nose with thumb and forefinger. "Now, tomorrow be all right?"

From then on they were flying over the front from the wing headquarters airdrome. It was bloody blue cold, the squadron using Sopwith Camels nearly as bad, Hike had said, as DH-4's, the goddamn notorious Flaming Coffins. The British and American pilots lived on milk and brandy, stinking of tension turned to sweat in black flying breeches, going over the Hun lines, escorting the heavy reconnaissance camera planes with the enemy's archies exploding high up, bursting in their faces. The legend that nobody lived beyond the first six weeks, Simon figured, was mostly true. The British Sixth Wing by actual count lost a third of its fliers, and it was worse before Cambrai fell; the Boche began mounting heavier Spandau machine guns in their *Jagdstaffel* hunting packs. They had replaced their older planes with the Fokker triplane. The Americans were still in the flypaper-and-canvas-and-wood Sopwith F.I. Camels. As Simon reported, it was the will doing the work of the impossible. All took to carrying bottles of brandy in their flying suits.

Flying on patrol, the long-toothed major got his ticket west, trying out over the lines a recently built Nieuport. A Hun dipped down out of the sun and began to pour it into him, and Hike said he saw the major's face, the Sandhurst mustache standing out. "Flying on his left tip, trying to come up to protect him. He just looked sad, mouthed '*Merde,*' the crate began to smoke and flame and slide down dropping wings and parts. He waved. . . . The buggering British—*that* gesture. . . ."

The letter Lieutenant Simon Bolivar Copperwood wrote to Dolly and Brewster was read (edited a bit) at a meeting of the Ladies War Aid Red Cross Bandage-Rolling Tuesday Session, Silver Bend, Montana.

DEAR FOLKS:

Scared knocked-kneed of flying in these muslin boxes, but I do go up. Yesterday with our best flier, Hike Harris, a roughneck who's been flying at country fairs since 1911. He says flying skill can't be caught like a common cold. We took off early morning, just milk and brandy for breakfast, with an egg in it. Got up high. A good clear day, but some woolly clouds, about like Silver Bend on a good day with not too much wind, but some phosgene gas in shell pockets below. I was dreaming, I suppose, wondering if I should in my report talk up as to how I felt about airplanes being a great military arm, I mean beyond what we use them for in this war. When Hike gave the plane wings a wriggle and banked the rudder hard left, and there was a red-painted machine cut my brooding, coming right at us out of the sun. I nearly shot blue as I heard Hike clear his guns. I got hold of my gun. Hugged it with a kind of spontaneous affection you save for a dog. I fired a burst to clear the barrels, and the blur of the spinning day seemed all right. The Hun was good. He tried to keep the sun behind him, but our petrol was clean that morning in our tanks and Hike circled and got on his tail, he twisting us after him, the Hun crosses on his wings black against the dark canvas. I pressed off right into him, and the sonofabitch didn't seem to hurt at all. I could see wood and canvas splintering off and falling away. We had become a deadly duet, stuck close, to the death.

The Hun lifted away to climb, and Hike throttled back, and I thought damn-damn-you Kraut, when I sensed something on our right. And there we were jumped by a *Staffel* of Albatross who were laying for us. Our pigeon had been a decoy. Hike kicked the stick over and went into a long, fast dive, wires screaming, did an evasion spin that began to strain the wings. There was a wisp of cloud nearby, looking no bigger than a bath towel, Hike started for that and it was bigger than it looked. I didn't want to die. Not before I sent you a picture of myself in my London-tailored uniform.

We went through the cloud and found ourselves with just one Hun. He had a skull-and-bones painted on his canvas side, and Hike fired and I automatically pressed the Lewis button and a burst caught him in the belly of his machine. We were just under him—in his blind spot—and he fell, all black smoke, flames redder than any new wagon paint job. I could see the flier's face as he screamed. Nobody carried chutes, and his right wing just touched ours—a kiss—as he fell away in a fast drop.

Hike scooted for our lines, me sticky with sweat. I vomited brandy and milk and bile all over. Yes, it's very romantic flying. Remembered Craig's old Sunday-school lesson: "Man is full of misery and all earthly beauty is corrupt because of the untiring abjuration of the Devil. . . ." My mouth, throat were sour-tasting, like acid and Hike set the plane down with a hard bounce. The ack-emma warrant officer came out in the windy cold among the trampled weeds, the gunnery sergeant at his side.

"The other major bought one."

"Oh," I said, climbing out, covered with my own slime.

I left Hike and walked toward the tin hut where the flight officer would want to hear all, and to kid me. It was too warm in the hut. Captain Gregory, MC, DSM, sat at a desk, a gray scarf wound around his neck, his Savile Row boots scuffed; a proper advertisement for the paraphernalia of war, only his eyes were bloodshot and he had a small tic on his right cheek.

"Phone call just came in."

I poured myself a brandy from the desk bottle, knocked it back.

"Who called?"

"A Holtzsomething. Officer."

I went to the bathhouse and fell asleep standing under the hot shower and nearly scalded myself. Left the flying jacket and the gear for the corporal to take to the laundress. I must have slept openmouthed for some time because when I woke up the sun was on the dirty windowpane and my mouth was the real Black Hole of Calcutta. A U.S. colonel, the flying officer, had his gramophone going: "There's a Long, Long

Trail. . . ." I felt rat-poisoned, my throat raw. The forms of the world's patterns were dim. All dimensions and echoes lost their reality for me. A sure sign I was scared taut.

I took a pick-me-up brandy and I wished I had a couple of raw eggs to go with it, the way Uncle Brewster used to drink, wink and say, "Simon, man is the creature of obligations and betrayals, but a good toot of whisky never did a soul harm."

This letter is too long, but I wanted you to see how it's going here with all the malignant eccentricities of flying, and what I've been doing. I'm only here a week or two more, then I want to join in the advance of the AEF—can't say where, of course. You remember me writing of my roommate, Bruno Holtzman, at the Point? He's got leave and I've got leave, and we intend to really hit—well, bend, Paris together. *Le bon temps viendra* (good times ahead). I'm doing fine studying French with a shaky old priest in the village. But my accent still stinks. You have to be born with a French mouth. Comes from sucking up snails, maybe. Miss you all.

Always,
Simon
(Somewhere in France)

A muddy car came up the wreck of a muddy road from the main highway and under the camouflage nets. Two officers in RAF dress were singing "The Bastard Kings of England." They were all young, very Anglo-Saxon. Bruno Holtzman took his hands off the wheel and waved at Simon. "On the way," he shouted.

He looked very solid, and there were flying wings on his tunic and French and English decor of gold and silver and bronze. He was opening the twisted wires on the cork of a wine bottle. Simon didn't know the two officers in the back, Oxford kids, pink-cheeked, foul-mouthed, very friendly.

Bruno slapped Simon's shoulder, smiling, showing the even

row of good teeth and the capped one he had once shattered. "Imagine, Si, you still alive. We're running low on petrol."

"I'll get the gunnery sergeant, that's his swindle. How's the leg?"

"You'll win the whole bloody thing for us, you Yanks," said one of the Oxford boys.

"That we will. Want to fight?" asked Simon. "Never stick it into an ally, old chap."

Bruno took Simon aside. "They're not bad. And they know the ropes in Paris. They also have connections for fuel and oil. You've been up in those kites?"

"Just a few times. I don't like it, but it's going to be a vital arm of the service."

"Borrow all you can, sport, from everybody. We're going to do this leave to the hilt. Wear your medals. I've been using mine. Fine for flashing on the mademoiselles."

The weather had been a great gray bowl of sky, so bad no one could fly any sorties over the front in that sector. The war lay under a lashing rain and the morning mists lasted days and below it men drowned in putrefying mud. He was happy to get away in the car Bruno had produced, a 12.5-horsepower Sizaire that had one big headlight over its radiator. Bruno, very smart in a clipped sheepskin coat, pink whipcord breeches, splendid Savile Row boots; if you didn't notice the tremor in the nicotined fingers.

A huge, shaggy dog sat on the front seat of the auto. "What the hell is that?"

"Genuine Boche dog, survived a crash when our RAF shot down a Heinie ace."

Simon said, "I've got to wangle leave from the CO. Three days enough?"

"More than. *Très gash, très likker, comprenez-vous?*"

The group major was sitting at his desk under the signed photograph of Guynemer and his Spad. His overbred face, like that of a racehorse, was tired.

"Paris? HQ is chewing out my arse about your chaps not flying right now."

"Must be at a wedding."

"Wedding?" The major did a slow assimilation of the words.

"Damn-fool idea in a war. Have the warrant officer give you the pass."

The canvas top of the Sizaire was fairly waterproof; with all trench coats on and between the bottle of brandy and some singing, and the dog, Fritz, barking, they managed to get stuck only twice in the foul mud the roads had become under four years of horse manure, army traffic, and shelling. It was sad, Bruno said, to see the long lines of boys and middle-aged men marching the other way, wet, muddy, burdened with firearms and war gear.

Simon agreed. "The French are scraping up old men now, ancient farts with whiskers, runty kids."

Bruno bent over the wheel of the iron monster. "We Yanks, we'll have to end it for them. . . . Now for Paris. The Louvre, Notre Dame. Wonder if they still have the old museums open on the Seine."

Simon took a suck of the brandy bottle and worked the windshield wiper by hand. *"Bien merci.* Jewboy, you out of your rabbinical mind? We're going to Paris to paint it red, marry off our dog, drink, eat, get laid. Eh, Fritz, *du Schweinhund."*

The dog barked and clawed at Simon from the back seat. Bruno steered the car around a horse-drawn 75 mired to the wheels. The flogged horses had given up; the muddy lumps of bearded Frenchmen cursed them out, but with no strength or feeling.

"I could open up this baby, open to a hundred miles an hour. There's the power of Niagara under the hood."

An English chap said, "Let's try."

"After the war, Simon, I'm going to take it down to Nice and open it up. After the war."

Simon took the nearly empty bottle. "Nobody, Bruno, unless it's the dog, may be around after the war."

Bruno grinned. "All I'm praying for is a nice clean wound, just a flesh wound, see, and a nurse with beautiful breasts and some English garden to convalesce in. I believe in prayer. I'll include you guys in when I pray."

An English boy threw the empty bottle out into the rain beyond the flapping curtains. "Gunnery Sergeant Peterson got his manhood shot off. I'd rather get it between the eyes."

They hit a rut and the car bounced so high they came down on the shoulder of the road. They went on singing, *"Viens, pou-poule"* and *"La Petite Tonkinoise."* The dog didn't have any voice.

A Senegalese company of black colonials, blue-green with cold and damp, were huddled over little smouldering fires. They jumped apart as the car passed splashing, scattering rifles, knives, little pots of condemned canned stew they were heating.

Simon threw some franc notes at them as they plowed back onto the road. "Poor devils. What are they fighting for?"

"The right to eat their grandmothers. What are *we* fighting for, if it comes to that?"

"To get passes to Paris," Simon said.

Bruno took his hands off the wheel and beat his gloved fists together as they passed a mired tank, its crew sitting under a canvas spread like shipwrecked sailors.

"Who the hell has a pass? I just went out over the place the dustbins go."

They detoured around the main gates into Paris and came up past the Gare de Lyon, crowded with returning leave trains, human cargoes going out to die or drown beyond the Marne. Hotels looked sodden in the thin green rain but the Ritz was busy and exciting. There was still a doorman, one empty sleeve pinned across his chest under his medals. They took Fritz in, but the clerk said they weren't going to be allowed to have the creature along.

Simon said, "This is President Wilson's dog."

They went for the lift without waiting to hear any more and came to a crowded suite.

They found it full of well-dressed, fine-smelling women, a few charming in lacy mourning black. There were assorted officers of all nations with that fine smooth look of desk riders, a Jesuit, a man who said he ran the prison of the Santé, staff pips, red-braided caps, fliers. A middle-aged French officer, one-legged and on crutches, was talking to an Italian major with plucked eyebrows. Simon quoted Donne as he sniffed: "And find/What wind/Serves to advance an honest mind."

"Lord," said Bruno, "all alive, and females!" There were sounds of humming, buzzing, the clatter of breaking glass,

[108]

voices singing some sentimental ballad. Bruno's eyes gleamed. "Girl laughter."

War or no war, Simon saw, money was money, and the red-carpeted hallway was heavy with waiters and maids pushing little tables of drink and food. The gold and white doors of the suite were open, framing a pattern of officers and smartly dressed women, standing in a haze of tobacco smoke, retaining their hold on glasses of wine. The women for me he figured, rapidly taking inventory of haunches, arms, torsos, legs. As for the men—one-third in uniform of some special HQ service, Red Cross, Admiralty, War Office, or some sort of desk work. They, too, fought a splendid war. "Basically," Bruno said, drinking from two glasses, "in war only *three* things matter. Sexual congress, drunken plenty, and avoidance of death."

Some of the women were in black, and the few men in frock coats had a sprinkling of mourning bands among them. They had survived their sons and seemed pious about it. Simon sensed a feeling in them of *we, too, have had our loss*, and so, chin up, drink in hand, carry on, the worst is yet to be.

They went to the buffet, smiled at the suckling pig, at the pink, sliced ham. Long kept alive on bad coffee, brandy, leathery eggs, canned offal from the Chicago packing houses, they grinned at each other and fell to, mouths greasy, stomachs at rest now that they didn't have to go into battle. Chewing, sipping, their eyes on stems at the sight of the clean women. A small band playing Victor Herbert waltzes under palms yellowing in gilt pots. They took it all in with the unanesthetized parts of their brains.

Bruno said with awe and respect, "You ever see so much woman even in your best dreams?"

Simon led him over to the seafood buffet. "Stop pawing the ground like a stud stallion. Time for *that*."

In later years neither Simon nor Bruno could remember very much what happened the rest of that day, that night, the next day. But it must have been pleasant, they decided. On the second night they found themselves in a *maison de tolerance*, a nice family whorehouse on the rue Faubourg Montmartre, treating the *maqueraux* and *souteneurs* to drinks, a whore on each lap stroking their cheeks and whispering, *"O, le pauvre bébé!"*

"You know, Bruno, I think we have fallen into a house of ill fame."

"Too bad our leave is up tomorrow, back to the war!"

"What war?"

The girl said, "You order *les alcools* all 'round, *chéri?*"

Bruno began to sing:

> We're here because we're here
> Because we're here, because we're here.

Which led to

> I love the ladies,
> I love to be among the girls . . .

A scratchy gramophone disc across the hall ground out:

> Oh, we don't want to lose you,
> But we think you ought to go,
> For your King and your Country
> Both need you so . . .

Simon looked down at the whore's face.

> We shall want you and miss you,
> But with all your might and main
> We will thank you, cheer you, kiss you,
> When you come back again.

Chapter 14

The Americans had been given the hard, nasty job of nipping off the Saint-Mihiel salient, that landscape hernia, to straighten the Allied front line. It had been there, in enemy hands for four years. Its western area was firmly anchored on the Côtes de Meuse, and on the southern flank flaunted the high places, Montsec and Loupmont, where the Boche had their observation and firepower posts in place. In the middle of all this, around Thiaucourt, was the shell-scarred earth, blasted into what could have been the moon. The soggy plain of Woëvre was a swamp of frog spawn and marsh gas in wet weather, and by mid-August the rains came often, creating a mired world all knitted together by overflown streams, with no sure information for the Allies as to how wide or deep the muddy waters were.

Behind all this mess and mud of the salient there perched the fortress of Metz, and the big rail center of Conflans. So the Germans could pour their soldiers, ammunition, supplies, directly to front-line troops, and heavy guns.

Americans massing for the attack heard the order of battle. One private to another doughboy, soaping their faces against mustard gas, lying in shell craters, "Pershing, he says he'll take Metz if it costs a million men." "Ain't he the generous sonofabitch."

Nineteen American divisions were to be in the advance against the salient—the French, in unruffled complacency, had sent a token of six divisions of their own.

Reports from patrols, crawling back with blackened faces, said that the Germans were dug in deep; revetted trenches, dugouts shellproof. Overhead buzzed *Jagdstaffel* planes in dogfights with Nieuports and Spads—as the soldiers watched, chewing chow or grousing. The Heinies, the patrols said, held brass-band concerts in their trenches a half mile away. Lieutenant Bruno Holtzman recognized Schubert's "Lindenbaum." American wire-cutting parties got close enough to exchange their egg-shaped grenades for the Kraut potato-mashers. Gas lay in poison-white mist in shellholes, with the old dead worried by weather and mold. The big guns on both sides, the nine-inch stuff, the 155's, kept firing, echoed by the French *soixante-quinze*. General George C. Marshall, Chief of Operations, moved the American divisions up to the line through the pulsating arteries of bad roads. The Ist U.S. had been at Cantigny and Soissons, the IInd had hung on to the Paris Road, the IIId was stomping up from the Marne, the IVth from Sergy, Bazoches. Other divisions also were on the move from the Ourcq, Aisne, Champagne, under field packs: horsing, beefing, pissing, as Captain Bishop put it, on stones where Caesar's men took a leak. Over 600,000 young Americans, backed by the confusion of long lines of lorries, chugging trains, ambulances, mountains of hard bread, canned salmon, beans, spuds, ammunition crates. Stretchers were stacked, still stained with dark blotches. More than 3,000 guns set tailplates in mud, and there was a promise of 1,500 planes; Se-5's, Be-2c's, Camels, Pups, Snipes. And on land from the British, 267 light Renault tanks with fume-sick drivers, waiting in the ditches.

Colonel George Patton commanded the 304th Tank Brigade, and it was already doing very badly because of a glue of mud, engine failures, and lack of gasoline at the vital moment. The weather continued to be miserable, the cantankerous rain beat down on supply depots; trucks mired, turned over, spinning wheels, throwing up great shards of muck. And accidents tore men, horses, and gear apart. The nights were soot dark, the days merged into the blind gray gloom of fog.

Lieutenant Copperwood knew history books would ignore the gigantic mess of moving into battle. Simon Bolivar Copperwood, on the night of September 12, came up with his company from Troyon, jolting along in hard-tire trucks, only soggy canvas over the men of the 33d Division. They came, following the Meuse most of the way, bypassing the enemy-held bulge of Saint-Mihiel, that vicious tumor, to bring themselves alongside the Ist Division massing at Beaumont to attack through the Remières Wood.

Most of the divisions were already in place at their jumping-off points, or trying to find their taking-off places. The colonels and majors, looking wise, stern, or bored, bent bleary-eyed over maps examined under tent flaps lit by smoky pressure lamps. Simon studied Lieutenant Wheeler's twitchy face; he was happy, he said, to get into action so soon. Young Wheeler kept sucking his long, horsy teeth. He was from Princeton ROTC, and had played right end on the freshman team, sung in the Triangle Show on tour, knew Scotty and Bunny, whoever the hell they were. Captain Bishop kept seeking comfort in his crotch-tight pants: chewed on a cud of tobacco. He was an Oklahoman, dealt in second-hand oil-rig pipe and rotary drills, and carried into battle a bunch of oil lease forms and acreage maps which he studied, and showed to Simon when he had a chance. "When I get back to Tulsa, I'll be a millionaire." He was a very good officer, had been with Pershing in Mexico, chasing Pancho Villa in 1916. "Sheet, we never even got a good smell of his trail."

Captain Bishop was short, but wide and overmuscled, had a good solid head with a nose bent to one side. He had had a dinner of omelet, Vichy, and peaches the night before, and felt, "the French know how to eat." Lieutenant Wheeler asked, "What do you think, sir, is it ever going to stop raining?"

"Never does if there's fighting to do in France, does it, Copperwood?"

"Seems so, captain."

"Bet you it shines like a hurr's gold tooth all the time in peacetime. You sorry, lieutenant, they didn't let you stay with the flyboys?"

"No. I'm a ground soldier. The air stuff is interesting, but has a long way to come yet."

"Got yourself the Crow-de-gear."

"A little late. But it came. Followed me around." Simon was secretly proud of the French award of the Croix de Guerre, even if later he had to admit to Bruno, "It doesn't mean much, everybody the French can stick with one, they do. Even HQ sweepers and swampers."

Some of the men were singing

> Black cat came from behind the bar,
> Gobbled up the little white mouse.
> Moral to this story is:
> Never take a drink on the house.

The rain fell straight down, steam rose from the blankets and raincoats of the company squatting in the shelter of a stone wall that had once had a house attached to it. The village street was cobblestoned here and there, but was ankle-deep in mud, mule litter, broken shell casings of French makes. All around hung rusting coils of old barbwire strung across garden spots, like the pubic hair of war, Simon thought; he clutching at the opening of his clammy raincoat as the rain from his tin hat dripped down his neck. As usual, while on the fringe of action, he felt cold fear, knew for certain he would die in the attack. As usual, he hoped he could just keep a stern face and keep moving forward. The fog touching the ground seemed to move in ribbons as a barrage continued in the east, west, and south. Not much light, only the flash of the guns showed perspective, a wider world than a stone wall, revealed the reach and pattern of the broken-apart landscape, the unknown danger into which they would move.

The guns had been blasting in increasing fury since one hour after midnight. A regular earth-tearer of a barrage, it was agreed. At 4:30 A.M., Captain Bishop decided the drizzle was ending. "Get the men to shuck their rain gear. Give 'em better freedom of movement. How you stay *so* calm, Copperwood?"

Simon said. "I work up a good sweat."

Ain't no use me workin' so hard.
I got a gal in the rich folks' yard.
They kill a chicken, she sends me the head;
She thinks I'm workin', I'm a-laying in her bed.

Simon moved down among the crouching company, a few cigarette butts glowing ruby-red in the dark. He found Sergeant Cuddy Price playing the finger game for dimes with Corporal Belli and Corporal Zandor.

"Sergeant, the barrage is starting to roll in front of us up ahead. We follow tight on its tail."

"Yes, sir. . . . Saddle up! Rifles on the ready!"

"No, the enemy is still far off. Just keep the rifles slung, keeps the men calmer."

"Yeah, sir, and the *nyushrs*—as we say in China—can't chop chop shoot each other's toes off."

Sergeant Cuddy Price was an old China hand, having done duty at the U.S. Embassy in Peking, where he had a Chinese wife. "A *syansheng* I can't bring back to the U.S.A., and three kids." Price ran the regimental crap games, and lent money Army-style, at one and a half. You borrowed ten dollars from him, Simon had heard, and paid back fifteen on payday.

[114]

All along the still-dark front hiding over half a million men, whistles were going off—7:01, Simon saw. The sergeants were moving the men to their feet. Companies were adjusting packs, noncoms were cursing the goldbricks and kicking a rump here and there. Lieutenant Wheeler went rushing around as they moved out. Simon followed the paths at a steady pace, the company ahead fearful of mines. Some men stumbled a bit as they crossed the garden-soggy earth, but the drizzle was down to a few scattered drops—rain seemed moored in the trees.

Ahead, the rolling barrage went on breaking up the ground into even more wet, smoking clods. The whole 4th Division was moving up beyond them, the 42's out of Seicheprey, the 89th out of Flirey . . . and all the others unseen. Simon knew they were flanked by the U.S. Ist on their left; beyond, he couldn't picture anything. The French must be coming from below, right for Saint-Mihiel. The going was on very rough ground, stinking of death and decay, of rubble. Somehow, Simon smelled it as wet wallpaper, old mashed-in privies, wet green brush. The whole world was red-orange in front, and hearing was lost to eardrums in the concussion of growing pain.

> Down in the henhouse on my knees,
> I thought I heard a chicken sneeze,
> But it was only the rooster sayin' his prayers,
> Thankin' the Lord for the hens upstairs.

"Shut them chowderheads up!" yelled Captain Bishop.

Enemy fire began to eat into the men and Simon ran forward, gashing a leg badly on old wire. Ahead were mounds of earth and brick. He waved B Company down for rapid fire in prone position, and then got them to their feet for a slow move forward. On both flanks, Boche machine guns took up a steady tat-tat-tatting chatter. A sergeant—it was Barney Shapiro—his face all mud, spoke to Simon, "Gonna go on gonna—" (as half his head seemed to burst like a flung ripe tomato) and the sergeant fell slowly, the whole body in a slow collapse as the vital juices spurted. Simon swallowed hard, waved his Luger as they all ran past fragments of furniture, wire, posts, stumbled over sandbags of a gray washed-out color. Below, and waiting behind the sand-bags, were animated metal pots which turned into helmets of the enemy, their bayonets pointing up. Surprise on both sides gal-vanized into action. Simon threw grenades down at the pots with the easy casual throw of a kid pitcher on a sandlot, and all over two hundred meters of the deep trench there were explosions. He fired his Luger at an unshaved face, and an open mouth showing yellow tobacco-stained teeth. It died away muttering, *"Das tutes."* Somehow, Simon next discovered Captain Bishop was leaning on him after a jump down. Both were standing on the wooden duckboards of the trench bottom among fragments of the Heinies in green-gray uniforms, and a German smell of lard cooking: Americans, Simon remembered, smelled of peanut butter. The captain was laughing, slapping his thigh in mirth. "Don't, don't, go overrun our first-day objective, don't. . . . Oh, Christ—this hurts. . . ." The captain sat down with a thud, a groan. He suddenly sank into a pile of wood ash some enemy batman had carefully piled up outside a dugout. Simon saw the captain was a runny red all down his left side, the tunic gnawed away, chewed up. He pulled at a pocket, held up bloody papers, collapsed muttering, "Spud in—the rotary. . . ." Sergeant Cuddy Price went by with two men, all panting, faces red. Simon grabbed the sergeant's arm.

"Get stretcher bearers, the captain caught a—"

"What the hell, sir, no bearers, just we've got a mess of Fritzes blastin' us from that connecting trench."

Everyone reflexed at once, ducked as there was a rush of trench-mortar fire all around. The captain fell prone, still mut-tering, and two squads came up breathing openmouthed, yell-ing.

"Leave two men with the captain, Price. Rest of you follow me."

The sergeant said, "Colonel's dead, the captain's hard hit, the major broke a leg—fell down some glory hole." Simon noted he pronounced it "hull." "And so what we do now?" Simon began firing at a matted group of arms, legs, iron hats, and weapons that were firing back. Then, at one identical moment, the group put up their hands and cried out, *"Kameraden!"* Sergeant Price kept firing his Springfield into the earth till Simon put a hand on his arm. "Get three men to march the prisoners back." They waited, all bent down, as the firing overhead was very clear to them—it pinged when it hit a tin can or iron hat.

> Been a-workin' in the Army,
> Workin' on a farm,
> All I got to show for it
> Is the muscle in my arm.

The sergeant asked, "Who's the fuckin' medder lark?"

The sun was well up when a half hour later Simon and fourteen men, some of whom he didn't know—stragglers—wingdings—sat in a big shellhole and the wan daylight, putty-colored, reflected on their faces. Beyond them, they could hear the Ist Corps fighting in Fey-en-Haye and Vieville-en-Haye, the chant-chant gunners keeping up a methodical fire. Several of the men were opening cans of bully beef, and Sergeant Price was frying bread and some dark lump in a mess kit, cooking up an Army standby dish known as slum. The sergeant had a nice fire going inside a Boche helmet. He shook his head as he stirred his cooking. "Anybody here got an onion, a few strips of bacon? In Chiner we'd add *syaryi*—bit of chicken to it, scrounged off a peasant."

"Futz off, sarge," said a fat corporal, "I'm hungry." Somehow Simon felt a memory loss, couldn't remember names. "And you got some Heinie blood all over that there hardtack."

"Close your eyes when you get your share, Skip."

A thin corporal said, "I ain't hungry, Cuddy. Take my whack."

A runner, puttees unrolling, came up, breathing from nose and mouth, his chest rising, falling from both fear and moving fast through the wreckage of ancient barns, foundations, the unremoved bloated dead. An Austrian 88 shell passed overhead as the running man flung himself at their feet and kept saying, "Sonofabitch, sonofabitch, why *me?*"

Sergeant Price protected his cooking. "Why not?"

Simon finished rebandaging his wire-gashed leg. He hoped the inch-and-a-half barbwire hadn't been too rusty; he hadn't had the open wound in the muck too long. The runner said,

"Everything's taken, sir, and the First Corps is in Thiaucourt. The French general said, *'Je les grignote.'* "* The runner had a good accent. Simon wondered if he was a college man. "Orders are, lieutenant, the six companies along map reading, L to P, move at noon up to the area marked *'Stumpf Lager,'* clear out machine-gun nests there."

"Where," asked the sergeant, tasting his slum off a knife blade, "is your bitchin' written orders?"

"Same message to all companies in the area, lieutenant. A major and two captains are coming up to take over. You're to wait for them."

Simon asked, "Ammunition boxes and grenades coming up?"

"A major, two captains."

The runner leaped to his feet, mumbled something else, ran off to the next company. Simon looked at his watch. It was ten to twelve. "What you figure is noon in Army orders, sergeant?"

"Figure twelve-thirty, if we get grenades and stuff fer the Springfields. Want some of this slum? Nice an' hot."

Simon shook his head. His stomach was knotted like a fist. Wait? He looked about him as he pulled himself up just to the lip of the shell crater, the earth smelling like an old Indian outhouse. There was gray-green smoke all along the ground—gas clinging to pockets in the ground, frayed ends of broken trees like giant toothpicks. The red spots were old chimney brick. Beyond all that was *Stumpf Lager*, where the Hun had his machine-gun nests tucked away. The barrage was creeping up all around the place, sending up shards, whole carloads of earth. The Heinie Maxims were safe enough—out of sight—most likely behind concrete and steel railroad ties, Simon decided. It was going to be a mean thing, and could bring on morose dissatisfaction at HQ, if they delayed here. The new officers were most likely back-area goof-offs.

*I'm grinding them up.

[118]

Chapter 15

THE damn desolation of it, this abomination of thicket, swamp, hidden danger; all disjointed his courage. . . .

He knew his limbs were trembling, yet knew his face was expressionless. He took out a plug of tobacco and bit into a good wedge, worrying it loose with his teeth till it gave. It was a new habit for him, a couple of weeks old, chewing a cud. But it was better than eating solid food when his nerves were so taut and his stomach seemed filled with ground glass and sand. He was learning bravery is an acquiescence, a resignation.

Second Lieutenant Wheeler was up, coming crawling over to him. "It's worse up to the right."

"They get Captain Bishop back?"

"He died on the stretcher. The major lost a leg. Sixteen dead and lots of wounded. Who's senior now?"

"I am. Any goldbricks?" Simon felt death is a horror to the individual; en masse, it's just addition. That helped.

"Huh?"

"Self-inflicted wounds, unwounded, wounded?"

"Didn't ask."

"Wouldn't be mannerly, Wheeler?"

Simon saw the boy was all right, taut, but game, and he held out a leather-bound flask to him. "Take two pulls on this, Wheeler. You get any chow?"

The lieutenant took a good belt of brandy—didn't even cough.

"Catted it up."

"You and me—we're taking the men forward."

The rim of the shell crater began to give way—as several nearby explosions took place. The men all rolled over and over as concussions spun them around. Sergeant Price cursed as he burned himself juggling the hot mess kit of slum. He howled in pain, sucked his dirty fingers. There was the sharp bite of explosives all around them—a butcher shop smell. Two men were dead, crumpled up, obscene stuffing escaping from burst-open chests. Two more screamed and rolled about. Simon asked Lieutenant Wheeler, "You see any ammunition carriers on your way up?"

"Three dead ones." Simon turned to the sergeant, who was winding burned fingers in a soiled scarf. "Get the wounded back and see if you can scrounge some grenades and rifle shells. I'm not waiting. We move out twelve-thirty."

A soldier was weeping—he looked fifteen—all of him was covered with mud, but he was unhurt. The rest of the company survivors were all reclining against the steep slopes of the crater that faced the enemy; they just waited, silently looking up at Simon from time to time as the big guns created rolling octaves of thunder all around. *My* men, Simon thought, they trust *me*, need *me*.

"Eat what you have. Don't drink the water in the puddles. Should find some stream ahead." Simon sat down, feeling at once the damp of the earth go up his spine. His wire-gashed calf was beginning to throb, and his whole leg was going stiff. He wound a bandage over wound, blood, cloth and mud, chewed his cud, spat, smiled at the company—some hacking at tins—others too worried to eat. He kept the printed smile he didn't feel. But it gave the men the idea their officer was comfortable, confident—like a good daddy—and the situation fairly normal, even if it could kill you.

At 12:32, Simon—Wheeler the only other officer—led the men out of the crater, the shelling from his rear letting up, and all along the line he saw other companies coming out of the ground, all wary, moving slowly. They had been rearmed. Simon's men had heavy gunnysacks of grenades and pouches full of rifle cartridges. There had even been a five-gallon can of hot soup with greasy beef fragments, some strange vegetables flotaing on the top, carried in on a pole brought up to the front by two sweating soldiers. Whatever it was, it was hot and it was filling. Better to die, Simon felt, armed and fed. There was a rumor going around that General Pershing himself was viewing the battle from Fort Gironville, a height to the south of the salient. A wounded French captain was carried past. *"Eh, bien, devore et branle-toi . . ."**

Simon's company ran forward into the last bit of cleared ground, all of them, Simon suspected, feeling naked. They moved over old logs, tree trunks, and around them leaves fell as the machine-gun nests began to seek them out. The brush was thicker, no birds sang.

Companies to the left, to the right, also moved quickly. Men fell with heavy thuds. There was no theater, no drama to their dying. The wounded sat, lay, fell prone, some calling out, some not too sure yet what had happened to them. Suddenly they seemed to belong to another race, the injured, the discarded.

The companies kept moving, taking their losses, not so many now as they clung closer to the ground, moved low, bent over, stepped out with care. To the west IV Corps' major forces seemed to be getting hell. The map readings marked off where patrols had reported the Boche had dug in deep, had used railroad iron, built concrete cellars, burrowed in for a long stay. There was no coherence or clarity in the advance, just power pressure.

Fifth Corps seemed to be barging ahead. Simon figured by West Point classroom standards they all were ahead of objectives set for the day's progress. And he had avoided a takeover by other officers.

Moving on, the world began to tilt on its axis. It was progress, unless you were dead or wounded, or. . . zabroooo! Simon gasped, choked, found himself alone—tossed—but alive with six men in a cloud of gas, lying on the bottom of a cup-shaped shell hole. He waved the men on, up and out, an automatic gesture, and after they left the gas pocket, and were once more in the open, they all just lay on patches of wild hay, choking, vomiting, eyes burning. The momentary troubles passed. They hadn't done themselves too much damage, the gas was old and very diluted. Simon got them up, waved them on, half blind, but there was nothing to do but go on, and keep his cud wedged in his right cheek. The answer simple; if they stopped to lament

*Eat and jerk off.

[121]

and examine themselves, they'd all report as gas casualties and be out of the battle. Four men fell as if they had suddenly run into an invisible stone wall, and been broken there, bones shattered. Simon fell on his left side and peered ahead as the explosion settled to dust clouds. Stabs of rapidly projected flame were coming from a pile of pine boughs. He sensed that was one of the main machine-gun nests. Bits of gray litter lying around showed there was a lot of concrete behind the boughs. He motioned Sergeant Price closer and grasped his arm above the scarf tied over his cooking burns.

"What do you think?"

"Oh, it's a beauty—three, four gunners."

"Get a sack of grenades, come with me. Lieutenant Wheeler, order rapid fire for four, five minutes. Price—can you make it?"

"I'd rather have a sharp stick poked in my eye, but I kin make it."

Lieutenant Wheeler began to give orders in a low, clear voice, effusive, yet serene.

Simon hung a sack of grenades around his neck, reloaded the Luger, and smiled at the surviving men. They had seemed to fray away into smaller and smaller groups. He wished he had known them better. But may be it was just as well they had died without his being too aware of them as fully human in habit, human in qualities you learn from men with whom you live closely. Jaysus, he was thinking like a gushing idealist bathed in sentimental cant; a soldier's full duty is completed *only* by his dying.

But die for a good reason. Simon began to crawl off to the right as the machine guns seemed to be firing in larger numbers. Must be a cluster, four, five nests set up to sweep in a crossfire, get everything moving up this goddamn valley. Sounded like the tapping of a million tambourines. What did *Stumpf Lager* mean? Something out of the Boer War, most likely. He didn't have time to think it over as a German officer stood before him in the weeds, looking down in surprise at the two crawling men. His pants were wrinkled around his knees. Simon laughed. The German had been caught bare-bottomed among his freshly made spoor; some chap too delicate or shy to use the proper latrine. Sergeant Price rolled away as Simon fired at the yellow underwear of the German—fired just at the bottom where the navel would be. The officer, a newspaper clutched in his left hand, fell backward as if shamefully, Simon thought, removing himself for being caught like this in the open. Simon crawled on, the machine-gun fire was now on their left, they were getting behind it. Some crisscrossing mill timbers were piled up, and the Americans saw heavy iron hats moving behind them. Both Simon and the sergeant lobbed in three grenades each, then rushed in, leaping the timbers. It was a pretty mangled mess, but no machine guns, just stacks of wooden boxes with German markings; RHEINLACHS, WESTPHALIA; a sort of supply depot, and several mutilated men who still stirred blindly in reflexes. Sergeant Price moved among them, cutting their throats with the edge of a bayonet, and then looked around, wiping his hands on his pants, kicking open some boxes.

"Cheese, ham." He pried a boxtop off, took out a wrapped bottle. "Vino."

Simon's leg ached. He could read the labels. LIEBFRAUMILCH, STEINHAGER, KIRSCHWASSER. "Must have been a high general's mess supply."

The sergeant put several bottles in the extra gunnysack he carried. "Just in case we find the work thirsty."

Simon motioned Price to the left. They crawled on and found several strands of telephone wire among the wild rye grass. Simon changed direction and began to crawl along the wires, following them. Suddenly they saw the helmeted heads and the tunicked shoulders of six men busy at machine guns, bodies vibrating from the concussion of the firing. One soldier, a young boy, turned, got to staring at the Americans. His shoulders were hung with belts of machine-gun cartridges. He pointed at them, seemed to have lost his voice. He tapped one of the soldiers bent over the noisy, smoking Maxim. Simon and the sergeant rose and flung their grenades, fell down, and flung two more overhand from a prone position. It was a broth of smoke, flame, fragments. The machine guns were pointed skyward among bent iron rods and wooden splinters, fragments of concrete. Bodies lay like scarecrows, joints all in the wrong places. "Lootenant, that put a wild hair up their prat." The smell of explosives was acid strong. Simon found the sight of the blasted

[123]

machine nest very unpleasant. Sergeant Price broke off the neck of a bottle. "This calls for a booze." He drank wine and handed it to Simon.

"Price, you're a good backup man." He drank deeply, being careful not to cut mouth or tongue on the raw glass edges. "A lot of guts, lootenant, in a body, sure is." Simon turned away. "Come on." They went on, Simon wondering if he contained some dubious puritanism about killing enemies. They put two more machine nests out of the war, and then lay in the tall grass finishing the wine in lurching spasms of swallowing, followed by the brandy in Simon's flask. The ominous thunder of a far-off barrage echoed. The sergeant had a slug in his right thigh. Simon had his head tied up in a German newspaper, the *Neues Berliner Tageblatt*, and a strip of gray blanket. Either he had a slight scalp wound or his brains were seeping out. Or, he figured, it was the glancing blow of a hunk of concrete, or a bit of steel. "Either, either" he sang to himself, and he remembered a gramophone record of Mistinguette singing *"La femme torpille, pille, pille."* They lay there as Americans and the 2d French Colonial Corps passed on a loping run.

By nightfall, the first day of attack, they had taken all positions that had been assigned for the second day. That night, while Sergeant Price had his leg amputated, and Simon's head was shaved, some small bone fragments that protruded from the skull cleaned out, and a dozen stitches made in his scalp, the regiments of the 26th Division moved on Vigneulles to cut off the retreating enemy in his pullback. The attack moved on to take Hattonchâtel. The 102d and the 28th joined hands for a solid junction and the whole Saint-Mihiel salient was American ground.

The mind in some insidious way was aware of a tottering edifice, menacing and shaking. The head done up like a balloon of pain, a vast swelling of spurlike pain under all the ether: the body lay on a bed under a yellow naked electric light bulb, lay in an atmosphere of delirium. The room had been part of the carriage house of a great estate and there were still red-wheeled gigs and berlins, and a state coach of dusty gold, enameled in blue, between some of the beds. The doctor, of a serene, admirable nature, kept coming back and taking his pulse, counting, worrying about gas gangrene three days after the battle—that gashed-open calf of the young officer looked bad.

The body was in a faroff place—in Silver Bend, at the Copperwood mansion, so damn rundown and friendly yet. So *déclassé*, so middle class, watch it—*upper* middle class. Uncle Brewster was saying, "Took fifteen thousand prisoners, two hundred fifty-seven guns, two hundred square miles of territory . . . think of that. . . ."

The body said, "For the rattlesnake skins you get a dollar each in St. Louis."

Uncle Brewster said, "A Chablis or Sauterne. . . . Of course we had casualties, too, about seven thousand is the figure . . . yes. . . ." Indifference, the body decided, comes from fatigue rather than from reason.

The doctor went on talking as he sniffed Simon's leg. "The carbolic soaking should do the trick, but if it begins to smell. . . ." He saw Lieutenant Copperwood's eyes were open and under the cocoon of head bandages the young officer was staring at him in a kind of parenthesis of silence. "Lieutenant, the general himself asked about you, General Hugh Drum . . . you did something very crazy . . . took, or destroyed four machine-gun nests or something. . . ."

Uncle Brewster was back. "Love fast and hot like fire in straw."

"You're still feeling the ether, lieutenant . . . a bit. . . ."

The ether went on singing through his body, for how long he didn't know—and he drifted out of the present and the sagacity of the cheerful doctor. Images formed of simple things like an apple and a horse. Merged to a house burning, to the sound of ringing bells. A bird's view of Aunt Dolly's deserted garden chairs waiting out a winter. Then the ether-gassed brain made fearful things happen . . . it said in every house at night there is a murderer upon the stairs and Bo Hue, the Chinese cook, was placing flowers with large, open mouths in a blue vase . . . a barking, and no dog in sight. . . . Coming suddenly on a glass of water with a set of teeth in it . . . as the full symbol of domestic misfortune . . . the old Starkweather boathouse, exploring the throbbing sexual oyster Mollie Ott . . . in the end life puts a finger

[125]

down your throat, Uncle Brewster warned, and you give up *everything* . . . and Craig's fat lips were near his ear saying you swine, you swine, you. . . .

It was morning when Simon, having recovered his body, opened his eyes. Sunlight made quivering patterns on a dusty crayon-blue wall. The muttering of voices in talk was mixed with sobbing and a groan. He had a vague memory he had survived a night full of strange terror. Yes—yes, lucky, lucky to be alive, muzzy and tipsy, but alive. Bruno had once said, "Simon Copperwood calls on luck like whistling to a dog." He laughed and his head hurt and he felt with pin-prickly fingers the bandages thick and tight on his noggin.

The doctor was bending over him, sniffing, still smiling. "Was it really four machine-gun nests, lieutenant?"

The last of the ether spoke, "Start with what you know, doc, and you have only to do well. . . ." Then he slept, free of all images, all fears, any desires.

Chapter 16

CAPTAIN SIMON BOLIVAR COPPERWOOD, the double bars of the fresh insignia of promotion on his uniform, was leaning on a cane, dragging one foot. Angry scar tissue showed on one side of his head, the hair still not grown out enough to hide it. He stood in the chilly November air of the HQ chateau, its courtyard filled with splendid military cars; Rolls, Cadillacs, a Bugatti, two Vauxhalls, Pierce-Arrows, Franklins, Hispano-Suizas, Isotta-Fraschinis, even two captured Germans, a Benz and a Daimler. He was a little mad about well-made motorcars. A new interest. Smoke made up of blue exhaust came from the waiting cars —cars that gave the HQ status and stature. The uniformed drivers stood under the leafless trees, cupping cold hands as they lit cigarettes and stamped icy feet on the paved courtyard. Twenty miles away, the front muttered like a bumptious deity.

Simon knew the conflict was moving toward its end. The Boche had been desperately, with that German dolorous ire, pulling back. The Ardennes in sight, the Argonne taken, the Crown Prince's armies with General von Gallwitz, pressed with his back against Luxembourg, driven out of Lyons. It was over. Simon touched the tunic where hung a new medal, besides the U.S. decoration and the Croix de Guerre, also pinned there was the Medaglia d'Argento al Valore Militare: most likely the British might give him something casually tasteful in bronze for his weeks of service at the shared airdromes. Certainly, if as this morning, he had been invited to attend their burial of the last of the Hun aces, Heinz von Kissingessel—from the late von Richthofen *Jagdstaffel 2*. All the colonels Simon had made friends with, lunched, gotten drunk with, would be there. Mitchell, Patton, Millhouse. Yes, he had made solid Army friends. It counterbalanced the hostility of some who had been critical of Simon Copperwood after Major Haber killed himself an hour before his first military hearing.

Heinz von Kissingessel's scarlet plane had crash landed near the Bray-Corbie road. Australian gunners nearby watched openmouthed. One Aussie, with a whoop, ran out with a rope which he made fast to the wreck. With a heave and a ho, they pulled the plane out of no-man's-land and gathered round for a look-see at the dead pilot.

An RAF pilot never claimed he actually downed von K., just that he fired at him and that pilots of his flight had seen the scarlet plane go down. Claims were later put in for the kill by some Australians manning a Lewis-gun post near the road, protecting a battery armed with eighteen-pound field guns. The Australians had opened fire with their Lewis guns and the artillery also fired on the scarlet plane; they watched von K's Albatross make a quick right-hand turn in the air and fall into a steep dive. So no one knows for sure who downed it. Most accounts give the credit to the RAF Captain Brown, however. Simon thought this bears out Tolstoy's dictum: "As soon as an event has taken place, it becomes as many events as it has witnesses, for they all tell different versions. . . ."

A rigid figure was still at his controls in the scarlet plane. From

[127]

the open mouth blood, thick and red, gushed as from some wine fountain. The body was searched, pockets emptied. Papers went around in grimy gunners' hands. "Jesus Christ! That's von Kissingessel, the last of Richthofen's aces!"

So it was decided by the victors to hold a grand funeral. Simon felt the entire burial was like some ritual scene from a Gilbert and Sullivan opera. The body, shrouded, lay on the bed of a military truck, bedded deep with flowers. A stiff, correct escort of six officers from the RAF's 209th Squadron, captains all, walked in solemn parade-step behind the slow-paced truck. Simon and the Americans, the French, followed. For interment, a choice plot had been picked in the shade of a lordly hemlock. The body had lain in state during the day, and hundreds of British officers and rank and file, ground crews, anyone interested, had filed past the dead enemy. He lay, it seemed, untouched, for the bullet that killed him had not marred his features. The postmortem showed, Simon read, that the slug had entered one chest wall banged against the spine, gone through the heart, and moved on through the other chest wall.

A reporter said to the Americans, "So when a staunch foe of long standing passes on, you find you strangely miss him . . . a certain piquancy is now lacking."

"Balls," said an American colonel.

Then came the actual burial in the French earth, with full military protocol. The coffin, carried by six air captains wearing black armbands, went into a Crossley utility car painted black. Wreaths were piled on the coffin, one lettered TO OUR GALLANT AND WORTHY FOE.

On command, off moved the fourteen-man firing party, rifles reversed in the traditional ritual position, to match the pomp of mourning, leading the cortege. Next came the carrier and the honorary pallbearers, the captains. All in bare sunlight at a slow regal pace. Simon, limping along, muttered, "Poor dead bastard. The German hero is dead." Well, Simon thought, to be tired of being one's self in defeat; a root in the dark, to die was lucky.

At the cemetery gate, the riflemen formed two lines facing each other. The captains carried the flower-draped coffin past the riflemen at salute position. All were lead by a neatly robed chaplain of the Church of England, prayerbook in hand. An

[128]

orderly crowd of soldiers, and whatever townspeople were available in the ruined village, gathered around under the best surviving hemlock tree, the Americans grouped together on one side. The chaplain recited the Church of England ritual for the dead . . . words, Simon felt, once powerful, now worn meaningless by constant casual use. A eulogy was said. The coffin was lowered into the fresh-dug grave. A crisp officer's bark stiffened the firing party into position, with the calls, "Load! Present! *Fire!*"

Three times in paced order volleys were pressed off. A bugler stepped forward, wet his lips, and blew "The Last Post."

A four-bladed propeller lopped off to make a cross, onto which was screwed a brass plate with the dead German's name and rank. Later it was found his age was wrongly engraved as twenty-two.

Official pictures were taken of the burial. A legendary hero easily destroyed by one burst of desperate gunfire from an enemy.

A photograph taken over the grave, filled with fresh flowers, was reproduced in the 1922 edition of *History of the AEF*. A copy is in the stacks of the old Signal Corps' records in Washington. The Americans in the picture are to one side on the right, a tight group with two French officers, Mitchell, Patton, Millhouse; three shadowy figures under the tree, unidentified. And Captain Simon Bolivar Copperwood, a slim handsome figure, very tight Sam Browne belt, medals in a row—neat, just enough, not flashy. He tall and elegant in a fresh Bond Street tunic, in laced boots because of his not yet fully healed leg infection. The very young Simon stares straight ahead, jawline firmly set, leaning on his cane, among friends, yet an isolated figure among all these incandescent warriors, all aware of each other's drive for position.

Perhaps in two weeks, even less, Simon thought, the war would end in an armistice. He had been tried in battle, had done a heroic deed, for all his self-doubts, made the best of connections with honorable soldiers.

That night he wrote Bruno Holtzman: poor Bruno, sinking into the mud of a base camp at Le Havre, ticketing wounded doughboys, dispatching ambulances, men being loaded into converted ocean liners for the trip home. . . .

Afraid of death, Bruno, as who isn't, who can be patient when you see how easy it is to drop your life in the mud; you have to feel it's all worth it. Right now, it's all winding up quickly. But our future, after it's over, it will come up on us like an ambush, arbitrary and contradictory. I've decided to stay in the Army. Maybe go back to the War College, maybe then go to China with the Embassy, or some cushy tea dancing and escort service with all the peace conferences that are going to come up. What I do feel is that I am making promises to myself that I carry around with me like heavy rocks. I'm learning chess—do you know the Van Kruit opening, the Chatard attack? Fascinating . . .

Simon also made three attempts to write a letter to the widow of Major Lester Haber. However, they all turned out to be so unfairly humiliating, so condescending about himself, that he mailed none of them.

Book Three

Woman changes and remains the same. She is inconstant and faithful. She ceaselessly moults in the shadows of grace. She whom you loved this morning is not the woman whom you will see this evening.

—JULES MICHELET

(From Simon Copperwood's notebooks)

Book Three

Chapter 17

In those years between Great Peconic Bay and the Atlantic, between Southampton and Montauk, the roads were still fairly primitive, and Long Island that far out was not crowded at all. The villagers, in 1922, lived in the Hamptons, away from the sandy shores. Sailboats tacking, pencil scribbles of smoke from some Cunarder or the *France*, moving with racked stacks toward Europe. Cars were the sports toys of the young men; the Kissel Gold Bug, Stutz, Mercer, Packard. These, with fornication, drinking bootleg hooch, country club, yacht-club dances, made a season "on the Island," or so the new tabloid press insisted.

Splendid cars roaring along the sandy roads toward a weekend at some great beach house, were social status—equal to an English butler; cars built at the turn of the century. Envied was the driver of a Bugatti Brescia; usually some young stockbroker out of Yale, who had missed the Great War. His uncle drove his Lorraine-Dietrich 15-C sports car, talking over a highball of the pushrod overhead valves, six vertical cylinders in line. One's bootlegger was also a topic of consideration in the early twenties.

The older folk stuck to their Hispano-Suizas or Cadillacs. The Clinton Rochs had an open Rolls-Royce. "Yep, a London-Edinburgh, six valves in an L head," Clinton Roch had bragged to his son-in-law, Captain Copperwood. "Three forward pedals. Jesus H. Christ—this season we're all car crazy on the Island."

The captain and his wife, the Rochs' daughter, Ada, had come roaring across Long Island in their Cunningham Eight. "Four speeds," the captain ironically reminded his father-in-law, "eight cylinders on elliptic springs." The Copperwoods drove out from Fort Hamilton, where they were in military residence.

Everyone knew great wars were over for good; the Treaty of

Versailles, a cant phrase perhaps here and there—was signed, the League of Nations inaugurated even without the United States, and in 1920—more shocking to most—Prohibition had begun. That caused more talk at Fort Hamilton and on the Island than the fact that Britain had granted dominion status to the Irish Free State, or that the tennis at Forest Hills was dominated by the French. "The quality of your bootlegger's product," Ada Copperwood had said at one of the Fort's afternoon bridge parties, sipping highballs with the wives of majors and colonels, "that brews a hell of a lot more excitement than this talk of what's-his-name? Mussolini going to march on Rome."

Ada was listened to—she looked like a Follies girl turned flapper —because of the Roch money, and there was Captain Copperwood. He had reorganized Fort Hamilton, put in cost accounting, more hot-water showers, and instilled a spirit of pride into the runty, pimply-faced recruits who were volunteering for the Army. It was amazing how soon—by careful selection and weeding out, the recruits were taller, handsomer, drilled better, and seemed to enjoy saluting Captain Copperwood.

They might beef—in the incongruous and absurd way of soldiers —that he was "a drill-crazy bastard, and what's this guff about shaving every day?" But it was good to stand at retreat, see the disk of orange sun die in the west across the bay; at the fort, everyone ramrod stiff as the flag was ritually lowered and Corporal Ron Welldin sobbed out taps on his bugle.

That Captain and Mrs. Copperwood played a fine hand of bridge only added to their acceptance.

The captain wrote long reports on the four airplanes the Army stationed there, still armed with Vickers-Maxim pom-poms. In private, he tinkered with the aid of two mechanics, trying to rebuild a wartime Sopwith Camel.

The Clinton Rochs were noncommittal about their son-in-law. He was a bit outside the perimeter of their experience. Roch Motors of Flint, Michigan, had been absorbed by General Motors at a good stiff price. The Rochs also held huge amounts of stocks in various blue-chip corporations. Clinton and his son, Willard, had land plats in Florida, where a boom was predicted by people Clinton Roch hired to write of such a boom. In the Carolinas they once hunted real foxes.

Clinton Roch, in his late fifties, still had a good head of gray hair, worn short and parted in the middle. He was tall, a bit portly in the middle. Had played halfback at Bucknell the years of that fine team, drank a bit too much of his wine cellar of au domaine moulin à vent, Louis Latour fleurie. He played tennis well, but never overdid exercise. He was a member of several clubs in New York City. There was a showgirl, Effie Saunders, from a George White show, he often took to dinner, and once a week to bed with indifferent results. As Effie expressed it, "The poor gink—hour after hour like sawing a woman in half."

Mary Roch felt Ada had married beneath her. "Some damn cowboy out of the West with medals on his chest." "But smart," Clinton added. "You have to hand it to Captain Copperwood. He has the makings of a future in the Army." Clinton, a solid Republican, took to tossing a word about his son-in-law to the Harding big shots around the War Department when in Washington, while sitting in on a high-stake poker game on H Street. His son-in-law could stand a little special treatment. Do no harm. After all, he told the President, laying down the three kings, Roch contributions to the party were no small potatoes.

"Now, Clinton, don't you start. Everybody wants something."

Mornings on Long Island, Clinton rose at nine. His morning glass of bourbon in his fist, he in apple-green bathing suit, yellow robe, canvas slippers, came down to breakfast in the garden facing the shore. He was gregarious, happy within the periphery of his personality. Hell of a good day to just sit and watch the young fry sail, sip his booze, stare at the pretty girls walking around the beach—he, who couldn't drink, couldn't screw. Those black stockings gave him the hots; he'd give Effie a good shaking workout on Monday. Buy her that fox scarf she was talking up. Clinton decided he was a happy man. He had a fine family, and his prostate seemed in order again, and maybe Ada would get pregnant and put on some weight. A grandson. He gave an insouciant hiccup. Better put some food over the bourbon.

His son-in-law and daughter, both in blue matching robes, were seated in the garden at the white metal table under the arbor. Eating Canadian bacon and eggs, laughing about something. She was, Clinton knew, crazy about that soldier, and you couldn't blame her, after all the jelly beans and hickies that had courted her. Looked like a good stud, handsome, never raucous, never loud. Always like a kind of spring wound up inside him—wound just enough. Clinton suspected depths of subtle insolence and self-assurance in this Westerner.

"When you get here, kids?"

"One in the morning," said Simon. "We blew a tire in East-port."

Ada took a cigarette from a Fabergé case, lit it, coughed. Jesus H. Christ, she was thin! He had always been ashamed he disliked her so at times.

Clinton kissed his daughter's cheek, nuzzled the shaved back of her head, the sleek black shingled bob edged by two earrings of blue stone. Not much, he mused, in the breast department, very good long legs and a grand figure if fed up. He kissed her cheek again and lied: "Ada, you delight an old man's heart."

"You're not *that* old, C.R.," said Ada. She had a thin, musical voice and a face as if ironed free of wrinkles every day—well, *that* was the famous Roch skin.

Simon sipped his coffee, smiled—aware Clinton was putting on an act. His own body was overtanned, the legs ending in rope sandals, showing on one hairy calf an ugly four-inch battle scar.

"What's running out of Montauk?"

"Sea bass, Si. . . . Getting all the planes you want?"

"No. Even Mitchell isn't getting through to those chow-derheads in Washington. . . ."

Ada rose, stretched—hipbones very prominent—waved to Hulda, the Swedish maid. "I'll have a shot of what Dado is drinking."

"This early?" said her father. "Why, Si, don't you kick her crosseyed?"

"I only beat her in private." He closed his eyes to feel the pleasure of warm sun on his eyelids.

"I'm not ritzy, Dado, I'll drink what you old folks drink. . . . We may go to China."

"Premature," said Simon. "I've applied for a tour of duty in the Far East. But those in Washington. . . ." He waved off the rest of his opinion of them.

"Don't tell your mother. She's got those duodenal pyloric

[136]

pains again. She wants you all here in her summer nest. What the hell is there in China, Japan, for the Army?"

"MacArthur thinks it's the kicking-off place for a war."

Clinton sat down, looked at the remains of his drink in the sunlight, as Hulda set a plate of eggs and bacon before him. "He know anything, Si?"

"Where's my drink, Hulda?"

"Koomin."

"Well, he's not mealymouthed. He speaks out."

"Kinda the cock of the walk, MacArthur, Met him at Newport." Clinton watched his daughter gulp her drink. "Don't know what's come over young people. It's revolting, Ada, the way you drink. My mother drank, loved the sauce, but she sipped. My grandmother liked her hot toddies, even if she dressed like Whistler's mother. Morals and manners, Si, all gone to hell in a hack."

Simon laughed: Ada was at her best slightly looped. "My Uncle Brewster used to say that. Only he doesn't really think so. He's a happy *péjorist.*

"What's that, darling?" asked Ada. *"Péjorist?"*

"One who believes the world is steadily getting worse."

"That's a snazzy idea. Isn't it, Dado?"

"He made that word up," said Clinton. "You believe that about the world?"

Simon looked off to where a group of children on the beach were scrambling over the backs and shoulders of two Shetland ponies. "Clinton, our conception of ourselves is never our true appearance, or so a teacher taught us up at the Point. Maybe he's right. Not a bad course—I began to understand the disparity between action and consequence."

"Pérjorist? Hulda, get my big dictionary," said Clinton.

"Let's get into bathing suits." Ada stood, the breakfast tray before her untouched.

"I'll just smoke a cigar," said Clinton. He watched them walk down to the bathhouse, they young, slender. A nice body on his bitchy daughter, and a good spread of shoulders on that cowboy popinjay. Well, he'd have to accept the marriage. Ada *might* have married a Catholic, or even a sissy from Cherry Grove in Great South Bay. She never was one given to restraints. He sat in the sun, a bulky, kindly man, glass in hand, cigar in mouth. He envied his son-in-law his youth, his perception, even his daughter's body that—forget it—so many had known since she was fifteen.

In the yellow dressing room of the Roch bathhouse, Ada and Simon stood naked, inspecting a row of drying bathing suits. Simon always was amazed at the crisp blackness of his wife's bush, and the smallness of her apple-sized breasts he called "the little Greeks," that from his study of the history of art at the Point.

She wriggled against him; desire could catch her like a cardiac spasm, and she asked, "Huh?"

He enjoyed her life of sensation rather than thought. "Huh, *what?*"

"A quickie?"

"Ad, only ranchhands in town on payday don't think loving should be done in leisure and with detail."

She banged a hip against him. He was already aroused and thought, she sure raises my hackles. They fell to on a canvas beach pad, not bothering to move to the faded studio couch. Ada cried out in exhorting erratic yelps: "Oh, hurt me, hurt me!"

He kissed her—was her mouth wet with the taste of money? What a crazy thought just now as he felt her hand grab his jock. "Hurt me, hurt me."

He said, "Ad, I'll hit you with a boat oar, okay?"

"You bastard," she cried out laughing, "oh, oh!"

"Oh, yes," he said; no other woman had ever had it for him like Ada, like Ada, like Ada. . . . This, she, was his dream princess —all but for a few faults. Not the boyhood dream—but the adult reality.

It was a fierce rolling and straining to come together. They both were ardent natures and felt full commitment to this pleasuring. In the heat of the bathhouse they began to sweat and go shiny with effort. They rolled from side to side on the beach pad. Ada said, "No, no; don't you, you damn stallion. I can't, *can't!*"

"Sure you can. Keep trying, keep trying."

But it was no use. Half the time Ada couldn't make it. Too

much reflection, Simon told her, self-awareness. She would, in disappointment, grow desperate and pant and bite her lower lip. He looked down at her, wondering at the precise logic of their relationship.

"Now," she said in a pleading voice. "Will you try again? Oh, damn, darling, will you?"

"You try too hard—*la belle gonzesse*."

"No wop talk, please. Please, *huh?*"

After a while she gave a long, long sigh, freeing her lungs of all air. When she could speak again, she said, "Oh, sport!" She had learned that term—"sport"—from Bruno Holtzman, "Oh, it's like that first time in the car after the Rutgers-Princeton game."

"Was it?"

"You, you said, 'Jesus Christ,' and I said, 'Crazy . . . crazy.' "

They had met eight months before, after a Rutgers-Princeton football game, met in a roadhouse in New Brunswick, New Jersey, on French Street. General Buckley Hollister had invited Captain Copperwood to join him and his party, a couple, Major and Mrs. Ned Chambers—Miss Silver and Charlie Norton, for the game, going down to Princeton in the general's open Paige. Buck Hollister was commanding at Fort Hamilton, a large, lean, red-faced man, with the last spear wound (on his right cheek) ever made by an Apache war party when he was a shavetail with General Miles.

There had been flasks at the game, Rutgers had a big Negro backfield player, Robinson, who impressed everyone. After the game General Hollister said, "We need a chill breaker. Back to Zoller's up the road in Brunswick." They all piled into the car and went north. Miss Silver and Charlie lost someplace, and raccoon coats and travel rugs all in disorder—felt freezing. Zoller's was an established Swiss roadhouse that was now serving alcohol in various forms from its ample cellar—not in teacups, but in the original bottles.

Upstairs at Zoller's were bedrooms with clean linen and thick drapes. Downstairs the lighting was discreet, the tablecloths crisp linen. There were several parties, most of which were from the game, shouting between each other's groups. "Damn fine game. . . ." "Hello, Chet." "Made a packet . . . drinkee, drinkee, drinkee. . . ." Buck Hollister waved to a group of four, drinking champagne and the two girls smoking through foot-long holders.

"Good game, Buck."

The tall girl with the dark bob waved. "Damn cold, Unk."

"Hell, you're not dressed for it."

Simon thought the girl was neatly undressed. A short gown, a very low, blue gown, rolled gray stockings, high-heeled shoes, a pale-blue silk band around her shiny winged black hair, bobbing earrings, a fur coat on the floor at her feet. Could have used a little more breast, but snazzy as the saying was, as she wriggled her shoulders to a trio playing "Avalon."

"My niece," said Buck Hollister. He snapped his fingers at the maître d'. "Andre, have them join us. Knock two tables together."

"No. No," said the girl, "I got stood up by Buzz Taylor. He musta gotten drunk. I just sat in over there. Andre, one chair." It was a pleasure, said Andre.

"A how-dee-do," said the girl to Simon as he held her slim hand with the one ring, blue stoned.

"Ada, this is Captain Copperwood. Simon, my niece, Ada Roch. Ada, you know Ned and Mina. Sit down. . . . Andre, what's cooking?"

Andre Zoller said he had several pheasants—well hung—on the spits, and would the general care for the splendid Burgundy he had put down in 1912. But of course! The real thing. Musty but not sharp.

"You play football at West Point, Captain Copperfield?" One foot out of her shoe was rubbing his ankle.

"Copperwood. Simon. No I was on the baseball team."

"Icky, baseball players get so sweaty. . . . Have them play 'Dardanella.' Dance, captain?"

"Go ahead, Simon," said the general. "That's an order."

Simon had learned to dance well at West Point. It was part of the education there, and he had polished his style in Paris and in London after the armistice. Later at the Peace Conference. . . . All a million years ago, and Woodrow Wilson in a saloon car with acetylene gas headlamps.

[140]

He led well, didn't crowd the girl. Just managed a grace, an ease. She smelled of gin, and deliciously of armpits and almond cream. She laid her head on his shoulder and said, "I'm tanked, bocoo tanked, but I like you, Copperfield, you're not ritzy like those grinds from Annapolis."

He smiled and they talked of horses and dogs. Ada owned two Airedales and kept a saddle horse at Piping Rock. He remembered a line from Lit. 2: *to describe the happy dawning of her thighs. . . .*

The food was good, the wine only fair. Buck Hollister smiled, his eyes a bit glazed: "Captain, don't want Ada to drive. You're ordered to deliver her to her home."

"Yes, sir. Where is home?"

Ada said, "Rye. Rye, New York, U.S.A."

Her car was a Stutz Black Hawk, which Simon had never driven. He had driven a Stutz Bearcat, but the Black Hawk was a pure delight, and Ada leaned against him singing from the depth of the fox furs wrapped around her.

Let me throw my arms around you
Honey ain't I glad I found you . . .

Ada delighted Simon, her casual conviviality, extravagant gestures. Generals, colonels, and majors usually had such ugly daughters and female relatives. Ada Roch was an exception. Pretty, very pretty, good bone structure. Her voice had a husky sensual quality, an invitation to comradery, to involvement, with that easy calm of the rich. He had been lonely, had been working hard. . . . He was unaware just how vulnerable he was. He adjusted his dream standards to the visible present.

She kept hunting for his chest through the heavy military overcoat—her hand like a varmint in the bush—she made throaty, beasty sounds. She laughed a lot as they passed through Metuchen, Rahway, Elizabeth, Jersey City. Her hand on his naked chest felt scar tissue. He said, "Shrapnel."

He even sang some himself as the wind—choked with snow—whipped around them. The Jersey Meadows, a horror of odors prolonged across a swampy void led to the lights of the city rigid in the night across the bay.

Ships in the ocean
Rocks in the sea
Black haired woman
Made a fool out of me.

On the Hudson the night wind was warmer. As they came to the outskirts of Rye, Ada said, "Stop here. Under the trees." The wind seemed calmer, a flute with plaintive notes.

They petted, they pulled the travel rugs over their bodies and under the coverings they fondled. At two in the morning, they made love. He was quiet, sure they did it well.

Captain Bruno Holtzman came up from Panama when they were married, three months later, in the First Congregational Church of Rye, New York, leaving under an arch of fellow officers' swords. ("Sorry, Bruno, they didn't cotton to a Jewish best man.") The noon wedding reception was held in the Clinton Roch residence on Hudson Drive, a huge Medician-Italian-Stanford White mixture of red brick, white marble, gray stucco, and much ivy. There was a buffet for a hundred and fifty, of *crêpes roulées et farcies*, cold turkey galantine, *homard*, brook trout, pressed duck à l'Américain on rings of steamed rice. "Hell," said General Buckley, "no American in Paris ever heard of it."

Simon had no relatives present—he regretted that.

The bottles were labeled "Chateau de Tours Brouilly," "Au Domaine Moulin à Vinet," and "Mumm's Sec." But were actually all from a local bootlegger. However, the raw gin, scotch, and bourbon from the West Indies, served most of the guests better.

Everyone had told how wonderful a girl Ada was. How lucky he was. What a success their life would be. He was sure they were all right.

It had been really a bad time for him—between the war ending, trying to adjust to peace, and being alone at the Fort. Now, all would change.

Uncle Brewster and Aunt Dolly had wired they had the flu.

Mrs. Roch, out of bed two days from a minor operation, suffering dyspeptic flatulence, looked pale and distant at the wedding. Clinton Roch kept clinking glasses and asked, *"That's* fifteen hundred dollars' worth of flowers?" Ada was a load off his mind: that poor bastard of a captain would learn about the duplicity of women. All women!

After Ada went up to change into a green traveling outfit and leopard skin jacket, a gift from her father, Simon put on a Harris tweed single-breasted suit, a snap-brim gray hat, two-tone shoes. Clinton took him to one side in the music room upstairs, and in between the Steinway and the Victrola, slipped him an envelope, trying not to act as if Simon were a headwaiter. "Don't you be mean to the little girl, Simon. She's a handful, some ambiguity—a bit loose in the head. The Matthews—her mother's folks—the Pottsville coal people—all a bit dippy. But you treat Ada fine, or you'll hear from me. You're the only stud she ever showed more than a three-day interest in. Yes . . . well . . . happy life."

Clinton Roch was drunk, Simon decided. He felt the envelope. Too thick for a check. He wanted to give it back, but his father-in-law was weaving on his feet, his gray cravat loose, the pearl stickpin coming out. Simon said, "It's all going to be fine." Clinton muttered, "You poor, poor bastid"—or something like that.

The Roch chauffeur and houseman drove the couple to the Jersey City pier. Simon remembered he had sailed for France and battle from nearby Hoboken. The big white ship they were taking to France waited. A dozen of the younger wedding party had followed. There was rice throwing and in the cabin, opening of bottles, flowers dying all around; "like a bootlegger's funeral," someone said. Huge basket containers of tropical fruits, apples, and pears, were set all round the stateroom. Captain Bruno Holtzman frowned at what passed for the champagne in his glass, lifted it up after a taste. "To the bride, the groom, and the Army way."

Ada kissed Bruno twice with happy insolence. "Love Army." When the siren had gone off and she was alone with Simon, the wilting flowers, the smell of pineapples and oranges, she held Simon very close, bit an ear without breaking the skin. "From

[143]

now on, darling, a nifty life together, no more problems making it."

"Yeah, yeah," said Simon unknotting his tie.

By the time the big ship was rolling in the tidal change off Kill Van Kull, Ada was too seasick to concentrate on their lovemaking. The empty wine bottles rolled around on the pitching floor as she vomited.

Hotel Crillon
10 Place de la Concorde
Paris 8, France.

DEAR DOLLY AND BREWSTER:

Yes, I've done it, the ultimate, gone and gotten married. Sorry you were too sick to come East. Up to a few days before the event, I wasn't too sure myself it was going to happen to me. I don't mean I wasn't sure, it was just that the world was all in a whirl here, the air full of feathers, and the family I've married into lead a life that you don't believe.

First things first. Her full name is Ada Audrey Roch. Or was, it's now Mrs. Captain Copperwood. She looks like a John Held, Jr., drawing—ate *pâté de foie gras* in bed with a shoehorn—lives on a merry-go-round, and wears hornrimmed glasses when she reads. She is a highbrow, been tossed out on her pretty tail from several of the best colleges. The last one, Cornell.

I have no idea how it all went to serious consideration from the first meeting—and the poet's line, "Love is a sovereign state of two—" liking each other around, a serious talk about life and all that guff, to a final idea we *might* try and make it in double harness. It's time I settled into a domestic life as a career officer, and add to it the fact I love the little filly, I hope to adjust to running double. It wasn't just a taste for order in my life, or too much high living here.

This is all too flip a letter of course, and I'm writing it in an unmade hotel room while Ada is just out of bed and downstairs getting her hair frizzed. But I do want

[144]

you both to know I'm as reasonably happy as man can be. As for career, my plans, frankly, are to suck up to enough high brass to get something interesting—an assignment overseas, at perhaps an embassy. It's all too bland—the Army here—and lazy.

Right now it's all Vionet and Poiret gowns and the Bal Negre on the Rue Blomet. But I think of Mitchell, Mac, Ike, all the men of promise or guile, who are just like me, marking time, waiting for some opening. I feel—it's no wild improbability—the Asian theater is going to boil over. The Nipponese are going to make a power play soon. It's only logical. If I were them, I'd do the same. China is rotten to the core, all this warlord, Kuomintang mess. The Bolshies in Moscow are wobbly with Lenin sick. So why not? The Japanese, if they're smart, and they are, I've met them at the Point visiting and observing, *ah, so—ah, so*—they'll begin taking bites out of the Flowery Kingdom. Which brings up our policy there—call it the amorality of imperialism if you like—and how much will we stand. But this War College gossip is not for this letter. I just want to be there when things begin to happen. As a Major Millhouse, who taught us at West Point, put it, "We should be defending our borders, not in San Francisco or New York but at Peking or Leningrad."

Ada just came in—ordered iced *vin rosé* and grouse paste for lunch, and said, "Say howdy to the folks," her idea of how we hicks talk in Montana. I'll write to brother Craig when I have a little more time. Funny me having a banker brother, I mean a real banker. I heard him being talked about by some Wall Street guests, silk tophats at a party. Something to do with Craig Copperwood's banks merging with the Cattle Trail Banks and he getting on the board of the M.Y. & Western R.R. That's what has come out of a quixotic principle of devotion to high interest rates.

I wanted to send you, Aunt Dolly, a hunk of the three-story wedding cake, but some Princeton bastard—the drunken twerp—fell into it and demolished most of it. Ada says we're off to *l'esprit pumesautier*.

As always,

Simon

He quickly learned how to live with a woman. How to expect the unexpected. He was a man of discipline, and besides he loved her. He loved her very much and he was sternly determined to have a good marriage.

He had laid out a pattern for the kind of woman he wanted and Ada—with a little adjustment—fitted the pattern. At least in most ways. She was pretty and at times beautiful. He was learning that no women looks the same at all times. She had a crisp wit. Her set called it wisecracking. Not profound but amusing. She was warm, comforting, responding to his lovemaking as much as she could. And it was getting better.

He was aware that all he had thought he knew about women was worthless or silly. Both. Domestic life, the shared bathroom, the unwashed looks in the morning, the damp towels underfoot, the stray combs and the intimate garments in the wrong places, all this he survived. If in some sudden rage she was unreasonable, he blamed a monthly mystery, and if she laughed too much and drank a lot and got sick, it was good to baby her. And wipe her face and hold her head when she upchucked. It was best at morning, in bed talking of the day ahead, smoking the first cigarettes, offering each other the bathroom. It was then that he knew he liked being a married man. In time he suspected he'd even become a nearly perfect husband.

Chapter 18

SEVERAL children were building sand castles. Simon sat on the beach under a striped umbrella, a tan pad of lined paper on his brown knees. He was writing rapidly with a soft pencil, racing his ideas to get them onto paper, disciplining the extremes of style and effects he permitted himself. Ada had gone back to bed—a migraine, booze flavored.

It has been said [he wrote in his strong, schoolboy script] happy countries have no history, but it is more than likely that nations without histories had no military establishments powerful enough to protect them. And so vanished from the scene. Not as happy nations but as disasters brought about by the neglect of their shields and chariots, and not by unsavory attitudes and extravagances.

He looked up, wondering over the qualities of order and authority a nation needed. A large woman with a floppy yellow straw hat was reading a novel lettered *Flaming Youth*. Beyond her, two little girls in blue frocks were rolling a red ball back and forth, while a black and white terrier ran between them barking ferociously. The surf was high, cream-foamed, and most of the people on the beach were drowsy and idle under umbrellas, or lay prone—larded with cocoa butter, tanning skins into leather.

Simon turned to take in the rows of well-kept houses, spaced discreetly apart by lawns and hedges—an Island community still isolated, protected from the people who were beginning to crowd the outer extent of the Island. Already the Model T, the popular flivver tin lizzie, was bringing in gawkers past the Roch house—rubbernecking to see how the rich disported themselves on their expanse of white sand. There had been talk, led by Clinton Roch, of closed roads, private gates, more police. Simon shifted away from the sun in his face, and began to write again.

The terrier was digging up sand, the fat woman, novel forgotten, was asleep, mouth open. Far out at sea, a liner inched along —looked like the *Rochambeau*.

He had been writing these notes for over a year now, collecting them, keeping them locked away in a bottom desk drawer at Fort Hamilton. Would they make a book? Or even some articles in the *Army Journal*? He doubted if he would ever publish them.

They were personal ideas by a nobody captain, extensions of some lonely philosophy, if he could call it philosophy on military theory.

> There are two simple ruthless standards by which the purity of any military action can be determined. What is required is, first, an indifference to all dated conceptions of military minds whose work has been completed—a disregard for those who have lost with success or age the will to think fully, and whose major accomplishments are of the past. There are too many repressive establishments of older men, traditional ways to do things.

He closed the pad as Ada—by way of a traveling dance step —came across the sands carrying two lime collins on a tray, and a newspaper. "Mah-Jongg going full blast at the house, darling. All those dippy people. My head got better so I tried to read *archy* to them, but. . . ."

"Who's *archy?*" he asked as she sank down by his side and kissed his neck and shoulders as he reached for a glass. She'd had a few already. He sensed that. He enjoyed her lively, darting, often scurrilous mind. Like a blue jay, he thought, busy here and there picking up bits of shiny paper, pebbles, and bitsof bark.

Ada took a good pull on her drink and flipped open the newspaper, stared, pensive, introspectively at a page. "He's a cockroach who's a poet. He types them out—the poems. But by hitting the keys of the machine with his head. Capish? But he can't make capital letters."

"Who?"

"Archy, that's who."

Simon nodded. "Because he can't shift keys, the bug—yes."

"You've read *archy?* In the *Sun?*"

"No, I just figured it out from your hints. So?"

Did she love as he did? Was he an overadjusted man.

"He has this friend, archy has. An alley cat, mehitabel, who's a kind of Village bum. . . . Listen:

[148]

          boss i believe
          that the
          millennium will
          get here some day
          but i could
          compile quite a list
          of persons
          who will have
          to go
          first

Simon took a sip from his drink as he watched two children finish making a huge sand castle. "That's the problem, Ad. Whom do you shoot to save the world? Why shoot? Who shoots first? He's a roach with a good head on him." The fat woman had given up sleep and was smearing oil on her arms and large mushy thighs (one would have to get into her, Simon figured, with a ladder). From one of the houses came a Victrola's version of "Japanese Sandman." Ada tossed aside the newspaper, began to sing the words, but discovered she only knew two lines. The grunting mutter of a saxophone solo caused the terrier to stop digging and began to bark.

Ada sipped her drink and watched Simon write.

> The original military mind hunts new methods—and so each of these methods can result in the isolation and, finally, the exposure of some essential—which is to say difficult—military problem. It is axiomatic among great soldiers that only difficult tasks are worth doing. . . .

He became aware she had seized the sheets and was tearing them to shreds.

Clinton Roch turned away from the bank of sun-porch windows that faced the beach, turned away with a chuckle. "Say! Si just gave Ada a real solid belt to the chops. Knocked her right back on her heels."

Mary Roch shook her head, almost as if with a palsy. She was a lean, pale woman with a kind of fragile beauty gone to wrinkles

[149]

and sagging skin. The victim of expensive doctors—over-drugged, addicted actually—she lived the life of a well-cared-for invalid.

"You needn't gloat so, Clint."

"She had it coming, I'm sure." He went back to look out the windows. "She's running, look at her throw up sand, and he isn't following her."

"You approve of his brutality?" Mary Roch spoke with a meticulous exactness, as if counting her breaths.

"Oh, hell, Mary. She's been asking for it. Always was so god-damn pernickety, and—"

Mary Roch rec'ined deep into a soft wickerwork chair and felt for her pulse with a thumb. "You always had unnatural desires for her, Clint. I was certainly aware of it. You're looking for peculiar pleasures."

Her husband turned to stare at her. "You're out of your mind, woman. I could hardly stand the sight of that girl."

Did he really resent Simon Copperwood in bed with his daughter? Deep down did he? No, of course not. He stilled the tremor of disquiet in his gut.

Clinton Roch, still outraged, went down to the beach. Simon was sitting, hands and arms wound around his naked knees, staring out at a scrubbed smudge of smoke on the horizon. Ada was no place in sight—sulking, most likely, in the boathouse—a childhood hiding place.

"Had a tiff, Si?"

"Bad reflexes."

"She deserved it. Should of myself done more of it."

Simon looked up at his father-in-law. "Oh?"

"I saw it from the sun porch."

Simon's gaze followed the flight of some scraps of his papers moving up the beach. "I was, you see—well—surprised. I reacted in a lousy way. You ever hit a woman, Clint?"

"Often wanted to bat one a few. Never had the chance. Would have liked to a few times." It was pleasant talking to another man. You don't have to aim for subtleties of behavior.

"She doesn't want to go to China," Simon said.

"You don't have to. Hell, I'll make you vice-president in one of our companies. No, no, not any fake job, I mean you'll be able to

[150]

work your tail off for us. You'll do things. You've got the oom-pah. Don't give me that insulted look."

"Not insulted. It's just. . . ."

Simon stood up and put the writing pad under one arm. "I'm Army. That's the way the game goes for me. I'm not goddamn truculent or self-righteous—but if Ad doesn't see it—"

"Oh, she'll go along. She was always this way. The Matthews women, Mary's folk, are, well. . . ." He spun a finger near one temple. He looked out toward where a small sloop was moving with a rising wind behind it.

"I love her, you know," Simon said.

"Willard has his boat out. Sea bass must be running with the tide. Care to come out with me this afternoon?"

"I was going to write. But I guess fishing will do me more good. You don't think I should go find Ada?"

"Worst thing you could do. Women need sulking time."

Ada made it up to him that night. She was ardent—as if in some compulsion—and comforting, forgiving, as if she had struck the blow. She was not abject, but she explained she did things without reason. Yes, Simon said, she did—he told her as they lay locked in each other's arms. He didn't mind moods. But if she ever tore up any more of his writing, he'd break her ass. Ada said he could do that any time. Simon suspected she was one of those women who were at their peak sexually after a dis-agreement and a reconciliation. She lay quivering, whispering, "Yes, yes. . . ." Her voice had just the tone of the sea outside, a sea sliding up with a rush and withdrawal on the beach, destroying the last sand castle.

Book Four

My son, if only two remain in the whole world to
study the truth, it will be enough . . .

—RABBI SHIMON BEN YOHAI

(From the notebooks of Simon Copperwood)

Chapter 19

ADA was happier in 1925 when Captain Simon Bolivar Copperwood was ordered to the Army War College in Washington, D.C., to take a series of courses on conditioning of troops for extreme climates. They drove down, happy, filled with facetious badinage, drove in a Cunningham eight-cylinder sports roadster with four forward speeds, rather sticky to shift. Simon had reconditioned the car and given it a maroon coat of paint. He explained to Ada it had side valves in an L-head, knowledge which didn't impress her. The open car made it a dusty ride in a crisp September day. Ada was happy to get to Washington and begin to move about in society there. "I have this old schoolmate—Cornell together—who is moving out the Negroes and redecorating the old houses for people who want real Colonial old brick."

"Real honest-to-God Colonial old brick?"

"And genuine worm-riddled oak rafters. I promised we'd stay with her till we get settled. Souki Miller knows just everyone."

"It's not going to be all social. A hell of a time to tell me. I wanted to stay near the War College at Fourth and P Streets. I've a lot of studying to do."

"I kept it as a surprise. Souki, I mean. . . . They'll give you a regiment or something, I suppose."

"Try and get the order of things, Ad. A sergeant commands a squad, a lieutenant a platoon, a captain a company, a lieutenant colonel a battalion, a colonel a regiment, a brigadier general a brigade, supposedly the largest unit one man can control within the range of his voice. And a major general a division, a lieutenant general a corps or an army group, and a general an army group or a supreme command."

"No wonder a battle is so confusing."

"Don't get smarty-pants, no flapper wisecracks. It's all damn protocol in Washington Army circles. The *grandes dames* of the generals are important. Cozy up to them."

They were going 85 mph past Camden.

"I can't make Army talk, Simon. I keep laughing out loud."

"Well, just accept them all as high-titted Southern darlings grown haggard in the stink of magnolia blossoms."

"I'll try out my Long Island accent on the broads."

"Their husbands decide on what young officer gets the thumbs up. So just remember a few facts to impress them as a military wife. A squad is twelve men, a platoon forty, a company roughly one hundred and fifty, a battalion eight hundred to one thousand, a regiment three thousand to five thousand, a brigade four thousand to five thousand, a division fifteen thousand, a corps two or more divisions, an army two or more corps, an army group two or more armies. Got it?"

"No." She pinched his arm, laughing. "Can't I just sleep —pretty please—with some of the generals? It's much more interesting than how many soldiers make an army group."

"Be serious, Ad—I want to make major."

"I bet none of them are the jock you are."

"Just don't try to find out. . . . Hungry? How about Bookbinder's in Philly for some shad roe, brisket of beef with horseradish sauce, and a Pennsylvania Dutch fruit pie?"

"I hope they have a clean john. I'm all windburned, and want to spend a dime."

They had a fine lunch, Two martinis each. Simon was keyed up about the War College and the Beefeaters drinks helped get them out of Philadelphia. Ada said she heard it was closed on Sunday. Before they came to Washington at dusk they had stopped for a tea at the Red Lion Inn at four in the afternoon, and had more Beefeaters.

Souki (originally Susan) Miller had inherited from her mother a six-unit apartment building on Q Street. A building erected sometime after Appomattox, solidly enough built but now settled and cracked by shifting foundations on a shaky subsoil. In need of repairs, but usually filled by tenants who took its lack of proper heating, painting, a full supply of hot water, because of its modest rents. They were mostly minor officials in obscure posts; some were often back-country Congressmen elected by some fluke or shift in political gambits, and not too sure they would be reelected.

Souki, a slim, elegant blonde, hard-eyed, full-mouthed, stoical and wise, lived in a third-floor apartment of her house. A high-ceilinged place of three spacious rooms, too hot in summer and often chilly in winter. Here, among three generations of value-less furniture, the Millers had existed after coming to Washington during Grant's administration. Souki's grandfather, a colonel of volunteers from Michigan, was one of the major organizers of the Grand Army of the Republic, that powerful veterans' organization. He had served as a claims supervisor director in the War Department and aided in the looting of the U.S. Treasury by the demands, many valid, of the ex-soldiers of the Civil War. The Millers were Army—had stayed on in Washington. Souki's father was in the Indian Department (during the Ghost Dance wars), several uncles served on military waterways, two cousins in regimental supplies. Souki, in silver lamé pants, hugged Ada to her and looked over at Simon, a cigarette in a short jade holder wagging in one corner of her too large, but attractive mouth.

"You both look damn windblown. . . . And not too sober. But welcome to Miller Court."

"It was a bit breezy in the open car, Souki."

Simon said, "The hooch kept us warm."

"War College captain? Going in for a desk job?"

Simon looked at Ada shaking out her shingled hair in a mirror. He made a noncommittal move of his head. "I'll just glide with the current until I really decide. I'll just observe for a bit."

"Scared? Don't blame you. The War Department is a bear trap. Well, I'll see you get the right information, and meet the right people. *Right* is the key word. You get to running around with the low-rating behinds grown to their chairs, people going noplace, and you'll get marked down yourself. I've got a turtle stew. Malvina learned to cook it at Miller's in Baltimore. And downstairs a two-room apartment for you until you decide if you

[157]

want to take a house. My advice is, don't, Simon, not until you make colonel. It's Liberty Hall here—so"—Souki laughed and smiled a trifle archly—"maid service and breakfasts."

The terrapin stew was delicious. Malvina the cook was large and coffee-colored, and no plantation mammy. Souki said Malvina had two sons in the government printing department and a daughter married to a naval inspector at Newport News.

"It's a black town—and getting blacker.... You must be tired."

Malvina showed them the two-room apartment over the back garden, the sitting room in rose-colored wallpaper, with chaise longue and what Souki called "some scarred original General Grant-period furnishing." There was a wide bed in the smaller room, a bed with pineapple-carved posts, which impressed Ada.

Malvina said, "Bathroom down the hall. Miss Miller, she couldn't crowd no more plumbin' in up here, with the house fallin' down. The winder screens are new; them bugs comin' up from the Potomac and the bay." She turned at the door. "Oh, I don't do breakfasts in bed, and weekends I visit relations in Alexandria, so you fix yourself. Goodnight."

"Thank you, Malvina," said Ada, kicking off her shoes while sitting on the bed. Simon lifted their two strapped suitcases onto the luggage stands. Their trunks would follow.

Simon said, "So far—so good."

Ada came to Simon and hugged him. "It's going to be fine, just fine. Generals are made in Washington, Souki says, not on battlefields."

"I'll be happy to be a colonel in ten, twelve years. Unless, of course, there's a big war."

He began to unpack his suitcase and wrapped some books on China and some large folded maps of the Western Pacific sections in two shirts, before putting them into the bottom drawer of a warped, marble-topped dresser. He felt some incongruous disposition of his life was soon to take place—that he was on the perimeter of fuller experience.

In the morning, Ada sleeping late, face crumpled into her pillow, Simon went out to the War College, walked down a hall full of old iron and bronze, oil paintings under too much varnish. The official green-and-chartreuse walls were faded but clean. He found at last the office of Souki Miller's friend, Major

Arnold Rosegold, a solid, well-muscled Kansas product, thirty years in service he told Simon at once, "and *not* a West Point man." His mustache was mink-colored and a bit on the English style, just missing being too long at its spur-sharp waxed ends. On one wall was a Navaho blanket and several photographs of Teddy Roosevelt with Major Rosegold.

"Captain, sit down—glad to have you with us. Souki is an old friend, and she did right telling you to see me. The college is a good one but slack just now. You can drift through it, or lead yourself to something in a career. We're loose as a goose's bowels here. Just coasting. This fellow Harding and his buddies are looting the country. But you'll learn here you take care of your department, remain loyal to the Army, *and* wear blinders." Major Rosegold, with well-cared-for hands, opened a folder before him. "You have a fine record, captain, and you have a probing mind. But. . . ." He twirled each end of his mustache in turn. "Old General Tjaden took me in hand when I came here, a shavetail with Crook when we went after Heronimo. He put it to me like this: 'Arnie, think if I had words to tell a fellow about how to get ahead in the Army, I'd say, *be known*. Take steps to be known by a large number of senior officers and *be known favorably*. Doesn't matter how. By polo, athletics, football, trap shooting, but get known all over the Army. You're going to a selection board in the War College. The board studies the names and the records and then starts talking about the people, and picks the people they know.' Well, I followed that advice myself, never forgot it."

Simon tried to remain expressionless: it was advice he had been getting for a week. "Thank you, major, Miss Miller says the same thing, and the officers at Hamilton."

"I'd say, studying your record, you're aching to make general some day. Well, maybe the best men in the Army are the majors and colonels who *never* made general. Oh, I'm not patting myself on the back, captain, I've gone as high as I want, high as my brain power and skeptic's laziness will take me. Three more years and I'm heading for retirement and Pasadena, go puttering at golf, and beefing with the other retired how the War Department failed to improve the Army with our splendid ideas. Now go see Colonel Wallie Elkins and get your program set. Wallie's weakness is old military prints. He'll wear your ear off about Lee's mistakes at Gettysburg. Very good teacher. So let's have lunch at the Willard next"—Major Rosegold flipped open a memo book—"next Wednesday, one pee-emma. Good luck, Copperwood."

It was a good handshake and Simon wondered if he'd end up a stylish gossip of a major at a desk, taking young officers out to lunch and looking forward to dying in Pasadena or Santa Barbara, or on a sea island off the Carolinas.

In the next few weeks, Simon got a good solid picture of the War College and how one survived and benefited by it. In his private journal he noted (while Ada bathed and did her face for a party a Senator heading military budgets was giving): "Two aspects of the WC—first an *unhealthy climate* of *caste* surrounding general officers, second the inability of lower-ranking officers to use their most energetic years in productive work. A third point is that the Army is compulsively anti-intellectual, as opposed to being anti-brains. Brains do count—but only on routine matters."

Ada stood naked and steamy before him. "You like my hair combed this way to one side?"

"I like everything I see."

"Oh, no, Si, darling—now? Oh, well, they can start without us. Um—that's nice—*so* nice."

Colonel Wallace McCord Elkins wore gold-rimmed glasses and was popular in his classes on high strategy. He was a handsome forty-eight. The class had been working out a military solution to an action in one aspect of a battle on the final attack against the Hindenburg Line.

Colonel Elkins shook his head as Simon gave his version of how the action had to proceed.

"It's not at all right, captain, not right at all. Captain Astruc will show you on the blackboard how the solution would go." Jeff Astruc was the colonel's assistant, and drew well.

Simon studied the diagram and shook his head. "Sir, interesting. But that solution would not be used."

"And why not, captain?" The colonel polished his glasses with a silk handkerchief.

"I was in *that* battle, and I fear we muffed that way of fighting it."

The colonel smiled, adjusted the blue enamel Slavic Order of Royal Merit on his chest, reset his glasses in place, smiled again.

"Ah, captain, nevertheless this solution is the doctrine one and here in class we do not run counter to doctrine. Prosaic, practical, obvious, *always* doctrine."

The colonel got to talking to Simon about it after class. "Our job here, captain, is to pour good officer material through a mixer and get a uniform product. That's why doctrine is sacred. We don't get any Napoleons or Grants. Hardly ever."

"Yes, sir."

"Now take George Meade at Gettysburg. He was the inferior general. Frightened. But he stuck to doctrine, hung on for three days of hell. Lee, free-rolling—well, it was all banners and bugles and Pickett's silly charge and some very bad errors."

Simon nodded. "We're attacking a shrine, attacking Lee. Grant, now, he would *not* have retreated on the third day if he had been in command of the rebel forces. Meade was near the breaking point. Actually speechless with fear, according to some of his staff."

Colonel Elkins smiled. "We *must* carry this talk further. Interesting point you have there about Grant. Now just remember this. If we seem slow here. The system wears most men as smooth as a pebble. In an institution as complicated as that of the Army, nothing is more excellent than sheer *competence*. The slogans reflect it: No *problems, zero defects*. The man who can make it work without making waves is a prize. It is from a system of such *rigid hierarchy* that the young rebel must be protected, taken under the wing of a senior in order to survive. The Army should take its most talented and make them staff men in order to serve the system; insist that talented staff men command battalions. A lieutenant colonel who has not been blooded is like a surgeon who has not operated. A good officer can be circumscribed by so many rules and regulations that he is rarely able to display either initiative or innovation. Innovation is *not* a working rule in the

[161]

Army. The most thoughtful officers have a common complaint: in its most extreme form the notion of 'the freedom to fail.' You follow me?"

"Yes, sir."

"How about dinner some evening at my place, meet Mrs. Elkins and get Mrs. Copperwood and her together? Show you some interesting Civil War woodcut prints by Winslow Homer."

"Yes, sir. Be good for Ada to get to know more Army wives. She's been going to tea dances afternoons, and evenings it's country clubs for us. The booze is terrible."

It was becoming clearer to Simon that the War College, the War Department (not yet pussyfooting it as the Department of Defense) was the best start to being a success in the military pecking order. A dress suit, a skill at the newest dance step, Souki Miller explained—eating and drinking with the right people was paramount.

Living at Miller Court was easy. Souki had a wise, penetrating acumen and enjoyed parties, men, good food. Malvina soon grew to accept Simon and Ada, as Ada turned over to her discarded hats, a soiled Paquin dress of unfashionable cut. Clinton Roch came down to see them for a day on his way to fishing off Key West.

"Snug, snug nest. It's all right here. Ada, you look chipper."

"Washington is wearing, but fun. Bocoo fun."

"Well, Chicky, you need any more money for clothes, why just say so. Don't frown, Si, I can afford it, and this Army social hullabaloo needs a good bit of window dressing."

"The closet is full now for all the elegance we need."

"Sure, sure. You wouldn't want to try and get time off and come fishing with me? Marlin, size of a barn door, bigger, been sighted."

Simon said no, and was happy to accept a gift—a large *croute* of *foie gras*—and to see his father-in-law go. He liked the man, but always felt if Clinton wasn't held back, he'd pour income and gifts on Ada, almost as if making up for some sense of guilt. Ada said her father was all right. "But a bit stuffy, you know, if you don't put the bite on him. Gifts settle everything for him. He's got this show girl stashed in some West End apartment, but tries to act as if none of us knew of it."

"He's one of those people who feel, 'Why cause pain?' "

Ada hugged Simon to her. "Well, when you get a chippy for quickies in the afternoon, you tell me and I'll get me a fancy man, some snazzy Latin like Rod la Rocque . . . huh?"

"I'll make a note of it."

Everyone, Souki and Malvina included, ate *foie gras* for a week.

Simon didn't mind their social life being a bit hectic. He worked hard at the War College and was given an office at the War Department under a wall of officers' photographs labeled KILLED IN ACTION, with dates and battles added. His job: to go through French and English military magazines and report on anything of interest in the hardware line—strivings, failures, and some pretension of prophecy.

Their closest new friend was Colonel Elkins' assistant, Captain Jeff Astruc. Tall, hair so blond to be almost white, a pose of a lazy nature ("We are only ourselves, chaps") and as a nephew and heir of a popular brand of beer, well supplied with money. At twenty-eight, Jeff escorted beautiful Washington women ("bachelor girls of experience"), hardly ever the same one for long. He had a reputation among the female employees in the government buildings as "a sleek sheik," or so Ada reported it. "You know women outnumber men in this town, damn unfair."

They would take long rides with Jeff and Souki into the Virginia or Maryland countryside on a weekend. Fauquier County, Westburg, along the Shenandoah, up the Muddy Branch, follow the Cumberland Canal. Either in Simon's Cunningham or Jeff's Packard roadster with its rumble seat. They ate heavily, drank a lot in the country inns, at country clubs, or at the fine estates below Mount Vernon on the Potomac, where Jeff or Souki—of old Army stock—seemed always to have hospitable relatives. Retired majors, gouty colonels, even a three-star general. "All you gotta be is Army to be always welcome here, suh."

Chapter 20

SIMON got used to Jeff's girls. Faye or Edie, Gladie, Shirl, Mary-Mae, all were jolly, all great drinkers out of silver hip flasks. Girls rangy, long-legged, full of slangy talk of "ritzy speaks" and "snitty cops," and approving of someone as "the bee's knees," the "cat's pajamas," and expressing disbelief by "horsefeathers," or "banana oil." Souki Miller, their landlady, for all her ironic qualities, Simon liked the best—she had a true elegance, a bit crumpled at times, he admitted, but always ready to party, always decorative.

They were as a class, these girls, Simon told Ada, high-class tramps. "Not whores, for they take only small gifts, seem to be known to every young, and some middle-aged, officers in the Washington district with a trembling in the loins." Sometimes, Souki admitted, one killed herself or died of a poorly done abortion. But in the main, as they approached thirty, they married or drifted off toward home. They were "Army all the way," knew the War Department gossip, wore favors of someone's Medal of Valor, Légion d'honneur. And Souki added, "What's wrong to die spent, in debt, all breath gone?"

They were all reading Michael Arlen's novel, *The Green Hat*, and copied its doomed heroine. For more settled social events, the Copperwoods attended dinners with the Major Rosegolds and the Colonel Elkins. Mrs. Rosegold was large, with puffy ankles. She raised sheep dogs in Maryland, and felt of the social flummery: *"Merde alors."* Mrs. Elkins was small, had stiff joints, walked with a gold-headed cane. She had once been a tennis champion, three years in a row of the Western Regions Army Posts, and kept the silver cups polished. She was a master of Army politics ("Be careful, Simon—inscrutable"). At these houses one met the young officers whose futures mattered, the middle-aged men who ran the Army. The older men sniffing at their brandy and holding their glowing cigars in a sure grip were those who ran the War Department, dealt with the Senators and Congressmen who headed committees of Army procurement and fundings, those men who cleared bills for massive weapon costs, sites for new bases, placed Army engineers in far places for hush-hush surveyings.

"Captain," said General (three-star) Raven (better known as Iron Brain) Saunders at a dinner of *sirloin grillé au feu de bois* and turkey Arlington, at Colonel Elkins', "we need somebody to bird-dog the Senators' Armed Forces Committee. You come along to Capitol Hill with me, around eleven in the morning. The new experiments for the 155-M field gun need more money. Know any politicians?"

"I can't say I do, general."

" 'But if the salt hath lost its savour, wherewith shall it be salted?' Matthew 5-13."

The general, a pious Methodist, looked over the dozen guests around the table. "Yes, salted, unsalted, the boys on Capitol Hill—to us are nice enough, mean too, at times. The fat cats there, you keep a firm rein on 'em, spur 'em a bit by showing it hurts very little to spend on Army, for it protects us, them, and theirs."

General Saunders, it was clear, was a unique, hardworking fanatic.

"I knew some politicians out in Montana."

"We have a weak Army I tell 'em, we could fall through the crack in the bottom of the world. . . ."

Jeff Astruc called to Simon from the other end of the table, where he and Ada were building comic modern sculpture out of a turkey carcass, celery stalks, and beef bones. "What say, Simon, we go to the Potomic Gardens later? Got this right sockem niggrah jazz band, real Dixieland. I want to try with Ada to win the Charleston contest. What say?"

Ada said, in her boopadoop voice, "Why lil me, Jeff?"

General Saunders frowned, as if suspecting Jeff Astruc, Simon thought, a fallen *soufflé*. Simon shook his head at Jeff. "I have some early-morning work. You take Ada."

The general seemed pleased with the answer, shook ash off his cigar into the dessert plate. "I'd like to send these Dancing Dan's off on a hundred-mile scouting ride in dead of winter, the way I was trained when I was a second louie out in the Dakotas. Young men these days just stand 'round and watch the country go to hell. Feckless *and* all full of promiscuity. We excuse it, calling it liaisons—it's just dirty goings-on away from home."

Simon was asleep when Ada came back at two in the morning carrying a tall, ugly, silver cup and a huge teddy bear with electric light bulb eyes. Her breath was rather too strongly bourbon.

"You night crawler." He tried to focus on the night-table clock.

"Darling, darling, you know, we won! Me and Jeff and we drank outa my cup and and . . . oh, my gosh . . . I'm going to cat up. . . ."

He heard her high heels go down the hall, and the retching in the bathroom. He was asleep again before she came back. . . . In the morning, Ada, in her pale-blue slip and rolled stockings lay snoring, tousled head on a soiled pillow, the teddy bear, one eye lit, beside her. Simon made hot coffee on the gas plate, and got Ada to sip it very black.

"I hope it pains you good."

"What a night, Si, what a night. They gave us bad Chivas Regal scotch that all—musta danced my feet off clear to my knees. Say, don't tell me you're glad I'm hung over?"

"Must have been some evening."

"Next time, you come too. You dance bettern Jeffie. Mucho so. Mucho better." And she was asleep again. Simon showered, shaved, got out his best Brooks Brothers tailored uniform, his London boots. He didn't wear spurs; only Mac and Patton still made a habit of wearing spurs with dress outfits. The Sam Browne belt was as yet regulation, but there was talk it would be out soon.

He met General Saunders at the War Department, and in a big, dun-colored USA Lincoln, they headed for Capitol Hill. The traffic was heavy; cabs and private cars coming from Chevy Chase just inside the Maryland line and going past the Woodner on 16th, the apartment house gleaming in the morning light, the heavy butt of the Senator from Alabama getting into a cab. They drove to the Shoreham, where there were some memos, and then drove on into Rock Creek Park, the hum of the day getting louder. The packed buses were heading for Constitution Avenue. Already, Simon saw, the visitors were out. The general said he enjoyed the serene monuments of the city offering ghosts of the great dead, the forgotten heroes. Passing the Washington Monument, he looked up as he always did and flipped two fingers at the granite shaft for luck, past the Bureau of Engraving, and they slid into the traffic across 14th Street, went by the Agricultural Department, and followed the buildings to where they linked over Independence Avenue. The Botanical Gardens had a few loafers and old soldiers in slippers sunning in front of it. Beyond was the Senate buildings, a monstrous disgrace to the beauty of the immense, luminous sky. The Capitol Plaza cops gave them one-finger salutes on the peaks of their caps. They moved along the halls, the news tickers tinging away, smelled the government floor wax (once cause of a costs scandal). The historic dust at home in the drapes.

The general was very serious. He was no figure of sybaritic dalliance. Simon felt here was a man as solidly sold on the Army as he was.

"Now, captain, get familiar hereabouts—you're going to be my eyes and ears—and nose—if you smell out a stink. Use tact and discretion—these Senators have to kowtow to big business, to do-gooders—bleeding hearts that help elect them. But, well—they practice a bit of moral ambiguity."

"Yes, sir." Simon tried to make it crisp, firm.

"Don't turn your charm on me, captain, I only want your brains. I get plenty of ass-kissing from men like Jeff Astruc and Major Rosegold."

"Yes, sir—I mean—"

"Whatever you mean, I know you're Army and smart. You may also get to know I am called a hidebound old bastard—but I'm trying to give this country an Army it will need in the next war. Not one of two wars back."

Simon nodded. Wasn't a place for a "yes, sir."

[167]

It was ten minutes to noon when they got to the Senate Chamber. A session was about to begin and the place was humming like a violin. There it was—the brown-marble oval that Simon no longer stood in awe of, with the pageboys distributing bills and legislative calendars to the historic desks, and here and there a polished spittoon, a tradition from the days when most men chawed and had amber-stained mustaches. Clerks and secretaries tried to look important or busy. The parliamentarian came in—a bit petulant—he and the clerk of the Senate and the sergeant-at-arms were in a huddle, most likely, the general suggested, cutting up a basketball pool. The majority side was filling, the other, too, had a good showing. The sound reached the obsessive haunting of a tuned orchestra.

Simon looked around at the public gallery: Girl Scouts, a bland Oriental face, and some Arabs—not much of a crowd. In the family gallery Senators' wives and a nanny with an ugly-looking child. The diplomatic gallery empty but for two fat British types out of P. G. Wodehouse.

The Vice President rapped his gavel. The Senate chaplain rose in dusty black robes and went into what the general called an unctuous, pious twang based on some prose style from the King James Version, asking His good and fervent help in this hour of meditation and the cries of our Jeremiahs as the nation faced grave problems—might now the Divine aid look down on this splendid body of lawmakers and inspire to complete victory the high hopes and visions of peace, kindness, and charity we held for all the world, and take unto His cherished haven those maimed and dead in far places, those killed and destroyed on sea and land in the use of those weapons which symbolized our simple desires for eternal peace, without ourselves demanding any gratitude or thanks for our crusades to set up order in far corners of this planet, and soon in deepest space.

The general smiled. "I have a bet on he ends with something from the Book of Psalms today."

"How much you have on it, sir?"

"Two tickets to the next tryout of a Broadway play in town. Ten dollars."

"I feel, sir, he seems headed for the Book of Job. Does that about every three weeks. Ah!"

And behold, there came a great wind from the wilderness
And smote the four corners of the house
And it fell upon the young men, and they are dead.

The general rubbed his brows and repeated: " 'And it fell upon the young men, and they are dead.' Oh, well—it's apt."

It needed fifty-one Senators for a quorum. The clerk began to call the roll. A Senator asked for unanimous consent to have the quorum call dispensed with, but there were two rings for a quorum and it turned out that a quorum was present. Simon looked down on the balding heads, the bodies looked like a cross section of the people in the streets—more portly perhaps, a bit more of a twitch or tic here and there. But solid enough and human enough, too human often, within the peripheries of their own personalities, prejudices, desires.

Someone cheered in the visitors' gallery, someone started a cough, but it was going to be a quiet day—unless Senator Lorser Pearson ("Our man, captain") brought up the Senate Armed Forces Bill before the Chamber and out of committee. Simon reinspected the galleries. Four columnists' legmen, National Military Foundation people, staff officers' faces were familiar. Yes, from the Chiefs of Staff. And behind them some pale faces.

The special interests were always present, their lobbyists there in rank. This season they had pretty much castrated the Fair Packaging Act, the Revised Auto Safety Bills, beaten down the policing of loan sharks and shady savings and loan companies, and more money for the Army.

A sharp debate began between Senator Monti of Texas and Senator Pearson. "I ask the respected Senator from New Jersey to yield so I may answer some preposterous rumors about the Army grab bill in works," said Monti in his county chairman's drawl. He had been a medicine-show singer—the General Staff said—in his youth, peddling a cure-all for man or beast till he was thirty. He was an expert office holder, with tact and forbearance, adored by the poor whites, the old, and cattle barons alike. "I ask to speak to refute those items of incredibility that have appeared in some Northern papers hinting that I am in league with the opposition party in my native state to loot the treasury. . . ."

Senator Pearson, at ease and earnest, said: "I do not yield. The item before this sitting of the Senate is the matter of bringing an Armed Forces Funding bill before it."

"I ask you to yield."

"I will not yield on matters not directly pertaining to the measure, Senator Monti."

An opposition member, Senator Hamilton Bellon (D-Indiana) rose. "If the opposition is in conflict among itself, I would like the gentlemen to yield to me. I have here some military figures . . . that. . . ."

Senator Monti said, "If the gentleman from Indiana is referring to certain trips to India to investigate the military roads of that country with a party of forty-two that used blocked funds at the U.S. Embassy in Paris . . . or for that clearing of the Old Keystone Canal by the Army engineers. . . . A bill of great merit; I'm sure no Senator here has not aided his—"

Bellon smiled. "No, I'm not using even the cost of the Cactus Park Historical Monuments Funding along U.S. highways, or the reconversion of land spoiled by strip mining. Bill A 4065 dash 9083, which is in process of consideration—"

Senator Pearson said, "I do not yield the floor, Senator Bellon."

The general explained, "It's all a ritual. They trade off a canal against some historic stretch of highway—your bill for mine. Some dam for a fish hatchery, some park to a dying town against a federal celebration of a major Indian defeat. This surface bickering covers some major policy, or a stand against some 'must' budget. The superfluous talk in the Senate will take up another hour."

With a lot of pushing forward and backing up, the Army Funding Bill was introduced—voted for debate. The general tapped Simon on the arm. "Now it will go into talk for a week. Some figures on it back to my office—and I'll give you some reports to follow up on it."

"You think it will go through, sir?"

"Not all of it. They'll cut it here and there. But enough, I hope, to get something for holes in our Army budgets. I'll try and get old Black Jack down to speak for it . . . he's a womanizer. . . . got about half a dozen women right now he's serving, and at *his* age. And a boozer too. But a ramrod. A *real* ramrod. I was on his staff

[170]

when he commanded the AEF and he faced that frog Foch and said to him, 'You send us into the line as an army—as an American expeditionary force, or it's no ballgame. No bleeding us to bits as part of the French, backing up your failing lines. . . .' Yes, a ramrod. Elkins tells me you want to go to China, a legation post?"

"I hope so."

"Why?"

"Things going to move there. The Russians are going to make a power grab for China. The Japanese, too. I'd like to know what goes there, close up."

"Well, if Elkins says yes to it, you'll go. It's his section. You think the Russkis can take China?"

"No idea, sir."

"Well, we'll keep you busy till then. No time for larking around. Spoil your social life. Women raise a fuss. But your wife seems to understand. She looks real Army to me."

It was dark when Simon came out of the War Department. The buildings around emptying; the lights set in the borders of the rooms gave off a melancholy, lambent glow. Simon felt lonely. The sound of feet departing, the whine of elevators emptying the vast bad taste of artless buildings. Small minds in outer offices closing up their desks, the departure of clerks. The heavier steps, he mused, were of the cliques of Robespierrists, bound not for the view of sport at the guillotine, but to clubs and cocktail parties, to roll reputations like severed heads on the rugs of the better apartments. All were leaving for the day and also from the buildings around; heading for alcohol, kissing the baby goodnight or . kissing elsewhere—all the departing paladins, princes, priests, merchants, artists, scholars, scientists, secret anatomists, and the average clerks and typists that run the nation—and rule the Army.

At Miller Court, Malvina told Simon that Ada and Miss Miller had gone to a Chopin concert by Artur Rubinstein, and Malvina had breaded veal cutlets warm for him in the oven.

Later, he stood at a window and looked out at the narrowed precincts of trees, and stood waiting as he often did late at night for the moment of revelation, which never came. Uncle Brewster's voice back on the porch in Montana came, with his insistence on the proper way to mix a drink, and a word of advice on parting: "Life is the total of what you have to pay for it. I think I read that someplace, but it could be my own."

At the window, night sounds and street noises mingled, fading down now to bearable mutterings. Simon could picture the late poker games on H Street, the lobbyists' call girls slowly undressing, and he could even name a half a dozen Army figures for whom they were pulling dresses over their heads, popping out nubile titties to be bitten by bad Midwestern dentistry. Could see Senator Pearson smoking his last fine cigar, the brandy in his balloon glass down to its last half inch, a volume of Gibbon's *History* on his lap. A wise, hard-shelled gentleman, aware death already had him in its teeth like a mother cat carrying its whelp. . . . And where was Souki Miller? Brisk, a bit soggy at a fine bar with a lot of Madison Avenue tramps, at home in her strange world of expense accounts, martinis, ulcers. And the single clerks in shoddy apartment houses in Maryland reading Dickens to mothers who stank like wet dogs. . . . In the State Department bored men were watching ticker messages being decoded, and someplace somebody was being bribed by flesh or money to supply items of secret value, someone was on the river watching the moon scud through moored trees, someone was feeling his way in the dark to a strange, rustling bed, some old soldier was dying at Walter Reed, maybe a dozen wornout beings or the remains of a young soldier frayed apart, or the barely alive nerve ends of an old general trying to swallow life through tubes in arms.

Chapter 21

CAPTAIN SIMON BOLIVAR COPPERWOOD, neat, serious, informative at the War College on Capitol Hill, or at the War Department, was a different man from the one who came roaring home to Miller Court at the cocktail hour, usually carrying a quart of coffee ice cream, a potted Cattleya orchid, or a bottle of wine.

Feeling a singing, shouting release, he'd rush upstairs to join Ada and Souki for very dry martinis. What had been a trim, attentive young officer all day, given to listening to General Raven Saunders or Colonel Elkins, and offering only well-thought-out answers, became at home a released person. Tossing his military cap in a long shot onto the rack of deer antlers in the hall, unbuckling belt and jacket, grabbing Ada for a kiss, snapping his fingers at Souki.

"What a day, what a day. Twice I almost pointed out errors in the Chief of Staff memos, and tore up three ideas I had pointing out we could move troops faster if each military zone region had a number besides a name. Mustn't get pushy, must I?"

"But you didn't, dear," said Ada, her bobbed hair producing two strands below the cheekbones like twin daggers, smoking a cigarette in her jade holder and jiggling the cocktail shaker —silver, and a wedding present from Uncle Brewster and Aunt Dolly.

"No, I didn't. I played it numb, played it cool. I'm there to learn, watch, observe."

"Keep your pants on, Simon," Souki said. "You're doing fine, Wallie Elkins says."

Ada poured drinks and they lifted glasses, smiled at each other, sipped the powerful, rather odd-tasting drink, made, Souki assured them, with "Booth's House of Lords gin stolen from the British Embassy."

For Simon, it was a slow unwinding from playing the earnest, bushy-tailed young officer all day. The pressure had to be loosened, like a spring in some clockwork toy—run loose a bit—before he became himself. They usually ate in Souki's apartment. By dinnertime he was chatting away, telling of minor mishaps at the college, of tangling red tape at the department, the ambivalence of attitudes one had to tune in on.

"I know things are wrong, some fatty degeneration of the military mind. Also know how they can be made right. It just mustn't move too fast, too soon. Hell, Roger Millhouse at the Point used to warn us 'without absurdity, there would be no universe.' "

"That's right," Souki told him, taking the roast-duck platter from Malvina. "Here, you carve these birds, Simon. Senator Pearson shot them in Maryland last week. . . . In this town the way to advance is to see which way the wind blows and take your cue from the drifters."

"Christ, it's the slow way, isn't it?"

"Don't mangle the birds so."

"Bridge tonight?" Ada asked. "Jeff's coming over."

"By all means, bridge," said Simon, slicing off wedges of breast. "An officer may not be able to understand the battles of Alexander the Great, but a good bridge player is the noblest asset of Army society."

"Simon," said Souki, "is a smarty-pants."

Sometimes Simon, feeling a mixture of absurdity and frustration, worked late. Came in around midnight, drag-tailed, muttering to himself. Dropping his attaché case with a crash by their sagging sofa, waking Ada if she had already gone to bed. "I don't know, I just don't know, Ada girl, why I don't go back to Montana and starve to death raising horses."

Ada, used now to his antics and idiosyncrasies, tried to keep her eyes shut. "It's after midnight, darling. Tell me all—huh? —in the morning?"

"Sorry, go back to sleep."

Undressing in haste, but neatly folding his clothes, an old habit, Simon shook his head, pulling off his socks. "I think, I feel I have something worked out. I expect *now* they'll see it. Now they'll understand. And what happens?"

"Yes, dear. Turn out the light."

" 'Proceed with the original concept', they say. 'Do not design group project 22D into new format. Hold orders for readjustment of plans on machine-gunnery school.' God, Ada! It's all so incredibly archaic. . . . You listening?"

"Uhuh."

He tossed himself onto the bed, nuzzled her shaved, shingled neck with his face, made growling sounds in his throat. He laughed, sighed and she waited—half asleep for his assault. He quickly adjusted their bodies for convenience. It was a kind of release he practiced and she was used to it. Somehow a sexual attack on her body compensated or salved a day of bad handling

[174]

of routine, the betrayal of his ideas. With her in this ritual of fierceness, of need, problems were soothed away in a climax of lovemaking. Lovemaking delightfully brutal, a frontal attack rammed home, that left her panting and pleased at their preposterous pleasure—delighted, and yet wondering if he was aware of her at all, or merely using her body to boil down his rage, his drive. He lay in a calm muscularity, relaxed to peace. It was not flattering to her, not afterward, trying to knot up sleep again. She would tell him so. "You bastard—you don't even ask!"

They would quarrel in loud protestation of their sensitivities, and then make it up with another assault, splendidly young and ardent, slaves to their appetites.

There was no time for sullen petulance, Simon explained, and the lashing aphrodisiac of "making up" became a ritual, made them very *simpático*—she had been reading early Hemingway —to each other. As she told Souki of their sex life, "Satisfying in the kip, yet never sated."

Their friends were young officers, their wives or girlfriends, journalists with social standing, young English, Rumanian, Italian rakes from the better embassies. Simon cultivated bright young engineers and scientists, those who were, like Simon, fighting the resident skeptics in their departments. Some were, as Ada admitted, "boozers *extraordinaires*." She enjoyed the new hedonists—pseudosophisticates down from Greenwich Village with talk of Edna St. Vincent, the *New Masses*, Floyd Dell, F. Scott, James Branch, Tutankhamen's tomb, Sacco and Vanzetti. The Europeans would talk of Baroque perversions, and of heteros and homos, with a *c'est la vie* smile.

"Waterheads," Simon said, "but fun at that." For he felt he was missing something—there was a world whose flavor, he suspected, was beyond the Florida land boom in which Clinton Roch was so busy selling acreage; or more disarmament talk: the League of Nations, toothless and talking nonsense. What of the world in which he didn't live? More flivvers on the streets, everyone buying stocks called Goldman Sachs and RKO on margin. And being told Paris was the place for Americans to really live: Passy, Place St. Michel, *à premier prix fix*.

[175]

Souki Miller sailed with a group of Argentinians one night to Europe. Their friends all drove up to New York, Jeff, Ada, Simon, Wallie Elkins, for the midnight sailing of the *France*. Everyone in evening clothes, and so many parties—one in every stateroom. The sailing itself; lights, sirens, tugboat horns, mixed with drunken partings of travelers and revelers.

Simon near dawn, sick with champagne and port and grenadine, was in no condition to drive their Mercer, a car he had bought after the Cunningham broke down. They stayed at the Astor, with no baggage, and woke up next day at noon, hung over. There was nothing to drink in the room but a half bottle of Almadén Chablis. After a slim breakfast (or lunch) served in the room, they discovered they were sexually carnivorous, and had orgasms, as Ada bragged, like coronaries. Near dusk, their noisy frivolity subdued, heads throbbing. Simon was due to lecture on the first use of tank warfare at Mons, in the morning.

They sat on the bed, jaybird naked—watching plum-colored dusk tint the city, that pale lavender-blue tone, as lights went on, animated signs leaped to life. The taxi horns from below were still able to stir up memories of their earlier headaches.

"God, Ada, we can't go on like this."

"Like what, darling?" She giggled. "You have a face like a crumpled drawing."

"The frigging social life, these whacked-up parties. The awful hooch we're drinking."

"Die young, leave a beautiful body, darling."

Ada inspected her mouth in a mirror, and with shaky fingers drew on a fuller, redder version with a gold lipstick. "You think Souki will like Paris? The Cole Porters said come on over, but will they remember her? And the Gertrude Stein crowd of cruds are a bit too sharp for Souki. She had no perceptible social intelligence. God, I'm getting old around the eyes."

"I'm going to ask for transfer out of Washington next year."

"Yes, dear. Next year. *Next* year. When you make major. My body is still fine, isn't it? The tush. The boobs. . . ? Hawaii is a good Army post. You can play polo. Or the Canal Zone. Servants by the dozen. All those wonderful cruise ships standing by for a day or so. . . . You don't want us to make a baby, do you, darling? The belly wrinkles up and you get loose—so loose."

Souki Miller came back from Paris in three months, with a cabochon emerald, a blue-paper covered copy of James Joyce, which she read out loud, at least Mollie Bloom's bed-talk thoughts, to Ada. Souki had a photograph of herself taken with Nancy Cunard and all her bracelets. She also hinted that Gertrude Stein, or someone who looked like her, had made a pass at her in the Gypsy *boîte* on the Edgar-Quinet.

"Ada, the embassies in Paris are full of whoopie. This um-um officer at the American Embassy said he knew Simon at West Point. Took me to all the real places, Rosalie's on the Rue Campagne, I mean, toots, where the tourists don't go. You ought to get Simon to take a post like that. *Très* gay and real Chateau Mouton-Rothschild like I mean no Cokes or Moxie. Simon, he'd do well—he's sexy as Valentino or Milton Sills." A remark which led to a quarrel between Ada and Simon. "Souki—she is too making passes at you. That bit of fancy cat meat!"

"Come off it, Ada, Souki is just the town Army mattress. Thinks she's Mata Hari and Peggy Hopkins Joyce rolled into one."

"She's just a juicy little piece been had by everyone including that high-pockets nigger jazz piano player. I don't trust her. Hanging round making goo-goo eyes at you."

"I trust myself, *and* I trust you. *You* and Jeff get seen all over town. At the horse show, embassy garden parties, the six-day bike races."

"Oh, nuts." She tore at a crepe de Chine handkerchief. "Jeff, he's damn kind to take me out while you work nights. Wallow in bureaucratic lethargy. I've seen those War Department bitches with their shorthand books."

It was a near thing. They were of late rasping at each other more. They made it up—again—with a shaky amity like time and time again. . . . Simon began to dislike the Washington life, set for him in pools of social boredom. Capitol Hill fascinated him, however.

The major Army funding bill, clipped a bit, added to here and there, was fully debated. With pressures from the right places, it was passed by both Houses in pious complacency. Simon went twice a week to Capitol Hill to talk to Senators and Congressmen, to act polite, and to offer advice if asked. God, he hoped he wasn't getting the oily tones of a Pecksniff. Simon learned the truth of how government functions exist, how frail was the illusion of true democracy, moving at a paralyzed. shuffle. As Senator Lorser Pearson put it to Simon and General Raven Saunders over a lunch in the Senators' dining room, after the President had signed their bill: "It's amazing that the whole shebang of running the nation works at all. This nation is still run by rules and procedures set up in the Presbyterian ethic, by agnostics in the eighteenth century to keep thirteen colonies going. Backwoods farming communities, hunters, fishermen, with no great love between the new states, even after 1776. A nation's laws made when it took weeks of country riders to bring news of elections and events to people—when the needs and uses of our resources were simpler. Now we're trying to run as a world power on these old-style casual town-meeting styles of trappers and Colonial cider makers."

The general smiled. "We're a cockeyed masterpiece of a country. The wardheelers and political bosses kind of shut their eyes to the sacred old rules, except in election speeches. While we're invading banana republics with marines for United Fruit. And look how we grabbed off the Sandwich Islands in the night, like raiding a chicken house—for the sugar and pineapples, boys, and call it Hawaii. . . . Senator, more important, what's going to happen to China?"

"Like it or not, we've got to stick our noses in, to keep out the Japanese; if not them, the Russians. It isn't just a matter of us being contemptuous of morals. For big or small countries, Judeo-Christian morality is for Sunday-school classes. National morality is survival, and the goddamn scientists are so busy inventing ultimate weapons for you folk that this is going to be the most messed-up century in history, corrupt and depraved."

"No," said the general. "The next war is too horrible to happen."

Simon said, "It's a sad truth scientific advances come quickest during wars."

"As you say, general, it is not moral. But the Army is to protect the nation—not debate ideals."

Senator Pearson set down his coffee cup. "Yes—well, I never

[178]

was worth a plugged nickel when given to prophecy. We'll just have to wait and see what goes in Asia and where it serves our best interests for survival to stand. Only Talleyrand would love today's politics."

Later, General Saunders said to Simon, "Someplace we have old war-surplus weapons for native underground fighters—dig up a report."

Rimming the city in stucco, steel, wood, and stone confusion, piled up in Maryland, Virginia, were somber warehouses, War Department storage areas, depositories, tombs of debris, some of red brick going back to the Mexican War, some of board and tar paper set up temporarily during World War I. Many huge and ugly ones of concrete and plaster, and these, larger than Roman ruins, existed, Simon discovered, to house, store, hoard, mothball, hide much that is no longer vital or needed, even the locked-away shapes of some great error in plan or design. SURPLUS OVERSEAS was a ten-story-high humpbacked expanse of hangarlike buildings, painted asylum dun-gray and guarded by twenty-foot walls tipped with barbwire growth suggesting man-made cactus. It all sat by the river, its tail end like the vent of some great historic creature ending in piers and loading cranes.

Simon got out of an Army car and went to a booth with a sign: SO.DIV. WASH. ENTRANCE. SPECIAL PASS ONLY BY WAR DEPT: An old man sat there eating sandwiches out of a waxed bag. He looked with unfocused eyes as he inspected Simon's credentials.

"I have an appointment with Mr. De Souza."

"Dept. II, X-11-A, up two flights to the left. Security guard takes you from there." He wrote slowly on a triplicate form, chewing on tuna on rye, and stamped it with the time: 11:32 A.M.

Simon followed his directions and met a sullen, very black Negro in fatigue uniform, who said, "Capin Copperwood? Foller me."

"You're Army?"

"I am."

"Then make it: 'Follow me, *sir.*' "

"*Sir.*"

He led Simon past vast dark spaces from which came the odor of rotting leather, mothballs, the acid bite of chemical preserving stinks. Strongest was the smell of old paper rotting; yellowing, crumbling, also machines and weapons soaked in protecting greases. The door they reached was very old, perhaps from some long-destroyed McKinley-period building. It had been cruelly sawed down to fit, and mutilated by the rape of a shiny bronze Yale lock, and by the letters R. R. DE SOUZA, DIRECTOR, SO. DEPT. X-11-A. There's a sense of servitude in civil service country, Simon thought, bifocals, carbon paper, constipation.

He went into an office with no windows, only yellow lights in a plywood ceiling. Two middle-aged women were doing each other's fingernails out of tiny bottles of cutthroat-red liquid. The smell of banana oil was heavy in the place.

Simon said he had an appointment to see Mr. De Souza, and one of the women waving a hand to dry her nails, pointed with an elbow toward another damaged door marked PRIVATE. Simon knocked, opened it, and went in to see a fat little man, egg-bald, silver-trimmed glasses on his nose. He was listening to a gramophone record of an Italian opera.

"Captain Copperwood. I'm from the War Department."

"Ah, yes. Yes, let me find the papers." He ruffled in a basket marked URGENT that was attached over one marked MUST DO, and took out a thick batch of papers of various sizes clipped together.

"Here we are. Dept. X-11-A Form 213. Storage form 45 . . . blue form—Reference Directive 870. Yellow form. You can follow me from your own copies of the directive. The blue sheet and then the yellow."

"I'm tracing 20,000 old-type Springfield rifles, Form KL-202."

"Captain, you should have at least Request Form 34, dated shipping order; that's the delivery form okayed by State and —oh, and the cost-accounting release."

"De Souza, what's wrong with KL-202—the rifles?"

"How long you been with the War Department?"

"About one year."

"That explains it. I'm a twenty-year myself. Remember when General Saunders he first came here. Well, a real foul-up some place. Now follow me. I'll reaffirm the route. All right, yellow form from War Department, 1917, to Sterling-Nash Bath Fixtures Company, Troy, New York. Order for design of 1,800 self-flushing, china-finish, white bidets. Next, War Department order 453987S, order for 1,800 items, use by Allied nurses, etc., overseas. Cost $320 each. Next, shipment, Bill of Lading —Overseas Transport, Liberty Ship *Dixon*, K2-22, Order 456, Department Women's Div: X327 Army Women's Service, 1918. Loading Order 876 on Hoboken Pier 74. You follow?"

"No."

"All it means is 1,800 bidets were ordered for Allied women serving in the armed forces. A bidet is a—"

"I know what a bidet is, De Souza."

"Let's carry on then. Search Order Wash Aid Form 23, May 10th, 1919. Storage form attached, stamped 546 War Surplus. An order to produce (ignored) bidets at Harbor Storage, Canal St., NYC."

"But they're listed as 20,000 rifles at the War Department."

"Whatever they are—they were never shipped."

"Why?"

"We don't know. Now come the lawyers, Office of Cost Control, July, 1920, in a federal suit—court order attached—against Harbor Storage and Sterling-Nash Bath Fixtures to recover cost of bidets, in a sworn statement, 1922, August 14, says control of objects passed to Port Control War Department, who signed for bidets at Fort Hamilton, Brooklyn, May 18, 1923. Sterling and Port Control Storage claim the matter of loss of delivery is not their fault. Fuller records temporarily sealed in USA Archives in Monmouth Cave, Kentucky."

"Damn the bidets. Where are the rifles?"

"Now, I have an order by the State Department as of last week ordering the delivery of the 1,800 bidets to the Indian Famine Relief Committee."

"What good will that do them if they're starving?"

Mr. De Souza looked at Simon with wonder. "Nobody asks why State does things. The bidets are to be shipped via"—he referred to some new papers—"via the Greek freighter *Monadokusi*, when repacked after testing. With instructions in English, Hindustani, and three Muslim dialects. War Department, Silverthorn, is responsible for the objects to be shipped. I've already ordered the instruction forms printed in two languages and the three dialects."

"The rifles no longer exist here?"

"You a married man, captain?"

"So?"

"I saw a French whore use one—a bidet—when I was supply sergeant on the Rhine. It's the goddamndest most amazing thing you ever saw, amazing."

"No one, De Souza, knows where the rifles are, if they still exist?"

"Oh, they exist. Nothing just vanishes in Washington. Indian war issue, weren't they?"

"You find them. That's your job. SO Department X-11 War Department Surplus."

The man sighed. "I thought maybe, captain, you could produce an order the bidets were broken up for rubble, or dumped into the ocean from the NYC rubbish scows. What I need is evidence, you see, that they're destroyed. Or the 1,800 bidets."

"Rifles, goddamn it: I'll send a search form out from our end, De Souza. You send one out from your end. Agreed?"

"I haven't the staff for it. I got two Congressmen's old-maid aunts, a mean-tusked nigrah making out lists of us he's going to kill some day, and an old man who's deaf at the gate."

"Find me those Springfields!"

"Everything's sealed off and locked. Civil War sabers, lifeboats from the battleship *Maine*, sixteen million feet of olive-drab tenting, ten thousand rubber life rafts, one million six hun—"

Simon turned toward the door. "Let's give it a try. Cut orders for a search."

"Use the pink form, Interdepartmental memo: the gray urgent form is no g.d. good. Pink is Expedite Immed."

Simon left with a firm dry handshake. Outside, the office dust, the smell of rotting papers settled in peace over the surplus in storage.

General Saunders was not amused. "The usual exquisite red tape foul-up. Take the sabers and whatever saddles they have, mess kits, all that truck, and we'll send it all out to the Philippines bases in case the State Department wants to send it anyplace in Asia to arm natives. Meanwhile check all Army warehouses, cross-country, for weapon storages. Hell, we must have a couple million rifles left over from Bull Run to the Rough Riders, and all the training stuff we had at Dix and other places from the War to Make the World Safe for Democracy. Wallie Elkins may help you. He's a Civil War nut."

Colonel Elkins, in full dress, was about to review an American Legion parade, his medals in order on his handsome body, the blue-enamel and gold Slavic Order of Royal Incarnatus (the prettiest medal, Colonel Elkins suggested). "Call all depots listed and have them ship all pre-1900 rifles, what they have, to ports on the West Coast for holding. A fine excuse for getting rid of the old junk. Bidets, not Springfields here, eh?"

"Never could understand how that mixup happened."

"Well, don't ship any of *those*. Might give the natives some idea we're decadent people."

In the end, Simon located 160,000 stands of workable ancient rifles, and no reserve ammo in any quantity.

Colonel Elkins, every year, gave a small Christmas party for his teaching staff, his best pupils, and a few old friends in the Army and government service. One wasn't expected to give any too-valuable presents, just items like old maps, an 1812 horse pistol. Christmas of 1926, Simon found a warrior's coupstick of the Hunkpapa Sioux, decorated with red flannel, feathers, and some strips of human scalplocks. The dealer in Baltimore had sworn it had once belonged to Sitting Bull, if not to him, then for sure to Crazy Horse. But Simon pointed out Crazy Horse was not a Hunkpapa.

The party was held in Colonel Elkins' big house in Georgetown. Colonel Elkins was delighted with the Indian coupstick. He gave the Copperwoods a *Harper's Weekly* woodcut of "The Sharpshooter," by Winslow Homer. General Buck Hollister was down from Fort Hamilton for the weekend, and said he was delighted with what he had heard of Simon's progress. "Christ, we need more of you firecrackers, Simon. Wallie likes you; Iron Brain thinks you believe in the true God and artillery barrages in equal parts. Good work."

"General Saunders is working himself into asthmatic spasms."

"Somebody has to. Civilians display insufficient gratitude. You know we still haven't got a goddamn rifle fit for modern infantrymen. . . . Ada looks fine, just fine. I think I'll whirl her around a bit."

The big living room was a wild study in warm rapport.

Simon drank his second cocktail and watched Ada, in blue lace, spin around with Buck Hollister. Souki, garrulous and petulant, in shiny green satin, was at his elbow, glass in hand, looking sleek and large-eyed.

"I'm ducking the Brazilian chargé d'affaires. He leaves fingerprints." She snapped her fingers to the gramophone music, her wrist heavy with bracelets. "Oh, that good, oh, that fine. That's King Oliver style. Bet you never heard of him?"

Simon was relaxed, thinking of Montana Christmas, deep snow, great big log fires, another more innocent life.

"Big black buck, isn't he, Souki? Used to play in Chicago —Royal Gardens, I think. Had this young horn player from New Orleans, Louie, with the scarred lips. Sweated a lot."

"You bastard," said Souki, leaning on him, kissing his cheek. "Think of you being so esoteric, huh?"

"Heard that whorehouse music first in France. This Army band with somebody called Jim Europe in control—a big dinge, and—"

Souki leaned closer, a warm healthy flesh smell, and musk. "It's just too bad, Simon. *Too* bad."

"What is?"

"Me, you. We don't mesh, I mean sexually."

"Don't suppose we do. Nice to keep it that way."

"I mean, for me no potentialities, guy. Some people they have it for each other—know what I mean?—you can almost smell it. Know what I mean?"

"Unhuh."

The gramophone began to bray out "Tea for Two."

"Right away when Ada brought you down here, I said here's a regular stud, but I'd hate him, I mean for loving. And he'd not like me, skin to skin. Know what I mean?"

"Chemistry," said Simon, waving to Ada dancing by. "No chemistry, Souki. I like you of course, enjoy your company as a friend, but—"

"No chemistry? Same here—sexually we're persona non grata to each other. Never get in the hay together."

[184]

"Besides, Souki—"

"Besides, Ada and me. Ol' Cornell together, so no feline prowling."

"Also."

"Also, you're not cheating on your wife." Souki lifted her glass. "Here's to that, *all* that."

They sipped their drinks and watched circling dancers and black servants, white-gloved soldiers off duty, pass glasses. "Simon. You're not playing around 'cause it's bad for a young officer bucking for a higher place, to be known as a disquieting cocksman—a sex hound—spending his time in the bed away from home, not doing his Uncle Sam best for the War Department, like Jeff there, just a social gadabout. Not you—you take it *all* home to Ada."

Simon smiled. "Bull."

"Not a moral issue with you? You're not an icky puritan?"

"Don't think it's moral with me. Have a code of course, but no self-righteousness. . . ." Lord, he was getting sloshed with this fancy bitch. "But morally; think a man does what he wants to do, if he harms no one. I mean, mean, well. . . ."

Souki bowed with absurd pomposity and almost fell as she went off toward Ada. "No chemistry," said Souki aloud. A young lieutenant came up to her. "You taken?"

"Let's find out, junior."

Simon and Ada remained on very friendly terms with Jeff Astruc and Souki Miller. If a Washington hostess invited one couple, they usually invited the foursome.

Chapter 22

May 19, 1927

Major Roger Millhouse
United States Military Academy
West Point, New York.

DEAR ROGER,

It was a grand surprise getting your letter (I still have your volume of letters of Helmuth von Moltke) hearing how things are in Asia, and Ada thanks you for the tortoise-shell comb. I'm sure you reveled in your four years in Tokyo at the Embassy. I am pulling all the goddamn wires to get appointed to our legation in Peking. Colonel Elkins who has the power to see I get it, has practically promised it this fall, for my reorganizing his section. I don't know how Ada will take it, but as a good Army wife (fingers crossed) she will, I'm sure, pout and come along. I suppose you are still the dandy collecting Utamaro prints, reading *outré* volumes, and smoothing down the rough edges of young louts they are making into officers at the Point. I know I owe you a hell of a lot. What I've been doing for the War Department is compiling reports from British, French, Russian military publications, turning them in. And that's the end of them, I don't know what happens to them from there on. The French have a crackerjack of a young officer, de Gaulle, who's done a marvelous text on the theory of tank warfare, beyond our half-assed ideas—but out own tanks are mostly just good for parades so far.

I don't want to reform Army politics. I'm too skeptical to think I can change officeholders. Hell, I think we've got to revitalize our armed forces before all hell breaks loose. I'm pissed off when at parties the military talk of the Wall Street Bull Market, but ignore the inflation in Germany and the closing British coal mines, and that general strike. It all points to a rigidity of the official mind—to it not being aware it's not the best of all possible worlds. Forgive my griping.

If there should come up a moment when you could say a good word for me about a post in Asia, do it for your old student. As Karl von Clausewitz said in *Vom Kriege*, write soon.

As always,
Simon

He was not feeling as cheerful as his letter sounded. Life had become a series of Chinese boxes, one within the other. The biggest box his career, inside it the Washington box of politics and positions, then the box of his personal life. He had come to depend on Ada and he wondered now if she knew it. Just how much he expected from her. The cheerful cocktail hour, the evenings, out or cozy in the place. The intimacy one could trust, talk to, say things that were bottled up inside.

Only she was aware how thin was his skin, how much his nerve ends were sandpapered, so that, under control all day, he expected, accepted the smoothing, the concern from the woman who had become his image of woman; if not the original image then the practical version of the one woman for one man. His public façade was role playing; the hard-nosed, stern soldier was at the core a wondering, worried human being, whose tenderness and vulnerability he never exposed in public.

Chapter 23

THERE were pickets in front of the White House protesting the execution of Sacco and Vanzetti. Simon, driving through the five o'clock October weekday traffic, was in a bad humor. Souki's phone call had found him on a bad afternoon of piled-up details at the War Department. He had to get the folders cleared from his Out box. For it was certain now he had the inside track for the appointment to the Peking legation. On the surface, merely to be in charge of the military detachment there. But actually he was to act as an agent to study in detail the various Chinese factions, the warlords, the Russian agents and interests, the drives of the Nationalists under Chiang Kai-shek to power. Captain Copperwood was to make contacts and to suggest when, if, and to whom—there were so many warlords—arms were to be handed over in order to frustrate the efforts of the Russians or the Japanese in China.

Souki's hysterical phone call had brought Simon's thoughts back to mundane matters. "You must come over here. Right *now!* It's vital. And damn personal. Don't screw around, and don't you shout at me, Simon Copperwood. I'm doing you a damn big favor. . . . No, Ada isn't here—" *Bang!* and she had hung up.

Simon parked the car and looked over the façade of red brick and gray stone, the overhang of rusting cast-iron cornices that was Miller Court. He had a respect for Souki's intellect in spite of all her malicious, corrosive edges. A playgirl, "solid Army," was the town's term, yes. Careless of her income, always in some emotional crisis, usually casually gay, too ironic, but no fool. How many like her had he met in Washington? Girls, women, attached almost as camp followers to Army, Navy, State, Justice, Indian Bureau, even U.S. Printing. He locked the car, walked toward the flaking lobby. Sometimes these girls married. But he knew usually they drifted leaflike into middle age as mistresses; fun-loving company, pals loyal to whatever section of government they had attached themselves to. "Maid Marions of Sherwood Forest, Washington," Jeff Astruc called them.

What was up? Souki drank, but could mostly control it. Souki was Army, War Department—the Army liked good drinkers, girls wise to the ways of military protocol, alert to officers' gossip. Souki, it was said, had influence in certain departments whose heads had passed her along—as part of the totality of human experience—one to the other.

Simon walked up the three flights of carpeted stairs, red Brussels carpets worn here and there. Souki's apartment door was painted crimson, scarred by key scratches and by careless kicks and scuffling at its base. Simon rang the bell. Souki's voice called from behind the door, "Come in, baby, expecting you. It's open." He was angered but swallowed his resentment like an oyster, and went in.

The room, called by Souki the party parlor, was long, narrow, high-ceilinged, with two wide bay windows on the street side. The furniture was old, of no actual period, and Souki's escorts and lovers had added large silk cloth dolls won at *fêtes* and carnivals. Spanish shawls as wall hangings. Kewpee dolls and rag dolls.

"Hello." Her voice was husky.

"Hello." He looked at the decor of Hawaiian war clubs, Japanese figures of geisha and warrior dolls, assorted shells on a really magnificent Adams fireplace salvaged from a ruin after the British had burned Washington and rediscovered in a Potomac junkyard. He didn't look in Souki's direction. No light was on, but strong sun from the west made dramatic Rembrandt shadows in the room. Souki, when he at last turned toward her, sat clad only in a slip, barefooted, reclining on a sofa, a glass of gin in one hand. She held up her arms and showed heavily bandaged wrists. "I was a bad girl."

Simon said simply, "Some day you'll hurt yourself."

"Oh, this was a serious try last night. Macky, the janitor, found me and tied, bandaged me up. He was a hospital orderly, you know, in the AEF."

Simon sat down on a low stool facing Souki. He felt he was talking to an echo of an echo. "People always talk about it, doing it. But they say—"

"They say those that talk, don't. Well, I tried with a razorblade. Bollixed it. That's me. That's me. Have a drink."

Simon sniffed the tacky half-full bottle. He judged it to be "panther's sweat," a cheap Negro product distilled in Washington. He poured three fingers of it into a glass and took a sip. Was he facing perfidy or indiscretion? Or an act? "Look, Souki, I had no idea what brought it on. You should be in a hospital. Or have some woman with you. Ada, or—"

"Ada—now I'm really browned off. It's over her dirty tricks why I did it. Ada! Damn the snotty bitch." Souki was certainly a woman with some grievance. Simon said nothing. He sipped the dreadful gin. Yes, a monstrous grievance sat on Souki's face, he decided. When faced with something you don't comprehend, wait, *don't* talk.

Souki adjusted a shoulder strap of her slip, set naked feet up on a low coffee table. "Ada, dear chap, she's been making time with *my* friends. She's been so goddamn social with my buddies—touching all the bases, charm rolling off her like dirt off a shovel. And you've been so busy making a place for yourself with the Army, you wouldn't see sunlight if you were lost in a desert. Oh, God." She sipped her drink and wept, blew her nose on the back of a hand. "God, I'm miserable—but you hear me out."

"Souki, don't say anything you'll be sorry—I mean, you're upset. Enough to try dramatics for some kind of satisfaction."

"You mean I'm exquisitely treacherous, you bastard?"

Souki leaned over toward him, her breasts escaping the slip. She smelled of gin, of a Souki just then a bit unwashed, and of an emotional civet odor he couldn't fully explain, akin to the smell of men under fire; yes, under fear, stress, men, they too had a different kind of smell.

"Look, fella, I always liked you. Kept hands off. That's lil ole Souki. A rambunctious tramp maybe, but honorable, know what I mean? Well, captain, I have a certain respect for myself. Pride, yes. I play by a code. I don't trespass—no six legs in a bed for me. But Ada, that bitch, she's having an affair with someone in the War College that's kind of mine. Have had my brand on him a long, long time. Oh, we meet and part. But, but—pour for me, my wrists hurt."

All Simon could think of was Uncle Brewster saying, "The end of everything is forgiveness." No: Simon, expressionless, half refilled the glass held out to him. Already he felt some skewed sense of pain. Ada?

"You're upset, Souki. And mean at times. And a liar."

"Paranoid, captain? Nuts? I'm crackers?"

"Something has pushed you to extremes."

"Baby, I caught that tight-up poker face of yours. You registered reaction as soon as I said Ada and a guy. You've been thinking of it too; little doubts, poor excuses by the wife as to why she's late, where she's been. Signs of a little tumbling in the kip, a disorder of the clothes, a bit of torn lace, showing a bruise here and there? Eh, eh? Well, she's putting it out right *now*—outside Alexandria, at the Royal George Inn. Go ahead, get out your horse pistol. Bang, *bang!*"

Simon stood up. Souki's dialogue was sputtering, spitting. "I'll get Mrs. Rosegold over to take care of you, Souki. You shouldn't be alone."

Souki fell back on the sofa, exposing long white thighs like veal sausages.

"Please. Don't want that iron-biddy here. I'm all right. Be good as new in a day or so. Didn't cut my wrists too deep, you know. Hacked just to get the gore to flow. And—hey. . . . Oh, kiss-my-ass."

Simon had turned and gone. Souki began to weep loudly, and all through her weeping she sipped her drink and casually watched her reflection full length in a Colonial pier glass across the room. She sniffed back tears—what fool would give up *that* body for a simp like Ada Roch Copperwood?

Simon stood at the curb, frozen in some muscled inadequacy, eyes closed, leaning on the car fender. Jeff! Jeff Astruc! Captain Jefferson Flornoy Astruc! "All our righteousness is as filthy rags" (Isaiah via General Saunders). Souki had been right; he'd had small doubts for some time. But had felt it was just his mind misinterpreting. Not Ada. Still, often that flush on her face when he came home, that overgay directness, the flowers on her birthday or some event, flowers from Jeff—a bit too expensive. The way Jeff held her arm at a party, at the theater. Small talk, jests that now seemed such deliberate disguises.

He felt like a bankrupt taking inventory of his past. Simon had long trained himself to depend on logic and reason. No emotional hysterical reaction to any event. Now, his heart was racing, he felt a throbbing in his temples, and he was horrified to find reason and logic were failing him. He was murderously angry. Like any clod, peasant, dim-witted, betrayed husband. He wanted to kill, to tear, to face the guilty pair in a melodrama of cheap theater, storm about in banal drama. All his controls seemed increasingly superficial, open to vulnerability.

He got into the car and sat behind the wheel to present to himself certain strategies. He must proceed calmly. These things happened. Men and women are, were, yes, creatures of drives, glands, nerves, compulsions. Victims—yes, that was it, unwilling victims of forces beyond their control (screw that kind of thinking). He kicked the car motor into life.

Simon drove toward a favorite bridge and found himself crossing into Virginia, heading for Alexandria. He had no plan, he told himself, he wanted no plan of action. Logic, reason, sensible resolve would take care; civilized thinking. Of course. Only he'd kill them both first. He had a Smith and Wesson .45 with ivory grips in the glove compartment. Blow their heads off. That simple idea calmed him as he tooled through the afternoon traffic. Virginia was beautiful. ("Over hill, over dale, as we hit the dusty trail, the caissons go rolling along.") Ada had talked of buying an old house and green acres, a brook, a house for her collection of milk glass (I'll smash every bit of it), his military prints, his—it was all *so* logical, like a military action. Surprise them.

Ah, execution—drumhead style; "the unwritten law" his lawyer would call it. What a scandal it would make. Witnesses, dates, places, bedsheets examined. Some wise-looking dolt of a head doctor talking of Captain Copperwood's unbalanced psychoanalytic makeup when faced with this traumatic betrayal. Captain Copperwood's loss of his senses, a blackout. Captain Copperwood's lack of knowledge of the actual kill. An amnesia of the emotions as he pumped out six slugs. Three in each head, neatly placed between the eyes. Yes, Captain Copperwood let them pull apart, disengage, before he shot—so he could skillfully, calmly place the nickel-jacketed slugs perfectly on the bull's-eye. The action of a man unaware of what he was doing —as if on the target range.

It would mean the end of his Army career. Why do it then?

After all, it was hurt male vanity, that was all. A woman with no moral sensibility, sharing her orifice with someone else, probably some obscene movements up and down, a little wriggling, some personal slobbering of wet mouths and teeth. *God, I'll blow them to shreds!*

Logic? Reason? Simon beat on the golden-oak steering wheel with his gloved hands. Logic, reason, don't desert me! What I am planning to do is a fool's way, a damn fool's senseless action.

Better to be ironic. Walk into the Royal George Inn grounds from the back, through the side road. The place had small bungalows where, for clandestine couples, according to the War Department office gossip, there was privacy, an icebox for drinks, a game bird baked, cold snacks. And then a hasty wash, and with slackened loins, home for dinner. Yes, Captain Copperwood (I'm talking to myself), play it calmly, detached, amused. Just tap on the window, or if the door is flimsy, just kick it in. Just stand, cigarette in mouth, not lit. Just, just. Light it slowly with the thin gold lighter, smiling on the sweaty copulating couple locked in their positioning. (a feather-trimmed peignoir on the footboard—handkerchief-linen underwear embroidered with fleurs-de-lis?) Tap your forehead, captain, in a salute, inhale, exhale, blow smoke into the lust-heated air. A little dialogue? "Sorry to interrupt." Something more pithy? "Just passing through." It was like a bad dream. . . . Slam the door. Still smiling, get into the car. Drive off. Spend the night at the Army Club. Take no phone calls. In a week, Colonel Elkins will have cut orders moving you, Captain Copperwood, to China. (The dream broke off like a screaming cat flung against a wall.)

Simon found himself in the yard of the Royal George Inn. From the main building came the chatter from the busy bar in the Tack Room Salon, the Rambouillet Hunt tapering off. Homeward-bound citizens of the Republic stopping for one more after afternoon conferences; lawyers, businessmen finishing off the day's doings with a horse's neck highball, gimlet, gibson, martini. Someplace a Victrola played "a chi amo a chi mi ama."

Simon walked toward the three cabins. Two showed no light—lots of dead leaves in the doorways. One, the last one by the small lake, presented just a sliver of golden yellow between

[193]

the slats of a wooden blind. He walked slowly—military-funeral pace—over the well-cared-for lawn, and was amazed to find himself under some elms, holding the heavy revolver at chest level: gun open, and spinning the cylinder to see if it was fully loaded. It was. He saw the tips of the ugly bullets. As he snapped it together, he couldn't understand why he had the handgun out. But it was clear. Something outside of his firm control; his sense of the foolishness of murder, was taking him toward a monomaniacal double killing. Life is not lived with ideas, it is lived with experiences.

Chapter 24

HE was aware of his audible breathing as he moved closer to the window. The slatted blind showed cracks through which he could glimpse a bit of an interior; lamplit, knotty pine walls, some hunting prints of red coats, liver spotted hounds. At the foot of a bed with bedclothes thrown back there was some sort of thrashing about. The main action out of sight. He inhaled slowly, listening to an amorous pulsating, groaning (female) and a rougher crackle of soporific (male) voice in rut.

It was the jocular overheated sounds, the scraps of laughter, intense, involved in love play, that made him aware of the gratitude he felt toward the weapon he gripped. Finger firm on trigger. *Yes? No?* Sanity returned suddenly, for all the adrenalin flowing in him. Perhaps because these two creatures in connection seemed so paltry a part of the universe—hardly the end of the world, or the bigger enveloping business of living and being. Degrading, but normal. . . . No reasonable logic governs our actions. Back off, man, back off. . . .

No killings, no murders. But let them know he was aware. Just burst in the door, show himself to Ada, to Jeff sweating jaybird naked, there just beyond his full range of vision on that tumbled bed. Then leave them, mouths open. He put the .45 into a side pocket and then, as the breathing from the room grew intense and labored, he focused for the first time on the military jacket carefully placed on the back of a chair—as if on display in a shop window—beyond Ada's discarded pale-green shoes. Saw first the blue enamel and gold of the Slavic Order of the Royal Incarnatus—then the colonel's insignia on the shoulders. *Wallie!* Colonel Wallace Elkins, his chief, his teacher! Not Jeff, but the man who was getting him the China assignment. Who held Simon Bolivar Copperwood's future in his hand, as if gripping a cuckold's manhood. With this base image in his mind, Simon turned away from the window and walked slowly back to his car. The rabbity, insatiable bitch. He had through Ada lost honor, lost love, lost a security, the vanity in being a well-hung man. But now he would not let her destroy his career, that appointment to Asia, not by a dirty little display of a face-off here and now. Great claws of despair gripped him, the bite of misery, of the wrong done to him. Betrayal, degradation. He heard from his own throat fluctuating sobbing sounds. His lungs seemed to seek air and not find it.

He lacked the slack romanticism to get drunk. He wandered—that night—in pain. He thought, Is anything so desolate as a city you know so well when you see it as if you never saw it before? He wandered around in a sudden rain that came up from the Potomac, whipping around the Washington Monument, and he went drifting off, not wanting to remember the dreadful event of the day before.

In Washington at night, in the dangerous hours, the drunk-rollers were out searching for necks to grab, heads to break, pockets to pick. He stood in front of the Smithsonian figuring his worth, pocket-held wealth. Dunhill lighter (plated), no fluid, a worn alligator wallet, six cards, two addresses of persons he couldn't recall, a faded yellow notebook with a red hat-feather stuck in it like a dried rose.

He went out to the river where the rebel troops one night crossed the plank bridge in the old war; someone had forgotten to pull up the planks that night and the Confederate troops had marched into Washington, ragged, barefoot bastards, found the city empty, silent; fearing a trap, they marched out again singing

"It's a rich man's war, a pore man's fight." And here Booth had ridden off, boot full of blood and a broken bone, down the road to the other side where Doctor Mudd's house had stood, and the doctor had set the bone. But Simon wondered, How do you set a broken life?

At the Corcoran they were having a showing of that season's modern art. He went in and at the buffet ate caviar in stale halves of hard-boiled eggs and drank very good brandy. "Valid," said someone in his ear. He feared it was Ada—it wasn't. At the German Embassy he stayed and then left in a taxi with a tall blond woman. She said, "Who he thinks he is, as if I didn't know he's screwing that daughter of the Texas bastard. That's all he thinks about, honey, since we came from Oklahoma. He tells me, standing in his underwear, his teeth in a glass, 'Oil is politics.' He and three men rule the world. Ha! Look. Look, you ever see the big Lincoln on that high marble chair? Me neither. Six years and never near it. What you say we go look? What do you say?"

So, in the wet, they went to see Mr. Lincoln, a grand sight, all lit up, the man sitting there. And the wife of the oil man had her shoes off; lost the shoes. Arm in arm they stood there, warm and fine all over, looking at Mr. Lincoln.

There wasn't anything to say. It was impressive and it had scale, you know. "Large scale," she said. "Makes you proud, huh?" They went to find some drinks at the Shoreham. "It's a lonely city, huh?"

The top of his head, like topping a breakfast egg—*rasp, rasp.* He lay staring at the ceiling, light coming from some nearby windows. He was on a sagging sofa. Souki, in a blue dressing gown, red-eyed, was looking down on him, her wrist bandages frayed, a big cup of smoking coffee in her fingers.

"Clap yourself around this."

Simon moaned, sat halfway up, sipped, burned his mouth, and kept gulping in some horrifying apprehension he had done some fearful thing.

"Did you kill them?"

He sat up, held the cup between his hands. Shook his head. "You don't kill a colonel."

"You chickened." Souki seemed only mildly disappointed. She

[196]

took up a cigarette, took up another—put it in his mouth, the other in hers. She lit them with a lighter set with mother-of-pearl and a division insignia. "Sonofabitch, I felt you'd really do them in."

"Wallie Elkins? I figured all the time it was Jeff!"

"Jeff?" Souki laughed. "You don't think, captain, that Ada, that cold-nosed bitch, would go off with anyone that didn't outrank *you?* No, she and Wallie have been moving on this collision course ever since Wallie and me had a. . . . Well, never mind. That's Wallie for you and his rapt sweetness. Gets close to a young hotshot officer with brains, as a pet. . . . Oh, you have brains, Simon. And while he is polishing his boy wonder, setting him up the command ladder, he's making it with the wife. That's how Wallie he gets his rocks off, gets his kicks. I've seen it at least three times. And you, you poor jerk, you thought it was. . . ."

Simon wondered at the mercy of instantaneous death and tried to stand. "How I get here?"

"You fell in through the door, smelling like a garbage scow. Then passed out. Wallie and Ada, how they react when you came calling?"

"What?"

"You did face them—you said your little piece like the proper diddled husband?"

"I didn't, didn't do anything. Just, *just* walked away without—"

"You flounced around without letting them know you were a Peeping Tom? I suspected that. Captain Simon Bolivar Copperwood, oh, a coming Army man. So was he going to upset his superior officer while that great man was stupping his wife? And get the man so mad, he'd not go through with whatever he had promised? What did Wallie get you in return for Ada?"

He tried to walk, felt himself fall, spun around. He was again on the sofa, on his back. Souki handed him a glass. "Here, a hair of the dog. You're a jerk, Simon. But a thinking jerk. Maybe you're right. Nothing gained by knocking down Wallie with his pants off—facing him. Men can lose their vanity when surprised like that, and they *never* forgive."

"Shut up, Souki."

"We're both up crap alley, aren't we? I wanted you to kill Wallie last night—and—well. . . . It's not important now, is it? I'll find another colonel. And you, Simon? You'll never be friendless and alone in the Army—not *you*."

"You think I didn't go in and face them because it might have blown up my China assignment? I'd hate to think that."

Souki gave him a glancing scrutiny, refilled his drink. "No scars will show in a little time on you, baby. Oh, you'll cuddle your little betrayal by Ada and Wallie. Feel good you were done wrong. Christ, I envy you being free of this rotten place. All the conniving, two-timing, double-crossing. Where they can pick your pockets while both their hands are folded in prayer. . . . I'll miss you . . . yes. . . . Do me one favor when you get to China."

"What's that?"

"Don't send me any ivory chopsticks from Peking, huh?"

She was weeping again, no longer petulant and erratic.

It seemed a simple promise to make.

Souki was wrong about Simon. The scars were there, the scar tissue never healed. Ada had been his first love, had been—and the fault may have been his, he admitted, that he had made her an image of his own design and she wasn't that person at all. He had loved deeply and he was not prepared for the sudden ending to his marriage.

While walking to the Army Club to take a room, he promised himself to turn into hard steel inside, to never again offer his whole love like a heart-shaped box of candy to any other human being.

He wondered if he was lying to himself. There were two people questioning each other in him. The first was the cheated-on male, confused, badly hurt, as if a huge balloon he has been blowing into had blown up in his face. And the second man, that was Simon the city knew, his fellow workers knew. A smart bastard, a very-high-IQ chap. Hard, hard, always thinking, always had an answer.

The first man said: "Go away, don't look at me." The second man said: "Face it, accept it. A woman is only a woman."

Said Number One: "That's what you think." Said Number Two: "That's what all people say." One: "Leave me be." Two: "It's for your own good. Logic, clean head, career, the service. Your intellect." One: "Shove it." Two: "That just now. When you come out of it you'll laugh at it all." One: "Ha! Ha!"

He got a room at the club. The radio someplace was playing Cuban music. He found out your heart doesn't break. It hits you instead in the kidneys and in the stomach. And between the eyes. Every once in a while you find you had to order yourself to breathe; you keep forgetting to suck air. Crazy, how all your life you've been breathing, and suddenly you find you need air.

He went down to the bar and had two martinis, spoke to a major about a polo game, and had dinner—a veal cutlet, half a bottle of white wine, a wedge of pecan pie and two coffees. He was surprised to find he had eaten a huge meal. He was a compulsive eater when under stress. Unaware of anything but gobbling.

He got an evening paper and read it carefully, not remembering anything he read. He left word at the desk he would take no calls. No calls at all, unless it was official business.

For a long time he lay fully dressed on the bed. He must have slept, for Ada and he were swimming in the Sound and, no, not the Sound—the ocean off Santa Barbara and he said, "Love me, love me, I need you, need you," and she was laughing and pointing as she swam spitting out seawater and crying out, "China, China. . . ."

He came awake and felt the shirt tacky with sweat, sticking to his body and the radio giving the results of some horseraces.

The meal lay heavy on his heart and he hoped it would kill him.

Book Five

Mean and mighty, rotting
Together, have one dust.

—WILLIAM SHAKESPEARE

Der Historiker ist ein rückwärts gekehrter Prophet. . .

—SCHLEGEL

(From the notebooks of Simon Copperwood)

Chapter 25

In the summer the flat, chartreuse-colored landscape became drier than usual. The heat was dreadful and the dust blew continually around the red-brick barracks. The major, a man of about thirty, had a heat rash flaring angrily on his neck. The two brass electric fans buzzed and whirled, but merely stirred and redistributed the rancid air. He was a deeply weathered officer, a bit too lean. He had had two months of fever in the post hospital the year before, and now, recuperated, had not regained lost weight. He sat at the battered teak desk in the main barracks of the 15th Infantry, U.S. Army, stationed in 1929, at Tientsin. They were sixty miles upriver, with Peking to the northwest. To the major, the post seemed set in a transitory mood, caught for a moment in a chasm, too wide to bridge, to his past.

"Wong Li!"

The screen door banged open and a tall Northern Chinese coolie came in, wearing washed-out blue, his teeth too large for his oval face, smelling of byar wine—a pair of sandals made from old car tires on his dusty feet.

"*Dzauaun. Ni hau ma syansheng majah?*"

"*Syesye ni*, I'm all right." The major had been studying Chinese in the post school for a year now and wore the patch letter CHUNG on his uniform as one who spoke the language. But he still wondered if Wong Li, his barracks coolie, understood him, or just smiled as if he did.

Wong Li was as unsure of his English as the major of his Chinese. "You wanna eatem *chr jungfan*, with *chr kafei*, or *chr cha?*"

"The tea and with lots of ice." He made the gesture of piled-up lumps of ice. "*Lots* of ice."

"Ice machine *dztsung shangtsz.*" Wong Li held his hands up, palms forward. "No fix yet *syansheng* majah."

The major motioned Wong Li out, to stop an argumentative debate, and scratched his rashed neck. No ice again. He'd have to borrow some tonight from the English in the Concession Area. They suspected Americans of sloth, foolery, and irreverence to the Empire. The American flag flew, shredding in the wind, over the three-story brick barracks and the always dusty parade ground. He looked at the papers on his desk, touching them with a sweaty hand, and wondered why they couldn't keep the ice machine running. He felt a blast of hot air as the fans in their buzzing movement on their stands crisscrossed for a moment.

There was a French dinner-dance tonight. Colonel Nast liked two Americans to be present. The polo team was short a man; Captain Bistrom, their best rider, had developed a hernia on a visit to Singapore. And the mounted U.S. patrol, sent out four days ago on those damn Tang ponies, was half a day late from scouting conditions near the shops of the Peking-Mukden railroad they were supposed to protect.

What the hell were they all doing here in Tientsin? Fifty officers, eight hundred men, and short of artillery, mortars, howitzers, truck parts. The joke of an airfield so dustblown, most of the time, it was suicide to try to land.

There was a tap of confidence—three direct blows—on the door frame and Captain Budgins came in past the screen door. Captain A. Budgins, but called "Sobbing Sam" by the men, behind his back of course. He had the innocent earnest face of one who cherished an integral personality—helped by pale-blue eyes, a body with large feet and hands. He was in proper duty-dress, carried the swagger stick under one arm, as demanded by Colonel Nast.

The captain's salute was perfect even if his shirt was, already, after three hours, sweat-stained under the arms. The way he moved to stand at ease made the major suspect the heat rash had hit the captain in the crotch. The major smiled at any discomfort in Captain Budgins. Sobbing Sam was the major's cross at Tientsin. When drunk one night at Madam Wu's, the major had called the captain "more real than real, more gold than gold."

"Major Copperwood, I have the report ready on the two battalions of the Fifteenth stationed here. I fear, sir, it's not a good report."

"I'm sure, captain, a hotshot voluptuary like yourself did a good hard searching job."

"The major knows me better than that—I mean my personal conduct. I've had very little cooperation, I may add, from anyone at the post, but I don't mention that in my report."

"Leave it, captain, I'll break it down for Colonel Nast and—"

"Major"—the captain's face flushed, even under the pork-colored peeling sunburn—"I wonder if we should forward some of the facts I have found. Almost all the men are cohabitating with low-caste native women. The situation here in the Concession Area and in the town is such that whores, intoxicants—that Kaoliang brandy—and narcotics can be obtained in their vilest forms for a few cents. And all kinds of abomination."

"I see you really worked hard, captain."

"Yes, major. Take disease—the venereal rate is very high, shocking."

The major seemed to lose interest. . . . The absence of the patrol worried him.

"That's a fine swagger stick you carry, Budgins."

"Colonel Nast posted orders: 'Officers will carry a riding crop or swagger stick and sergeants will carry sabers while on duty.' We're getting the sabers from Peking. About the men, we do try—give them four movies a week. You'd think they'd stay at the post."

"The mounted patrol report in yet? Any telegraph news?"

"No, major, those little Manchurian ponies make our men look rather foolish. In Kentucky we raised up proper mounts, Morgan Reds and fine quarter-horses."

"American horses die here. These ponies are native and can live off the land. Inform me the moment the patrol gets in."

The captain saluted, set down on the desk his neatly typed report, properly stapled. "We could get us a better chaplain —punish the men who get infected."

"What, you've never had the clap or the Canton crud, Budgins? How long you been in China? That's bizarre—you're letting the Fifteenth Infantry down."

[205]

"Sir, don't jest. I'm engaged to be married next leave—and my father is a minister in Lexington."

"It's fine, captain, the way you avoid low, vicarious satisfactions. But, as Kipling said: 'Single men in barracks aren't exactly plaster saints.' They have normal desires. Just be sure there is a medical short-arm inspection twice a week and profacs are available in the canteen. How's your rash?"

Captain Budgins automatically touched his crotch and quickly withdrew his hand. "I feared at first it was some native filth infection. I've limed the latrines—but still—"

"You'll find the singsong girls and the whores in the Jade Dream and at Madam Wu's very healthy. Try the French houses or the Italian Legation sections. It might just be repressions."

"Sir!" the captain shouted, turned, and started for the door. The major was in a mean mood and the captain's austere moral principles were bad for morale.

"Have Doc get you a mixture of baking soda and calamine lotion. Nothing to be ashamed of, captain, if you caught it from a toilet seat."

The captain went out, carefully seeing to it the screen door didn't bang. The major knew Captain Budgins was one of the few officers who didn't have a girl in some room on Race Course Road in the British Concession. The captain had once publicly announced, after two martinis, last Armistice Day, at the officers' club: "It is not to our national interest for the white men to fornicate in lechery with yellow women." Which remark had been greeted by a series of lip noises called "Bronx cheering."

Major Simon Bolivar Copperwood tossed the captain's report into a desk drawer on top of a pile of neglected or held-back similar reports that would have done the 15th no good with the USAFC (U.S. Army Forces in China) or with General Gerald Comkin, a society-connected officer with a rich wife, political ambition, and a trust in his horoscope—drawn weekly—hinting that he had some great destiny to fulfill. A bit deficient in common sense, but General Comkin saw to the officers' whisky supply.

Simon panted and itched in the heat; he imagined great iced schooners of Pilsner beer in the Pink Poodle Bar in Shanghai, the frosted Tom Collinses at the Smoke Jade in Peking, and with a sigh and a scratching, the cool mountain streams of Montana. He settled for the tepid water in the desk thermos, water tasting of the barracks chlorine filter system. Sipping, standing at the window observing the parade ground being policed by a squad of coolies, he wondered at the post's self-indulgences. Everything but drilling seemed to be done by coolies: washing, cooking, cleaning, and fighting over the rich contents of the latrines, which were sold by the barrels to farmers as fertilizer. Simon studied the patch of garden in which, with pale-yellow flowers and red-leaved plants, there was spelled out the motto of the 15th U.S. Infantry: CAN DO!

Can Do. Simon turned from the window. He had been eleven months in Tientsin and had brought order to the place, while Colonel Nast worried about swagger sticks, riding crops, and sabers. The mounted patrols Simon had activated were functioning well. And Simon had his agents moving south and north keeping track of warlords, the Nationalists, and the Communist underground setup, which was growing more powerful than the legation men in Peking, or in the legations here at the main port of North China, admitted. It was all surface spit-and-polish in the Concessions. Policed by Sikhs, manned by well-fed and sassy Europeans or Americans who lorded it over the Chinese. The 15th was stationed just a block from the former German Concession. Kaiser Wilhelmstrasse was now Woodrow Wilson Street, and there was a Victoria Road, a rue de France, a Via Italia. Yet, any day, the major feared, either the Japanese or some warlord could come down and make things truly dangerous. Simon had worked out a plan for moving the 15th in full armed force up to Peking at half an hour's notice, *if* the American Legation there was in danger. The trucks were always in need of repair, and stealing of gasoline and parts didn't help. He'd run the infantry on foot on the double to Peking if he had to. He had to be wary. What was General Feng Yu-shiang up to? and General Wu Pei-fu? and that sleek weasel, Chiang Kai-shek? . . . Chang Tsung-chang, the Shantung warlord, was on the U.S. roll, but on the Japanese one too most likely. Simon, as a special legation attaché, felt he'd have to make an inspection of what was actually going on beyond the range of the 15th and their pony patrols.

[207]

Wong Li was back with a tray, playing his game with the major. Simon had studied Chinese cuisine as he had studied the Chinese language, with better results, he hoped. But Wong Li liked to test his ability to eat new dishes. Simon had tried the boiled bear paws and the fried fish lips. Tried them once. Actually he preferred deep-fried Peking chicken with ginger root, braised fish steaks with bean curd, stuffed bitter melon, stir-fry beef and bean sprouts, and relished the crispness of the shrimp and lobster dishes with black sauce.

Wong Li uncovered the dishes. "Szechwan beef hot pepper, wine sauce chicken, egg flied lice with *huijyau.* . . . No ice for *yisye cha.* . . ."

Simon, head to one side, listening, had heard the clatter of pony feet on the parade ground. He waved off the tray. "Put it down."

"You no eat?"

"*Yesyu.*"

The patrol was made up of thirty-two men, and they trotted, with no ostentation, across the burned-out turf on their small, shaggy Manchurian ponies. Men and mounts were dusty but in good order. The troops had the morose wariness of twenty-year men. Wide campaign-hats from the Philippines supply depot, home base of the 15th, were battered into all kinds of individual shapes. The men looked rugged enough, but bushed. Simon had picked them, and they now were a bit ass-sprung, he saw, as he walked toward them.

Lieutenant Ollie Wallibee cried out, "Prepare to dismount."

Top Sergeant McMaster, a big Negro with a smashed-flat nose repeated, "Prepare to dismount."

"Dismount."

"Dismount."

Simon saluted the young officer who, feet on the ground, pressed on his kidneys with both gloved hands, and smiled through a mask of yellowish dust.

"Sergeant, get the troop to the stables, see the horses are rubbed down well by the coolies, have a weapons check, and get the men to the showers and to tiffin. . . . How do you do, major?"

Simon petted a hairy pony who tried to bite him in return. "You've been having all the fun, Wallibee."

"Of course. Somebody fired at us out by the railroad shops. Might have been Kuomintang. Talk is they have some officers from the Chang-Whampoa Academy out on the road—gossip, anyway. Don't really know. Might have been somebody just letting off a round at us for the hell of it."

"Hear anything on General Feng?"

"Nothing but lies—the usual accumulation of crap. More lies than fleas. And there were *fleas*." The young officer scratched himself under his shirt.

"Madam Wu's dance on tonight, major?"

"I don't know. Get your report done first. I may go out scouting myself. Want to come along?" He liked the lieutenant's style; elation, candor, a complete commitment.

"Sir, of course—if it's not too soon. I've got this marvelous half-White Russian, half-China doll of a dancer giving me tango lessons."

"Three days' leave at least. Now go dust yourself. I have to contact Peking. And there's some real scotch my man Wong Li is holding for me. Be free to test it."

"Thanks, major. We've been drinking this Kentucky bourbon made in Japan." He rubbed his kidney area again. "I gotta soak first, and have *this* much ice in the tallest glass in China."

Simon grinned, scratched his rash. "*Wo hen gan sye Wo hen bauchyan.*"

"Huh, sir?" The lieutenant turned over his pony reins to a stable coolie.

"Sorry. Ice machine again broken down."

Lieutenant Wallibee did know *some* Chinese, and he spoke his favorite fearful oaths.

Simon Bolivar Copperwood was a bit of an enigma to the old salts and shavetails of the 15th, career soldiers living in a foreign atmosphere where sensations become unwontedly acute, insights a bit warped, even abnormal. And each officer usually had his own individual maladjustments, not helped by a China of rumors and chaos.

Major Copperwood seemed to exist in some potential

urgency, in an armor of purpose while on duty. Strict, but Army-wise, relentless, but fair to the enlisted man. A discriminating connoisseur of all the old Army dodges of the rank and file malingerer, the latrine lawyer. He presented a seamless shell of irony against the blather and loose talk of the officers trying to adjust to China, while drinking, going to the racetrack, reading copies of *Collier's, College Humor, Review of Reviews, Saturday Evening Post*.

There was gossip of course about Major Copperwood. That he was a divorced man whose society heiress wife had been a niece, or "something," to a President, or somebody with power in the War Department. She a Dupont, or Ford, or Mellon. That the major had more medals and awards than he wore, and had been a favorite of General Pershing in the Great War, or was it General Foch? A sergeant who knew him at Hamilton said he had been a stern breaker of tails among his former posts of service, tossing the book at any goldbricking doughboy who shirked duty and was unprincipled about his place in the service. The major had the added reputation of being a bookworm, a reader of thick, small-print volumes by military historians —given to love of footnotes—books one had been forced to study up at the Point. Books that weren't of much use, the officers told each other, in protecting Socony Hill for Standard Oil in Nanking, or trying to shoe a Manchurian pony, or an aid in kicking a coolie back into order when he went a bit wild on four cattees of bygar wine and began yelling, "*Yao-ho!* Kill the white devils!"

It wasn't that the major was a recluse; he did gamble, booze a bit, in fact he was trying to keep from seeming a drunk, or so the messroom talk hinted. It was the major's enthusiasms that weren't really Old Army. His interest in Sung pottery, picture scrolls, the flatulent Chink food he'd try, the coolies' *po-po* dumpling, or using chopsticks. Of course for all their griping the enlisted men liked him. He'd talk a noncom with a cheating wife at home out of apathetic depression, find AWOL's in some rickshaw puller's *hutung*, passed out in his own puke among gongs, drums, flutes, and the stink of joss sticks and Chinese garlic.

Major Copperwood wasn't exactly alienated from the mainland, but he never warmed up to talk, as many officers did, of their sexual adventures back in the States, of marvelously depraved sweethearts, of wives won or lost. It was a mistake, as some made at first, to charge him with a touch of misanthropy, or to blame his silences on modesty. He actually, they learned, had a good bump of ego, and he damn well knew his worth. He was liked for all the moods and mysteries some saw in him.

He was human and he felt *many* feel, *few* think—and there were times when his sensibilities were rubbed raw. Of his failed marriage he never spoke. It was, as the post chaplain, Roscoe Norman, put it to Rabbi Finkel in Peking at the YMCA there, "A marriage, a past to Major Copperwood is like a mean child fallen away from one's heart." The Reverend Captain Norman was wrong. There were lonely night hours when Simon anguished, and the limits of existence seemed blurred. So in the morning he'd often insist on a thirty-mile hike—full pack—and himself join the blistering column.

Chapter 26

IF one knew the way out beyond the British Legation, its pavilions, moated gardens, and made one's way in a quick rickshaw past Race Course Road and Nin Chieh—Cow Street—to Kan yo Hutung (Alley of Sweet Rain), there were discreet houses with blind front walls, overhangs of dragon eaves, and roofs of greenish tiles. Here, for a few liangs of silver a month an officer could have a flat, a few servants, and set up if so inclined, a menage, not a liaison exactly; rather, an unblessed marriage. Simon usually spent, as a compensation for his duties, two nights a week in his flat, a flat which in season looked down on a courtyard of blossoming peach and plum, a zigzag bridge under which swam bugeyed goldfish of smoky hue sporting great lacy tails and fins, swaying like living kelp in fruit-green water.

Simon walked down the lane from the road after dismissing the rickshaw boy—the "boy" usually a thin wreck of thirty, his clothes wet with sweat. Simon inserted his key in a blackwood door and went up twenty steps and found another door on which he tapped. The Amah Chang, a fat, middle-aged woman with large yellow teeth going in all directions, as if spreading her smile, let him in and bowed. *"Wuan, majah, syansheng."*

A gramophone played:

> Don't let anything bother you
> It's something I never do.
> Your little troubles
> Are only bubbles.

"Wuan, Amah Chang. Syesye ni." He handed her the bottle of Haig and Haig, the tins of Danish sardines, and, in oiled paper, the sliced, smoked salmon Kao Mah liked.

He walked down the straw-matted little hall and past a doorway protected by strings of beads and a scroll by a calligraphist. Kao Mah turned off the gramophone and stood smiling by the potted gingko tree in her blue silk trousers, long loose gown, white-soled slippers on her rather-too-large but graceful feet. How right, he thought, of Roger Millhouse to think that chastity is the meanest of perversions.

"Ching jin dzai lai, darling." She pronounced it "darring." She ran toward him, leaped up like a gazelle, and he engulfed her in his arms. She chattering in Chinese, mixed with Legation Quarter English, kissing his cheeks. Her well-cared-for fingers went digging at the base of his skull, where the close-cropped hair merged into a sunbaked neck. Her voice had perceptible shadings of suggested passion, a gossamer hint of bliss.

"Kao Mah, Kao Mah," he answered, holding the slim young body close, enjoying her smell, so strange and different an odor from women he had known elsewhere—gradations of musk, civet, bursting sap-filled pods. The face so close was a fine tan tint, the eyes on a slight, fascinating slant, the shiny black hair almost varnished. She held one leg bent behind her as she had seen in an American film. There was a butterfly tattooed on one of her ankles.

Kao Mah was eighteen years old—as far as he knew. Amah Chang was her aunt, maybe. He did not pry too much into the establishment he had set up. It satisfied his nature, it calmed Simon after the wearing tasks of his Army duties. Kao Mah gave him an invulnerability, nearly, to despair. He adored the girl without being very much in love with her. There were too many incomprehensible categories to her views of life. To Simon she was rather like some marvelous jointed doll, of fine flesh and perfect parts. The shaved pudenda at first seemed a bit of a mistake but she proved a splendid lover full of incessant body play. She was better for him, he decided in an ironic moment, than a membership at the Pa Poo Shan Golf Club. As she said it—quoting a Chinese novel she had read—all life is expression—and all expression is life. *Shr? Bushr?* (Yes? No?)

Amah Chang came in, arm enfolding a beautiful six-month-old baby with large, staring, but unfrightened black eyes, over-fed cheeks. A tiny red silk cap on its perfect oval of a head.

"Little Elegance has been waiting up fo' you, majah." Simon looked at his son, if he was his son. He felt a tug of the acquisitive instinct. He called the boy Edward, not by the too-pleasant Chinese name of Little Elegance.

"I think you're overfeeding him. He's got cheeks like a behind."

Kao Mah clapped her hands. Little Elegance stared on. "I buy him a fighting cricket—Little Golden Ball—in a cage, come the peddler who cries '*Heng*,' and Little Elegance, some day, grow up to be a brave sojah like you, darring."

"Well, that's an assumption. Hello, Edward."

Simon smiled at the baby, patted a fat cheek, and the child stared back, unblinking. Simon thought: Accept this—it is good to have issue, to have done what we, I and Kao Mah had done to make it. Uncle Brewster had always insisted a man wasn't a man until he'd killed someone, planted a tree, and produced a baby. Don't like to think of Uncle Brewster or of Aunt Dolly; they had died of a strain of animal anthrax that had killed off most of the Silver Bend, Montana, horse herds, and infected them, too. Just a year ago. So do chance and decay hem us in. . . . Now all the family he had was just his brother Craig, from whom he hardly ever heard. But for a tasteful Dickensian card—in full color—at Christmas, signed "Craig and Laura, Charles, Nancy and Robert." He supposed Craig was two up on him in the matter of children. Fat Craig with his stertorous breathing, on Nob Hill, where he now lived immersed in well-calculated dealing in banks, mines, oil drillings. Craig Copperwood, a power in California and national politics; overweight, balding, quoted on international relations, national defense, and, of course, the tariff.

"His nose is running a bit, isn't it?"

"Nothing, darring, he take a pill, the Triple Yellow Precious Wax. Cure anything, *Dangran*."

"Damn it, I wish you'd use the legation doctor, but I suppose in all this *cloisonné*, celadon-bowls culture you may be right to use sorcerers."

"Bedtime summah time."

The baby was withdrawn, still silent, but now restless in Amah Chang's arms, not willing to react to any badinage.

Simon changed from uniform to a dragon robe; the girl slipped out of her jacket and pants—like naked fruit from its husk, he thought. Someplace in a nearby teahouse someone was playing a stringed instrument, in that nerve-racking Chinese musical scale of five notes called, he remembered from lessons, the *shang*. Simon took Kao Mah in his arms, both sinking to the low, red, lacquered bed. He was ardent and strong in the sequence of events that followed. He tried to hold back his desire, and wished the girl was not so gracefully submissive, and yet so skilled in touching, caressing him. Almost—oh, goddamn puritan American memories—obscene in her businesslike skill. He, huge-bodied, white, she small, tan, birdlike, in a nest of bedding, he brushed away any thoughts or doubts; the hell with where she came from, or who had trained her.

She came to him from an Englishman who wore his hair rather long, wrote sardonic poems, and was commander of the Sikh police of the International Settlement. "Her father, an unemployed noodlemaker, sold her to Madam Wu Hai last year —these slopeheads—no decencies, what?" The Englishman had kept the girl "her first time out" as he admitted to Simon. "Well, it's expected, you know, but I'm rather, well, major, hard cheese, to admit it, getting on—rather slack in the jock I suppose. But

[214]

for buying woman here, she's bit of all right for a slanteye."

Later, Simon wondered, Am I as crass and revolting as this Englishman?

They were making love, made it on the lacquered bed, then Simon felt relaxed. They drank Kao-liang brandy made of millet, and he hoped it wasn't true that it was flavored with pigeon droppings. A crosseyed servant girl brought them sour prune soup, mimosa cakes, a candy called Sugared Horse Blossoms. They didn't feel very hungry after making love—just felt some hidden seed of affection germinating. Perhaps it was the alcohol, he thought. They switched to drinking scotch. The next hour passed in wild talk and laughter, and some hilarious sensual play.

Simon was drunk when he fell asleep, or at least, as he dropped off, his mind seemed to suggest he had been drinking a hell of a lot too much. But off duty one did sink into a calculated outrageousness. He came awake in the morning, hearing the three-pipe whistles, the *shao-yzu* these damn people attached to pigeons flying about someplace close on the roof. Jade Wing and Bronze Back the girl called the birds that he had bought her because it was good luck, Amah Chang had told him. "Much good!" He felt just a mild headache. Kao Mah lay sleeping on her side, displayed fully in just a short, yellow, fingertip jacket. Her mouth open, a slight drooling of dewy moisture, a steady healthy breathing. She seemed locked off, nebulous, elusive, yet alive flesh. Her perfect small breasts, like tepid gold in the morning sunlight, the round little belly protruding proudly a bit—to show she fed well in a hungry land. The delicate rose-petal lips of her plucked sex, he decided was a work of art, Chinese, but art.

He felt a surge of sexual probabilities and moved over her while she still slept. She came awake, alert, smiling, delighted.

After which, in a swift deterioration of his early mood of well-being, he bathed, rather *they* bathed, pouring warm water from blue porcelain pots over each other while standing in a large cedarwood tub. Her delight brought back his amenity. In shantung robes they ate stir-fry pork and bean curd, wine and ginger cod, with "red-sand" rice rolls. Simon insisted on Amah Chang getting the cook to produce his favorite breakfast tidbit:

[215]

Peking pancakes with apricot filling. What the hell, he thought—go all the way in the spectacle of man in pursuit of diversion and pleasure.

It was noon before he was dressed in Army tailoring and ready to go back to the barracks, swagger stick in place, per Colonel Nast's posted orders.

"Kao Mah, I'm going away for about two weeks. On a trip, you understand? *Jege ywe*, this month."

"*Dztsung shangtsz* time you go away so long."

"Duty, Army. Understand? You'll have everything you need here. I'll leave Yinhang ma-bank money with the *Amah*."

"Nothing to do but play *mahchiang*. I buy for Little Elegance fire crackrahs, called Five Devils Resisting Judgment. He like to see bang bang. You go—I unnestan."

"Yes, well, I'll be back." He held her close, kissed her, and his loneliness came back to him, his isolation, like a blow on the back of the head with a hard-rubber club. What was he to this Chinese girl but an organ backed with money. And she to him? Yin and Yang, a basic pattern of man and woman, this and that. And time passing.

"Bring you a bit of jade, Kao. We'll have, have fun."

"I teach you gambling games. Pawning the Jewel, and Nine Cards. Ooh-kay?"

"Okay."

He made his good-bye to Little Elegance. Said, "Boo, Edward, be a good boy." This time Little Elegance opened wide a toothless mouth, showed amazingly pink gums, and let out howl after howl, real Chinese howls. As Simon walked past the red cassia trees beyond the lane to find a group of rickshaw boys playing the finger game for cigarettes, he felt depressed as always on leaving the flat, and he thought of Ada, and Washington, and what had been, and now was not. But why? He had here love of a pleasant, skilled kind; a male child. And as a soldier, he could not avoid the thought there would be a great war with its sure, swift promotion; and his manuscript on theories of the future of tank warfare was to be published by the Military Press of Pittsburgh, in the fall.

As his rickshaw boy moved swiftly in the heat of the day past the Confucius Temple of the Azure Cloud, past men with Kalmuck, Mongolian features, past Indians and Sikhs, cockney Tommies and Kansas farmboys in uniform, seeking adventure in native quarters . . . past the shops of fake Tang art, yellow and purple brocades, he began to plan his trip out of Tientsin, and so for a time, for him, the past receded, lost its color and intimate odors.

> God what a rain of ashes falls on him
> Who sees the new and cannot leave the old!

Chapter 27

THE two-week planned journey stretched out to six weeks of a harrowing, dangerous expedition. With Lieutenant Wallibee, Sergeant McMaster, and Wong Li. Major Copperwood moved out boldly with several sets of credentials from various sources, credentials that no one took too seriously. Not the warlords, the louse-scratching generals, or the wandering southern detachments they ran into. Nor the Red bands, furtive groups moving here and there in the night from village to village, often to end as corpses in the ditches; tortured, heads shattered by slugs on Chiang Kai-shek's orders. Great disharmony existed in the countryside and death was easy to come by.

Simon never forgot the lice that seemed so lewd and jocose in his skin at Tainan, the firing squads at work outside the inn at Kaifeng: the near drowning of the party on the Huanh Ho when their ferry was caught in midriver in a sudden cloudburst. He grew to accept the constant undiminishing phenomena of China in agony. No one seemed able to grasp the essence of the vast chaos; the leaders' derision for the peasant, the denigration of the population. Simon estimated troop sizes, arms, the validity of the aims of the various semibandit generals; the numbers of White Russians in their service, the handful of 1914-1918 crop-haired, fat-necked, cynical exiles who felt no hope for China or for themselves. The Chinese people lived, ate, bred, and died accepting the pathos and grip of old myths.

Nanyangfu was for Simon's party a week of dodging Red bands, who felt the Americans were spies of the Nationalists. Crossing the Tasha Ho in a leaking motorboat, Lieutenant Wallibee caught a bad cold and his fever never seemed to go below 102°, until Simon threw away the sliver of measuring mercury. Szechow was a rest base: good food, a native amenity. Here Simon expanded his notes, met two agents to whom he turned over copies in the hope they might get back to the legation in Peking. In Mingkwang he was sure they would be murdered after an arrest by a band of army horse-drovers from General Hai's army. The general himself came to see them, the "white devil" prisoners, in an old Standard Oil compound where he stabled his best horses. Stern at first—a preening little butterball of a man—he was impressed when Simon pointed out to him he was being sold some bad riding stock. "A general like yourself," Simon said, removing a straw from his coat collar, "deserves better horseflesh."

General Hai smoked Russian cigarettes in long cardboard holders, spoke a Shanghai English, explaining "I was head-waiter, maître d' there in the Crown Club in my youth." He slapped the rump of a brown gelding standing sadly, shivering on three legs. "What's the matter with the horses my agents buy?"

Simon took a long time inspecting the stock, remaining poker-faced. "In Montana where I was raised, general, we knew the tricks horsedealers have."

"So?"

McMaster looked at Lieutenant Wallibee and frowned.

"This gelding," Simon said, "I'd guess he's been doped with arsenic or lobelia to hide the heaves. Now the dark horse next to him, he had bad bone spavin, so he's been given gasoline to perk him up. But it will kill him soon. Smell him."

"Petrol."

"That's what I figure, general. Also—feel here—someone has

[218]

put in air with a hollow needle attached to a bike pump to fill the cavities above the eyes so he'll look younger, more fit."

"*Heng!*"

"Watch out for a horse that looks good, general, and then gets stiff joints. The painful joint can be frozen so he can't feel it, with chloroform. And if a horse seems too frisky, he's maybe had a rubdown on his balls or ass with an ammonia rag between the hind legs. Still, I'd say you have six good horses here, out of the twenty."

General Hai howled "*Heng!*" again, turned on his high-heeled boots and went out followed by chattering staff officers all talking at once.

Said Lieutenant Wallibee, "That was strong stuff, major."

Wong Li said, "Oh, general, he in bad bad temah. Trouble for us, sure."

Simon was awakened just before dawn by one of the staff officers shaking him until he sat up in the hay bin. "Come! come! Wakee up."

Lieutenant Wallibee and Sergeant McMaster were also being pulled to their feet. The three of them were shoved outside into a straw-littered courtyard with an old well. Kneeling in a row on the hard earth were three Chinese, hands bound behind their backs, heads down. Over them stood a giant Chinese, eyes open, expressionless. General Hai waved to Simon in the light of acetylene gas lamps. "My three horse dealers." He waved a gloved hand at the giant who stood, his hands crossed on his chest, a huge wide sword in his grip. The lamps hissed, smelling like the Fourth of July in Silver Bend, Simon thought.

There was a flash of steel coming down and a head fell from a body. Another swooping *swish!* and another head rolled in the dirt. A final stroke with, Simon thought, the grace of a ballet gesture, and the third head left its neck. The three bodies, still in their kneeling positions, sprouted fountains that smoked in the cold of dawn just touched by the first sunrays.

General Hai came over to Simon and Ollie, offering a cardboard box of Russian cigarettes.

[219]

"So they no more not fix for me horses, not no more buy for me doctored animals."

"I'm sure of that," Simon said, looking beyond the wellhead as he smelled the blood.

"What do you think of Yee Hing, my swordsman? There is a story he once presided over the beheading of great, famous bandit, most famous one. And this bandit said, 'Please, Yee Hing, I am impatient—get it done with.' And Yee Hing laughed—said, 'Nod your head.' And bandit did, and head fell off. Yee Hing had been so fast, so skillful, the bandit never knew he had already passed from this world to his ancestors. . . . You going now, Major Copperwood?"

"Mingkwang, Anking too, if I can get through, and then to Yüchchow."

"Ah, Yüchchow. My dear friend, General Chang Tsung-chang, rules there. Do not trust him. A vessel of lotsa evil."

"If you could honor us with a letter to him, General Hai."

"Of course, we are, he and I, as I have said, old friends. But he is too tall a man, much too tall. I think so tall, there is snow on his head so his brain is not always in the same mood."

It had been as an official military attaché that Major Copperwood went out for the American Legation to seek fairly reliable estimates of just what was going on with the various warring armies of China. The missionaries' reports, the consular letters with their unreliable details, were at best confusing. There seemed to be, in a China in deep distress, a rising cloud of antiforeign fanaticism.

Lieutenant Oswald Wallibee and Sergeant Floyd McMaster, the sergeant in charge of extra bed rolls, medical supplies, and their emergency rations, were still with Simon when he at last got to the city of Yüchchow with his credentials. And Wong Li was there to interpret beyond Simon's skill to understand Chinese.

"Now remember, Ollie," said Simon at the Yüchchow railroad station, "this warlord Chang Tsung-chang in control here is a bastard. So just smile."

"He really seven feet tall?"

The Negro sergeant, pushing off coolies trying to carry their baggage, smiled showing teeth outlined in gold. "Yes, sir, major.

They call General Chang Tsung-chang 'Three-Things-You-Don't-Know.' "

Lieutenant Wallibee looked about for rickshaws. "Why?"

"You don't know how much dough he's stolen, how many soldiers he's got, and how many what they call concubines here, he's servicing. I met this colored fella what's boss in a river steamer engine room on the Yalla River—and he said the general he's got forty-four of them gals, in his hair-um. Jap, Koreans, and over twenty White Russians and one American. Hauls 'em round in two private railroad cars. That's fat livin'. *Yeah*, fat."

Simon looked over the malodorous ruin of the town. The general's armored trains, steam up, were just outside the station. Simon could make out around them Czarist White Russian adventurers who had fled the revolution. Big blond men with eyes from old icons, moving about as if from some nonspecific infection. Dressed in the remains of Imperial uniforms and added Chinese tailoring. It was clear these professionals were the general's best mercenaries.

"Major, major." A little Chinese approached. He looked like an oversized old dwarf, smoke-dried, with a face under a flat-brimmed straw hat like an old valise sagging in the wrong places. This man pushed his way toward Simon, past soldiers sleeping on the brick platform. He held out his hand, wriggling it free from a blue, over-long sleeve, and Simon shook it.

"I am Mistah Lao Dock, just now in charge of the Baptist Mission here." Simon found that Lao Dock had a breath like a dog—and he averted his head and released his fingers.

"Mr. Dock, we're in your hands. The legation at Peking has great confidence in your reports."

"Yes, I do try." His English was precise, clean—an education abroad, no doubt. "The mission is deserted just now, not functioning. But you will find some comfort, safety, too, I hope."

Simon introduced the rest of his party, and soon they were all in rickshaws, including their bundles, moving through a confusion of very young soldiers chewing and spitting out sunflower seeds, peddlers of night pots and steaming bowls of *po-po* dumplings. Simon observed mean little shops and a great deal of rubble. The smell of decay and rot, excrement was choking.

"The general, he feels the southern armies will bypass him here—go to the west to fight the Red Spears," said Mr. Dock, a Christian of long standing, he explained, and one of the Baptist Mission's best caretakers, also representing Singer sewing machines. "You will present your credentials to the general. But do not brush him the wrong way. He is a cruel, witty man, and a laughing man who does bad things to people."

The mission was old and not impressive, battered, but the thick-walled inner rooms, bare, dusty, could be made comfortable. Simon had Sergeant McMaster and Wong Li hide their supplies in an attic, and set out their bedding on low cots that seemed free of insects. Ollie Wallibee tried to figure out ways to defend the courtyard. "Hopeless."

Simon said Mr. Dock would provide them with figures as to the number of troops and the kind of arms the general had.

Simon wondered as to the worth of this collecting of information. They had come through a mournful countryside of dust mounds accepted as the tombs of kings. All of China seemed in these last years of the 1920's gripped in an aggressive, paranoiac fear, and a tedious grievance toward its leaders—men hardly aware of the external world beyond their borders.

The warlords, as they banged together, plotted, drew blood, made of warfare the most delirious of professions, with few real professionals. Simon had witnessed whole armies advancing in a drizzle toward battle under oiled-paper umbrellas, corpses hanging like overripe fruit on a mile of telegraph poles, even ritual serious dancers under flowering catalpa trees giving a Chinese play on the rim of a burning town. In China, he decided, history is past the point of irony, and rape a spectator sport. And there were so many Chinese; like that year in Montana when the locusts in the billions came out of the ground, and the family elms were dying of Dutch blight.

Carefully, seated on his bedding, he wrote out his notes in the Baptist Mission. The black sergeant got friendly with one of the general's machine gunners—originally from an Alabama chain gang.

"Sergeant, you're a mine of information."

"Yes sir, major. That General Tsung-chang, this 'Bama boy

says he's got this big tool for love what takes eighty-six silver dollars piled one on the other to measure its size, so they call him Ole Eighty-Six, in gook talk, *Lao pa-shih liu*."

"I wish," said Lieutenant Wallibee, smoking the last good cigar, "we knew more of his war plans."

"We'll know." Simon prepared to shave as Wong Li brought in a bowl of hot water. "We're going to dinner at his *yeman*."

They gave up their weapons on entering the party—and never got them back. It wasn't a dinner that Simon, or any of his party, was ever to forget. The brandy flowed and the champagne was in cut-glass cups. Officers: White Russians and Chinese caroused with town women.

General Chang Tsung-chang, seated on a Mandarin chair throne, looked even more than seven feet tall. A magnificent barbarian, he beamed at Simon, offered cup after cup of brandy. Simon decided this overuniformed hulk of muscle and guts was mad with living, packed with cruelty. Cunning, too, and with an army that might be powerful enough to make it worthwhile for the Americans to humor him. As one official in the legation had once put it to Simon: "What we need are limited massacres here—no one big man."

The general held out a fresh glass of brandy to Simon. His interpreter said: "General drink to Mr. Washington, to Mr. Rinkin, Mr. Voodroo Werson."

Simon held up the glass, tried to be heard over the din of the party. "I drink to the general's prowess, of which we've all heard."

The huge general, face carnation-red, chuckled, made some obscene remark in an officer's ear. Simon went on. "To China, the Middle Kingdom, the Center of the World, to its great past, its flowing future, to the general."

"*Dangran!*"

The drinking went on. The Russians gave Cossack howls, women screamed, Turkish cigarettes were smoked. Java cigars were lit, servants hurried around with trays of strange delicacies. The interpreter said: "General would like you view his coffin."

"His *what?*" Simon and Ollie Wallibee had just rejected two Japanese girls, faces painted white, smelling of unwashed gar-

[223]

ments and sweat. "Coffin. Always general with it. Very much teakwood. Also fine carved and lacquered. Coffin on train car outside. Very grand coffin like for Ming king."

"Yes, I suppose it is worthy of him." Simon grimaced out what he hoped was a smile at the general.

The general gripped Simon's shoulder in one ham of a hand, gently, and began a high, whining speech ending in uproarious laughter. The interpreter bowed. "He say he, the honorable general, always returns from battle sitting on coffin, smoking and happy drunk. If he not ever win victory, he will return inside coffin. . . . You *Lao mao tze*—now come see coffin."

Simon leaned toward Wong Li hovering behind him, offering him hot, wet napkins. "What the hell is *Lao mao tze?*"

"Mean Old-Hairy-Fella. That what the general call white devil foreigner. You—major. You go see train now and coffin."

The train car was paneled in bird's-eye maple. Simon remembered the huge crimson coffin and the last glass of brandy of the night. The general filled the world like the giant in Jack and the Beanstalk—bending over him, bottle in hand, and Simon muttering "Ho, ho, hum!" Next morning, Simon had what Wong Li called the grandmother of all gong-banging heads. Ollie Wallibee, lamenting the loss of their weapons, was drafting Simon's notes of the past two days:

"Lots of carts with safe-conduct flags . . . means local bandits or war conditions. . . . Bandits are blackmailing the villages . . . mud walls being mended in fear of raids. Soldiers all over railroad yards. No discipline, apathetic young conscripts. Order kept by official executor with very huge wide sword called a *da-bao* —lopping off a head here and there. Hope to recover our service revolvers."

"Don't talk so loud, Ollie. Your voice jars me. What did Mr. Dock report that's vital to our mission?"

"White Russian cavalry, drunk most of the time. The city of Yüchchow is one big wreck filled with camps of refugees . . . crippled ex-soldiers every place. Merchants hoarding food, supplies are very low. I counted ten dead bodies in the street this morning. Famine is already here. People just step over the dead—nobody cares—population starving. Eating the pressed-bean residue usually fit only to fertilize the fields. Farmers' carts and horses and young men have all been seized for the army. Houses are torn down for firewood. The Russky cavalry are some show, major—dark-green uniforms, yellow leather boots and lances, honest-to-God pigstickers in stirrup sockets. But armed with long-barreled Mauser pistols."

"How many horse soldiers are there?"

"Just a hundred of them. Also a Russian infantry brigade under a Russian General Netchaeff, a child molester, a cocaine-sniffing bastard."

Simon smiled. "No place for clean, unarmed Americans like us, eh? What about native troops, Chinese?"

"Say three thousand on four armored trains. Mr. Dock says run by Russians. Also he counted twenty locomotives, two hundred freight cars."

"Soldiers well armed?"

"Thirty, only thirty out of a hundred men have rifles, says Mr. Dock, and half the soldiers are under fourteen—lots of them shoeless."

"But what are they up against?"

"Armed peasants called the Red Spears, major. Fighters from the countryside. Got organized to fight off the general's looters and rapists. They kill and fight pretty good. Impression is the general's army is scared of them. The general's army hasn't been paid for a year, and they're living on mantou, rice, and water —lots of water. Rumor is his rival, Feng Yü-hsiang, holds Chengchow. So our general may ride inside his coffin yet."

"Feng is damn good, Ollie, has been to Moscow and heads the Kuominchin. Trained two hundred thousand men in Shensi. We better move on."

"I hear Feng, he'll double-cross everybody, this Christian general."

"Maybe, but he doesn't let the soldiers abuse the people like Tsung-chang does."

Ollie Wallibee went out to the telegraph office with Simon's report in code, to send it to the legation. He came back shaking his head.

"No dice, major, office closed and the operators all gone over the hill. It looks like the general is pulling out—harem, coffin,

[225]

and all. I saw six trains leaving. When they're all gone, the southern army will come in and we'll be in danger of being shot."

"That's cheerful, Ollie."

Mr. Dock came in, face sunken in as usual. "I tried, major, to get you on one of the troop trains, the *Tuchun*'s train. Offered money, tinned goods. No good. Madness in the railroad station and yards. People clinging to roofs and windows. Saw some run over when they fell off. Little boy's legs cut off. And no luck in getting your weapons. General's orders—no."

Simon wondered about the world of the irrational, patterns of incongruity. "I think we stay and wait for the southerns."

"We can go west," Ollie Wallibee said.

Mr. Dock shook his head: "Red Spears there. And Russians to the east. Major—I have been in touch with the southerns. I think for you all to stay is safer. But—" Mr. Dock made a gesture suggesting hope is the last sin. McMaster winked at Wong Li.

That night, looting and firing, some shrill dimensions of screaming took over the city. For two days the general's army and camp followers moved out, going north. The only break in the tension was a stray Nationalist plane that came out of a pink cloud and dropped some bombs that splattered dirt on people. The Russians held the station with a steel-clad armored train bristling with machine guns and with a naval cannon mounted in the rear. The Russians were snap-shooting for fun, leaving bodies all over the tracks. Some Russians moved off, massacring villages, stealing what they could. Simon and Wallibee were shaken by the callousness of the White Russians, and by the brutality of the retreating Chinese. Sergeant McMaster and Wong Li were placid—as nonwhites they seemed to accept and wait.

Mr. Dock took risks in watching the railyards and station. Simon wrote reports—feeling pent in, powerless, reflecting on the immediacy of death. They hid all the notes in the cracks between bricks in a deserted house next door. They lived dyspeptically from cans and some undercooked, filthy rice Mr. Dock managed to get to them. It was clear to Simon that Mr. Dock was playing both sides and profiting in rice sales.

On the dawn of an overheated morning, Mr. Dock, his facial creases red with excitement, his hands way up his sleeves, came to them with a bag of little bean-and-honey cakes and a bottle of native wine.

"Oh, it's a fine morning. God's morning. The Kuomintang army is here!"

"When they get in?" Simon began to get his boots on.

"Late last night. Very good army. No looting, no fornication of virgins. No beating anybody, just shooting a few hoarding merchants. But I think you all better stay in here. Soldiers don't know you're here." Mr. Dock began an elaboration of what white men had done to lose face in China.

Simon refused to stay indoors. He decided to go out and make contact. Ollie shrugged. Sergeant McMaster smiled a gold-toothed smile and unbuttoned the flap of his empty pistol-holster. "Be prepared, major."

Simon adjusted his crumpled uniform, rubbed a chin needing a shave. "I'm going out alone, just with Wong Li. If I don't come back in an hour, Ollie, Mr. Dock will get someone to lead you to the south, Shanghai. That's an order, lieutenant—and close your damn open mouth with some rice cakes."

Mr. Dock, in a bleat with a lisp in it, said, "I would not advice it, going out, major."

The streets were full of Kuomintang flags. Welcome banners in red were blossoming on shops and buildings. There were even gangs of workers repairing shop fronts. Dead and dying were still underfoot. Simon stepped over them. The railroad station and yards were bare of trains, of any rolling stock. Refugees moved like walking corpses, begging, offering what they had. The stink of death, of rotting animals, of human flesh in burned-out ruins was choking. Simon and Wong Li pressed through the packs of frightened, beaten people, smelling of their own offal. A patrol in loose uniforms, floppy caps, came around a corner, to suddenly face Simon and Wong Li. A southern *ping*, Wong Li said, of boys. Mostly looking about fifteen years of age. Even the officer, runty, thin, was bug-eyed at the sight of Simon. *"Ni dzar dzwo shemma!"* Wong Li lifted his hands, palms forward, and cried out something. The officer yelled back. Wong Li said to Simon, "Ah, good luck—majah. They like Americans. They say Americans will help them fight a good war."

"Tell them anything they want to hear. Also that we're friends." Simon's face remained calm—but he had to admit to a stomach stuffed with ground glass.

There was more talk and a shaking of hands by Simon, hands, most of them never washed. The scent of garlic like a gas attack in the Great War. Simon smiled, the boy soldiers smiled, the officer grinned, took Simon's offered pack of Camels. Wong Li bowed and waved. As they walked away, Simon asked, "Anything you learned from them?"

"Majah, there is one train coming, going south. Only train left, freight train. Coming through here, officer say, five o'clock, six o'clock, who know."

"We better get on it."

"Very hard to get on. But I talk to station massah. Cost a lot." Wong Li rubbed his two thumbs and forefingers together. *"Kumshaw."*

Simon lifted an arm as if to slap the coolie, then smiled. "Just leave your share of the cut out of it. Or I'll drop you off here to the mercy of the army."

"Majah made good joke. *Shr?*"

"Bushr," said Simon. "Major one sonofabitch about chiseling bastard of a servant."

Chapter 28

ELEVEN days later Major Copperwood and his party made contact with a mounted infantry unit of the United States Army, to the west of Shanghai. They were not in what the major called "perfect marching order," being without arms, having been abused by some peasants at an inn, and having just escaped that morning from a band of Kuomintang soldiers hunting supplies. But wrapped in a soiled shirt and carried tied around his

[228]

stomach were Simon's notes and several rude maps. He had not told the lieutenant or the sergeant about the maps because it was a damn foolish thing to have maps that could get them executed if captured. He blamed this selfish detail on the fact he was suffering from a fever.

Major Copperwood's journey—six weeks of investigation —became famous in the Chinese world of legations and international settlements. His technical and political reports on the southern armies, the warlords, the military appraisals, were later pointed out as classics. He wrote them all out in the Peking Legation, suffering from some obscure tick fever—working from notes, a solid, no-nonsense charting of the Kuomintang, the Marxist forces. He gave very good judgment to the Kuomintang for morale, confidence, and discipline. They were, he wrote, head and shoulders above any other Chinese military force. They did not loot or rape, the people welcomed them, the officers were young and full of morale and ideals. Perhaps not as well-armed as the northern armies—they had a better fighting spirit. He noted they were short of trains, both locomotives and cars, and so were stranded for the time being in Yüchow. He added that in his opinion, when they moved onward again, they would destroy Chang Tsung-cheng, as only his White Russians would really stand and fight. Chiang Kai-shek remained an enigma—a buttoned-up question mark.

Washington was impressed. There was an official set of laurels to be garnered by Simon, a letter for a few important desk trays, from the general in command of the USAFC, speaking of Simon's and Lieutenant Wallibee's "intrepid magnificent Army qualities and personal courage.... Major Copperwood showing the highest type of military efficiency, splendid intelligence, determination, and conduct in six harrowing weeks of work in the interior. ... Major Copperwood presenting the highest courage of an individual Army officer who, in close, dangerous contact, and with a small party, unaided, moved among thousands of hostile, anti-foreign Chinese soldiers of several contending armies, collecting information. He was the only person available to us with that necessary combination of military knowledge and skilled in the Chinese language and background.

He and his group carried out a mission to hostile areas and returned with the most vital information. . . ."

Colonel Roger Millhouse read the letter to his classes at West Point.

Lieutenant Oswald Wallibee—with a touch of dysentery—was given a three weeks' leave to Japan. There was a promotion to captain in the works. Sergeant Lloyd McMaster, on his return, got into a wild crap game in the legation garages in Peking, and was slightly knifed, a slash across his right cheek. But he got back from the regiment his top-sergeant's stripes—which he had lost twice before. He was sent down to the coast to instruct some newly arriving companies from the States, in the proper attitude to the Chinese population. "Now you pay attention. Remember, you'll find 'Old Hundred Names'—that's what they call the fella in the streets, not a bad Joe at all, and as for the women. . . ."

Wong Li took up his duties again in the barracks, expanding into a moneylender, taking a second wife. Simon and Ollie had a last dinner of *Jow Jing Chuen-aap*—duckling steamed in a white wine, and *Fooyung Haryun* shrimp, at the Rabbit-of-the-Moon eating place near the Peking railroad station. "It was touch and go, Ollie, with General Tsung-chang. I didn't trust Mr. Dock, and later when we were on that train unarmed—it looked bad."

"Well, if I ever again am stupid enough to go volunteering for such a butt-kicking mission, I hope it's with you, Simon."

"Don't go haywire in Japan—you're on sick leave."

"Going to Kyoto, hunt up old junk, Buddhist prints. Take on a load of the geishas in the Yoshawara, try the saki. What about you?"

"I want to set down some text on the future of warfare here and elsewhere. Ideas on mechanical brigades I have, and moving whole divisions by air. Maybe drop them by chutes."

"When you're a general, Simon, remember me. I'm loyal, clean, and think your ideas are daffy."

"I hope we can get together—chew the fat again."

Simon never spoke to Oswald Wallibee again. After several exchanges of long letters, their destinies seemed to separate.

(Colonel Oswald Wallibee died in 1944, moving through the minefields of the Hürtgen Forest. General Copperwood, in command of two divisions of the Second Army, moving his armored columns down from Aachen in the blue-cold November, had pointed out to him the body of his companion in the Chinese adventure, lying by a burned-out recon car. A portly, gray-haired corpse, badly mangled. The general turned away with a mind suddenly packed full of long-stored-away memories of when he was young and in China. And how after that, through his own fault, his career went all haywire, all wrong, with no hope of rising in the Army chain of command. A discard, shoved off to obscure posts far from the center of things.)

It was after returning from Yüchow that he met Sarah Upchurch, the wife of Senator Chester Upchurch.

Chapter 29

"You can always rile the British," Colonel Nast used to say to his officers going on leave, "by referring to it as 'Hong Kong, China,' and not, as they call it, 'Hong Kong, British Crown Colony,' or just 'Hong Kong, B.C.C.'" And it was a difference, Major Copperwood thought, even if still, in 1932, ninety miles south of Canton, this splinter was called "Hong Kong Island," the "Kowloon Peninsula," and the "New Territories." United States Army officers, delighted to go on leave there, favored the Miramar and the Peninsula, the Repulse Bay hotels. There was too much of a jam in the crowded city itself; in Victoria, packed tightly just under the Peak, with the yeasty spawning of humanity. It was so given to vice and sensuality, Lieutenant Wallibee insisted, that it would "stir the gallstones of old virgins."

Major Copperwood always told the officers there were no subtleties in Hong Kong, just intriguing fun, and to avoid the Rotary International, but scrounge guest cards for admission to the Toya Hong Kong Club, the Jockey, and the Cricket Club. "Don't go after girls in the Sai Ying Pun and Wanchai sections.

Better ask your doorman of the hotel or the club stewards for proper poontang." He made it clear to all ranks that Kwangtung, Macao, was out of bounds; the Portuguese colony's citizens had the bad habit of drugging and robbing, and the police of tossing guests into their jails. And of not being impressed by American Legation demands for setting free a member of the United States armed forces in China without paying enormous fines. Simon was expecting promotion to colonel; time, too—after all that work he had done on his reports, the great exploit of his six weeks' expedition. But delay seemed a strategy in the War Department.

Hong Kong represented to Simon and for the legation people an escape hatch, an assembly point far from the prying eyes of their superiors. There were new girls, both native and European, also traveling American flappers, debutantes. And one's credit might be stretched beyond what one owed Chinese moneylenders on the mainland. Simon, always short of cash, managed to avoid any heavy debts.

He had saved up his leaves and had three weeks free—on his own. He stayed in Hong Kong, not at one of the big hotels, but high up over the harbor at a pension run by a French couple. (Or, at least, Jean Paul Balbac had a French grandfather, a sailor and smuggler.) His wife, Vicky, was Chinese, the daughter of three generations of Hong Kong servants at the Victoria Club.

While serving Simon breakfast, she spoke of her pride in her island status. "Bloody mainlanders, con't pronounce an *r* properly, and smell of garlic. Don't know how you stood them, major."

"I like them, Vicky." He looked down at the breakfast tray she had set before him. Pink ham and golden eggs, grits, toasted French bread, good yellow country butter, English marmalade, and a Queen Anne silver pot of hot coffee.

"Too much of that soy and bean curd, major, and your eyes will begin to slont." She laughed, jiggled, all her two hundred and ten pounds, enjoying her poor-mouthing of Chinese cuisine. "This cum by special messenger."

Simon took the stiff linen-paper envelope, sealed with yellow wax in which was impressed an image of a lion wearing a crown, and the letters V.C.

"Victoria Cross?" he asked, hefting the envelope.

"Victoria Club. Smashing posh club too, no naggers or Buddha-faces. My grandfather was maître d'hôtel there. The Prince of Wales, grandfather of this one, gave him ten golden coins, sovereigns they were—still in the family. Must be having a bloody fine party at the Victoria."

Simon was reading the enclosure on the stiff club paper:

DEAR MAJOR COPPERWOOD, the American Consul in Hong Kong invites you to the Anglo-American Society's Dinner Dance honoring British and American guests in Asia. Your presence has been suggested by General Buckley Hollister. The Legation staff and its guests will be most interested in your adventures in the interior of China.

Anne Burgmeyer,
Sec: to J. Hapgood Ott, U.S. Consul

"Dinner Dance. Hell, it's an order from the War Department that I attend."

Vicky nodded. "Block tie. But you'll go in uniform, of course. Medals, all of that."

"Damned if I'll go at all. Anglo-American hogwash." He attacked the ham and eggs. He hardly cared for fancy parties. Had enough of those in Washington, years ago. Simon preferred some cheerful gung-ho with some fellow officers, not-too-discreet drinking. If in the mood, some of the Chinese girls later, with their carved-ivory skins, slit skirts, all charm and skills. It was not fully satisfactory for him, and rather routine. Somehow he had not been in the condition, or the situation for having anything like a liaison with European or American women. Truth was, he admitted, he feared entanglements. He wanted no more of marriage. No, not just yet. Perhaps when he made major general. *If, when.* Meanwhile he'd better go to this party—Buck Hollister was pushing that promotion to colonel.

Simon said to Vicky Balbac, "Yes, the full-dress uniform, all the ribbons and medals." He permitted himself a large dollop of thick country cream in his coffee.

"The things I do for the Army, Vicky."

The pipe major of the Cameroons was playing his solo pibroch on his bagpipe: "Desperate Battle of the Birds."

As was only fitting for the wife of a United States Senator, Sarah Upchurch, escaping during the solo, came striding across the hallway off the ballroom: music by the Royal Scottish Orchestra (half Chinese). She was in, rather than wore, a daring gown of sheer blue moire sea silk to set off the red-gold of her hair, which she wore not in the prevailing fashion of the bob or shingle, but twisted to the side and caught up in a glistening chignon behind one ear. She was large . . . and young, with a spontaneous, casual walk. The Senator had married her when she was twenty-four, the older women present had whispered—right off two thousand acres of fairly good upcountry tobacco land. And, added the U.S. Consul's wife, "on which he held a hefty mortgage." There was about this tall girl a jocosity and enthusiasm. Simon felt it while standing under the painting of Warren Hastings mounted on an Indian elephant. Simon was holding a glass of scotch, enjoying the sight of the girl. She had a familiar kind of country-bumpkin charm done up in a Bergdorf-Goodman gown, and a fresh hairdo already a bit in disorder. Yes, she looked as if she didn't give a fiddler's damn about her appearance. He bet with himself that those magnificent, but by no means slim, legs would perhaps have just a hint of wrinkled stockings. But no, only a run moving toward the right knee. It delighted him—it was his third scotch—to find so magnificent a creature in some human disorder. He figured she was a bit bored by the unctuous, sleek ladies of Hong Kong's white, ruling, old-China-hands class.

"Where in this hothouse monkey cage can I get a drink of bourbon, soldier?" She was addressing him in a country drawl, not "youall" and fake magnolia blossoms, but in good-natured near-intimate tones, not hurried.

"I'm sorry, but maybe it's in short supply here. Pérignon Curé? No? Dom Pérignon? No? You want that bourbon on the rocks, with branch water?"

She smiled and took his arm. "Well, here's somebody that doesn't talk through his nose. I'm Sarah Upchurch."

"Major Copperwood. I've seen your pictures in the papers, Mrs. Upchurch, with the Senator."

"My coloring doesn't show in those pictures."

"It doesn't," he agreed. A tan on good pink. Gray-green eyes and that twenty-dollar double-eagle gold-coin hair. At the busy bar he got a glass of what passed for bourbon and water in Hong Kong, and ice cubes, and from under the thrashing ceiling fans, they went out onto a terrace. Below was the deep purple of the bay and the junks, the two proud intruders, white around-the-world liners. The city itself was clinging to the hillside—dark, deep olive-green in the shadows. The streetlights were beaded together in the descending loops of a necklace.

Sarah sipped her drink. "You like this brawl, captain?"

"Major—gold oakleaf, Mrs. Upchurch. No, I don't enjoy it. But maybe like you, I'm on duty, ordered to be here."

"You too?" She sipped and laughed, a good open-air laugh, showing fine white teeth with just a little spacing and a faint wet glint of a gold inlay way back. "Duty's children, aren't we, major? Is that China off there in the dark blue?"

"This too is China under our feet, in a way. Yes, across there, if this were daylight, you'd see something that is the mainland."

"The Middle Kingdom. I learned that at the university."

She sat down in a wicker seat and slipped off blue slippers from very small feet for such a large girl. Her hands, too, he noticed, were small. In the light of the lanterns, he enjoyed her cleavage and experienced his bleakness, loneliness like stabs in his lower guts.

"Jesus, look, a run again. My last damn pair of silk stockings."

"There's a Japanese shop—Jennie Hokusai's on On Lan Street, that is said to have the best silk stockings in Asia."

There was no vacillating about her. "Let's get away from here. All they talk about is polo, servants, recognition or nonrecognition of Manchoukuo. What the devil is *that*?"

"*That* used to be Manchuria before the Nips seized it this year. Before they invaded Shanghai."

"I should know, shouldn't I? Since the Senator helped draw up the Stimson Doctrine."

"That doctrine—it really doesn't mean anything. Sorry, no offense to the Senator—us not recognizing the gains achieved by armed force. The Japanese don't give a hoot."

[235]

She held up a small evening bag of meshed gold. "Let's go buy the stockings."

"Should you leave before—"

She hooked her arm in his. "You don't want to lead me in the Lancers' square dance, do you?"

"No, rather have you all by myself."

"Listen to *you*, major."

He felt it's all so commonplace and enjoyable—no smart London-Washington dialogue that stings with scorpion tails.

From the ballroom came the first notes of some Irving Berlin tune. Hands clasped, moving quickly, they fled to the hall where Chinese servants passed with trays of pungent tidbits. They moved out to where small taxis waited.

"I've always wanted to own black-lace stockings—they're so *outré*, major. Is that the word? Had a French teacher at the university used it a lot."

"That's as good a word for black lace as any."

They were naked in bed together in Simon's room at the Balbac pension by half past midnight. They were in the grip of mutual spontaneous drives—very much taken with each other, using to the full the revelance of their passion in splendid accelerating desires, delighted with themselves, the living immediacy. Sarah muttering, "Oh, God, Simon, oh, God, if you only knew how long it's been since I've had a real deep feeling for this—Oh, God, had it like this, *this*. . . . God!"

He mouthed her cheeks—he was locked in some marvelous vertigo—kissed her strong neck, her hair—a green-apple-and-wood-ash smell—hair once so carefully prepared for the ball. Now in a mess of golden disorder in the light from the bronze Ming lantern that hung over them, a light swaying a bit in the humid air.

"Oh, you be good to me, Simon, you bastard. Good like this. It's been such a nothing. . . . Washington, being a Senator's wife. Not Chester's fault, he's too old for me, sixty-two. And so damn busy and goddamn excited, sitting in the catbird seat on all those important committees. . . . You do really love me? It's not just you were horny? You don't think I'm a cheap lay, do you?"

He buried his face in her hair and mumbled, "MMM, mmmm. Mmmm."

It was a week, ten days, like that—the patterns of the moods, images of their emotions, physical kaleidoscope, always confusing, yet pleasing.

For the first time in a long while he thought of his betrayal by Ada. Forgiveness is a great luxury, he decided. He was meeting Sarah Upchurch for lunch at the Cathay Seaview, which specialized in Szechwan cooking, then he was going to show her the Tiger Balm Garden. . . . Christ, I fall in love the way some people fling themselves out of a window. He tapped at the glass pane of the French door of his room, standing in a dressing gown, smoking a small Java cigar and feeling a flow through him of a lifting of spirits. An exhilaration he had not felt for a long time. That had brought on the thoughts of Ada. How he had felt those first months with her, the total, virtuoso delight in the games of love! After their divorce, Ada had gone to Europe with her father, made some headlines with the Cole Porter, Elsa Maxwell crowd in Paris. There had been a fistfight over her in the Brick Tops nightclub and, reported the Paris *Herald,* she had met Hemingway at Jimmy's Bar. She, a bit high, had said, "An infinite world aware of its infinities." And Hem had answered, "Yep." A year later, Ada married the chairman of the board of an aircraft firm bidding with the War Department for the design of a fighter plane, something improved over the Grumman F3F's. Souki Miller had written Simon news of Ada from time to time; "Ada and her husband live on a dandy country estate, Grayoaks, in North Carolina. They ride with the Pickwick Hunt, have two children, and Ada is slim as a snake."

Simon was sure he no longer had any feelings for Ada. She had no intrinsic significance for him. He did not even have contempt for her—their life together was all just a blurring of fast-moving images, as in a motion picture film strip projected on a screen when it runs at too fast a speed and out of focus—just before it tears. He had not wanted to ever go through such a time again. He lifted up an arm and looked at his watch, beating like a heart. He was at the moment of decision. It was damn clear he was deeply in love again. Deeply earnest. Maybe in love to the

[237]

point of madness. In love you don't recover your personal existence, as from a dream. He had come to believe falling in love, and the whole incubation period of love, was a kind of insanity in which the lover and the loved find a change in the colors, in words, in tones of voice, all different.

And the love object; a touch, a blue vein on a slim ankle, crisp crackle of hair seemed more precious than life itself. Christ, he sighed as he turned from the view, mashed out the remains of the little cigar in a green soapstone tray. Its color, its texture, made him think of the Chinese girl, Mai—and his (?) son in his little Sung cap, and the staring infant Buddha-baby eyes. That was—he shrugged evasively—at best a caprice; good word, "caprice." Good as Sarah's *outré*. At worst a selfish indulgence in a Chinese custom—without love but, truth is, with much feeling. Nothing repellent in it—it was another time for me, tainted by place and situation.

Simon had no doubts he must have Sarah. She was—silly comparison—like the hot potatoes his Aunt Dolly used to put in a sock and push against his shivering body on cold Montana nights. He was ten at the time, and the warmth of Aunt Dolly's love and the hot potatoes gave comfort and a sense of being comforted—a warmth in his groin, the first sensual awareness of the rightness of a thing.

So, too, that was the warmth of Sarah's long, solid body, part of the perfect coordination of their emotional drives and needs, too, for each other. A drive, he was to realize, much later, that pushed from his mind any idea, or much interest in, what the situation would appear like to gossip in Hong Kong, or how Senator Upchurch would take this breakup of his marriage. Simon, at some precarious emotional peak, felt the Army understood that a man is a man and not a gelded cat. It would all work out. He had friends in power in the service, men who thought of him as a future general. Jeff Astruc was now a well-positioned staff officer. Buck Hollister, Roger Millhouse, Arnold Rosegold. (No, Rosey had retired to grow old in Pasadena.) And Wallie Elkins was dead, and buried in Arlington. Simon saw his situation as a sort of reward; oh, maybe a sticky moment or two, here and there—but it would be all right once one saw the natural perception of things. Yes.

After lunch—and sips of Grand Marnier—he and Sarah went out to the beach resort at Shek-o in the old village of Dragon Back Peninsular, and they lay under a beach umbrella in their damp bathing suits; so good a feeling in the humid air. Sarah's tight, one-piece suit was a royal butterfly blue, her hair was golden coins in the white sunlight, loose on her shoulders. She sipped on her Tom Collins, looking to Simon like one of those old paintings of the cornfed Goddess of Plenty one saw on the walls of country banks; a goddess holding a horn from which hung local wheat and apples and pumpkins to overflowing. Sarah, with her usual casualness, Simon observed, had repaired one shoulder strap with the wrong color thread.

"Seriously, Simon love, I can't file for divorce until after the next November elections. Chet is running against some Populist hayseed, the farmer's friend. So you can see—"

"November, hell."

"It's gotta be that way, love," she said, smiling, rubbing the spot on the sunburned top of his head where the hair was thinning.

She shifted her position; they lay hip to hip.

"You like war?" she asked.

"It's too murderous, yet fascinating, to ever like."

"How's that?"

"War is just the most dreadful disciplined thing on the planet. So much so that I sometimes wonder if man isn't nature's biggest mistake. War stains loyalties, wipes out decencies, yet guarantees no permanent peace."

"Why, then, are you a soldier?"

"I like Army life. War has a male challenge—for some of us a groin-tightening kick. Also, it's an affirming attitude, Army life—no slackness like you find among civilians. I can't see myself selling Packards, or brownnosing a chairman of the board of a firm that makes cornflakes or sparkplugs."

The fruit-green waters, the odor of thyme, sweet basil, drainage was in the air.

"In a sense I know somebody has to protect the fat people of the Republic—who in peacetime despise us—don't understand it's a world of wolves, Sarah. Yes, and somebody has to be ready when trouble comes to see they don't get gobbled up." He made grunting sounds and began kissing her arm from elbow to shoulder.

"I used to think generals made wars, love, but it's politicians, don't you think?"

"It's adrenal-filled neurotics who seize power by votes or bayonets. Doesn't matter how—they set history in motion."

He took her hand, palm up, traced her life line.

"To me, the Army is like the protective abrasive between opposing forces. Or simply, it's a bulldog you keep to drive off dangerous tramps, protect the family herd. You hope the tramp never shows up, but it's good to have a bulldog at your feet with all his teeth. . . . No chance of us not waiting until after November?"

"It's that kind of a state Chet comes from, where a divorce before an election would just blow him out of politics ass over teakettle."

"Pretty holy?"

"Everybody is always playing around till their feathers shine—all sorts of running around after dark pronging high-yella girls. But in hard daylight you'd think butter wouldn't melt in their mouths. It's churchgoing white Protestant morality. Just like that."

"I was planning to go back to the War College in Kansas for a year after we get married. I'll be a chicken colonel—the eagle on my shoulders then."

She led his hand to her stomach and he scratched lightly.

"Kansas doesn't sound too good to me, Simon. I've had all the farm culture I want. A wheatfield, a grove of trees, doesn't het me up like a good chic Parisian shop. My ideal is a really high-tone city apartment with servants that really are servants, not dumb Doras brought in off the fields."

"The War College is pretty cozy."

He bought her a cheongsam—a charming Chinese dress. They took one more dip in the tepid sea, and made love in the hired room.

Sarah said she was beginning not to feel any sense of sin. He told her she was someone he would delight in educating into all the nuances of love. They dressed, laughing, eating nectarines, juices flowing down their faces, and took a ride on the Peak Train to the top. Below them was a wide expanse like a child's toy modeling hills and hillsides, and a city of building blocks, a sea made of a mirror on which model sampans and junks were set, and the white luxury ship needed only to have its spring wound up to move out onto a glass surface. The painted backdrop of green and clay-brown distance could be the Chinese land mass. Then several objects moved and the illusion became reality. The sky was too perfect. "A Maxfield Parrish blue," Sarah called it, "with little woolly lamb clouds."

They made an impressive couple standing on top of a land mass. A Hindu photographer with an ancient camera on a tripod took their picture, arms around each other, leaning very close, cheeks touching, smiling. The photographer developed it on the spot in little chemical containers, washed it in a pot attached to the tripod, waved it in the air to dry, then inserted the picture into a yellow cardboard frame lettered in false silver. SOUVINEER OF HONK KONG, 1932.

"One dollah, please, sahib, sir."

It was the same picture Senator Upchurch's lawyers produced—with other evidence—nine months later, after his reelection. Vicky Balbac of the Balbac pension had stolen it and sold it to the detectives. The Senator sued for divorce on grounds of adultery. The picture was reproduced in his hometown paper, the Tefftallow *Weekly News*. It brought him over three dozen letters of condolence and one, block-printed in crayon, with the message THE WAGES OF SIN ARE DEATH.

On his wedding day Simon sat in his shorts in a room in San Francisco's St. Francis, thinking he had reached safety again after dark. Back in Montana, as a small boy, coming home late from the Empire movie house, he wondered, in the shadows of an early-winter twilight, if he could reach home and warmth and aunt and uncle before some monster ate him. It was again that feeling of reaching the warm lights of home, making it safely once more. Sarah would be there from now on, aware of his soft underside, the hidden self of doubts that was coated with a hard shell. In her arms, comfort, in her respect, a sureness of purpose, in her solid physical shape, knowledge that the earth was real and old values had a truth to them. A man could even get some change back from what he gave out of himself. He laughed and went to prepare himself to become a husband.

Book Six

We withdraw our wrath from the man who admits that he is justly punished. . . .

—ARISTOTLE

(From the notebooks of Simon Copperwood)

Chapter 30

IN all his bad years, Simon Bolivar Copperwood never got used to the clammy mists drifting in from the Pacific up the Golden Gate, the choppy water moving past seal rocks and wet cliffs. It always seemed to be raining or about to rain. Yet there were clear summer days there and visitors crossing to Marin County from San Francisco, coming for soft-shell crab, the good bouillabaisse in Sausalito. Offshore, sailboats tacked and turned. There were even old cannon by which to have one's picture taken at Fort Barry, the Fort Cronkhite Military Reservation, and in the city itself, Fort Winfield Scott, and the Presidio, which had once held a Mexican garrison.

The tourists never came to Fort Custer, farther to the west, set low on a bluff over shore boulders; a post overlooking the Pacific. The waters, residences of the sea lions, roaring in rutting season, collecting harems. The whirling gulls giving their *awk! awk!* calls as they hunted in the kelp beds for something to salvage from the fort's sewer lines, which emptied into the sea. No one seemed to care about the fort—far from the more populated places to the south and east; serviced by improved tarred and concrete roads on which trucks carrying Army supplies made contact with the Bay and the city. Soldiers talked of places to "spend oneself"—Oakland, Berkeley, Richmond, as if recalling Bombay, St. Louis, or Singapore.

Fort Custer was the Siberia of the American War Department. Two hours by only fair roads by car to San Francisco, the fort was set on sterile rocky earth where even the wind-torn Australian bluegum trees had a hard time flourishing. It was hardly a fort; rather a storage area of great plank sheds with tarpaper roofs. Barracks, in some sections, which were built for the Spanish-American War, and at a time when Americans were fighting in the Philippines against natives seeking independence. They were World War I warehouses, and high, chain-link fences surrounding ancient tanks and ambulances with wheels removed, set on blocks of wood. Simon found a park of gray-painted 75's with iron-rimmed artillery wheels, guns that had followed Pancho Villa into Mexico under Pershing in 1916.

A Congressman had said, "Fort Custer is where the War Department hides away those items it can't either destroy without accounting for them, or piles up those items it has contracted for and never found able to function in the field."

This was unfair. If the need ever came, Orderly Sergeant Peter Blacker used to say, after his sixth pint of steam beer at the Ferry Landing Bar and Grill, "For, say, wooden-hulled hoss saddles, Spencer rifles, two-ton cavalry blacksmith outfits, complete with two-hundred-pound anvils and portable bellows, mister, we got 'em at Custer." Orderly Sergeant Blacker was an ex-coal miner. He was all bone and muscle except for a huge beer paunch.

In command at Fort Custer was Lieutenant Colonel Copperwood, under some disgrace with the big brass in Washington. There were also two captains who drank, but not enough to get them kicked out of the Army; six lieutenants, mostly earnest young men unlucky enough to have duty here: four were low-graders from West Point, and two risen from the ranks, but not keen enough as yet to be tried elsewhere. The sergeants and corporals were old sweats, wise as foxes. Twenty, thirty years in the service, with shoe-leather faces, usually great drinkers, fornicators, supply stealers; stuff to trade, to keep their vices up to snuff. Splendid NCO soldiers, they lived mostly on the outer boundaries of callous indifference.

Fort Custer was a perfectly run place. Green grounds well policed, no sloppy uniforms, work clothes, or parade dress. The little lawns were close-cropped, the decaying buildings painted once a year a listless gray, and on file were the huge volumes listing inventories and rare withdrawals; kept in order. Siberia or not, "Lieutenant Colonel Iron Face," as Simon was known to the two hundred twenty enlisted men—sluffoffs, goldbricks, malingerers, bughousers (slight mental cases) and just plain morons—he kept them busy, punished fairly—by the book. It was soon clear after Lieutenant Colonel Copperwood took over a few years back that it was better to shape up and go through the motions than get confined in the stockade and miss the passes downcountry to dance music from jukeboxes, wide, careless waitresses and whores, and a chance to get charged as "Returning to fort drunk and disorderly."

Colonel Copperwood, his orderly sergeant insisted, was "pure black dog," an Army term for a man who was humorless, sunk in a kind of ritual despair. Iron Face knew he was on the S-list in Washington. Sergeant Blacker knew. But the colonel saw to the proper reveille flag-raising at dawn; turned out even the black cooks. Taps was preceded by a last inspection as to sloppiness, and the wobbling at attention caused by drinking of "moon," a deadly brew of secretly concocted alcohol, made by the cooks from yeast, prunes, and, it was rumored, flavored by Old Mail Pouch chewing tobacco. Simon fought hard a spongy pathological decay in the men, in himself.

Rain, of a dark-tea color, swept the parade ground, and the mist hid the ugliness of the old storage sheds packed with relics from the last Indian wars, tropical pith helmets tried out in the latest Latin American invasions by the soldiers sent to protect the United Fruit company's banana trees. The monthly morning visit by the traveling chaplain had occurred (Jesus homilies and an issue of condoms).

Simon's command room, with two outer orderly offices where two-fingered typing on World War I-model Underwoods went on, was of pine planking, a tin ceiling with embossed patterns, several wooden ceiling-fans, varnished oak furniture, metal desks, and filing cabinets. In his office there were two huge, yellowing photographs going into ghostlike fading: officers of the Sixth Cavalry, Pine Ridge Agency, 1891, and a Chippewa and Sioux peace treaty with William Cody, taken at Ashland, Wisconsin.

Simon, settled into rancor, was thinner than he had been in China. His hair was receding from the top of his head—there was a half dollar-sized bald spot, usually hidden by a careful combing. He never blamed his ruin of a career on his impetuous, importunate act with Senator Upchurch's wife, the Senator's appointment as Chairman of the Armed Services Committee, or with that committee's power to cut or advance Army budgets. Of course the Senator had worked to get Simon exiled to Fort Custer. And he had some pressure going that kept Simon from becoming a full colonel, to stagnate as a lieutenant colonel. "But the War Department," Simon told Sarah. "They didn't have to give in to him! I was tapped out by my own friends."

By that logic which even the clever men bow to at times, his friend Roger Millhouse had said, "Simon has twisted it all around to throw the blame on a betrayal by us, his friends."

Yes, Simon saw as unscrupulous, unctuous, General Buckley Hollister, General Raven Saunders, even Captain Jeff Astruc. They had all let themselves be steamrollered by Senator Upchurch and his Armed Services Committee into isolating Simon Bolivar Copperwood to a ghost camp. Fort Custer—named for that George Armstrong Custer who was another disaster to the Army. Senator Pearson, who did feel the unfairness of the situation, could not help Simon, for he was confined by a coronary and failing health to Walter Reed Hospital. When Simon had gone to Washington to rally forces to his aid, he had not been permitted to visit Senator Pearson. For three days he returned to the hospital waiting room on the fifth floor, and on the third day was told, "Senator Pearson died this morning at four twenty." He attended the services with a metaphysical, sepulchral feeling; he wished he were in the casket.

Jeff Astruc, with whom he and Ada had been gay and young together, was changed; gone plump, nearly hairless, baggy-eyed, and with a set smile. As they put on their gloves after the burial services, he said: "Hell, Simon, it's not as if you kicked an ambassador in the duff, or burned down an old soldiers' home while drunk. You humiliated a powerful U.S. Senator who, frankly, holds the balls of the War Department in his grip, and if he presses—*ouch!* We have to play footsy with him, sidetrack you. Of course this is all unofficial, off the record."

"I bet. What about my record? I'm no nonentity. My awards, the work I did in China. Jesus, do you know Fort Custer? It's a garbage can for Army misfits they can't press out of the service. Why are you all playing the sanctimonious bastard with me?"

"Upchurch is a swine about this. But officially, Simon, you've just got to take it. Give us a little time. You play it quietly—close to the vest—and you'll be back. You are a lieutenant colonel. That's something. After all, you stole the man's wife. Weren't the two of you thinking of consequences that—"

Simon moved toward a row of taxis. "Good-bye, Jeff." He turned and walked away. Astruc shrugged his shoulders. Simon didn't cool off until he was sipping martinis with Souki Miller in the Mayflower Hotel lounge.

Souki seemed sleeker than he remembered her. Harder too, in gay summer linen, a hat the size of a crepe pancake, with bracelets on both wrists, modern Indian work of silver and blue stones. She sat smiling, legs crossed, twirling the stem of her martini glass. "Up that famous creek and no paddle, sweetie, and nobody here can help you. General Raven Saunders tried. No dice."

"They could if they all stood up to the goddamn civilians."

"Come off it. You know better. Capitol Hill holds the Army-Navy pursestrings. Nobody in uniform is going to enrage those fat cats, not for a dame-crazy officer. Why—level with ol' Souki—why did you do it, Si?" (Simon, full of too many drinks, thought: Everything is falling away in spirals like the rind of a carefully peeled orange.)

"Waiter, another round." He looked over the plush crowd, the heavy, polished wood panels, all the cheerful people. Men with briefcases, women with beautiful made-up faces, clothes tailored to hide their imperfections. He sniffed the air; it was as the Chinese said: White people smelled too strong, did foolish things in draping their bodies so tightly. He turned toward Souki as she repeated the question, "Why?"

"Why? Oh, *why?* I don't have to explain that to every screwball in Washington. But truth is, Souki, it's a simple thing—like an apple, a snowy day." He smiled, tapped her knee with a light blow of a fist. "Plain old love as it's called in parts of this country. Maybe we just didn't place it all in the right perspective."

"You poor bastard," Souki said, as their fresh double martinis came. She lifted her glass up to eye level. "A toast. To love. To you and Sarah. I liked Sarah. She didn't like us, I mean Washington. A big farmgirl, married to that picknose slob. But she is lovable, as you know."

"There isn't much farmgirl left in her after the year we spent at the War College in Kansas. Wears shoes in Frisco, doesn't pick her teeth at table."

"She'll do great—playing bridge with the Native Daughters in San Francisco, and giving nice little dinner parties. Of course you'll take a place in the city—don't bury her at Custer. They have marvelous cracked crab and swordfish out there."

"I'm not keeping the Custer assignment."

She pressed his arm, her bracelets rattled. Her scent brought images of Ada. "Oh, come on, Si, it's old Souki you're talking to. You going to resign from the Army? Become a second-hand-car salesman or sell lots in California? You're Army and nothing *but* Army. You and Sarah, you'll make a place for yourselves. Remember Roger Millhouse spouting: 'God will find us, even behind a thousand walls'?"

"You think I'm shelved for good?"

"Let's just say you're on the Don't Open file, and your chances for getting back in your stride are fifty-fifty, sixty-forty, maybe, *against* you."

"Thanks, Souki."

"But you're young yet. Not yet forty. You'll outlive the creeps on Capitol Hill. And if someone doesn't take over old feuds, hell, the Senate is an exclusive club of atrophied lawyers, you know that. . . . You just, *just* might make it, seeing you, say, brigadier general when you're sixty, just before you retire."

Simon left Washington dreadfully depressed, determined to somehow get out of Fort Custer, but escape was hopeless. By 1937, he knew it. He'd journey to perdition without selling second-hand cars.

Back in 1933, when Hitler was made Chancellor, Simon had submitted a report analyzing the new balance of military power forming in Europe, and some reports of tank warfare the German generals were writing about. A simple note came from the Chief of Staff's office, "Noted and filed." When the Germans withdrew from the League of Nations, when Dollfuss was assassinated in Austria, when Hitler in 1935 smashed the Versailles Treaty and openly reestablished universal military training, Lieutenant Colonel Copperwood memos went to Washington.

When Italy invaded Ethiopia. When Franco brought his Moors to Spain, to cut Christian throats, he offered to go abroad to report on the armies, the new planes, the whole new kind of military philosophy he felt the Germans and the Italians were establishing. The last Chief of Staff memo sent him, read: "Army Intelligence is furnishing credible reports on all aspects you mention. Please desist. . . ."

A torpor of his mind took over. He was silent for a while. Then Hitler sent some feeble columns of German troops into the Rhineland, denounced the Locarno Pact. Simon wrote with obstinacy to Buck Hollister: "For Christ's sake, going through official channels has gotten me nowhere. It's not for myself I now write; if the Europeans let that bastard Hitler get away with the Rhineland march, it means war in Europe in five years, maybe *less*. Back the British, the French to act. This is no schizophrenic dialogue I'm presenting and I haven't got a crystal ball, but you must get the French and British to push him back now. You just may knock him out of the ballgame. He's still only working with a shell of an army. This is a bluff. Get FDR to see it. I know I'm out of it. But it's right now you have to stop a war that may ruin the planet. Don't vacillate. The Russians will be kissing Hitler's rump in public—you watch, *if* he gets away with this. If you like I'll outline what I think his real strength is in tanks, planes, big guns. I've been studying French and Russian magazines, and also what appears in German Army journals—we're facing times almost too large for life and men—and so—"

General Hollister never answered. He was busy explaining the Spanish Civil War, and later the Rome-Berlin Axis to Capitol Hill. Simon sent him a telegram: EACH AGE CREATES ITS OWN GREEKS.

The general took no action: "The poor bastard, we can't kick him out now."

Simon wrote two more letters. By that time he was drinking heavily, deep in black-dog despair, and didn't mail them. The first when Edward VIII abdicated, Simon predicting the end of the British Empire; the second warning that the execution in Russia of Marshal Tukhachevski and seven generals by "a mad dog Stalin" brought Hitler closer to owning Europe. Simon knew he was close to being dismissed with disgrace from the Army when Major Roger Millhouse flew out and spent two days talking to Simon. No one ever knew what was really said. Şimon took a six weeks' journey to the Marcus Drood Sanitarium in La Jolla. He came back thin, pill-taking, and for six months didn't touch alcohol. After which he drank socially when off duty, attended his wife's parties in their San Francisco house, with its steep stairs, at least on weekends. And made Fort Custer a hell for goof-offs and slack officers.

It was then that he began to experiment with tanks. He had a dozen old tanks in storage and he got the motors rebuilt with a crew rank and file to whom he fed weekend passes, and didn't stockade for drunken Mondays. He stripped to coveralls and got two motors put together in new ways. He had sheet-steel plate shaped to make armor for the side of tank treads. He invented a bracing bar to control wobble while going over rough ground. It was called (many years later) the Copperwood Bar and was standard on all tanks. But at the time no one paid him any attention. And he didn't write public reports on his work. He kept private files. He made blueprints of a dream tank that could move faster, spin on a dime, be watertight and air-conditioned.

He not only wrote of tanks, he built them, or, rather, rebuilt them. He himself could take apart a complicated ten-speed clutch, trace a fuel line in the dark. He put in rocket racks, even if there was as yet no rocket for it.

In three years he made himself a tank expert, a tank designer, and had moved into the future of tank planning. He wrote up a 55mm gun that fired easy and fast like a pistol and consumed its own casing, so that no brass empties would clutter the interior of the tank in battle. He welded instead of using rivets, he hunted for a perfect air system, and failed. He dreamed of a motor that would work both at 40 below zero and in the desert at 120. On paper he thought he had such a motor, but didn't dare ask Washington for parts to build one.

He was forgotten, or nearly so, and when gossip did drift out to Washington of his mad tank-games, officers who had known him just shrugged, and one or two would, at some party, say: "Copperwood? Old Sport? Buried someplace. Not all there upstairs. Had a hard show in China years ago. Yes, some scandal . . . some woman."

Then, one morning Simon locked up his files on his tank work and sent what remained of his tanks into dead storage. He took to reading Pepys' journals, and working the crossword puzzles in two-week-old copies of the New York *Times*.

Chapter 31

THE Copperwoods, or rather Mrs. Copperwood, gave what the town's society columns called marvelous parties, dinners, cocktail hours. Simon didn't take delight in the events. ("The unraveling of undistinguished minds.") He usually came in from Fort Custer only for weekends. As it seemed to delight Sarah to have ten to twelve people in for dinner at their three-story narrow house near the top of Nob Hill, with its splendid bay windows, he never objected. He remained taciturn rather than reticent.

Sarah had inherited some money salvaged from the family tobacco acres, just enough, she explained to Simon, "to have a good solid town house and to entertain a bit."

It had been a bit rundown, a house of compressed grandeur built in the nineties, that had escaped the earthquake and fire of '06. A pervading use of mahogany and teak, walnut paneling, steep sets of dangerous stairs of ebony wood imported by some shipowner, even down to the deep cellar. Simon had felt it would do Sarah good to develop a new social setting. All her Washington "friends" and acquaintances had mostly turned away from her after the scandal of the divorce.

Sarah bought the house and brought in paperhangers and painters and rolls of Paris and London wallpapers, ignored the services of decorators, installed copper plumbing and new light fixtures, broke out walls, enlarged windows for views of the bay, bridge, and city. For Simon there was what she called his "trophy room" where medals and large photographs shared space with Hokusai prints and Chinese scrolls. But no weapons; he was no collector of such things. There were shelves of books, a vast array of volumes on military subjects in French and German, which he read, or, at least, "could work my way through"; also Russian volumes with sections translated on onionskin paper, even a set of manuscripts in Japanese that a Berkeley student was digesting for him in long memos.

Sarah herself had, over the years since their meeting in Hong Kong, gone through a metamorphosis, a thinning down, a firming up of her character. The divorce, the brutality, or was it military fears and apathy? in the treatment of Simon, had given her a kind of a cause. A desire to prove their right to their way of life. Also to bring out their social side. Her ability to organize a home for Simon, to give them stature among the city's hosts and hostesses that attracted the right, most interesting, people; she fed them gourmet meals, knew wines. ("Yes, it's the true Châteauneuf-du-Pape.") She could carry on a conversation to bring a shine of gratitude to someone she was flattering.

It amazed Simon to see the change in Sarah—to wonder just how much he really knew of her, beyond the warm, wonderful companion in his bed, the good companion, the personality that had attracted him from the beginning. Socially, she presented the purity of a complete vision with extraordinary buoyancy.

There was stern stuff in Sarah, he realized, when he found one of the "work sheets," as she called them—firmly typed pages—that were handed out to the Mexican maid, Conceptia, and to the Chinese cook, Jimmy Lee. Even the Negro waitresses. The Philippino barman, Chico, who came in for the dinners got a sheet Simon cherished:

BAR, Daily servicing chart
    1. TRAYS:
        a. Round gold tray with clean linen doilie and 4 linen cocktail napkins
        b. Round silver tray with clean linen doilie on which should be:
        1. Pitcher of Arrowhead water

2. Small paper cocktail napkin
3. 4 Steuben highball glasses

2. ARTICLES NEEDED FOR MIXING DRINKS:
  a. Jigger
  b. Long spoon
  c. Small knife
  d. Bottle opener
  e. Strainer
  f. Corkscrew
  g. Bar hand-towels

3. ICE BUCKET:
  a. Ice cubes (made of Arrowhead water) and ice tongs beside bucket

4. LIQUOR TO BE STOCKED:
  (One bottle of each on bar, one bottle in storage under bar.)
  a. Gin, House of Lords
  b. Scotch, Old Rarity, Martins or Ballantines
  c. Bourbon, Harpers, Old Taylor
  d. Vodka
  e. Vermouth, Nouilly Prat, dry
  f. Vermouth, Lêjon, sweet
  g. Sherry, Harvey's Bristol Cream, Dry Sack

4a. BEER:
  Heineken's. (Keep six in refrigerator and an extra supply of six in storage.)

5. LIQUEURS:
  (Only the most frequently used are shown here. In the event of entertainment a larger selection should be available.)
  a. Creme de menthe, green
  b. Creme de menthe, white
  c. Cointreau
  d. Brandy

[255]

6. MIXES:
    a. Soda
    b. Plain water (small bottles)
    c. Ginger ale

No really famous, or notorious, best-selling freak author passed through the city on tour, without Sarah trying for his or her being a guest at one of her dinners. French and English diplomatic and military men were hungry and easy. Some of them had read Simon's little book on tank warfare; it was much more respected abroad than in the United States, and a few had read his articles in the French magazine *La Guerre*, and the Swiss publication *Kriegstat*. Welcomed were actresses, news commentators, even drifting professors with strange ideas that the world was using up the resources of the earth, this long before the subject was a vital topic at most hostesses' tables.

Orderly Sergeant Peter Blacker drove the big Cadillac through the Friday-afternoon rain and up the steep San Francisco streets, the colonel wrapped in his greatcoat (collar up) and gloom, in the back seat, the second cigar of the trip in his clamped-together jaws. The sergeant took a look into the rearview mirror. The old bastard was acting black dog, all right. A puss on him as long as Kelsey's nose. Why so dragass? He was heading for a nice booze party, the missus was a grand-looking piece of tail. And it was a long weekend till Monday morning and the mud of Fort Custer. The sergeant swung the car past a clanging cable car. It was an okay town, a boo-coo burg for a couple of days to make the rounds. If he didn't draw KP at the CO's house for the party, he'd take on a few schooners of real steam beer, the last city in the United States they still brewed the stuff; go down to North Beach and look over the quiff, toss the cubes. . . . ("I need a seven from Decatur.")

The intercom of the car barked at him. "Sergeant, Mrs. Copperwood could use you to help out this weekend. Unless you have something planned. It's an all-volunteer setup."

Bull. "Yes, sir. Be happy to, sir." Try and *not* volunteer and get the CO in an uproar. Well, maybe I can get one of the niggrah maids, one of them beginner browns. . . . He turned a corner swiftly. Blacker's people had been Cornish miners brought to the Pennsylvania coal mines seventy years ago, and he had no prejudices as to color or breed in anything female.

"Big party, sir?" The car stopped before the brown house.

"You get drunk before Sunday night and it's your stripes, Blacker."

"Yes, sir." Well, the colonel never minded too much what was left over in the bottles, Three Star Hennessy, Courvoisier, Rhum Negrite—it went to the help. He tried to smile, a smile of amity and complacency into the mirror, which showed the colonel's mug.

Simon ran up the steep steps, ignoring the cast-iron handrails, let himself into the house, the rain falling in that silent steady spill that meant it would continue all night. After Orderly Sergeant Blacker put the car away in the garage under the house, he hightailed it around to the kitchen where Jimmy Lee, the cook, handed him one of Sarah Copperwood's instruction sheets.

"You help the bartender tonight, soldier."

An hour later, Simon, in his dressing gown, comfortable on a low chair in the third-floor bedroom, sat watching Sarah make up her party face. She sat in her slip, her gun-metal-colored stockings already on, attached to a garter belt, feet in white, high-heeled slippers. A splendid figure of a woman, he decided, pleased and serene. They had been making love just half an hour before.

Simon was aware that body contact with Sarah was to him a kind of release of pressures, a dose of medicine, a treatment. In a sexual attack on her flesh, he seemed to salve himself, through physical love for Sarah, of his doubts, his miseries, the situation that exiled him from the world where he belonged. At least for part of an hour anyway. Sarah seemed to know what his violent lovemaking meant. To her it was a delight—never reprehensible. She didn't mind if she was the anvil on which he beat iron rages into shape. (Oh, hell, she thought, using a pale old-rose lipstick—what a lousy image. He was Simon, and they only had each other. Her family, what was left of it, old aunts with smelly dogs, and drinking uncles, had turned from her. Only Pappy had seemed to understand and left her the only two farms free of mortgages, assessment, and debts.)

"Who is it tonight?" asked Simon, sipping the one scotch he permitted himself before dinner. (To "cut the phlegm" was his excuse.)

Sarah, inspecting her jewel box, named a famous bisexual actress. A Frenchman who had sailed across the Pacific in a rebuilt rowboat. Two local art dealers, a radio news commentator, and a professor from Stanford who had just returned from Alaska where he had been taking the rectal temperatures of hibernating bears in their winter sleep (on a Ford Foundation grant).

Simon made no further comment. His humor was bitter these days and he knew it. It pleased Sarah to have this circus and he wanted her happy. It didn't matter to him. He needed her at ease, to assure himself he was still interested in remaining alive. Someone had once said—he couldn't remember who: "What does it all matter, as long as the wounds fit the arrows." There had been the three dreadful weeks of separation, when she had gone East to be with her dying father. Simon had promised her not to drink. He had locked himself in his trophy room—in among his military histories, his pictures of Uncle Brewster and Aunt Dolly, of himself and Bruno Holtzman in France in 1918, the rattlesnake skin Indian Charlie had mounted for him on a board of mountain oak laurel, the snapshots of the great old cars he had once owned, even rebuilt. A Haynese, Stearns-Knight, a huge Pierce-Arrow.

The first two lonely days he was in no condition to go up to Custer. He hadn't drunk all weekend—just doodled on paper. He remembered in China a Captain Hennsinger, who was slowly going mad in an isolated post in the western Nan Shan mountains, he once told Simon, and who sent away for some Mexican jumping beans advertised in a magazine. The captain named three of the beans Winkin, Blinkin, and Nod, and talked to them seriously for four months until he was relieved.

There were no Mexican jumping beans in San Francisco, or at least he couldn't find them in any of the shops. He bought instead a three-dollar windup Japanese tin alarm clock. It had a loud metallic click. In some contemptible travesty of sense, he talked to it. It had a friendly ticking that he grew very fond of. He wound it faithfully every night with a lover's touch, feeling the tension of its spring getting tight. He talked to it for hours, and it cheerfully ticked on, as if nodding, agreeing with his conversation, knowing he had unrealized potentialities. The alarm clock's ticking kept him sane and sober until Sarah came back. She was two days overdue, having had to bury her father in Presbyterian dignity and attend to legal matters with the estate lawyers.

She had plainly been worried about Simon. He said he had been outlining a book he planned to do one day on Grant's Vicksburg campaign. But she saw later that it all actually turned out to be meaningless doodles and words of old popular songs in a loose-leaf notebook.

As he finished his scotch, and Sarah slipped into her gown, he asked her: "Whatever happened to that alarm clock that was on the shelf in the closet of my den?"

"Alarm clock? Really, Simon. Get into your evening clothes."

"What happened to it? I notice it's not there anymore."

"I gave it to the cook when he asked for it; when I sent Jimmy over to the Salvation Army with the other stuff."

"I'd like it back. I wish you—"

She turned, wriggling to adjust her gown, looking fastidiously amused, miraculously transformed, not at all the farmgirl scared of Washington life, the Sarah of their first meeting. The hostess now, the proper social presence, stance, frame of mind. "Really, Simon, on *one* scotch."

Simon forgot to ask the cook about the alarm clock, for the radio commentator, a fussy, round little man, came to dinner with the news that the U.S. gunboat *Panay* had been sunk by Japanese planes on the Yangtze, and two Americans had been killed and over two dozen wounded. He spoke with a staccato solemnity as if his words were immutable, eternal.

"Will it be war, do you think, colonel?" the man asked, almost with ecstasy.

Simon looked up from his shrimp in curry sauce. "Depends on events in Europe."

"What events?" asked the professor from Stanford. "Europeans, you know, have an average temperature of .24·higher than people in the United States. It isn't much, but—"

"Hitler, the ol' swine?" asked the actress rattling the ice cubes in her highball glass. "That psychic crap he believes in?"

Simon said, "France, England, should have stopped him dead when he marched troops into the Rhineland. He'd have collapsed, retreated."

"What good could that have done, colonel?"

"The German Army generals would have jumped him, made a putsch very likely, seized power in a junta. And, knowing German habits to keep clean, most likely would have executed him and his top boys." Simon slowly chewed on a very crisp nutty shrimp. "Yes, history muffed it."

"Barbaric," said an art dealer. "To talk of executions as easily as that."

Simon grinned, showing a lot of teeth. "Yes, isn't it primitive? And just to stop a madman of genius who's also an art collector, I hear. Anyway, he outbluffed them, the whole *corps diplomatique* of Europe, and he's running wild."

"Genius, colonel? That paperhanging clown? Really. Have you seen Charlie's *The Great Dictator?*" asked the actress.

"Genius," said Simon, helping himself to the duckling à la gelée. "He *is* a genius. Evil has its geniuses too. Benedict Arnold, a great general; Jack the Ripper; the French Bluebeard; Al Capone—"

Sarah frowned at Simon mocking the guests. She motioned to one of the Negro waiters to serve the wine. Orderly Sergeant Blacker, in a white jacket, handed over linen-wrapped bottles he had uncorked.

"What happens now?" asked the professor.

Simon lost interest in the conversation, which was now moving into spacious intellectual bypaths. There was no reaching people, he felt, on a gut level, at a dinner—beyond the food. They were either gloom-chasers without knowledge, seeing the future—but not in their generation—as horror. Or Yahoos, the millions of nice people who lived their dull lives and hoped for the best, paid their taxes and let the fat-cat leaders put nose rings on them. It was their sons he might lead to their deaths.

The tournedos of beef Huntington seemed overdone, he thought, and he didn't want to talk about China. The actress had been there on a world tour, playing Noel Coward. "Marvelous girls in the treaty ports. Long-legged darlings, beautiful faces of carved rosy ivory, inky-shiny hair that looks like Ming lacquer. . . . You keep a girl in China, colonel?" She handed her glass up for a refill, with a gesture famous on the stage of two continents. "Or, Christ, am I indiscreet?"

Simon chewed slowly. "One can't be indiscreet in this house, can they, Sarah?"

"Liberty Hall," said Sarah, giving the actress a very overcharming look. "Liberty Hall, my dear."

That night as Sarah creamed her face and neck for bed, inspected her teeth in her mirror, and looked at the roots of her hair, she asked: "You think there's going to be war?" She still had to make out a list for what the maid had to do in the morning, but a last conversation before sleep seemed cozy.

Simon was almost asleep. He lay on his right side, the pillow mashed down just right, one of the goose-down feather-filled pillows he and Sarah always traveled with. "What's that?"

Sarah took up paper and pencil to list the maid's duties. "Honey, I asked, you think that there's going to be—"

"War? As a military man I hate the actual business of war as the worst way to settle things. . . ." He was hardly awake, hazy in some state of knowing he was still not asleep but also that he was falling down into the comforting warm darkness of sleep. "Huh. . . . Oh, war. . . ."

He went under into sleep, with images of shrimp in curry, wine glasses gleaming, a celadon Tang bowl, his giggling Chinese mistress and a Chinese son (his?), the ticking of a friend—the alarm clock, loud metallic ticking and it changed into the banging on a brass gas-warning shell in a trench of decaying old dead, he rushing forward, so much younger, fear pouring sand into his bowels, behind him the AEF in their tin hats highlighted all aslant in the glare of a bursting star shell. . . .

Orderly Sergeant Blacker and Jimmy Lee sat drinking champagne in the big ground-floor kitchen. The dishes, pots, pans, were all washed and stacked, the used cloths put in hampers by the two Negro girls, neither of whom showed any interest in the sergeant's departing suggestions. They were, Jimmy said, "Both college girls from Berkeley. They don't put out for anything but a professor."

The sergeant nodded, sipped, burped; he was carrying a load. "Tail ain't what it used to be, Charlie, like when I first enlisted. I mean hookers respected the business then—took pride. Now you'd think they was a union."

Jimmy Lee—his great-grandfather had helped build the Central Pacific Railroad, and Jimmy himself was a high school graduate, trained as a cook by his father—refilled their glasses with the last of the champagne left in a bottle of Mumm's.

"What do you think of your colonel?"

"He's all right, Jimmy, not a bad Joe—know what I mean? Too good a soldier for Fort Crap where we are. But he's got something biting him up *here*." The sergeant touched his right temple, tapped twice. "He's fair to the enlisted men, but hard. Any goof-off or muck-up and he's got you up the short hair. How's the missus to serve under?"

Jimmy lifted both eyebrows, giving himself an expression of a man in doubt. "She's got this habit, sergeant, this habit of always writing out lists of what we have to do. And what's right for the colonel, is right for us all. She's always thinking what will please him, and he doesn't give a damn, doesn't care much, so she has this habit."

"How they make out?"

"Like mink, sergeant, mink. Anything left in the brandy bottle?"

Sarah was finishing her list for the maid for a small lunch party the next day:

MIXES:
7-Up
Coca-Cola
Tonic water, Schweppes
Lemons and limes

Cherries
Cocktail onions
Tomato juice

TOWELS:
Always have at least 6 white towels hanging in bar.
Supply is kept in cabinet to the north of ice-maker. Also
have 2 regular bar towels for mop-ups or emergency
spilling.

COCKTAIL NAPKINS:
Always have a supply stored in the cabinet where towels
are kept. Be sure they are mended and destringed.

COASTERS:
Keep 4 of these on top of bar. Keep supply on lower
shelf of sliding cabinet at northwest corner. (Be sure
these are not used as ashtrays.) Coasters should be
polished and free from ash stains.

Chapter 32

WHEN General Raven Saunders retired, with the three silver
stars of a lieutenant general, and was on his way to Hawaii—he
was going to live with a married sister—he stopped off to visit
Simon at Fort Custer. The general had withered a bit, his back
was bent in a slight but permanent crick. They sat in Simon's
drafty quarters at the fort. No rain was falling, but through the
window they were aware of a constant battle between a weak
sunlight and scudding, mauve-smeared clouds that threatened
but did not deliver. The general had lost his spontaneous vitality.
He was just an elderly man. "No future in old age." There were
two shot glasses of bourbon between the two men, but neither
was drinking.

"I couldn't leave the mainland, son, and not come see you for a little pontificating."

"That's more than most do. Oh, it's not self-pity. I'm just a fool for hanging on."

The old general seemed all lined wrinkles under close-cropped white hair with a life of its own. "Feel it's a stretch in Purgatory? Hell, I tried it outside after 1919. Grace and me, we'd lost three babies in Army posts. Went into the insurance business in St. Louis with a brother-in-law. Lasted six months. Back me and Grace went to Army camps. Panama, Alaska, Philippines. She's buried outside Manila. No enlisted men or women in Arlington now."

"What the devil holds us to the service? Waterheads running the War Department. Civilians spit on us in peacetime."

"Call it service, Simon. Don't laugh."

"Who laughed?" Simon put his fingers on the glass. "I didn't laugh."

"They can't keep you here forever."

"Do they know that?"

"You're coming up for promotion. I did some desk pounding. You'll be a bird colonel soon, silver eagles on your shoulders."

"Thanks, you're the only one who put up a fight for me."

The old general fixed his wrinkled features into a smile. "Just a token gesture—a bit of shadowboxing. I knew it would do no good, the Senator is pathological. Understand, son, there are times when to an officer, the service has to be unfair to an individual for the good of the Army."

"What goddamn good?"

"Comes before our personal likes or antipathies, the Army needs a lot of money for new plane designs, and the tanks are deathtraps. You pointed that out; riveted, not welded, so a shot through them would drive the rivets right through the crew. And they're rubber-lined for comfort; rubber which would burn or smoke, kill the crew. . . . So we had to brownnose the moneybox for new models."

"Senator Upchurch."

"He and his committee. He put it to us in private: 'Sidetrack Copperwood.' "

"Damn."

"Don't feel too bad about the Army men who did it to you. Some day the decision could be placed in your lap, Simon. You may find yourself in the position where you sacrifice a friend for Army welfare or morale."

"I don't think I could do it to a real friend."

"Do it, Simon, do it *if* you have to. Just close your eyes and swing the ax hard and fast. A good clean chop."

"You didn't."

"I didn't have to. I knew the staff would use the ax for me. I just wanted to make a gesture for all the times we worked together on Capitol Hill."

"Christ—seems a million years ago."

"Look, there's a hell of a war coming. They can't keep you here when the shooting starts. They'll have to drop out a couple hundred peacetime dandies, polo players, the saluters of the flag at Rose Bowl games. They'll clean house and—"

"I don't know, general, if I can hold out much longer. The doc is hinting I go on chloral for insomnia. My synthesis of observation is getting blurred." Simon held out a hand at eye level. "No tremor yet, sure. But, if I'm here two, three more years. . . ."

"I figure you're made of good metal. You dent, but don't crack."

"I don't want a war to spring me from here. Funny, I'm antimilitary in the sense I know war doesn't settle big problems. Army should be a defense against war."

"Well, don't write anymore about how you feel. *Don't* publish. Take dumb-lessons, son." The general lifted his glass. "To all good soldiers who agree with you and me." Simon lifted his own glass. They drank, neither smiling.

Chapter 33

MRS. SIMON BOLIVAR COPPERWOOD was giving a party, a buffet supper, and then, as was added on the card: "Games and Fun."

The invitation read: "Lieutenant Colonel and Mrs. Simon Bolivar Copperwood" but everyone knew it was Sarah's party in the charming three-story house the Copperwoods had done over. They were aware it was Sarah who thought up the exciting dishes, the wacky games, the recalling of old ones like Simon Says, and Red Rover, and, one New Year's night, Post Office and Spin the Bottle.

There were sixteen people, mostly important in San Francisco's social or artistic circles. Several of the guests were even on the national scene. A lobbyist against rigid rifle and pistol control, and for the cutting of imports of autos. A Congressman and his wife who worried over their poodle being left alone for the evening. Present were several writers, one of whom had published a book, and a tax lawyer from Los Angeles with the nose of an anteater; advertising copy writers (two), a lady poet from Big Sur, and some women with blue-rinsed hair. Popular were two young girls, one of whom had met Tyrone Power, said she smoked reefers at Mills College, and had some prime muggles in her handbag. Sarah hoped the barman and the waitresses had digested her memos.

Simon was in a good mood. He felt there was a thaw in his situation, his exile. Yes, Simon felt the staff officers in Washington might be looking over his record in the Defense Department. He might be sprung from Fort Custer as the world condition worsened. He could not get used to the new label: "Defense Department" for the old, realistic "War Department." It was, he had told Sarah, "such goddamn pussyfooting. Making things sound what they are not. Those careerist hotshots." But he made no comment outside the house. He had lived too long on an official tether.

The tax lawyer lifted his beak from a glass of sherry. "Colonel, I'd say Hitler is satisfied now he's seized Czechoslovakia."

"I remember you felt he was fully satisfied, ready to settle down, when last year his armies occupied Austria, and he proclaimed *Anschluss*."

"Well, he's got his belly full now. He's going to feel he has all he can hold on to."

"That's great news for your Polish friends."

[266]

"Now, colonel, that's a most cynical outlook, and—"

Simon went up to the bar where the Negro barman—new to the house—and Orderly Sergeant Blacker were setting out glasses, serving some drinks. The heavy drinking that would precede and follow the buffet had not yet started.

"Sergeant, if you—"

"Yes, sir. I know sir. I'll be fully sober to drive you back to the fort in the morning."

The barman asked, "A libation, cul'nul?"

"A scotch on the rocks."

Sarah, in yellow silk, hair piled up—Simon suspected it was being touched up these days to keep its fine gold-red color—was greeting people and carried some large cards under one arm.

"Now everyone pay attention." She tapped on a crystal goblet with a silver fish fork—*ting, ting, ting.* "We've got a most marvelous set of English games set for the evening. Melburn here—" She put down the fish fork and put an arm around the shoulders of a young man fidgeting with his bow tie. He had high color, blond hair, and very long teeth. "Melburn, on a visit here from the British Embassy in Washington, has been delighting me, explaining the games they play at parties back there." She smiled, pressed the shoulder again. "Across the Big Pond, as they say."

"Gawd," said one of the younger wives.

"Now, if you will first all attack the buffet before gametime. Yes."

It was a splendid buffet, several tables on which trays displayed rows of Jerusalem artichokes; shrimp, very white and pink; various sauces, hot and mild, yellow and red in which to dip them; whole lobsters already sliced, their claws used as decor. There were two turkeys that seemed oversized and varnished like boat hulls; a Virginia ham stuck with cloves.

Melburn turned down a plate a maid offered him. "No, thank you."

Simon always ate before a buffet party. He nursed his glass; he'd have two more scotches, his quota at a party. He'd have to find a place to avoid the games. There was a room called the Music Room on Sarah's memos, because it contained a spinet, bought at a bargain price by Sarah, and that she always meant to have put back into playing order. In the Music Room Simon found the lobbyist, a portly figure with broken blood vessels in his nose, either a low-fallen chest or an overlarge stomach. The man was trying to pick out a tune on the spinet with two forefingers. He banged a dead key. "Half of these don't work, colonel."

"Sarah is going to have it repaired some day."

"You don't hear songs like 'Mighty Lak' a Rose' anymore."

Simon liked the lobbyist; cynical, wary.

"Gregory, how's Washington taking FDR getting the brush from Hitler on the Polish question?"

"With egg on their faces. Washington, you wouldn't know it. They have the wind up. The English have a great slogan going round: 'Why should your son die for Danzig?' Catchy, eh?"

"Christ," said Simon, gulping his drink without being aware of it. "If Hitler moves now, it means—" He gave a whistle.

The lobbyist nodded and turned away from the spinet. "Maybe all the gossip about the Germans and the Russkis signing a Nazi-Soviet nonaggression pact has some truth in it. I need another drink, colonel."

"A pact between the Devil and Dracula? Like an attack from Mars, on that Orson Welles radio show. You know my wife was packed and ready to run to the hills from Martians."

They went to get fresh drinks.

The party, guests told Sarah, was a success, a smash. After a great attack on the buffet tables, plates and glasses lipstick-stained, napkins being carried off by the maids, several broken wine glasses swept up, everyone was gathered in the living room for games. A fire was flaming up in the black-marble fireplace, Sarah standing in the center of the room with her cards, motioned people closer. "Now, you have to enter into the spirit of these games. The English play them weekends in their castles and manor houses, after riding to hounds and grouse shooting, and all that sort of thing. Correct, Melburn?" Sarah sipped a brandy, her second, third? The new barman came over and kept handing them to her.

"Well, more or less, Mrs. Copperwood," said Melburn.

"Now, we'll begin with Sardine. Sardine is an old Edwardian child's game."

"Goes back, actually, to Tudor days."

"Thank you, Melburn. Now in Sardine we divide into two teams. It's played in the dark, just hall lights. You face an opposite number. One team of players are the sardines. The other side, the big fish. In this version—"

"Rather different, really—from the way it's done back there."

"The lights are put out, and the sardines get three minutes to hide, all rooms up and below are open for hiding. The kitchen and pantry are out. Then the big fish try to find the sardine they faced in the lineup. No other one counts. First one back with·a sardine wins. Oh, thank you." She took the drink the barman handed her, only to take a sip to be polite. "So now, number off, odd numbers the sardines, even, the big fish. No changing over."

In the Music Room, the published writer had joined Simon and the lobbyist. "Why all this strange emphasis on games?" The writer wasn't feeling too well. He had stuffed himself at the buffet; he lived off freeloading, as his novel was only a critical success. Now he felt the Norwegian smelts on top of the black olives and two thick slices of overbloody rare roast meat did not set well on the caviar and raw onion, the slices of turkey breast and Mexican hot peppers.

He wiped a damp brow and stood with his mouth open, wondering, Simon guessed, should he bolt for a bathroom. "*Very* hot in here."

Simon heard the sardines scamper off, saw the lights go out, then dim again in the halls. Sarah had a dimmer on a master switch attached to the house's entire lighting system, except for the bathrooms and the kitchen. The Music Room filled with shadows. The only light was from a small, pink lamp in the hall that gave a ghastly color to the men's faces.

There was laughter from all over the house, upstairs, downstairs—a shrill giggle. Simon set down his drink.

"Faulkner, now. I don't read novels as a rule. But *The Sound and the Fury* is a great bit of reading."

[269]

"But you admit, don't you," said the author, "that as a rule you don't read novels. It's conspiracy of the—"

Someone was screaming. It seemed to Simon to be two women's voices—as if competing with one another. Men's voices too, in rippling, questioning tones, sounds that plucked at nerves as if at taut harp strings.

Simon turned, ran out into the hall, went past the steep staircase leading to the upper stories, and around to a huddle of people all talking in excited bits of sentences; hurried talk. Simon elbowed his way, muscled through into the middle, gestures as if swimming past them.

Sergeant Blacker stood at the top of the cellar stairs in the open doorway, his arm blocking people trying to push past him.

The sergeant saw Simon, and he said softly: "Jesus."

"What is it?" Simon asked, trying to see down the dark of the cellar steps. A little light fell on them. A woman with short gray hair, wearing horn-rimmed glasses, rolled her head around as if it pained her. She said: "She must have become confused playing the damn game in the dark. . . . Hiding. Instead of opening the closet door here, she opened the cellar one next to it and—"

Someone found the master switch. Simon reached in and pressed the cellar lights on. A crumpled bundle of yellow silk, with long legs awkwardly crossed like a doll's, lay on the cement floor thirty feet below. Lay unmoving. Simon tried to call out, *"Sarah!"* But couldn't from suddenly uncooperative vocal chords. He tried with inept intensity. He saw Sergeant Blacker remove his arm from the doorway as Simon ran down the stairs, wondering if this was going to end as a dream with the alarm clock ticking.

Sarah was taken away by an ambulance, and the doctor (called from his residence across the street) had kept saying to Simon, "She's very concussed. Very much concussed. . . . But she'll be all right. A few days in the dark, in bed."

"She unconscious?" he had asked as the stretcher moved her down to the steep front steps.

"No, no, she's moving a bit. Moaning. Nothing to worry about but an aching head."

He wanted to ride in the ambulance with Sarah. But Gregory,

the lobbyist, drove Simon to the hospital. They didn't speak on the ride. He kept pressing his hands together, palm to palm. Gregory's cigar had gone out. He seemed unaware of it.

At the hospital entrance, in a drizzle, a rain like dew drifting, lights haloed yellow, Simon went up into the lobby, was aware of the smell of wet wool, Lysol, floor wax, was aware of strained faces sitting on benches. The information-desk woman said for him to go to the second-floor waiting room. Gregory took his arm. In the waiting room Gregory threw away his cigar. Simon looked out at the bridge, all alight, cars moving like glowworms, the whole thing very toylike.

He felt it was like the night he stood with Sarah on the Peak in Hong Kong and nothing below there, too, seemed anything but children's toys. Christ, how we pull memory toward us, like a lifebelt thrown to us in a rough sea.

"Colonel, when I was a kid, I was four, my brother Hal was chasing me once, and I ran into a wall on a run. I lay three hours not moving. Next day I was out delivering newspapers. Only I was tossing them onto the wrong roofs."

Simon asked, "Wrong roofs?"

"I was a mean kid. I always tried to toss the paper where the customer had trouble getting at it. One day—"

A tall man came in. A narrow face. Simon noticed the crop of silver hair and the trim triangle of mustache. The man was wearing a white operating-room gown. In his gloveless hands he held a cap and mask. He seemed to see what he was holding for the first time, and set them down on a small table by a radiator beginning to whine.

"Colonel Copperwood?"

Gregory pointed to Simon, who turned to face the man.

"I'm Doctor Prentice."

"Yes?"

"She never"—the doctor shook his head——"she never regained consciousness."

Simon felt Gregory's hand grab his arm; he heard himself say in a very controlled voice, "Thank you, doctor."

Book Seven

Man would fain be great and sees that he is little; would fain be happy and sees that he is miserable; would fain be perfect and sees that he is full of imperfections; would fain be the object of love and esteem of men, and sees that his faults merit only their aversion and contempt. The embarrassment wherein he finds himself produces in him the most unjust and criminal passions imaginable, for he conceives a mortal hatred against that truth which blames him and convinces him of his faults.

—PASCAL, *Pensées*

(From the notebooks of Simon Copperwood)

Chapter 34

THE general had a toothache, an ache with the heavy grossness of stabbing pain. He thought, as the car rolled on: The weather of a Simenon novel; black rain, greasy highlights on wet cobblestones, the stripped trees of autumn between whose dark limbs—that heavy expenditure of black—the sky was the color of congealed fat. He had lost a gold inlay after D-Day, and the French town-dentist at Livarot had packed the cavity in the molar with silver. But not very well. The general eased a bit of Jack Daniels from his leather-bound pocket flask into his mouth and over the aching tooth, while watching the back of the head of his aide, Captain Angelo Joseph Spinelli; Angie, the hammered-down little firecracker who was his chief of staff (since Caen, where he lost Captain Zimmerman). Angie sitting up by the red-eared driver of the Army Lincoln puddling through to HQ, the big meeting at Maastricht, moving among dank German trees. The general worried the aching tooth with his tongue, then forgot it as he thought back on all the goofups of the invasion and what followed, from Supreme Commander, SHAEF, to getting new car-tires.

He had argued himself hoarse at senior headquarters, after the breakthrough in Normandy, that the line of attack and advance should have been along the Antwerp, Breda, Zeke, Rotterdam line. Not the foulup of the one the brain-boys insisted on; Brussels, Nijmegen, Arnhem (ask the dead paratroopers about *that* one), Zuider Zee. SHAEF was at times like a debating society of Chasidic rabbis. . . . Yes. . . . He sipped whisky. Christ, why did our military talent approaching genius stop with the Civil War? No Grants, Lees, Shermans, Stonewall Jacksons have come upon the scene since. Good men and true, in some places now, hard workers or prima donnas. Going back, no great AEF commanders in Europe, even in 1914. . . . And now? Monty? A

[275]

travesty at times of military caution. The Supreme Commander? He wouldn't really ever fully exercise his power of command. In London, with patronizing superiority we called him The Chairman of the Board. A nice enough guy, no ideological sophistication. Social enough; pretty WAC girl drivers, the right booze at tap for VIP's, and his good old country-boy smile—a basic need to charm, give affection.

The heavy car skidded, and the general felt a stab of pain in his tooth. He cursed. Captain Spinelli turned half around, his dark Borgia fox-face, bound by silver-rimmed glasses, smiling. His family ran a splendid fish stand in the Fulton Fish Market. "Gas tankers been beating up the road. Patton's tearing the ass out of supply service for gasoline. Calls 'em cookie-pushers."

"A lot of what he wants is on the bottom of the Atlantic."

Patton. Most likely the only man in the war really able to command. Brad had the most brains. . . . Patton, in his aggressive adolescence, could not manage a group of armies. That was the damn trouble, as I reported to Supreme Command. Boiled down: Don't ask what command *is*—ask what it *does* to the individual general.

He remembered his notes as he put away the whisky. Certain constant factors of command are clear in this war. "The promotion of battalion commanders to take over brigades is hard to make smooth. Moving a battalion is not like moving a brigade, and the commander usually gets uptight. Observation seems to show the command of a division is about the limit of the abilities of the best men we have at this time."

That got the staff off their prostates in the London club-chairs. And all the while the fancy-dan newspapermen, "veteran journalists" as they were called, were reporting a marvelous victorious end of the war after D-Day. So now the folks back home were getting an idea the Germans were melting like butter on a hot griddle. Like hell. The U.S. 1st Army was dying, survivors held up in the Hürtgen Forest area, an icy inferno. A belt the enemy held to protect the river Ruhr and its seven dams. They ever open those dams, they could flood out a hell of a great part of the war. To the south, Patton had been wasting a lot of ammo, and there was a real shortage—a scandal—in the slow

[276]

production and transport of ammunition that worried everyone. The general felt the tooth bite at its nerve—Patton had had
very heavy losses in men and armor. Patton, he'd never be more
than a George Armstrong Custer, but a *very* good Custer if you
could get him to get away on an open-field run.

The U.S. 1st were fighting in mud, ice, snow, sleet, and floods.
The torrential rains mostly never stopped, never let up. The
U.S. 3d was now weeks in the wild country, soaked, tangled up
like loco sheep on barbed wire in Texas. Stalled around Metz.

The general decided on another nip, and maybe a cigar. For
all the headlines and broadcasts by Edward R. Murrow, the
Germans had achieved great defensive victories, were still an
integrated military organism.

It all seemed to General Copperwood like a fantasy journey;
propelled from the gloom of Fort Custer and its relics in storage,
promoted to the one star of a brigadier general. During that
period of hurried preparedness for a war everyone was sure the
nation under FDR would enter. Before Pearl Harbor, Simon's
hard work was a kind of antidote to the spleen and ennui of his
years of exile to the California Siberia. The work held down the
heavy agony of the death of Sarah in a foolish game on a set of
steep San Francisco cellar steps. There had been emotional
incoherence and black-dog despair. He had permitted himself
remorse, but not regrets. Then had come the war, and he was in
London, a ruined city; smoking nights of blackout. The work he
did was deep inside ETOUSA (which he found out to mean
European Theater of Operations United States Army.) Twenty
Grosvenor Square, where G-2 Military Intelligence lurked. Here
he taught young officers what he had learned in China of the art
of gathering information and analyzing it. "We can use any
absurd and ridiculous information, gentlemen—if we invent an
answer that fits it."

There were fools and sluff-offs in every service, but he ignored them, and worked hard with good men. The anguish of
uncertainty of life without Sarah was dimmed. He desired to get
into the battle areas. He hoped he'd die in battle. He rather
looked forward to death—at first with satisfaction and impunity.
That was his attitude the first two months in London. He had a
bed sitting-room on Oakley Street, Chelsea, and became in-

trigued by the way the people lived, drank, screwed, and bitched between the all clear and the next alert. In the pestilent blackness he felt the world was stumbling into oblivion. That revived him. Go down with his ship. The planet is the *Titanic*.

The old dormant desire for power and position came back. One night at the Wheatsheaf pub, a tall blonde in a long leather coat, impatient of the crush, asked him: "Would you be a luv and get me a gin and lime? I kent get to the bloody bar."

"If I can buy."

"I dun mind." A self-deprecatory shrug.

They had one—nodded for another. Her name was Caroline. Her accent was from around Leicester. "Not really, it's Joan. But nobody named Joan calls themselves Joan, you know."

She was twenty-eight, ran an Army department at Imports, near the India Dock. Had lost first a husband in North Africa. "Yes, make it a pink gin this time." And then a lover. "A major, Roy was, in one of those blazing failures, bloody raids—you know, commandos, on the French coast."

He felt he loved her adenoidal voice. That was after they went to the mat in his bed-sitter, making it while the gas ring, fed by the shilling meter, heated hot water for toddies they drank, made with a fifth of Kentucky bourbon Simon had gotten from Colonel Bruno Holtzman, who was up-country (near Coventry) training hush-hush groups to drop from gliders on D-Day.

Carrie, as he called her, gave him comfort and a great deal of sex. "I kent love you, you know, luv, but I like you."

She had been two years to some Manchester college, was very bright. "No luv." He settled for that. He told her of Sarah—said he didn't want any deep love "that could stab." (He was drunk at the time.) He got a bigger bed-sitter on Charlotte Street, among the pubs, and they liked to make the rounds when off duty. It was cozy. They lived together. She sang silly songs for him:

> There was an old man named Michael Finnigan
> He grew whiskers on his chinigin. The
> Wind came up and blew them in ag'in,
> Poor old Michael Finnigin, begin ag'in.

Her stockings hung in the tiny bathroom and his pipes lay

among her knickers, as he learned to call her drawers. And she called suspenders "braces," and his undershirt, "a vest." They liked to hole up when they had leave together, were free, hide away in the room with the dusty blackout curtains, feeding on kippers and rashers of Irish bacon and boxes of Ryvita, a rare egg or two. To drink and roll around in the bed, stay there even when the bloody alert was on, not go down among the moldy, beery, shitty smell of drains, and rot in the shelter by the greengrocer's.

Simon was very close to all intelligence information on the *Oberkommando der Wehrmacht*. He wrote reports and went out on two airraids. One, a day raid with Flying Fortresses out of a field near Malmesbury, to bomb a ball-bearing factory and some dams, and the other on a night raid in a Wellington to hit a *Sturm Abteilung* camp. Both times his fears were great and he was happy they had only encountered flak. When later he read a poem about a dead turret tail gunner, whose remains were sloshed out with a hose after a raid, he never regretted avoiding trips to Germany by B-17's, B-24's, Stirlings, or Lancasters.

There was no longer in him that long-accelerating process toward self-destruction.

Caroline, in an anxiety-focused predicament, missed two periods and then had a miscarriage. Six weeks later she went to Malta on a three weeks' check of import stores space. Simon moved "lonely as a cloud" around to the pubs; The Six Bells on King's Road, the Fitzroy, and bought soldiers and the whores drinks. The "tart's special" was Canadian Club with creme de menthe and white curaçao. But he wasn't happy about the gregarious life-style of London whores during the Blitz. He wrote Caroline he wanted to marry her. She wrote back: "Oh, ducks, I'm not sure the blinking major is really dead. And didn't you say one night in a pub crawl that bigamy is actually a desire to bring respectability to a criminal conclusion? Malta is *très* messy and the local garrison are poor sods, unhappy."

Simon searched records: The major was listed as three months dead in a German prisoner of war camp near Metz. Simon wrote, "Why not now?" She wrote back: "Finished my work here and am flying back in two weeks. Gather some damn orange blossoms. Steal some nylons, and a brace of Beefeater's gin."

Somewhere between Malta and Gibraltar the RAF plane Caroline was on disappeared. No trace of its crew or passengers was ever found. Most likely Messerschmitts or Focke-Wulfs had gunned it down, Simon was told.

General Copperwood became a little more ungracious in a calm despair, no bluster in public about the death of Caroline. He hadn't been in love, he assured himself in the night—just lonely. Very—yes—for that peaches and cream complexion, those pink-skinned nights together. D-Day was coming and there was the chance of the second star of a major general. He appeared very often at SHAEF with vital intelligence for the Supreme Commander—a charmer who called him Simon at times and offered him a scotch. Colonel Bruno Holtzman, as Simon's aide, was good with the charts.

Bruno had a wife and three children back in New Jersey. But he felt, he told Simon, he'd die in battle soon. "Bullet or shell fragment for this Jew mustn't come before I've led an attack column."

"Bruno, you always were a goddamn romantic. In this war we'll wear our rumps out explaining things at senior headquarters."

"Martyred to desk duty?"

The two of them would pick up WACS and WAVES in Charlotte Street pubs, feed them blackmarket food in Soho dives, and roll down nylons in discreet bedrooms. Girls named Honoré, Gladys, or Phyllis. And one pert little dark-eyed half-Burmese named of all things, Faustina Jedangir, who smelled right and read *A la recherche du temps perdu* in bed and left Ryvita crumbs between the sheets. "A fast life, sahib, yes? But yet not dissolute."

One morning Bruno came with a small bit of paper into Simon's office at ETOUSA, "Well, *Gruppenführer*, we're dropping the banana skin for Hitler."

"D-Day?"

"Set." He handed over the paper. "Not to leave this office. Lock it up in your safe."

[280]

"About time—we're all saturated and soggy with waiting. We *go!*"

"Me, Si. *You* stay behind. You come in D-plus-something with special radio gear and recon maps based on what we find out for you."

Later, in heavy-weather coat, on the wet docks of Dover, Simon went to find Bruno on the deck of a battered tug with a lot of hush-hush G-2 staff on it. He turned over the latest batch of intelligence on enemy panzer and *Luftwaffe* locations.

Bruno gave him a batch of letters, an old hunter watch, grimaced and said, "My old man's watch. His *tata* brought it out of a Polish ghetto after the Czar's Cossacks did in most of the family. The letters are for Myra, the kids, the family circle."

Simon fingered the letters, the tugboat swayed. "I saw this letter scene in a lousy movie, Bruno."

"I'm going to work with some of Monty's boys. Not a bad general—but lacks intellectual flexibility, don't you think?"

A siren was wailing a steamy howl, the tug smelled of fuel oil.

"He never got Egyptian sand out of his boots. Good luck."

The great invasion came two days later and Simon heard it over the radio. Sat scowling at his desk, sweating and sorting intelligence reports. Bruno was wounded north of Gold Beach. Not badly, but some day they would have to rebuild his right knee. A month later, General Copperwood and two aides, Captain Spinelli and Lieutenant Rosen, crossed to France.

Lord, it had seemed the war would be over before he could geacto' make contact with the enemy. But now it was hard winter and the dead GI froze to the earth, and there was something wrong with the confidence at senior headquarters; enigmatic, extremely imperceptive. Simon had distilled his idea of warfare down to a simple formula in his notebook. "Military victory involves the proper skill in the appreciation of a situation, in the taking of decisions, and issuing of proper orders."

General Bradley is good, has the best brain. As for the Supreme Commander, he is window dressing—"a chairman of the board," Simon wrote. Patton was the only real soldier, with Mac marking time in the Pacific, waiting for the Navy to bail him out. "A world at stake and sometimes it all seemed to be essentially a situation of farce."

(He had said to Captain Spinelli, one night of heavy bombing, "I get hit or knocked off, you see this notebook is destroyed. Capish?")

The Germans had made victories out of Arnhem, the Scheldt, Aachen, and Metz. Simon puffed the cigar into life as the car skidded in greasy mud. Captured German leaf. (Where the hell could *they* still get prime Havana?) A gift from the Supreme Commander's staff, a whole box of cigars, back there in August when SHAEF G-2 had issued that jolly absurdity of a report:

> The August battles have done it and the enemy in the West has had it. Two and a half months of bitter fighting have brought the end of the war in Europe within sight . . . almost within reach. . . . The German Army is no longer a cohesive force, but a number of fugitive battle groups, is disorganized and even demoralized, short of equipment and arms. . . .

A dream fantasy. Intelligence reports that Simon summarized were that the Germans were moving great masses of armor, some of the *Oberkommando des Heeres*, the newest tanks, their biggest guns, and were setting up depots for something fancy and very big. Beaten, demoralized? Now here. A million German casualties on the Russky front in three months. That's mean losses, and here in the West, say 300,000 killed, wounded, missing. Yes, it had looked easy when in August the Allies had crossed the Seine and cleaned out all of Northern France, Belgium, and Luxembourg. Then had moved up 200 miles to hit the German border in the harvest weather. Looking at German corpses, a major had joked, "There are just enough deaths, general, as there are people who qualify for them."

"Too slow, too slow," Simon's reports had read. "In hardly any respect are the Allies prepared to take advantage of the great opportunity offered to us to destroy the German forces before winter. . . . It would appear there is not now time to make the necessary readjustment in the logistic machinery that will bring the speedy victory spoken of. . . ."

"Sad Simon" they had called him at SHAEF. ("Too much Mao Tse-tung he got watching war in China," Colonel Jeff Astruc had told Brad.)

Simon tapped with his malacca cane on the back of the front seat. (The cane often brought memories of the swagger sticks the old colonel in Tientsin used to insist on.)

"Angie, let's all take a leak."

"Here?" They were on the outskirts of a ruined village, rimmed by shattered lanes of trees. Here and there the red fragment of an ancient brick or roof tile lay to suggest old ruins of other wars.

They stood, general, captain, (sergeant driver five yards to the left), in the light drizzle, hunched in their waterproofs, making water on dead leaves. Their breath and the warmed-up leaves giving off vapors.

"Jesus, Angie, it was just like this in 1917, rain, ruins, pissing on Europe. They always go to war in rainy weather, from the Merovingian kings on."

Captain Spinelli shivered and zipped.

"It rained after Waterloo, after Gettysburg, sir."

"I wish it would rain on some of our big victories. *When* we have them." He turned away. He was talking too much. No use getting too friendly with staff. Better to be just Iron Face, a know-it-all, with a special roving command to inspect and evaluate the capacities of the *Wehrmacht*'s armies. Maybe if he did it well they'd give him a couple of divisions on Patton's flank, and they'd roll to glory on to the Rhine. And get over and to Berlin before Stalin's divisions did. He dug his cane into the earth; here, once, battles were fought like a gavotte—in lace, scent, and smoke from primitive cannon. But *this* war was far from won, even if they were selling victory flags back home. The Germans had just pulled out to safety an army of 100,000 tough soldiers from the failed Pas de Calais trap. The great water-barrier of the Maas was still flowing there, and to the south the Germans were counterattacking the overexposed U.S. 3d on the Moselle.

They resumed their journey. Ahead was only the discontent of an icy winter, battles of attrition. Beyond that, the West Wall, the Siegfried Line. In his dispatch case, Simon carried rough notes of the new plan, a joint British-American plan, to move up and cross the Rhine.

He opened the case, as rain battered on the car's windows, and he took out the sheet that contained his warning against any idea the plan was a pushover. Another "Sad Simon" text, he thought, as the damaged tooth reminded him it needed attention. "Despite crippling factors, shattered communications, disorganization, and tremendous losses in personnel and equipment, the enemy has been able to maintain a cohesive front to exercise an overall control of his tactical situation. His withdrawal, continuing, has not been a rout or mass collapse. New identifications on contact in recent days have demonstrated clearly, despite enormous difficulties under which he is operating, the enemy is still capable of bringing new elements into the battle area from other fronts. . . ."

Spinelli half turned around. "Sir, how does this war seem, I mean compared to the first one?"

" 'The Great War'? '1917-1918'? as it was called? You interested in history, Angie?"

"Naw—not history. Was it a great war?"

Angie Spinelli was short, dark, with crisp curly hair, weak eyes behind heavy glasses. He had a great brain for map detail. An elephant's memory of almost-forgotten reports. Spinelli was also able to spell out theories about *Sicherheitsdienst*, captured intelligence reports that sometimes proved vital. Simon wondered if he actually remembered it all properly.

"I guess it was the last romantic war—if you were not dying by the hundreds of thousands in one prolonged attack, in a stinking mud made up of manure—millions of horses and mules were killed in four years—and the remains of soldiers, many years dead. And fighting going on over the same few hundred yards of trench. The doomed French singing *'A bas la Guerre, morte aux vaches.'** But there was excitement and a feeling among us innocent Americans, fresh, well-fed that it was a crusade . . . that war. . . ."

He let the sentence peter out. He could bring up Hitler, the

---

*To hell with war, kill the swine.

bestial, music-loving Germans gone insane, as a good reason for a new crusade. But what was the use? He took out a pen and added to his text: "It is clear from all indications that the fixed determination of the Germans is to wage a last-ditch struggle in the field at all costs. It must be constantly kept in mind fundamentally the enemy is playing for time. Weather will be one of his most potent allies, as well as terrain, as we move in to narrowing corridors. . . . Barring internal upheaval in the homeland and remoter possibility of insurrection within the *Wehrmacht*, the German armies will continue to fight until destroyed."

Chapter 35

BRIGADIER GENERAL SIMON BOLIVAR COPPERWOOD didn't look forward with any degree of pleasure to the big meeting of the allied commanders to be held at Maastricht. The bitter fighting in the Hürtgen Forest had left three divisions of the 1st Army with over 21,000 casualties, the Ruhr dams had not been taken, and there was no crossing the Ruhr without them. The situation, he felt, wasn't as bad as the optimist on a sinking ship taking a bath—still, it wasn't promising either.

The 8th Air Force, too, was not fully up to the job of both holding off the German Air Force and continuing strategic bombing. The rain had let up by the time the general's car reached Maastricht; water seeking gutters, a gray drifting miasma over all. Big muddy cars: Lincolns, Caddies, Rollses, various other expensive machines dabbed in Army tones, stood in the stone courtyard of the Second Empire Hohenzollern mansion where the conference was being held. MP's tested clubs on gloved palms, and jeep patrols circled the area. There were, inside the building, great logs burning in deep fireplaces ornamented with Teutonic gods and trolls. The marble floors rang with military heels. Telephone and radio panels connected the meeting with the various battle areas. The radio section, manned by gauche, sleepy-eyed specialists, was active. The floors were still lifes of cigarette butts, candy wrappers, crushed paper cups.

Simon was assigned a small, cold room. "Eisenhower has arrived," Captain Spinelli reported after a visit to the kitchen and the wine bins. He carried some bottles under his arms and their sergeant driver was putting other bottles under the bed. Captain Spinelli skillfully used a corkscrew on a bottle of Burgundy. "The Supreme Commander, sir, had a wild hair up his butt. He came through—on December seventh, in the Ardennes, he saw holes, unheld positions all along the lines. No transport, regiments missing, installations all haywire. Blew his top. Said it looked just like the goddamn condition we were in when we got clouted at Kasserine in North Africa."

"Brad knows there are gaps in over two hundred miles of front. Yet he's weakened the First to give Patton priority."

The sergeant produced some glasses from someplace and the captain poured. "He do right, sir?"

"*If* it works, Angie." He motioned the sergeant to pour himself a drink. "If not, it's sloppy. Monty here yet?"

"Oh, everything British and high-toned at their end. He's in with a staff, all very red-tabbed and they say there's a Scot regimental piper too. I haven't glommed on to him."

Simon sipped the wine. It was a bit corked. "Get out my report, suggestions for plans for Veritable."

"You sure pulled together a lot of ideas to please all the staffs. Only they won't. I never saw such an Alice in Wonderland megillah, sir."

"I wonder where the hell the Krauts have the Sixth Panzer Army really set? Chrissake, this wine is bringing back my toothache."

"There's a Polack dentist, Jon Casmir, I knew back in Hackensack, sir. He's a cook here with the HQ Corps. If you want him to take a look at your tooth."

Simon shook his head. "If he's a cook and not with the medics, he must be a pretty lousy dentist. I can bear it till we get to Paris or London."

The first meeting of the staffs of the Allies at Maastricht was at five o'clock, in what had been a ballroom. There was an impressive array of all the brass, with their decor on caps and chests, battle bars, and the tailoring. Medals of Honor, Silver Stars, even a Victoria Cross. It was clear to Simon the American and the British approaches to war were not meshing. Colonel Jeff Astruc, bald as an egg now, and some of the Supreme Commander's staff came over and shook Simon's hand as there was a shuffling around, a hunting of the place each had at the big, waxed, mahogany table with its place cards.

"Sonofagun, Si," said Jeff. "Haven't seen you since landing in England."

"Living fat, I see."

"Can't say it's too bad at Claridge's, as long as the nookie and scotch holds out. Even with the buzz bombs thumping. What do you think of this clambake?"

"No idea."

They turned as Field Marshal Montgomery came in, leaning forward, Simon thought, as if in a great wind. A small man, tam on a turtle's head, he waving a swagger stick in greeting. Giving the impression of a fierce runt of a litter of pups who felt he was better than the bigger pups. More of his staff followed, and hands were shaken with almost an inherent austerity above the small jests.

Simon said, "The perversities of military allies."

"The difference between Ike and Monty, on what's to be done, is giving Ike headaches. He hates headaches."

"They'll work it out, Jeff. It's Brad who gets too bitter when the British drawl and try to bugger up our ideas."

"Think they'll buy Plan Veritable?"

"I wouldn't bet on it, even at good odds. I've tried to pull it all into a reasonable plan. But they'll nitpick at it."

"How was Huřtgen? You had an army corps there, lucky bastard."

"It's no place to put an American boy raised on the idea football and eating his Wheaties will win over everything. Jesus, our casualties. You remember Wallibee, Ollie Wallibee? No, I guess not. Was in China with him."

Jeff was greeting people with nods and waves.

"Yes, yes, that crazy Chinese investigation you made."

[287]

"Got it in a tank—poor old Ollie. Direct hit from a 155mm self-propelled. Jesus, he had turned into burned bacon by the time I saw him."

"Gentlemen," someone said loudly.

At the head of the table there was a tapping for attention. Tobacco smoke drifted in large arabesques in the room. Simon sat down and listened to several short welcome talks. To cheerful words from both commanders. To friendship messages, and to a lisping English colonel who stood up and spoke from notes. "Having met here, first contact—yes—we will all meet again at dinner. There will be a short meeting of specialist groups as noted on the bulletin board—yes—in the lounge hall. Ten ac-emma tomorrow there will be the briefing of the study of the direct plans for the first of the year. . . . Righto."

There was a pushing back of chairs and a forming of small groups that collected, and noncom orderlies passed out trays of cocktails and small bits of something eatable on crackers.

The SHAEF people spoke to Simon, and the Supreme Commander pressed Simon's arm and gave him his famous smile. The Supreme Commander's face looked a bit wrinkled with worry while he talked. Simon didn't try to prolong the conversation, just saying he had some rough suggestions on the plan to present. Another pressing of the arm and the Commander was off, whispering in Bradley's ear. Brad looking more than ever like an elderly farmboy—wary of all talk—just listened and nodded. Simon knew his qualities of reason and authority were kept buttoned up.

Captain Spinelli met Simon in the hall with the convulsed, overcarved marble trimmings and a fireplace burning huge fir logs. The litter underfoot was worse, more candy and gum papers, empty cigarette packs, and the English seemed to have brought along strong-smelling cheeses. Simon's tooth ached. He thought of a line of Dante's: *"Vos temps de ma dolas."*

"The Sixth Panzer Army is in a wide arc covering Cologne, sir."

"Recheck that, Angie. Something is up. Let's get some sleep."

It was two in the morning when Simon had the Polish dentist-cook sent for. His head seemed bursting and a spear was jabbing at his brain stem. Sergeant Jon Casmir was a powerful-looking little man with red curly hair, a broken nose, and dishpan hands.

"I always carry my dentist gear along, general. Yeah, sir, I got me a full set of dentist probes, and I got fresh disinfectants from the Limey first-aid unit. A toothache, eh? Real bad. Just sit up in bed, general, and let me take a peek at that molar. Captain, please hold the flashlight here. Yeah, right *here*—Hmm. Nice set of teeth, general. Them inlays, very nice work. A-one."

"Can you pull it, sergeant, and stop talking? Og, *og!*" The probe was digging and the big Slavic face of the Hackensack dentist was close, smelling of brandy. "Pull? Not that beauty, general. No, it's just a lousy French silver-pack. Ah, got the silver out." The dentist sniffed it. "The butcher boy that did that didn't prepare the cavity at all. I'll give you a dose of something to deaden the exposed nerve. Antiseptic, and I'll put in a nerve guard to cut off the air hittin' it. Cement it over. Yeah, till you get a gold inlay molded."

Simon closed his eyes and sweated as the dentist worked in his mouth. Jon Casmir seemed to know what he was doing. He had Captain Spinelli mix on a glass slide some fine white powder with a liquid from a little bottle. "Keep mixing, captain. Don't let it harden. When it gets tacky, yell out—lemme know. Mix, mix, sir."

There was a strong hospital smell as a swab held on tweezers entered Simon's mouth and spurred a jolt of pain that broke off. A calm came. More pressing and packing went on. "Okay, captain, just you hand me the mix. Oh, open wider, general. Yeah. Now this will harden real quick. It's dental cement. Feel anything, general? No. Just sit up in bed ten minutes."

Simon opened his eyes. His head felt larger, but there was no pain, just a powerful medical smell and sweat. The red, damp face of the sergeant was grinning. Captain Spinelli handed the dentist a glass of brandy, which he knocked back quickly and wiped his face on a sleeve, staring at Simon with detached contemplation.

"I wouldn't trust a dog to a European dentist, sir. Nope, not even a mutt. Don't talk, sir, just let the cement dry. If I had mold material and some dental gold and a little furnace, I'd make you a jim-dandy inlay."

When the cement had set to the dentist's satisfaction (a thumb in the mouth for testing) Simon swallowed a brandy himself and flexed his jaws. "Tell me, Sergeant Casmir, why aren't you with the medics, instead of with the greasy pots?"

"Trut' is, sir, I hate looking in people's gaps—mouths—that is, pardon me, sir. I got tired of it long ago."

"I'll get you assigned to an active medical unit if you want."

"No thanks, general. Tell you the trut', sir, between you and me—I'm kind a nut for cooking. I'm doing up a beef Wellington for tomorrow's lunch. How was the pressed duck for dinner tonight?"

"I was in too much pain to notice, sergeant, but everyone said it was great. Captain, give Dr. Casmir a couple of Havana cigars. And if he wants to join our unit as cook, work it out."

"Cigars? No thanks, sir. Smoking, it destroys the taste buds, see, sir, for tasting the real flavor of food. But I'd like getting away from here. I gotta do windows, too."

When the sergeant was gone, Spinelli said, "You meet all kinds in a war, don't you, sir? If you mean it, I can get Casmir finagled to come over to our unit."

Simon didn't answer. He was prone in the bed, and sleeping soundly.

In the morning at 10 ac-emma, to a select group of the high commands, Simon presented ideas on Plan Veritable.

Some maps were up and several charts by Captain Spinelli were set on stands. After twenty minutes, with an almost detached contemplation, Simon summed up. "Ten U.S. Divisions to be made available under the Twenty-first Army Group for a right hook northeast from the Ruhr. Secondary attacks will be mounted in the south. Certain elements of our armor [he suspected they knew he meant Patton] will not be checked as long as forward progress is made toward the Frankfurt area. It could resolve the pattern of chaos our maps show."

The Supreme Commander nodded. "We have sufficient forces, gentlemen, to support the northern thrust fully, and still mount subsidiary attacks."

The British faces were expressionless, but it was easy for Simon to read disagreement. Well, let the Supreme Commander work on them with his subtle persuasion and charm.

The field marshal tapped the table with his swagger stick, and spoke briskly. "I really think the experience of the last few months has actually demonstrated the lack there is of sufficient resources for *both* attacks, don't you see? It seems to me this doubt is the difference between success and failure, and that, may I say, is fundamental."

All attention was on the two commanders. Jeff Astruc whispered to Simon, "A bit of grandstanding. Ike has all the cards. He's in a position to make *his* views prevail."

Monty, having spoken, seemed to grow more cheerful. They all broke up happily for a lunch of Dover sole, grouse, and endive salad. Monty actually was bouncy when the next day it was time for the two commanders to go back to their HQ's; in some agreement on a bleak and necessary logic.

Jeff came to say good-bye to Simon. "Do hope, sport, we meet again. It's back to London for me with the SC. We're meeting Air Marshal Tedder and Winnie." Jeff chuckled and pulled some radio report flimsies out of a pocket. "Winnie sent this to FDR, in code, yesterday about this conference. Just got it out of the code room. Don't ask how."

Simon read:

I feel that the time has come for me to place before you the serious and disappointing war situation which faces us at the close of this year. Although many fine tactical victories have been gained on the Western Front and Metz and Strasbourg are trophies, the fact remains that we have definitely failed to achieve the strategic object which we gave our armies five weeks ago. We have not yet reached the Rhine in the northern part and most important sector of the front, and we shall have to continue the great battle for many weeks before we can hope to reach the Rhine and establish our bridgeheads. After that, again, we have to advance through Germany.

Jeff refolded the paper. "Grim, huh?"

"I'd say he's got the truth by the tail."

"Ah, but FDR sent back a cheerful note reading: 'I've bicycled over the terrain in the old days . . . and our agreed broad strategy is developing according to plan.'"

Simon said, "Jesus H. Christ. Maybe FDR should send us his bike."

"The British hit the ceiling on this note—haven't come down yet. Well, good-bye."

It was like shaking hands with a long-gone past. Simon thought of Ada, Souki Miller, the War College days, and so many dead or retired officers who had missed all this muddle. *Were they lucky?* He tested the cement plug in his tooth with his tongue. Nice and hard, a bit rough, but no pain. He ordered the captain to alert their driver. He wanted to contact George Patton in person.

Chapter 36

ON the morning of December 15, General Simon Bolivar Copperwood, upon awaking in his trailer, a square shape, camouflaged, in a wood near Hansenfeld, was handed by Captain Spinelli a report from SHAEF G-3 Operations, beginning: "There is nothing to report in the Ardennes sector."

He felt lonely, introspective, looked up at the little Italian handing him a mug of very hot, sugarless, milkless tea. There was a wind pushing at the trailer under its denuded winter trees, while to the south of them the clang of some of Patton's reserve armor moving was audible.

"Haven't they been reading my reports back at SHAEF?"

"Sir, you know how they do pile up, reports."

Simon got up off his cot, his woolen nightshirt and pajama bottoms badly creased and, he feared, rather smelly. He felt a real poop-out—an erosion of ego—*why* don't they read my reports properly? He went to a battered field-desk fastened to the wall of the trailer and took out a heavy cardboard portfolio, began to rummage through sheaves of carbons of reports. "The bastards. I don't write these to amuse myself."

"Eggs and bacon, general? Got some English marmalade, too."

"I want copies made of some of these and get them by fast dispatch to HQ. Hell, you or Lieutenant Rosen take them yourselves. Promote a fast car and driver."

"Patton doesn't like his motor pools broken into. I'll use one of our crocks. I've got a captured Mercedes, repainted."

"Don't tell me. Against regulations." He began to reread a report out loud.

Captain Spinelli put on an interested look: the general could be a pain in the ass; hypertension, sure as hell.

"One may well ask what additional information the Allies will need to predict a major attack. In many ways the information is highly accurate. Most of the units which made up the panzer armies had been spotted days and even weeks forming up. Air reconnaissance, while hampered at times by bad weather, has marked the steady stream of men and supplies westward across the Rhine. Despite clever deceptive measures of the enemy, Allied intelligence experts had correctly analyzed most of the German dispositions and are aware of shifts toward the Ardennes area and of the arrival of new units in the zone of VIII Corps."

"That's pretty clear, sir."

"Damn right it is. Plain as pigeon droppings. Make copies. Here's another:

"Reinforcements for the West Wall between Düren and Trier continue to arrive. The identification of at least three or four newly reformed divisions along the Army front must be reckoned with during the next few days . . . it is possible that a limited-scale offensive will be launched for purpose of achieving a Christmas morale

[293]

victory for civilian consumption. Many PW's now speak of the coming attack between 17th and 25th December. None of this should be overlooked and is sufficiently definite to induce us to take action, and one wonders what one can expect from intelligence advisers. It is the role of intelligence to discover as many facts as possible, to keep track of enemy troop movements, and to evaluate the courses open to the enemy. This our staffs have done with remarkable accuracy."

Captain Spinelli set to typing (keep the general happy), battering away with two fingers, making copies of the reports. Simon dressed, bundled up in a long sheepskin jacket with the woolly pelt on the inside. He buried his neck in a scarf and got the sergeant driver to warm up a jeep motor with a blowtorch.

It was bitter cold under the elms and linden trees, driving past the clanging tanks, the scout cars, the turtle-shaped tracked Weasel, and the 155mm self-propelled guns of Patton's left flank. The crews were huddled in dour discomfort, overwrapped against the bitter frost. MP's in their jeeps were patrolling the armor like cowhands guiding a herd of moving cattle. An officer with a long pipe smoldering in one corner of a blue-lipped mouth waved to Simon and made a short mock-salute.

"Great day, general, for bringing in the brass monkeys."

"The general in the vicinity?"

"Hell, yes. He was up at dawn passing through, standing in his command car—flags flying, stars shined up on his helmet, jolly as a grig. What the devil is a grig?"

"I'll write you a letter, Miller. Where is the general now?"

"Go up the road six kilometers—we've cleared it of mines —turn left at a village, Schmidtdorf, and if there's a fairly good hotel, there's the general. Say, he's tetchy about supplies. Gasoline mostly."

Simon nodded to his driver to move on. Patton was *always* tetchy about supplies. George knew the value of momentum and could spin his tank columns on a dime and head in any direction' as long as he had the stuff to fuel up his iron. Had a neat schizophrenia—divided war into politicians and military men. Not bad.

[294]

The Wagner Hof was an impressive bulk in the village, Grimms' fairy tales in style. Once white, part of the roof missing, but inside, the dining area was cheerful, warm from the tiled stove. Chairs were piled up on tables—except in a corner, where George Patton, ivory-handled revolvers worn at hips ("Only jackasses would call them pearl-handled") was standing over a couple of yards of unfolded maps, his gloved hands bending his short hunting whip back and forth. Some of his staff stood around the table, most of them holding large mugs of very hot coffee, judging by the steam. Patton's HQ column carried its own ground coffee beans. The staff made small talk, pointed to areas on the map. Patton beat down on the surface of the already tattered paper with the butt end of the hunting crop. "We'll go *this* way in three columns, so if the *Herrenvolk* have mines in patterns *here*, we'll outflank the shitheads, and if they have the antitank guns in big supply at *this* crossroads, bring up our own self-propelled and blow them to the devil's privy for breakfast."

He turned as Simon entered, smiled, a smile that always gave Simon the impression there was a clown's mask pasted on the sharp fox-faced features—and that the strange brain of this remarkable general peered out only through the narrow eye-slits.

"Hello, Simon. What got you out of your warm bed this morning?"

"Wasn't warm, George."

"Come have breakfast. A duck-egg omelet, sunflower roots."

Two rather frightened young German girls were setting down on one table—Patton's silver coffeepot and covered trays on a crisp white tablecloth. It was, Simon knew, the general's own silver and cutlery, china with his family crest on the blue-flowered plates. George believed in the proper etiquette of civilized eating.

"Stay for lunch, too, Si. Managed to scrounge up some real Philadelphia scrapple and a marvelous Bavarian smoked ham."

"Thanks. I'm a bit off my feed. Gastritis I think."

"What the hell, in battle areas keep your bowels open, your fly closed. . . . Where are all the gas tankers? I'm moving on tanks dry as a bone." They sat facing each other over coffee cups.

"It's bad weather, torn-up roads. They'll make it. . . . George, something is brewing up north. Von Rundstedt is up to some illusory backfield play. Lots of movement, massing along the Ardennes sector."

"Ever read Nostradamus, Simon? Has some marvelous prophecy on the Ardennes." The general buttered a hot roll and chewed on it slowly. "What good would that do von Rundstedt? He'd be carrying the ball the wrong way."

Simon carefully broke his roll into bits. Began to arrange its fragments and some butter knives in a pattern. "I'm Hitler with my intuitive temperament. Okay, nuts. I want to make some big *big* movement. Here's the Meuse, here's Antwerp, here's Brussels. I package say a half million men, piles of supplies. I cross the Meuse in force, separate the Allied armies, split them in two. Force the British, cut off in isolation, into another Dunkirk. The drama of a charismatic charlatan—but daring, really. Admirable as a military move."

"Impossible, Simon. Too late for the Huns."

"Impossible? But probable. Chancy enough to bring a big defeat to us—if done with vigor, to even attempt it. And, George, we're spread thin as poorhouse butter and the generals are badgering Monty to—"

There was a great explosion nearby. Windows rattled and far off a rattling series of more explosions went on. A staff officer came over. "That's the panzer ammo dumps at the railhead we were after."

"Make contact, Jojo, and see if they've found any gas there." He looked up at a shaking waitress with a large platter of duck eggs and sausages in her hand, the plate vibrating. "Easy, girl, whoa, Nellie! I've carried that platter through three campaigns. *Kein Rauch ohne Feuer.*"*

"I'm going to contact Brad and say there should be some rethinking done about a big counterattack from them."

"You sleeping badly, Simon? I've latched on to some Spanish absinthe—Gojai special. Give you a bottle."

"You may have to change directions and rush divisions north."

"Don't you go putting any ideas like that into SHAEF.... Like a pup? I've got a bitch whelping in a couple of days.... All right,

*No smoke without fire.

all right, I catch on. You want me to hang loose—maybe you're on to something."

All the way back to his trailer Simon brooded. He hadn't been sleeping well. The Spanish absinthe—milky, sweetish, licoricy, didn't help. He had been dreaming he was back in China with that Chinese girl, and he would have meetings with his (?) son. A slender young man who kept calling, "Father, father." In that dream, Simon kept repeating: "Let me see your face, boy." The young man kept turning away, so his features were just out of range. Simon wanted very much to see if the youth had Chinese eyes, a Copperwood nose, and just when it was nearly possible to clearly see, Simon would wake up. He did not contact SHAEF. He was getting a reputation as a doom sayer.

Chapter 37

It was still dark, a cover of black-velvet freezing atmosphere, December 16, when German storm troopers, under the glare of massed searchlights, came in solid formations of armor and battalions out of the Eifel forest. Swift in surprise, they at once overran the forward American positions in the Ardennes. Little battles of shouts, the sharp rattle of heavy weapons, handarms, thud of bombs echoing to the dying cries of the Americans. In the south and center, the corps of von Manteuffel's 5th Panzer Army enveloped a thirty-mile front, from Wiltz to Prüm, and began to prepare to smother Saint-Vith, Bastogne. For the Americans it became a traumatic horror, as messages went back to the still sleeping American generals, hastily awakened to climb into their pants and Bond Street boots.

The 6th Panzer Army, which had so worried Simon Copperwood, was moving on a fifteen-mile front, tanks snorting blue smoke, the coal-scuttle helmeted troops breathing out white vapor as they crossed snowy ridges. General Dietrich was pressing all along the front from Mönchen and Malmédy.

Simon, like so many American top officers, came awake in his trailer to hear the banging bark of hundreds of guns the Germans had positioned for rapid fire. The barrage was the biggest the enemy had been able to mount since D-Day to *umkrempeln* (get around) the Americans, as they put it.

Simon came into full awakening to find himself staring open-mouthed into his shaving mirror that had fallen to the floor from the vibrations of the cannon fire. It was, he saw, uncracked as he bent to pick it up. A new and more sinister sound was overhead, a chilling sound of insouciant, almost flippant hatred.

Captain Spinelli, tucking his shirt into his heavy ski pants, came in. "Sir, V-1's overhead, a hell of a lot going by, radio contact reports."

"Headed *where?*" Simon polished the mirror surface with a clothed elbow.

"Liège, Antwerp, they think by the direction."

"Must get through to HQ. General Bradley's in Luxembourg. This catches us with our pants down. What's the weather?"

"Snow falling heavily to the north, sir. And coming in fast all over the Ardennes. Means fighting a defensive pullback—if we have to regroup, doesn't it, sir?"

Simon nodded. Spinelli was a very good staff officer, hammered down in size, but solid and never in panic. Not too much condescension; thinks I'm a too-precise old fart. . . . (Unknown to the two men, unseen, unheard, V-2's were also passing, speeding to put their high explosives into Antwerp.)

Suddenly, Simon felt claustrophobic in his trailer. He unfolded maps. "Holding anyplace?"

"No, sir, from the few reports so far. Overrun. What do you think, sir? The Krauts, they gone crazy?"

Simon was lifting a phone as his fingers traced a riverline on a map. "No, I think— Hello, get me HQ in Luxembourg—highest priority. General Copperwood at position Dark Horse point 5G." He turned to face the captain. "As I see it—my cockeyed evaluation—it's a last big throw of the dice. Hitler plans to split the Allies, drive the British into the sea, and he figures then maybe he can get a peace to his advantage. If he kills and destroys enough of us. That's his consuming vanity—his crazy hope. He's wrong to think— Hello, GH? Give me Colonel

Holtzman. General Copperwood, urgent, URGENT! . . . You see, Angie, the Hitler boldness, his maladjusted thinking. 'Screw military science and logic as taught in the books,' he yells. He— Hello, Bruno, Simon here at point 5G. Yes, yes. The goddamn barrage is creeping closer. Get Brad to look at the maps of the second section—R-4 to R-9. And dig up my reports of the last two weeks. What. . . ? The Germans? Plans? It's easy if you read their spoor." Spinelli handed some fresh reports an orderly sergeant brought in. "They're out to seize the crossing on the Meuse, cross—" He looked at the reports. "Cross the river most likely between Liège and Huy. . . . Why not? I would. You bet I would try if I were on their side. They'll push the Sixth Panzer through to Antwerp on the right, and the Fifth Panzer, after they take Liège, *bang* through to Brussels. . . . No, I don't say they *will*, I say that's what I read as their plan."

Lieutenant Rosen came in, saluted.

"Rosen, any constructive evaluation on corps radio?"

"No, sir, not so far. General, the barrage is coming closer, and is very precise, orderly in its arcs. They'll zoom in, hit us sure as hell in five minutes."

"Too bad, lieutenant. I've got to stay in contact and keep communications open. Move out the nontechnical crews and the cooks, and— Hello, Bruno? if what I said happens, you'll see a balls-up split between us and the English. Find out what Monty's reaction is. . . . Yes, yes, that old bastard von Rundstedt is going for throwing winning seven's at the crap table. *Es geht ums ganze,* which is: *It's all or nothing.* . . . Call me back after Bradley is briefed."

Captain Spinelli was at the window as a shell fell nearby, exploded into a rose of fire and earth. Trees came crashing down. "It's beginning to snow, sir, heavy as chicken feathers from a ripped pillow."

"You have a gift for lucid exposition, Angie. Get me Patton, and don't take any crap from him that he's busy on his own problems. I want him to hold—stop—where he is until I hear from HQ."

"Lousy weather. It's so bad we've not been able to send up any observation or bomber planes."

"In this, what the journalists call 'the cacophony of war,' the Germans are going to find their armor isn't going to move as fast as they planned. And snowdrifts are as bad as mud on tanks. They must cross the Meuse with no delay." Simon turned back to the maps. "Have to by the third day—before we can recover. And they'll have to depend on capturing our fuel dumps for gas. Get me?"

A phone buzzed. Spinelli picked it up. "Hello. Who? Yes, sir. Senior headquarters, General Bradley." He held out the phone to Simon, who took it almost with jubilation.

The day progressed badly; for the Americans, dank despair; and brilliantly for the Germans, wild optimism. The weather kept observation planes grounded. It was plain that the outposts, thinly held lines of Americans, had expected no attack and had gone down, been ground out, captured, bypassed. The Germans, as they advanced, clearly expected the disruption and confusion of the Americans would continue to grow worse. The heart of the enemy advance that day, Simon's maps showed, was toward the key road centers of Vith and Bastogne. Then, if these were evacuated, German thinking at the Army High Command was the Americans would not be such fools as to try to hold them. The Panzers would go on, smother Monschau and so have a clear set of roads through Eupen and Verviers. Simon, marking up his maps as reports came in, felt maybe they could do as they pleased.

By noon, the Germans were finding unexpected resistance in spots. Here and there, for all their confusion and snafus, the GI's were holding, dying. Some disruption of regiments and cross-road positions was taking place. HQ sounded as if it was gaining some sense and velocity, Simon thought. A bit confused, but who could blame them? He suggested some troop movements—take the beatup, unlucky 28th Division, great losses in the Hürtgen Forest battles and overloaded with raw replacements, bring them down from the north to Bastogne. Also, the 8th Corps headquarters would have to make some hard decisions. Simon remained calm, merely drinking too much coffee and breaking pencil points.

Regiments got badly bloodied holding some roads. But the Germans couldn't get through according to some timetable; not always. The enemy soldiers died in clumps in the snow—like broken crows on wintry farm fields—snow here and there turned strawberry-colored.

Simon suggested to HQ that they order up reinforcements from Luxembourg and from Rheims. More than suggested, as the day wore on. Headquarters put him in charge of some regional forward sections.

He and his staff—at last driven out by barrages—were now in a great stone warehouse smelling of wine vinegar. Wireless and phone crews were kept busy. Bleary-eyed, unshaven officers moved about with maps. Simon, his long sheepskin coat belted tight, drank mug after mug of coffee, unaware of just how much he put away of the strong brew. He waved off momentary distractions with almost a snarl.

Captain Spinelli had a big bruise on his forehead; he had fallen hard on the icy earth when his jeep was fired on at a stream crossing by Germans dressed in American uniforms. He had gotten away and limped a bit, but kept turning up the map references Simon asked for. For all the tension, the place took on a boisterous vitality smelling of dill pickles.

"Our Seventh Armored Division, sir, came rushing down from Aachen, picking up stragglers. Lots of battle-beaten sections."

"Where is it right now?"

"It's reported just outside Saint-Vith. It's fighting a pretty good withdrawal action."

"Don't tell General Hasbrouck that. He doesn't like the word 'withdrawing.' How's it look to you, Angie? *Me?* I think we're slowing them. HQ reports Dietrich's panzers got flogged by our Fifth Corps near the Ruhr dams.... I hope it's true, not whistling in a graveyard. Christ, our rear organization is all haywire. We've got no apparatus for withdrawal. The whole rear section sounds like a rout. Groups out of control and seeing Germans where there are no Germans. Where's my coffee?"

"Sir, you're hitting the java hard."

"Change to tea. . . . There are about two hundred Krauts from airdrops behind our lines, disrupting communications. I want them annihilated, pronto."

"Every man we can spare is out on patrol."

The twilight came too, dark and dank, the cold grew cruel, deadly. The American confusion was still growing. At the end of the first day, the panzers had cut all the communications of the 12th Army group. Bradley's HQ in Luxembourg was cut off from control of his 1st and 9th Army in the north. The 5th Army was still under orders to attack the Ruhr river dams. Simon wanted it to turn away to face the greater danger of the panzers. His request was refused by senior HQ staff that still did not realize the size and power of the German drive for a gigantic breakthrough. There was still no Allied concentration, rather a dispersion of interests.

Simon drank tepid tea, went out himself into the cold with a jeep and recon convoy—moving warily to the sound of guns. He came back to the vinegar warehouse HQ just before dawn, frozen, to drink brandy and coffee, sip overboiled soup and brandy, and find he had rocks in his bowels. He had a pretty good impression of German success, of what was shaping up. All night German armor had moved forward. Blasting to their control of the battered roads, moving on swiftly and with so much firepower, they could not be stopped in vital areas. Some American high-ranking officers went into paranoiac fantasies.

Simon tore a section out of a huge map and began to mark it up with red crayon. "Angie, they're still moving *Oberführer* and *Standarterführer* riding in leading tanks. They've bypassed Bastogne at last report, taken Houffalize and Wiltz to the south. And the defense of Saint-Vith in the center has split them into two columns. They're near our Army HQ at Spa. The news is all little sour green apples."

"What's General Bradley's reactions—direct action?"

"Damn if I know. Get me a scout plane and an escort of two machine gunners. I'm going to fly to HQ. I still don't think they see how big this thing is."

"Monty seems to, sir. He's stopped his Thirtieth Corps from

going north and is moving around to make his southern flank solid."

"That's something. Monty has a great sense of self-preservation."

There were sounds of scuffling outside. A muddy squad of six soldiers in sheepskin jackets came in, and between them three other soldiers in topcoats. Lieutenant Rosen followed them, his face scarlet with frostbite.

Lieutenant Rosen saluted. "Sir, these men claim to be American soldiers separated from their units."

"Are they?"

Simon merely glanced at the three stragglers.

"Papers look all right. They were in a jeep with the right markings, only. . . ."

The soldier with the buck teeth said, "We've been fighting, sir. Just got shot up. Lost contact with our unit."

"Only *what*? What the hell's biting you, Rosen?"

"The uniforms, sir, are regular issue, but don't seem to have been issued at the same time by supply."

Rosen was a CPA from Brooklyn in peacetime, and played chess from a portable board he carried.

One of the soldiers, smoking a cigarette, smiled. "We just picked up gear—it being so cold—what we needed from a depot that was burning, sir."

"Get rid of the cigarette," Simon said.

Lieutenant Rosen offered Simon a bit of paper. "I asked them to write out their names and serial numbers."

Simon thought: Rosen is worse than those Vienna Jewish analysts and their canting attitudes.

Walter Neyland	23546-987
Martin Bodie	68523-890
William A. Rome	54692-684

He looked up from a close scrutiny of the writing. "The seven, Rosen?"

"That's right, sir. No American draws a line halfway down the leg of the number seven."

A dark young soldier said, "I come from St. Louis. My folks

are refugees, and I enlisted to fight Hitler. I only had two years' schooling in St. Louis, so if the seven, sir, is—"

"Where did you go to school?" Simon felt his gut rumble.

"St. Louis."

Captain Spinelli shook off his attitude of passive tolerance. "I never heard too many people call it anything but St. Louie, not St. Louis."

The dark soldier said calmly, only a grimace of mouth muscle active, "I am not too sure of proper usage yet." He fumbled at a pocket, got out a letter. "A letter from my girl, sir."

Captain Spinelli looked at the postmark. "Two months old. She doesn't write often, does she?"

Simon turned to the other two soldiers. "You too refugees?"

"No, sir," said the blond boy. "Born in Brentwood, California. Attended UCLA and played Little League baseball as a kid in Gilmore Stadium."

"And you," he said, facing a tall soldier with a long jaw, chewing gum.

"New Brunswick, New Jersey. Apprentice carpenter at the Ford plant at Metuchen. I have my union card." He slapped his pockets, dug, handed over a crumpled green card. "It got wet. A F of L Local Forty-three."

Self-confidence, but no audacity among them.

Simon thought a while. "That Polack cook, Casmir, around? The one we took over after the conference? Go get him, captain. The dentist from Hackensack. And see if there are any packets of prunes around in the kitchen."

He turned back to his map study. Hell, it wasn't his job, these soldiers—let the MP's take them to Intelligence—if—

The soldiers, the squad guarding them, stared at each other.

The war outside was still in confusion. The day was dawning, reports showed, with great sections of the line torn to bits, panzers struggling successfully through ice and snow to keep moving. And, Simon noticed, they were moving. They were bypassing road points no one expected to hold, to be crushed later. The war aims of the Allies seemed a fragile continuity in mad hands.

Sergeant Casmir came in, rubbing cold hands in a soiled

kitchen apron. He gave the general a sloppy salute. He was wearing a heavy wool cap, a leather jacket and nonregulation boots. "Yes, sir, general. Trouble again with that molar?"

"Sergeant, as a skilled, knowledgeable dentist, I want you to look into the mouths of these three soldiers. If there are fillings, can you tell if they're American work or European?"

"Don't see why not. Open up, you guys; you, *wider*."

Only one did, the dark boy. The cook-dentist held a hanging naked light bulb close to the open mouth. He turned and shook his head.

"Schlock stuff, sir. Aluminum fillings. Never could be ours. Jesus, I never saw that recommended, no real protection to—"

The three soldiers had suddenly stiffened to attention, flung up their right arms, and all cried out, *"Heil Hitler!"*

Simon said, "Take them out under close guard."

Spinelli motioned to Lieutenant Rosen with a gloved hand. "Have them shot. We're moving out and we may be surrounded at any minute."

Simon didn't counter the order. In this world anyone can find himself victim or executioner. Casmir handed him a brown paper package. "Here you are, prunes, sir. Costive? They work better if you boil 'em."

Chapter 38

IN hundreds of square miles on a front of over two hundred miles, the battles went on, and from above to any frozen hawk circling in wonder, or Simon flying to HQ in a Piper Cub, it was a world ghostly bone-white, broken here and there by burned-out areas where tanks still flamed, their crews consumed inside or dying roasting alive, rolling in the snow. Simon, at dawn, had gone up. He saw along the road and paths the dead, inky blots—Germans and Americans, and some British. Still bundled against a cold now turning their blood to ice, their woolen scarves, rags fluttering in the cold wind. The scout plane flew low—vulnerable, unarmed, in weather too mucked-up for fighters or bombers.

Here and there, in shattered woods, men still alive fired at each other. Often they ran forward to throw up their hands and sink into drifts almost as if practicing calisthenics. Backward and forward, groups desperately pushed each other through ravines, over hills, and across patches of broken and shelled timber. Closer to towns, half eaten away by cannon fire, tanks were dug into the frozen earth. They fired into opaque pockets of mist, turning their turrets toward each other if of different markings—turrets like rusting knights' helmets in search of foes. The ditches and paths, Simon observed, were rimmed with wrecked vehicles, armor with blasted-off treads, recon personnel cars whose burning rubber sent up black, feathery plumes of smoke. Weasels, tracks broken, sides battered in like sardine cans, and various heavy guns upset off their mobile mounts, gun barrels shattered, so much junk, filled country lanes. Living shapes crawled around or lay moaning with messy wounds, the protruding ends of shattered bones.

Along a couple of hundred miles of shifting front, by the bigger villages, whole regiments lay or charged, crawled, dug themselves into rubble, the snouts of their rapid-fire weapons poking out and blasting. Men skidded on icy stone roads and fell, their loosened helmets went clattering and skimming across the cobbles. In the village street of Klemstadt, a priest, still chewing his breakfast, in melancholy contemplation recited the last rites to men dying along the curb.

Thousands and thousands of men and machines became merging clots as the engaging companies and divisions neared the two crossroads blocking the Germans' advance. Those stubborn junctions where the enemy had to divide his forces and go around the resistance points. At such points, the dead piled up and were pushed aside as medics, in the bitter cold, probed half-naked bodies, exposed torn flesh, carried dripping stretchers to collection points, places that resembled open-air butchers' shops. Men, like confirmed inebriates, staggered to field hospitals.

Simon, floating like a ghost over such scenes, felt at some end of Armageddon. There was no clear line of battle, no true front. Here and there, like some levee-destroying river overrunning icy fields, the panzers had punched their way and flooded forward streams of armor and men quickly, setting power and strength against mounting counterpressures. Some panzers went on to keep running, moving over towns and across ridges, the exhaust of their engines blue against white landscape and in muck turning brown on the overused roads.

Many columns, stolidly twitching like dying snakes, expired quickly as they ran out of fuel. Some heads appeared from the shells of their tanks and cars. Often, men piled out to look about them and wonder just where they were—while radios crackled and messages were sent or advice sought.

Some of the advance columns blundered into fixed-fire positions and were engulfed with flame, the direct blasting of cannon. Often the enemies own ammo in the armor took to exploding; men were flung to bits; others were standing in surrender—with arms up, black figures against the snow, and sometimes they were marched off, and sometimes there was revenge taken for those Americans executed after giving up to SS squads roaming deep behind the advance of the major fighting. Sometimes pockets existed where war was only a sporadic haphazard business.

The forest creatures died, too, or dug deep into the cold earth. Here and there one saw a dead deer, a tread-crushed rabbit, a dead cow in some farmyard, legs rigid and pointing up, the great udder unmilked. Chained-up dogs had long since stopped their strangled barking, and those still alive whimpered, noses on the ground.

The few planes, like Simon's, that could get up, skimmed burning woods, flattened-out villages, and from among rubble and along trails, observers could see the flashes of fire; below them men searched for other men, to destroy them. All along

[307]

hundreds of miles of sky and land, crushed farms, the various red tones of fires sent up great fountains of smoke. Guns firing at zero range tore holes through entire villages—sending spurting stones and earth, household goods, farm machinery, the remains of houses into the air. It became an increasing desolation, desperation; the grim purpose of men hunting men. Machines crushing machines, that was the full purpose of the day.

Bradley had come back from SHAEF and a conference with the Supreme Commander. Facing his staff, Bradley appeared settled in the conviction he was in trouble. Simon was on one side of the big room in Luxembourg, trying to thaw out his freezing hands from the miserable trip in the jolting Piper scout plane.

"Well, General Copperwood, you said we should be set for a counterattack."

"Yes, sir, it looks like we've got it. More than a minor inconvenience."

"A counterattack. . . . But, well—I'll be goddamned if I wanted one this big."

"It may be more than a counterattack. The size so far would indicate a full turning around in their plans. It's a hell of a major offensive."

"Yes, Copperwood, yes. Take it up with General Strong."

It was clear to Simon the Supreme Commander did not yet believe it was a major offensive. But Bradley did and began to regroup—contacted Monty and Patton—yet still insisted it was only a counterattack and a bogdown for the Germans. It took two more days before he accepted Simon's idea on the full extent of the German offensive.

SHAEF acted nobly—the Supreme Commander recommended Bradley's promotion with an added star. To General Marshall he sent a salutary message: "The 12th Army, Commander, General Bradley, kept his head magnificently and proceeded methodically and energetically to meet the situation. In no quarter is there any tendency to place any blame upon Bradley. . . ."

Simon merely made a comment to Colonel Bruno Holtzman as they redrew battle lines on new maps:

"Nothing wrong in generals trying to save each other's hides."

Later it was a sour note, however, to have Bradley claim: "No one came to me with a warning of any danger of counterattacking there in the Ardennes. I commanded nearly three quarters of a million men spread out over a front of 230 miles. It was impossible for me even to scan the intelligence estimates of subordinate units."

The reports of Generals Copperwood, Bedell Smith, and Strong, contrary to this statement, were buried in official files with defunct and defeated controversies.

It took General Bradley three days to come around to the bald fact that a major and deadly offensive had been mounted against him. Once he accepted the fact, he moved skillfully, with coherence and clarity, to counter it. Simon had been set up in a large, ornate room of a Luxembourg castle; however, so far from most facilities that his orderly-driver had to heat Simon's shaving water far below and come running up magnificent but badly chipped marble stairs with it, by the pint.

Simon was sleeping, not dreaming, frowning as he slept, when Captain Spinelli shook him awake after midnight. By Spinelli's side was Colonel Jeff Astruc, his frostbitten face half-buried in a dog-pelt collar.

"Christsake, Jeff, I need sleep. . . . Bent over those damn maps trying to find where we're holding, where the panzers are."

"Forget sleep. The general wants to move Patton north. You're to organize the routes and work out the maps, where we can rendezvous our gasoline tankers with him. It's all yours, baby."

"That bad? Patton to the rescue?" Simon sat up and rumpled his hair, scratched his chest, yawned, then shivered. Spinelli handed him his sheepskin coat, which he put on cape-wise and stood in naked feet, then paced around his map table, stopping to make some minute analysis on the scrawled-upon maps.

"Move him up from the Saar. Pronto?"

"Right. Rational strategic motivating, we call it. We're worried over deep snow and his rate of speed. Saint-Vith and Bastogne may go at any moment."

"We can't fly six armored divisions north."

"It's your problem, Simon. Get Patton here and in time. *All* yours."

"Be sure to thank the general for me." He picked up a map. "Patton, he'll have to swing north at right angles to his present line of attack. Six divisions. Give me that big-scale map, Angie. Who else is pulling HQ chestnuts out of the fire?"

"Dever's Sixth," said Jeff. "Moves to fill the breach left by the Third. It's that kind of a ballgame, Simon. Hazardous, and just now very problematic."

"Hell, that uncovers Strasbourg and the Alsatian plains."

"Maybe. The Seventh Armoured and the Tenth are racing for Saint-Vith and Bastogne. We hope to pile in all we can get there, hold in the end, and push the Germans into defiles."

"Where's the Eighteenth Airborne?" Simon felt the stone floor turn his naked feet to ice.

"Refitting at Rheims. They got clobbered at Arnhem."

Simon stuck his icy feet into frayed red slippers. "Get them into the fight." He accepted a mug of hot coffee Spinelli poured from a thermos jug. His teeth clicked against the cup's rim.

"Get Patton north, Simon." Jeff seemed overfatigued. "That's the important, vital thing. The general will see you before you take off. There's a plane waiting."

Simon felt he'd never be warm again. "In this weather, flying again with my queasy stomach. Damn it, my feet are freezing. Angie, some place I have fur-lined boots."

The morning of December 19, Simon and Captain Spinelli, Lieutenant Rosen, and Simon's orderly were flying south. The fog was thick here and there, trees too close; like apparitions, eerie, unsubstantial. Below, when the day cleared a bit, were burned-out landscapes and shattered armor. Roads torn up by treads of personnel carriers, mobile guns—yet still busy with scudding cars and clanging tanks.

"Can Patton get through, sir? In the next few days?" asked Lieutenant Rosen.

"I don't know. I feel sure of one thing. The Germans have to seize their bridgeheads across the Meuse in the next two days, and exploit them, or their whole advance is kaput."

Captain Spinelli was reading a letter from his family.

[310]

"It's going to be tough tittie for them. But they've come through so far."

Simon felt feverish. The plane shook as it hit an air pocket, or what wasn't an air pocket; there were doubts, Simon remembered, that air pockets existed. The plane had a rough time of it. "I'm going to take out a tank column, part of a division I trained in the States—when we turn Patton north. You're both invited."

Captain Spinelli took off the glove on his right hand and blew steadily and hard on his fingers. "Sure, sir. Glad to. Damn cold. General, the butter-fingered jerk I am, I've never killed a man. Have you, sir?"

Simon's thoughts were elusive, vague. He pulled them back. "That's my trade in part, killing. Survival too. I hate wars and the people who cause them. But I've always felt an army was set up to prevent wars. And fight the debacle of common sense when things got round so peace wasn't in the cards. . . . Yes, sure, I've killed men. World War I, Colonel Bruno Holtzman and I, we had some mean times in the AEF. We between us, killed a good number of men. . . . In China, on a small scale, close-up, four or five."

Lieutenant Rosen asked, "How did you feel? I mean, the first time, sir?"

The plane banked to the left and Simon caught sight of, far off through the streaked window, a column of greenish-dark smoke spiraling into the air, then strong winds tore it apart. "The last time was not like the first time; you reconcile easy to killing. You feel good it isn't you that's dead. Bad, because maybe I've always felt human life is unique."

Spinelli smiled. "What you Hebs call a *shlimazl*, Rosie."

Lieutenant Rosen made fists of his gloved hands. "I killed a man. My father." He looked around, expressionless. Simon noticed a pulse active someplace close to the lieutenant's jawline. "I was ten. My old man once or twice a year liked to go out on the beach, out on the Great South Bay past the Hamptons. To shoot at tin cans, driftwood. He was no hotshot deer hunter—just a furrier on Seventh Avenue. Been a sharpshooter in the Russian Army in 1914, came to New York after the Revolution. . . .

Anyway, he liked to shoot at tin cans and driftwood. Had this Czar's sharpshooter's medal at home—never wore it."

Spinelli watched the white vapor of their breathing, and said nothing.

The pilot turned toward them. "Landing, sir, in a couple of shakes. There's a pretty neat airstrip the Luftwaffe buggers left behind for us."

Lieutenant Rosen was shaking his head, working the corners of his mouth as if trying to relocate something in his memory. "This one day, late June, we were out for the day, sandwiches, a jar of soup, bottles of beer. My old man, he went up on a dune to set up empty Del Monte stewed tomato cans, and me, I picked up the .22. A Sears, Roebuck Savage, I remember. My old man had put it down on a rock. He was careful of firearms, never let a little kid hold it."

"Everybody belted down?" asked the pilot.

Lieutenant Rosen was bent over, but eyes held on Simon. "I was holding the .22 in my hand, just took it off the rock, and then aiming it at clumps of shore grass, rocks on the dune, yelling *bang! bang!* It went off."

Captain Spinelli said, "I wouldn't have a gun in the house."

"The slug got my old man right in the base of the skull. Right *here*. I was ten, not big for my age, either. . . . It was set down as an accident. They didn't even send me to juvenile detention. Nothing."

The plane was low—very low—skimming over pole pines and wrinkled ridges where the snow had been blown free by the winds from chocolate-colored rocks. Lines of cars and Weasels, antitank guns on treads appeared below—growing larger, then, like a rolled-out soiled bandage, was the airstrip from which snow had been scraped.

"Christsakes," asked Spinelli, "it *was* an accident, Rosie, wasn't it?"

Lieutenant Rosen said, "Everybody said so."

The plane's wheels touched down. The airstrip wasn't too level and they were jolted for a couple of hundred feet.

Chapter 39

GENERAL PATTON was having his boots polished by a Negro sergeant. Preparing to leave his trailer, his belts, straps, and fancy weapons on hips were all in place. He had listened to Simon, and kept nodding while he replaced some new puppies in a padded basket on the trailer floor—while the bitch, with the litter tugging at her dugs, watched him with confidence. "Damn best batch of pups this ol' bitch ever threw. I lined her with Willie Wilson's stud, Art Work. . . . You like truffles? Woods here full of them. . . . I'm listening, I'm listening. Go on, Simon."

"On paper, turning six divisions north with no confusion, or loss of time, is textbook dreaming. George, really—can you do it?"

"Your schedule seems a good *maybe*. Hell, of course I can do it. Those simps and pukes at HQ they have an idea I wear Indian feathers and carry a wine cellar. I *do* have a few bottles of burgundy. . . . Simon, you look lousy. Go see my medical chief."

"Just a bit of fever, gut ache—off my feed. . . . If you don't object, I'd like to command the Second Armored section, right off its ass. I trained with it."

"It's your baby. Find staff work superfluous, eh?" A colonel came in and saluted. "General, all divisions report turning north on routes indicated."

Patton was in some depths of revery over the pups. He looked up, grinned. "Good. We'll hit 'em right on their snouts. General Copperwood is taking over the Second Tank Group. See he's filled in and put two bottles of burgundy and a terrine of *foie gras* in his grub pack. Sure now, Simon, you don't want a champion Patton pup?"

The next two days Simon had a feeling of living in a surrealist drama of queasiness and excitement, extreme agitation. He refused to take his temperature, and felt his body sweat, turn hot and then cold. He rode in a command car over rutted trails and took a position in the lead tank of his column on a secondary road among ancient trees. He heard Captain Spinelli report road mines and Lieutenant Rosen speak of German Army Group H moving to assaults across the Waal and Maas. He remembered muttering, as he swallowed aspirin: "We have to keep Antwerp, need it for a supply harbor. Supplies and re-placements and reorganize, regroup our losses through the damn place." His columns were grinding through forest villages, three prongs of vehicles and gasoline tankers, tons of bridging equipment. Signal Corps wire too, loads of assault cable, and submarine cable to lay across rivers. Also repair trucks and mobile machine shops, as some of the armor was flawed in manufacturing.

Simon gave orders. "Any tank that throws a tread or conks out, shove it aside. Keep going. Keep the columns taut and moving (and the fever sang an old high school song in his head: '*Ann Marie Jones . . . Queen of the Tambourine, the cymbals . . . and the bones!*' ").

On December 25 ("Birth of the Prince of Peace," Lieutenant Rosen reminded them) they were moving downhill in closely planted forests, visibility cut down, for the clearings of before the war were now overgrown with heavy scrub. Maps proved unreliable among the roots of the deciduous trees. The going was harder for all the tracked and wheeled transport.

Near noon a scout car reported it had observed men in white winter coveralls backed by German-marked tanks in a wood ten miles ahead. Simon ordered a turning aside of his columns to get around the threat of having to do battle there. He couldn't stop to fight some small scouting contingent of Germans that were this near his columns. He had to keep up with other Patton divisions running north, spectacles of elephantine power among the big timber, bouncing on bad roads, the men freezing in tanks, personnel carriers, open jeeps. Sometimes great fires were lit and the men fed as they danced and beat their arms for warmth. Sometimes it was a night run if the section looked good and the roads were in fair condition. From Luxembourg came coded messages that the situation was desperate, losses heavy.

Lieutenant Rosen touched Simon's arm. They were riding in armor—behind two scout tanks, turrets open. The stink of fuel oil, wet wool, unwashed body odors was coming up strong to them.

Simon felt ready to throw up. On the pressure of Rosen's touch, he turned. "Huh?"

Rosen pointed to where a scout car lay on its side by a steep ravine—a white cross painted on its olive-green body.

"Accident," Simon said. "Get me map 74-A and—"

Just then a whole side of the road among some beech trees and low shrub took on a black ball of violence—the center of it glowed red. There was something like stones falling, clinking against the tank as Simon and the lieutenant both ducked in a furtiveness of shock—and they both at once came erect.

"It's a 155mm," Simon said, grabbing the radio mike. "All tanks in column Fox, attention. May be running into rat-pack scouting group. Button up. Stay in radio communication. All other columns keep moving north."

Two black objects had appeared ahead on the forest road. Medium German tanks. Simon was pleased they weren't the big babies, the Tiger IV's. The enemy was firing and the column split as had been planned if attacked, split to right and left, the Weasels and the scout cars and supply trucks fell back. The tanks on either side of Simon's were firing. He could feel the bang of concussion over the clatter of the diesels. He shook his head as Rosen tried to pull him down into the tank's interior. "No, I'm staying on top." He lifted in numb hands, the icy field glasses to his eyes. A tank to the right of him took one on its left tread, which broke with a dreadful grinding metal sound. The tank began to spin like a child's toy out of control, and the orange core of flames enveloped one side of it, paint blistering. The top flipped open and a burning man came howling up, as if propelled, shedding flaming cloth. He fell into the snow, crawling and rolling—all the time howling, all the time he was dying in flames. As Simon's craft passed the disabled tank, another figure came up out of it, hair on fire, its hands turning to cinders on the red-hot iron rim. Then it lay still, charring, and the stink of the cooking flesh filled Simon's throat with bile when they passed

[315]

on. He had a deep consciousness of purpose: no miscalculation, no miscalculation.

Great blows were being struck all around, the exploding shells on short fuses expanding to crimson, Chinese red, royal scarlet, all rimmed in mourning black and containing steel fragments driven by forces beyond the speed of sound.

Over all this rain of destruction, the heavy machine guns on the transports and wheeled cars were firing. The *zong! zong!* of bazookas had the perversity of a mean sound all their own. Another American tank took a blow that seemed to stun it and then stop it in its tracks. Like a turtle out of control it slowly zigzagged toward the left just before its fuel, ammo, and shells exploded in a great roar and a blasting. The disintegrating tank seemed to sigh as it crumbled away to the buzz-saw sound of metal breaking up.

Simon, eyes to field glasses, found four German tanks ahead in a clearing—in ambush—and he radioed his right flanking-columns to take shelter under some great oaks. His left column he ordered to turn and retreat. He did not call for aid from the two outer sections moving north. They must go on.

"Rosen, get the hell into a scout car and tell Major Colman to hold his fire until the Krauts give chase to our retreating armor, then pour it on them. His radio is out. Everything in action. Everything he's got to fire. His recon boys to set up mortars. I want every bazooka fired till it melts, the 155's rapid fire, rapid!"

He ducked a blast of flying earth, leaves with a center of steel.

The general seemed unhurt. He had seen several direct blows of American shells pound strike against the enemy iron, not enter. Damn fuses were set wrong or he was getting some lousy ammo the factories back in Detroit were screwing up.

A German tank did become a column of fire as little black figures ran from it and a machine gun played its tune like cicadas late at night, and the black figures lay still.

Simon felt something strike the tank and his back teeth seemed to go loose for a moment. A fresh dent in the steel armor was just below him on the flank of the tank. A voice from below in the belly of the machine spoke up.

[316]

"Duck, sir. If they hit them chains we have piled up on the front of the crate, they'll come apart like buckshot."

"Keep on rolling, soldier."

Simon picked up the fallen radio mike—he didn't remember dropping it—and began to give new orders. Two more of his tanks ground to a stop. He looked back over his shoulder. One was circling like a wounded rabbit with its mind gone, the other had just opened up like a sardine can at the seams and lay on its side, thick gray-green smoke pouring out.

He saw his retreating column hightailing it, and he ordered it to get out of sight, turn around, and come running when he gave the signal. A German tank went too close to a deep ditch that turned into a ravine. It fell away like a stone, went skidding down a hillside. It rolled over and over with a grace hard to believe for such a heavy object; absolutely unique, Simon thought. No attempt was made to unbutton the escape hatch.

Now the advancing German tanks were moving at a good rate. Simon had his tank pull over. From the wood there came the fast and furious fire of American mortars, antitank guns, the heavies from the big tank turrets. Simon had his tank move up to the action and was unaware one side of his face was singed and blistered from some close shell burst.

The German armor was dying quickly as tank after tank hissed, roared, two exploding very close, so that he had to duck down into the smell of the interior—a tank in battle, an engine grinding, gunner sweating acid and the echoing inside the iron closet brain-bending. There was an incessant nibbling away of his sanity. He hoped he didn't become incoherent. When he again put his head out, the battle was coming to its end, the once retreating American column was coming up fast, firing, the group in the oak forest was in the open now, picking off surviving German armor. A cold rain began to fall, turned to sleet, to pelt them. The three surviving German tanks were taking evasive action, smashing against trees and barging over sapling and second growth. Simon felt a serenity without smugness until his entrails seemed on fire. He doubled up in pain.

The firing had died down and he panted, stood erect, felt his fever had become a great heat and he climbed down, nearly

[317]

falling by the side of the road. Captain Spinelli came riding up in a scout jeep, his helmet strap flapping around his Adam's apple as he leaped out, saluted, smiling. Spinelli's body was twitching, he almost hysterical, for he kept moving about, crouching at times like a boxer, Simon thought, dodging blows.

"We did it! sure did it, sir! Clobbered them but good! Got seventeen of their tanks. Got one undamaged when its motor conked."

"Any prisoners?"

"Six wounded. A *Hauptsturmführer*, two *SS Waffen* bastards. Most aren't going to make it. Burns. Hey, sir, *your* face!"

"Just singed a bit. We took a bit of blasting."

Simon became aware of a German officer, part of his jacket burned away, hair singed, a stare of idiocy, some blocked-out horror suggested by his eyes. He was a major, by his torn shoulder tabs, or a colonel—a *Standartenführer*. He seemed in deep shock as he stood there among some shivering, oil-stained prisoners. Simon stepped forward and saluted. "General Copperwood."

The major did not move. He said in a gritty voice, "Swabian, Swabian." He made twitchy mouth gestures before he spoke again, then in remote tones seemed to be seeking remembered words:

> *Uber allen Gipfeln*
> *Ist Ruh . . .*
> *In allen Wipfeln*
> *Spurest du*
> *Kaum einen Hauch*

"What the hell," Spinelli said.

Simon motioned toward the rear. "Get him to some medics."

"Christ, he's got a whole side of his head caved in."

"Die Vögelein schweigen im Wald. . . ."

The German major seemed to react to Simon's closeness with grotesque inconsistencies. He rolled his eyes, then fell backward, his face as he lay was upturned and it was clear to see the left side of his head had been crushed and dripped gray matter into the dirty road snow.

[318]

"I don't know, sir, how he could even last to get out of his tank. He's way out of his nut." Spinelli bent low. "He's dead."

"Angie, check our own losses."

Simon felt it could be himself lying there. Lying with a split head, me dead, *dead* and I'm frightened now and the pain *is* bad.

"What—are—our—losses—Angie?"

"Yeah. Some right guys gone who were looking forward to being in on the kill in Berlin."

A tank passed, throwing up shards of packed snow, its commander giving the thumbs-up sign to the group around the dead major. "Missed you in the fight." Spinelli grinned, and held up a middle finger, yelled cheerfully, "Up yours, Charlie-boy."

The commander shouted back: "My nose bleeds for you."

Simon was freezing—between the heat of fever. "Bury the dead. Get the wounded to the ambulances. Serve rations. Something hot. I want all but the worst bunged-out tanks to form up in three hours. Get me General Patton on the radio."

"Man. He'll eat his ass out for missing this."

Simon took three aspirins and drank big gulps of water from a canteen the captain offered him.

On the morning of December 26, General Patton's advance columns led by General Simon Bolivar Copperwood's tanks reached Bastogne. The Germans began shifting the weight of their armor and firepower to the south and southwest. The enemy divisions were still fighting furious actions. But the salient that the Germans had made, from Bastogne through St. Hubert and Marchen to Malmédy and Elenborn was getting them noplace. Their desire to get to the Meuse was blocked. While the fighting was murderous and heavy, it had peaked, was turning against them. Some kind of order—for the Americans—was coming out of chaos. In less than a week, HQ reported the Allies had set back the most powerful offensive yet mounted against them since the invasion of Europe. Confused and overrun American divisions had taken great damage, casualties, and fought back. Had held in the most vital spots. It was admitted two-thirds of the houses in Antwerp were hit, a lot reduced to rubble. Liège was even harder hit: VI's and VII's killed thousands.

General Simon Bolivar Copperwood, settled into the ruins of a convent near Bastogne, was a sick man. His face was blistered and his inability to eat anything was complicated by a high fever. He refused, for all his onerous condition, to stay in bed.

"Gotta be at the meeting—the official Donnybrook—at Hasselt on the twenty-eighth, Angie. Supreme Commander going to be there. Field Marshal Montgomery. All the big monkeys on the stick . . . never mind my fever."

"It's snowing heavily, sir," said Captain Spinelli. "Real heavy snow. You're in pain. You keep holding your side. No doc is going to let you travel. A doctor is coming over, sir, to examine you."

"Goddamn it, Angie, get me a clean uniform, shaving water, and some brandy. That's an order, soldier."

Simon stood up and wondered at the lack of intensity of response in his legs, and where he was. A great stabbing began to move through his body. He spun slowly left. He suspected that was the way the earth rotated on its axis, left. Or was it the other way? That was the last thought Simon remembered as his knees folded up neatly like a carpenter's ruler. He experienced the feeling of being propelled as an amorphous mass through a dark, moving tunnel, a channel made of some red living flesh, wet, warm flesh. It was contracting like a womb expelling a fetus—pressing him, confining him. By the time Simon hit the stone floor he was unconscious.

The man in the hospital bed in Luxembourg had a deep, deep thought that was on the theme of alienation. It was clear, it hinted this was a moment of rare virtue—one had to simplify oneself. It was as if this was a time when truth was still oscillating, weighing the final self-confrontation. The man knew he was dreaming, he knew he had come a long way out of some searing pain. The rest was as something he had heard in China; had he actually been there? Once, as he remembered it, three wise old sages with brushed-out whiskers were drinking vinegar from a jug. The Buddha found it sour. Confucius had no reaction at all to the drink. Only Lao-Tzu smacked his lips and found it life-giving.... The man was then in Henekey's wine bar in the Strand in London playing Shove Ha'penny—no it was in the Chelsea pub, the Crossed Keys. The girl by his side said, "Our color is much better this morning, isn't it?"

The man opened his eyes—he had no idea who he was. He looked up into the face of a wide, middle-aged Army nurse with captain's bars on her collar. She was holding one of his wrists, casually taking his pulse. "Yes, indeed, our color is so much better, General Copperwood."

He wanted to ask, "Does wolfbane still bloom in the Carpathians?" Instead, he turned his head and saw he was in a kind of stone vault, a room with rafters, and in other beds were two bandaged officers. One with a leg in traction. The smell was of carbolic, also an oily odor; stale lemon peel, bedpans, the starch in the nurse's uniform.

"What's this place?"

"You've been asking that, general, for three days in your fever. It's the Ninth Army hospital in Luxembourg."

Emotions made of tenuous membranes filled him. Luxembourg, Patton, Bastogne, the Meuse. I am General Copperwood. "Thank you, nurse, I'm back in my skin."

"Now we'll have a good wash-up and try and eat our breakfast. And—"

"Oh?" The features of Jeff Astruc from senior headquarters appeared behind the nurse, who was looking at her wristwatch as she counted Simon's pulse.

"Well, Simon, you look vital enough this morning, It was touch and go there." He flipped a gloved hand right to left.

"What happened?"

"What happened? Your appendix burst, that's what happened. You've been riding your damn tank with an inflamed, pus-filled gut, and it burst wide open. Blew like an overinflated tire."

Simon tenderly touched his bandaged stomach. It seemed not to know his fingers. He wanted to say, "No woman winds a clock properly."

Instead it came out as, "Burst appendix?"

"Don't know how you kept going the last days, full of poison.

[321]

Anyway, today is big stuff for you. . . . Get the general shaved, nurse, and propped up. If he can stand it."

"Fever down, pulse good. But he's still a bit drugged—keeps saying odd things."

"How the battle go?" Simon asked. "The *Blitzkrieg?*"

"Still mopping up. The Kraut bust-through failed for the panzers, all the Germans. *Kaput—alles.* Costly to us, of course, your losses very heavy. But for them. . . . The final end as an offense force. Brad's coming at noon to see you."

"Is he?" (He almost said, "Napoleon at Champs-Aubert.")

"You're getting your second star, general." Jeff handed the nurse a bottle of champagne he took from his greatcoat pocket. "Give him a slug when he can handle it, nurse. He's turning green."

"The second star?" At first it seemed irrelevant, then magnificent. He'd act polite as old pie. The *second* star!

"Congrat," said the nurse, shoving a thermometer into Simon's mouth. "Don't talk."

Simon took out the sliver of glass. "My tank action was really a kind of standoff, permitting George to move faster. Keep rolling. The Germans turned tail and—"

"You're not getting the star for that roughhouse butchery. It's for you designing, planning for the Patton divisions to left turn and come north on the run. Had a hell of a lot to do with swinging the whole battle."

Simon quoted Churchill: "Nothing in war ever goes right except by accident. . . . There is only one thing certain in war, that it is full of disappointments and mistakes. . . . There are no safe battles."

The nurse shoved the sliver of glass back into Simon's mouth. She had blue agate marble eyes and a downy upper lip; *that's* a sure sign of passion, Uncle Brewster used to say; even if she was middle-aged and wide, and looked tired. Two stars! He was still peeling off the layers of his last dreams, not sure this scene itself wasn't a dream. Two stars! The slow climb up the Army wall, stratum by stratum. Three stars? Four stars? Voluptuous swarming stars spun him into dizziness as he closed his eyes.

He lay overcome by a happy inertia, like warm milk in his

veins. To live respected by one's superiors and die lamented by the folks.

He heard the nurse say, as she took a temperature reading: "Now you've made him excited, he's up a half degree. We want him nice and calm for the general, don't we?"

Book Eight

It is not the critic who counts, not the man who points out how the strong man stumbled and fell, of where the doer of deeds could have done them better. The credit belongs to the man who is actually in the arena; whose face is marred by dust and sweat and blood; who strives valiantly; who errs and comes short again and again . . . and spends himself in a worthy cause; and at the best knows in the end the triumph of high achievement, and who, at the worst if he fails, at least fails while daring greatly. . . .

—THEODORE ROOSEVELT

What experience and history teach is this —that people and governments never have learned anything from history, or acted on principles deduced from it.

—HEGEL

(From the notebooks of Simon Copperwood)

Chapter 40

THE Casslins of Virginia were names historians thought of *after* they mentioned the Fairfaxes, the Lees, Jeffersons, the Washingtons, the Patrick Henrys. Not of great fame, but old respected stock. Not given to heroic deeds or very bad habits. They were solid merchants who made, and lost, fortunes; tidy sums, but not a great amount of capital in rice and molasses, indigo, salt fish, timber, wool. Enough had died in American battles since the French and Indian War to fill a genteel graveyard. There had been a major who lost his life in Paris, after a mysterious fall down the Ritz elevator shaft. Since the turn of the century one remembered a Senator, three Congressmen (one who helped form the Bull Moose Party).

Margerie Rose Casslin was thirty-two, unmarried, a graduate of Smith, whose gracious poetry several times a year appeared in some small magazine, a publication of which she once said, "Like human nature, not permanent." She had corresponded with William Carlos Williams, Ezra Pound, Robinson Jeffers; once had received a letter that baffled her from Gertrude Stein and Margerie had never replied.

She was a tiny woman with beautiful aquiline features, large hazel eyes, and wore a fringe of her chestnut-colored hair in bangs across her forehead, as she had seen it long ago in a photograph of Katherine Mansfield. She lived near Alexandria, Virginia, in her father's (the family's) Colonial mansion, called by the press, "Senator Casslin's nest." She attended few events in Washington, twice a year went to writers' and poets' conferences in New England or New York. If in that city, she'd have lunch with Edna St. Vincent Millay or Margaret Anderson at Polly's or Romany Marie's, and with people whose names she forgot at Elinor Wylie's uptown. Robert Frost had once said a word in praise of Margerie's poem, "Autumn Heat." Also, a large woman poet who smoked cigars had offered her the pleasures of Sappho's love in a room at the Martha Washington. Margerie had fled in horror to the Pennsylvania Station and taken a midnight train. She took to her bed with a low fever for two weeks, writing in her journal, "I am in an emotional *cul-de-sac.*"

For her highly strung nerves, she took some long trips on boats, to be by herself, away from relatives, friends. She enjoyed watching the fox-hunting, hard-drinking, hard-living neighbors: members of her church, the country club; the sound of Virginian social events. Margerie had a firm core of strength, integrity, the ability to surmount those recurring periods of depression after she had completed some small cycle of poems, working for weeks on them.

Then, at release from work, falling into moods that caused her doctor—as he unbuttoned her blouse and listened to her heartbeat—to shake his head. "Damn it, Marge, *why*"—he thumped his fingers held against her chest—"(cough, inhale) didn't you get married like all the healthy old family fillies, raise dogs or horses? You like Yeats?"

"Very much." She buttoned her blouse, head down, smiling. Old Doctor Chubb didn't cause her any shyness or shame. He had brought her alive *and* weeping, so he swore, into the world. "Beautiful and bawling—real tears, I swear." Prescribed enemas for her costive state as a schoolgirl, and pried just every place with rubber-clad fingers; prescribed for her late and painful menstruating, and added she had the heart of a prize racehorse. Doctor Chubb was an old-fashioned doctor—his monthly medical journals unread—drove an ancient Packard with the dangerous daring of one who needed stronger glasses. Dr. Chubb felt that "every woman should have a great deal of sexual pleasuring and bring up large, healthy children." He had six daughters, who provided him with many grandchildren. He was a great reader of Balzac. He too wrote poetry but never showed it to anyone but Margerie. He told his housekeeper (he was a widower), Mrs. Ryedell, "That Margerie Casslin needs children, a house to run, meals to prepare, a wider world than just other neurotic poets, and/or solitary, lonely trips."

He prescribed for her gin and tonics, horseback riding, "And dancing lessons. Keep those beautiful legs active, and get a car of your own."

Margerie found the gin and tonics too strong for her, settled for Spanish sherry, and acquired a small English car, an MG, which she drove with great skill. She became a lover of sports cars, and traded up three times. During periods of musing and personal fantasies, she often found herself driving off the road, hitting a fencepost, or just escaping mashing herself into the tailgate of a tobacco-hauling truck.

It was at a big show, in Baltimore, of imported sports cars, that she got to know better Lieutenant General Copperwood. A large man in hairy tweeds, silver hair thinning, tanned face, a neat, clipped English military-type mustache. He was standing in front of an overdone Jag. Her brother Ned had once had him to the house. He swayed ever so slightly, smiled at Margerie. The officer was just now, what her brother called "looped," or "smashed." Her father said he was "not a proper gentleman."

"I'd love to own an Isotta-Fraschini," she said.

"Good girl. Buy you a drink? I'm General Simon Copperwood."

"My father, Senator Casslin, talks about you. My brother, Ned, had you to the house. I'm Margerie Casslin."

"You sat in the garden, I remember now—way off."

"Father doesn't like you—I mean your ideas on military spending."

"Don't like them myself. What about the drink? You can tell me all the lousy things your father says about me."

Oh, he was really looped, but walking perfectly, holding her arm.

The bar off the main showroom of the auto exhibition space was overlit—deep ottomans, booths, game heads. And too busy. But the general, after pushing to the bar, came across to her in a booth, carrying two scotches and water. As they sipped, he kept studying her. "Something about a writer. Yes?"

"Really. . . ."

He smiled, a good smile, as he snapped his fingers. "Yes, novels?"

"General, poems."

He snapped his fingers again. "Of course. 'The Eye of the Storm.' Didn't read it. Saw a review, something about 'the perils of our appetites for the unknown.' Shame on you."

She laughed. She had a small laugh, a soft, plausible laugh, he decided. It came, he figured, from a some secret corner of her body. Her tiny body; he had always liked large women, well-made; *stacked.*

"Do you drink a lot, general?"

"I drink too much, but not a lot. Only today I've had a kick in the ass—the Pentagon rejected a plan—"

She felt he knew women, too well the way he asked, by his tone, for sympathy. What he was feeding her was a "line," as her friends called this kind of conversation.

"I worked for a year on a really good airborne-division system—"

"Airborne division, old cars, general?"

"Simon."

"You're certainly an odd type of general. Are you a good one?"

"The best. I'll get us another round." He reached for her glass, and she pushed it away from his fingers. "I've still a lot left."

"I'd better taper off myself. I've a report to write tonight. Can I give you a lift? I've a car outside, Oh, safe. Staff sergeant driver."

"No."

"I meant I'm not driving."

I wonder, he thought, what she thinks of me? Destructive? Full of boozy flippancy? I wonder what I think of myself. Does she care I'm within reach of fifty? I've had enough women in my life. I mean this kind. The *rest?* call it entertainment.

They sat talking easily of old cars, of new sport jobs. Surface verbal ice skating, the petty orthodoxies of first meeting, she thought, this kind of chatter. But it was pleasant and it passed time. She had nothing much to do, and her poetry came slowly—at odd moments. It was one of her fallow periods; she dreaded them—for she seemed to sense a kind of hovering dread, some hideous event coming. Her nerves would become taut. The birds in the garden of her father's house would appear to be talking French. Not modern French, but the French of Villon. . . . The general, Simon, was talking to her earnestly—she began to focus on his words. He was talking about some women at the bar, loud and sumptuously dressed. He was rather aggressive—and so large a man. A type she disliked—the professional soldier. The other Pentagon brass; generals, majors, that Senator Casslin and Ned brought out to the house, at times when some military bill was on its way. (They never said anything more than "It's a hell of a nice day," made clumsy gallantries, and noted the price of everything was too much. . . . "As for the young people, they're a lot of Commie freaks, Miss Casslin, believe-you-me.")

"You're married?" she asked Simon.

"I've had two wives."

"You loved them?"

He smiled, patted her hand. "Margerie, on one mild scotch, you're pretty nosy. Of course I loved them. First one has four grown kids today, by someone else. The other? The other died; an accident. Oh, *before* the war. Lady, you have a husband?"

She shook her head. She looked at the tiny watch on her thin wrist. "I really must—"

He stood up. Not a sway, any sign of the load he was carrying. "Be happy to get you on your way."

She looked smaller than ever by his side as they picked their way through the growing crowd.

Jesus, I've still this feeling I overreact when I pick up a woman, he thought.

He still typed with only two fingers, after all the years. Typed swiftly, bent over the portable, frowning. He was in his shorts, in the small, overmodern hotel room, the scars showing on his torso, some sunk into smooth patches, one still angry red with welts like overbaked bread crust.

"Almost certainly [he typed], any two historians would disagree in significant ways if asked to give a description of a thinking officer, and each would disagree with what the other had said on the subject before. It comes down to the fact that

[331]

soldiers are whatever a nation needs in battle. But there is never any doubt about who is and who is *not* a creative soldier."

Jesus H. Christ! He stopped typing and rubbed the palms of his hands together. Oh, the damn imprudence of the aging mind in heat. He fingered his chin and got up and found the bottle of Jim Beam in his bag. He took it right from the bottle, a small good tot, swallowed, and stood as if listening to himself. He heard nothing as to an answer. What psychological quirk was up his prat? He picked up the phone and asked to be connected with the Shore House. He could understand a hard-on—but *love?* Now? again?

On the phone Margerie sounded sleepy.

"Simon here—Simon Copperwood. It just came to me you, we, might be going down to the horse show tomorrow in Clearwood. If so, give you a ride, a lift down."

She made that little laugh again. "With, of course, your sergeant driver?"

He too laughed now, relieved, as the tightness went from his chest. "Look, Margerie, I'm sober now, fairly so." (To himself he added: But not too sane. I've walked into an old trap.)

They were married two months later in the parlor of the Casslin house, by a Presbyterian minister, with General Roger Millhouse, now the President's military aide, as best man, and only a select group of people present, Souki Miller, plump and sassy, a few Casslin in-laws. *Newsweek* noted briefly: "MARRIED. Lt. Gen. SIMON BOLIVAR COPPERWOOD, most decorated Pentagon officer, Commander of the Washington War College and MARGERIE ROSE CASSLIN of the FFV political family; poet (the Compton Prize), six volumes of avant garde verse; the latest, *Aristotle's Waltz;* daughter of Senator Colton Casslin.

Her father had taken Margerie aside just before the wedding ceremony, taken her by one elbow to the "Washington Room," the family called it; for on a paneled wall hung a framed letter addressed to Captain Silas Casslin, Continental Army, 1st Virginia Line: "It has been called to my notice that your camp is often known to drunken disorder, an influx of doxies, and much

[332]

given to the playing of games of cards, which conditions I now command you to remedy with no delay.

Yrs urgently
George Washington, Gen."

"Margerie, you're marrying a sonofabitch. But an intelligent one." The Senator's face, she noticed, glowed pink as a baby's rump from the wedding morning's tots of bourbon.

"What kind of a wedding present is this, father?"

"All right. I just want you to know if you keep him on a straight course, he'll end up a four-star general. He'll have to beat out Mac, and Brad is at the moment the top man. But as for Simon, if you'll have him keep his temper and not go thinking too much independently—thinking beyond the rules isn't too popular at the Pentagon."

Margerie kissed her father's cheek. "I don't give a hoot if he's broken to sergeant."

"He does."

Man and wife that night went to bed—ignoring a teal-blue sky over a mountain camp near Mount Jackson on the Shenandoah. They stayed in a small lodge that Roger Millhouse used for weekends in the warm weather.

Margerie was very hopeful she wasn't showing any emotional strain at bridehood in all its intimate immediacy. Simon was rather surprised to find she was not a virgin. She had, she explained to him at breakfast, been molested by a cousin when she was twelve (the first time) and at fourteen, when the cousin came back one summer from Yale.

Chapter 41

GENERAL AND MRS. COPPERWOOD settled in, after Simon's tour of duty in the U.S. European embassies—first at a secret testing ground for guided missiles in a Georgia pine forest, where Simon proved the missiles were, as yet, not nearly so good as the Russian versions. After a year they moved back to the Casslin house near Alexandria, and a year later the Senator signed the house over to them. He preferred to live in an apartment hotel in Washington now that he was heading two powerful committees and was being spoken of as a Presidential prospect at the next convention.

Margerie suffered fewer attacks of nerves than before her marriage, but did have one major "period of close observation" (Dr. Chubb) eighteen months after they were married, when Simon was away on a tour of duty. Simon flew back from Vietnam, where he had been an observer with the French military forces backing Emperor Bao Dai, fighting the Viet Minh rebels.

Dr. Chubb spoke of "sensibility" to Simon in the cheerful sunroom of Blue Skies Farm (the word "sanitarium" was never approved of). The doctor was sucking on a short briar pipe, looking earnestly at Simon in his well-cut English tweeds ("a proper soldier figure") staring out at the smooth lawn and at two Negroes pulling a bucksaw back and forth across the trunk of a dead tree.

"Why the hell don't they use a chain saw?"

The doctor looked at the workers. "Oh, general, that would make a disturbing noise, and time is of no immediacy here."

"Can I see my wife?"

"Course you can, general. It's all just"—the doctor made a stabbing gesture upward with his pipe stem—"well, it's just Margerie is such a highly strung organism. Talented. A touch of genius, you know. That can produce incongruous diversive moments. Yes."

"I know about these—these periods. Had them since childhood, I gather?"

"Even more often when she was sixteen, twenty." He looked at Simon. "Also at thirty. She feels more the discrepancies between appearance and illusion than we do. I think she's now leveled off. This one is showing signs of ending."

"Can I take her home?"

"Perhaps, perhaps. She's dressing, doesn't want you to see her in bed. Go on in."

"What can we *do?*" Simon disliked this jolly old fart of a family doctor with his smug medical orthodoxies.

"Not a damn thing, general. You love her. That's better than any Freudian rigamarole. Get her working, pumping verse. A new book of poems. You don't write poems, do you general?" Dr. Chubb was a fusty, kindly liberal, who felt military men were superficial tax burdens.

"Hell, no, doctor."

"I write a few. Nothing to be ashamed of, or publishable. Margerie has been good enough to—"

A splendid-looking woman with red hair, very white skin —one couldn't call her a nurse at Blue Skies Farm—appeared. "This way, general."

Margerie, in the pale-lime-colored room, was standing by a dresser looking into a mirror and was placing a bit of Kleenex between her just-lipsticked mouth. She turned, said "Um!," discarded the tissue, and came into Simon's arms. "They shouldn't have sent for you, darling."

"Happy they did, before I got jungle rot."

He kissed her cheek, a skin smelling of milk, bath powder, and her own personal odor; the slight, tart, juice taste of some exotic fruit. A nectarine? Aunt Dolly grew them in her garden, and he and his brother Craig—dead now of a coronary ten years—ate them without end till colic came.

"I was getting bored. The French aren't getting anyplace. They treat this war like maîtres d'hôtel snapping their fingers."

"I felt a good rest, Dr. Chubb agreed—"

"You're eating?"

During the worst of Margerie's periods of "disassociation" from reality, she refused to accept food, to eat anything. ("The danger from starvation," Dr. Chubb said, "sometimes seems to be a bigger problem than her tuning out, as it were.")

"Had pancakes this morning—also sausages, whole-wheat toast, coffee, a danish, didn't I, Mrs. Duskin?"

The redheaded woman—she reminded him of Souki Miller (why?) smiled, set the bottles, jars and a Kleenex box into some sort of order on the dresser. "We left most of it. But we're going to have a good lunch, aren't we? Lamb chops."

Margerie held one pale, thin hand on her forehead, letting

[335]

just her fingertips touch. She waited until Mrs. Duskin went out, gently closing the door behind her.

"A motherly sneak, Mrs. D., a sixteen-jewel bitch. She's been stealing the torn scraps of paper—ruptured poems I discard —from my wastebasket and giving them to Dr. Mullins, the rumpot who runs this place.

"Most likely he wanted some original manuscripts of a major poet."

"I hope he didn't get the part of a poem about us—me, *you*. I never could get more than eight lines on intimacy, that worked."

"You're not going to try and get a book out for the fall?"

She studied his face, kissed his nose. "Oh, I must. I'm all right, darling." She whirled around, did a schoolgirl's curtsy, put a forefinger on her chin. "Come on, soldier, smile, and what's all that yellow doing in your eyeballs?"

"Touch of fever. I think I'll take a rest myself. I'll move in here with you."

"No, no. I want our home, our room, our bed. Oh, Simon, I'm only half me without you. I'm only whole, of guaranteed durability, with you. It was Swedenborg, wasn't it, who said each celestial being is both male and female in one body?"

She looked up at him as he held her close, she with that expression he knew—of one who wanted an answer that would wipe away all the problems of existence, so everything would then become as it was in good dreams. ("Jam today, every day, and the *Bhagavad Gita* doing the housework," she had once told Simon.)

Of the three wives that Simon Bolivar Copperwood had lived with, he loved Margerie the most, the deepest, and he knew her the least. Much of her was set apart from him, lived by itself, he thought. The Poet's Corner, he named her psychic quirks. Yet he was part of her secret places, as he saw that fall when Margerie Casslin's (she kept that name) new book of poems, *Stone Sunlight*, was published. Several of the sonnets were involved but joyous tributes to her love of her husband, their warm rapport. The bittersweet short poem, "Thunder in The Milk," opened with a direct quote of four lines from the poet George Peele.

Who has beheld fair Venus in her pride
Of nakedness, all alabaster white,
In ivory bed, strait laid by Mars his side
And hath not been enchanted by the sight.

Margerie's volume was spoken of as being considered for the Pulitzer Prize, which it didn't get, being beaten out by some verses about the plight of farm workers. She was honored by a membership in the National Academy of the Arts.

She was present when Simon appeared before a Congressional committee and spoke against the half-billion-dollars-a-year military aid to the French in Vietnam in 1950. "From a diplomatic viewpoint we are backing a corrupt regime. The native Bao Dai are greedy and lining their pockets, and I include the French merchants and officials, From a military view, the French *cannot* win. It's all built on a superstructure of flawed concepts. The Ho Chi Minh forces know how to fight in jungle. No modern military force ever can. The French are involved in a hopelessly losing war in Indochina, may lose the entire peninsula."

The French got their yearly half billion anyway, and General Copperwood was sent to study a new tank, still called X-4, which had developed problems that would keep it out of production.

When in June of that year the Korean war broke out and the United States decided to intervene—blessed by the United Nations—with troops, Margerie asked Simon not to take part in it overseas. They were sitting in the big front room with hickory logs unlit in the red brick fireplace. Simon thought all it needed was a dog at their feet to make a popular magazine cover; but their two hunting dogs were not permitted in the house. They sat sipping Gibsons that Margerie mixed to Simon's satisfaction.

"Darling, they want you here in the Pentagon."

"Mac is going to be U.N. commander, and I could get, maybe, Chief of Staff, or second in command. Damn it, I want it. I'm good and I've waited all my life to earn my keep. All the money spent on me."

"You don't think much of the U.N., you said so."

"It can't ever function with the Soviet bastards, their stooges taking up too much room. But it's all we have where the freeloaders, the talkers, can at least gather."

"You've no faith in the war, Simon, so why go?"

He refilled his glass from the glass pitcher. "Why? Because I'll be ordered to. Mac will see to that. Because I'm a damn good soldier. Because Mac knows he is a little too prone to show off. Oh, he's damn good. The best we have, maybe. But he's like poor ol' Patton, a grandstander, all is applause and *maya*. So. . . ."

"You're going out to play nursemaid to him."

"Marge, this country is so goddamn smug, curled up in safety between two oceans—it doesn't know it's a burning world out there, a burning world of tin, rubber, oil, copper we and the Russians are after."

"You sound, Simon, like you're speaking of Imperial Rome."

"Maybe."

"Stay where I can find you when I turn over in my sleep."

"Soon, soon."

A log disintegrated in the fire, broke apart into red fragments—flames rose up stronger, flames whose yellow and blue centers wavered and curled up into the sooty maw of the chimney with reckless speed.

She settled back in her chair and laughed softly.

"I'm no warrior's wife. Chin out, ass up, bushytailed. No, not me."

They did not make love that night, not at all in the two weeks before General Copperwood flew to Seoul. Margerie sent him a basket of old brandy from the family cellar, and a quote from Thoreau: "As for doing good, that is one of the professions which are full!"

On September 15, when Douglas MacArthur made an amphibious attack behind the enemy lines at Inchon, General Copperwood was in charge of the landing beaches, getting tanks ashore in great numbers and establishing two major pipelines for fueling them. At the end of the month, the "U.N. forces" ("It is a false title," Simon wrote Margerie. "Our American efforts and casualties give the U.N. credit for the fighting") in South Korea, under MacArthur's control, against General Copperwood's advice, invaded North Korea in force. He tried once more to object, one night in a Lao Tre-lai monastery used as a command post. . . .

"What if the Chinese come south in force, general?"

Mac insisted they wouldn't. They hadn't changed since warlords like Tsu Li-fo held power.

"General, we'll be up there in bad weather, exposed, near the Manchurian-Siberian borders. Long supply lines and the snow and ice up there isn't a Central Park skating rink."

MacArthur shook his head, insisted there'd be no Chinese coming into the war. "Be all over by Christmas."

Simon went to the mud room he occupied and wrote Margerie a long letter with a very poor ballpoint pen.

"I feel like the damn Charge of the Light Brigade—that it's going to happen to us. I figure the Chinese can put nearly a million soldiers against us. Easy. So write a poem about the vanity of power in even the best of men."

Actually, in late October, the Chinese put 700,000 well-armed, well-supported troops against the freezing, overextended U.N. Forces, and began to drive them back toward the 38th parallel.

Simon came awake coughing, felt the cold bite as if it had wolf's teeth. He had lain all night behind a mud wall, wrapped in two blankets, cocooned in a sleeping bag. His command trailer was wrecked, upside down in a gully. The splendid trailer (what he needed were tanks) had been hit by mortar fire, and two divisions were someplace, separated from their supply sections. Simon and his staff had for three days been eating the tacky koo-soo, native meat and fruit mess, and kinchi, some pickled horror. Now all that was gone, too. He looked around him in the remains of the hut, beating his arms together to get back the circulation. What was left of his staff were waiting for him to issue orders. The radio sergeant was bent over his set, an officer with a bandaged left arm tried to warm life into it over the charcoal fragments still warm in the smoke of the Sen-soonlow brazier. (Simon had wanted to send a bronze brazier like that back to Margerie, but the Chinese attacks, and the dreadful hurried retreat, had put that out of the question.) Now he was figuring out how to extract full divisions, what delaying tactics to advise.

The black orderly sergeant was handing out iron rations, his ebony face almost gray under the big Chinese fur hat with its earmuffs that he had scrounged up some place. The sergeant was a great scrounger. Simon began to write out orders for divisional commanders, a plan for HQ. He'd have to get on a wire.

"*Gochisosama, gochiso sama,*" said the sergeant, handing out iron rations.

"Good eating?" said the wounded officer.

Simon tried breathing through his mouth; it didn't help. His throat was lined with glue. A hell of a time for a cold.

He motioned to the sergeant. "Get me my maps. We're moving." And to Lieutenant Wystan, "I want a clear line to HQ."

In the worst of the Korean disaster, he remembered the cold most. Never had the general been so cold. Never so full of the agony of military command, and a corrosive contempt for the misjudgments that had left them here in the blue-green cold of Asia. Men dying, frozen stiff in the morning so that lifted up from the stone-hard earth they seemed made of cement, not of flesh and once fluid blood. He, in bronchial paroxysms, kept the survivors orderly, as their jeeps and trucks used up their fuel.

His throat, wrapped in blue scarves, never gave him rest. That was bad enough, but enemy radio someplace was broadcasting over and over an old, worn record of Kid Ory's "Savory Blues." How to analyze our anguish, he wondered. Why to die here among the sawtooth mountains in some stinking native hut with pots of human crap saved for some spring field planting. Out in the open, everyone huddled around smoking, blinding fires —wrapped in blankets, rags, lice-filled sheepskins, whatever would serve against the dreadful, penetrating cold. Wounds were lacquered shiny red as the blood froze. The foul breaths of the men escaped in clouds of vapor as they struggled on, or tried to talk. They ate the last of the iron rations, garbage and dust. When he asked his orderly sergeant, Jake Waitley, how he liked it, the sergeant said, "It's better than a poke in the eye with a sharp stick, sir."

In the end, sensing a Jonah hang-up over them all, he led the survivors down the icy slope, on their asses, and into a Chinese advance—a mile-long blue file moving on them. They exchanged fire for an hour, and broke through, shuffling on feet wrapped in burlaps. Walking on the frozen creek. They began to filter through to the rear of some of their own battalion lying in the path of the enemy columns.

Simon thought, A proper battle is expertise and preparedness and irrational optimism—*this* is nothing. They were fired on by the American units, for they looked like scarecrows, bundled up, belted up, tied off in their own piss-and-shit, worn down. Caught between the Chinese fire and the Americans shooting at them. By now, counting noses, most of the survivors of his HQ unit were wounded.

Simon took an M-15 slug through the flesh of the right forearm. He ordered two regiments to infiltrate on the right flank to escape the double fire. It was a cold, gray day, a nadir of bitterness, fog rising from the icy paths, the cruel mountains all around. They moved along to the sound of their own hard breathing, just trying to evade the enemy—the Chinese, in their blue-padded dress, and the Americans, bunched too close, so a lot of the time they lay pinned down, losing some men, dropping off the badly wounded. Simon, finishing a half pint of neat Courvoisier. Gesturing or writing divisional orders for the few moments he could bear to free one hand from his dogskin gloves. He shared a tired commiseration with no one.

After a long time, three days later, they stumbled into the 120th Evacuation Hospital. No one could tell the general from a dogfoot private. They just fell down; fell down in the red brick schoolhouse with part of the roof gone, the torn Red Cross flag flapping in the wind above the roof tiles. All, a doctor felt, were nearly paranoid. But they didn't stay long. A general evacuation had begun at Hamhung, and they lay in trucks for days, with Korean wounded smelling of gangrene. Jake Waitley, whose toes on his left foot had frozen solid, had them amputated to the metatarsal joint.

Chapter 42

THERE are today still men in Washington, at the Pentagon, and in various Army depots and bases around the world, who believe it was General Simon Bolivar Copperwood who suggested to the President of the United States that Douglas MacArthur be removed from command in Korea. Others know this is innocuous cant, and that at no time did Simon actually have that close a position of intimacy with the President. Nor would he have made such a suggestion. While he felt MacArthur carried a personal burden of omnipotence and was active against his C-in-C's orders, turning a blind eye to the dangers of an invasion of China, Simon's code of military fidelity was such that one did not offer information against a superior, unless forced to in times of crisis. Some remembered how he had reorganized divisions and mapped the retreat that saved an army.

Simon, in Japan, and convalescing from his arm wound, his bad cold, at Shizuki, at the Shimada Hotel, taken over by the Army, was ordered to fly to Guam for a top secret meeting with the President. There he found Roger Millhouse, the President's military adviser, and several other top Army brass. Simon had half an hour alone with the Commander in Chief. Neither Simon nor the Chief Executive ever revealed the contents of their conversation, nor anyone else's part in those meetings on Guam. General Douglas MacArthur was removed from command of the Korean War. Simon, to a few close friends, always insisted the President made the final decision on his own.

Skeptics said Simon Copperwood was given his third star not for the rallying of the retreating, beaten forces at the Yalu River, but as the wily counselor setting up the removal of General MacArthur. Simon knew enough about Army politics and gossip not to fight the rumors, not to try to explain under the scrutiny of those who envied or disliked him. He flew back to Margerie in July, when the first truce negotiations with the North Koreans began.

She was not bitter at his long tours of duty, but, rather, withdrawn as if in puzzled apprehension. Their first night together—the oversweet smell of lilacs from the garden in the room—they lay in bed and she ran a finger over the scar tissue on his arm.

"You weren't frightened?"

"I was, right down to my toes. I always am."

He sensed her close scrutiny in the dark.

"Death, Simon. It's so accessible to *all*."

"Damn incomprehensible, too. So much vitality down the drain."

"You're not going back?"

"Well, we're going to try to get a real armistice going at that hellhole, Panmunjom."

"That's table-thumping—it's for the State Department, not soldiers."

"It's a Pentagon matter while it's just a truce. The boys from Harvard come later."

"It sounds like such an inchoate land. When you are gone, I keep an atlas by the bed and recite: 'Tarden, Masan, Chemilpo, Shingishu.' "

"Neither side is worth a dog's whistle. Truth is they deserve each other. Stealing, lying, opium dealing, black marketing. But we have some sort of policy to put out an oar in everyplace there."

"You sound like a Machiavellian cynic."

"I'm fed up with Asia. But I can't step aside just now. When this is patched up, you, me, we'll go out to the Northwest —Whitehorn Mountain, Granite Falls, Glacier Park—into the high mountains, I promise."

She seemed nearly asleep.

Later, near dawn, that hour he felt when hopes, aspirations sag, Simon came awake and heard Margerie whimpering, punctuated by a hiccupping sob. It was the last night they were to

[343]

spend together. He left the next morning for Panmunjom. He heard from her just once more. An airmail postcard with an overcolored picture of the long, empty beach at Rehoboth Bay on the eastern shore of Maryland. They had spent some fine times there, loafing, loving, during two summers. The card contained, in Margerie's small, neat, dollhouse handwriting, just the words: *Reality is not an experience. M.*

Two days later, Roger Millhouse called Simon from Washington to tell him that Margerie had taken out a small motorboat from Baraclough Landing below Hawleytown—she was staying a weekend with the Willard Baracloughs—and three hours later the motorboat had been spotted drifting in the calm bay, with no sign of Margerie on board. Her body was found next day off Bloodworth Island, floating serenely among a school of minnows, unmarked. Her face was set in an expression of tranquillity.

Of personal loss, Simon decided, there is only the staring into the great pit of nothing, of being left behind by a spaceship on a chip cut off a dead star. A feeling that against the gods, a man has a total inadequacy. Those ancient buggering Greeks said it all with their belief in the fates and furies. It was worse when the images of her, him, they together, came into his grief.

In his despair, he was in Walter Reed, having the infection, in its latest appearance, on his arm drained, and taking massive doses of miracle drugs. I have, he decided, plenty of time to think out the enigma and paradoxes of human existence. It isn't worth a cat's old litter. I am left alone. Aunt and uncle long gone, brother Craig resting in a solid bronze box with the best people in Forest Lawn. I never made many friends. Bruno, settled as a family man, up to his navel in grandchildren. Roger Millhouse, thinner, more delicate, looking so overrefined, already preparing for his passing, hinting of some incurable disease making frontal attacks on his vital organs. Rather looking forward to Arlington.

Roger had come. To see Simon, the old man, relaxed, indifferent to events, on the arm of Lieutenant Wystan. Sat there, my

[344]

old teacher, in his well-tailored uniform, the stars on shoulders—two—the battle ribbons and campaigns all in rows. . . . Wystan handing him a folded handkerchief when needed.

"Simon. All the nonsense people say when someone dies will do no good, or help. So I'll say nothing of your loss. So what now? Retire, as I'm doing? Whatever time is left, well, why count how much, I don't. There isn't anything anymore these days for a good soldier to do. Ah, thank you, lieutenant. . . . War is the discovery of that moment when the direction of things will change." (An old West Point lecture of his, Simon thought.)

"You think we've done with our games in Asia?"

"Of course. China isn't going to make it. Incompetent amateur do-gooders and killers. It will go back to the warlords, and taking bribes."

"What about the Russians?" asked Lieutenant Wystan.

"Dear boy, forget them, and romantic 1917. Marxism is finished. They've a Czarist fascist empire. Read Orwell's *Animal Farm*. You can't ever admit Russia into civilized Western society. Show them the whip. Oh, they'll snarl, but come to heel."

Simon asked, "And the bomb?"

"Worthless *if* they have it, and *we* have it. Cancels out. Oh, some smart Heb or Arab might make a cheap-John version, I suppose. But we—the Russians and us—would move in on them together and flatten them. It's an interesting idea, Simon. I shan't be here to see it; which side we pick. The Russians against the Chinese? Or the Chinese against the Russians? Then, of course, some day the two winners take on each other. Yes, well, I'm getting as addled as a village gossip in my old age. I'll be back. Your arm, lieutenant." Roger's dry, thin hand shook Simon's and pressed, it felt like a fistful of chicken bones.

Roger Millhouse, leaning on Wystan, walked slowly from the room; a thin old man with unsteady steps. Such fusty generalizations in his thinking. Simon felt too sleepy to brood about it all. Somehow the future is always all incoherence. He was not as sure as some in the Pentagon that there was a domino theory that matched reality, or that "retaliation in strength" would mean much in the earthly smell of rice paddies and jungles.

I cannot get Margerie's image out of my mind for any length

[345]

of time. And the nurse smelling of starch and sprays somehow suggested the odor of chypre and lavender that Margerie's closets held.

My problem, he thought, while his pulse was being taken, is that I have too much memory. I'm honeycombed with discordant details. I remember the women I laid when I was at West Point. The jazz age speakeasy nights of hasty love after Army-Navy football games. In brownstone flats. The whore at the Ritz, in Paris, in 1918. ("My sex is international, but my heart is French." Or was it someone else? Someplace else?) The wives, the greatest vitality and potency of my life—I loved them greatly, even the bad one.

Not going to retire. But I'll get the hell as far as I can from the Pentagon—go to work perfecting that messed-up tank, the X-4—still not in production. . . .

He slept at last, just after figuring out the weight of armor on treads; what proportion of weight to thickness of steel, to speed, to load, came too.

Chapter 43

SOUKI MILLER—had been a Mrs. Willem Van Glickendorf, and a Mrs. Mervyn Conserdine, and was now back to listing herself in the *Washington Social Registry* as Susan Miller. ("I was lucky both times, they died natural deaths before I got tired of them or they of me.") Souki had grown wide and fat but remained resilient. She was a celebrated hostess to a certain level of the Capitol's population; people much seen at the non-black embassies, *fêtes*, charity affairs, and often consulted in lobbying circles on Defense Department contracts. She lived in a remodeled 1810 red brick Georgian house in Georgetown; Souki admitted it had been so rebuilt that only the front door and the cellar steps were from the original structure.

"I tell you, Simon, it's not our Washington anymore. The Snopeses have taken over Washington."

"Do you care?"

"Hell, no. As long as I can find their absurdity entertaining. You don't look as if you're having much of a time of it."

They were seated in a sort of plant room; ferns, green-spurred items, cactuses, facing a garden of ragged, petal-dropping roses and splendid hollyhocks. Souki, rather over life-size in pale blue, hair done up and colored by an artist, gave him a wide smile over her martini glass. Simon sat facing her, in a suit of gray-and-blue mixture cloth too tight for him. A suit Margerie had insisted he buy in Bond Street in London years ago, when they had gone over to England for her to read her poetry at an event. Some plaque being set in a wall of the Bloomsbury house of some dead, unread novelist. And Simon to inspect a new version of a missile the British were developing. Simon hadn't worn the suit very often, not much, actually, until after Margerie's death. He was rather fond of it now—and he'd get some tailor to let it out a bit; he was getting bulky.

"You're going to retire?"

"No, I've been tinkering with a new tank."

"Like to pick up another shoulder star?"

Simon helped himself from the pitcher of martinis. "I suppose so. But the itch isn't as strong as it used to be."

Souki laughed the old-time 1920's laugh. It was, Simon thought, like seeing a strip of Take-Yourself-Photos they used to pose for in those days. (Six for twenty-five cents; the girls in their helmet hats or coque-feather toques, Clara Bow shingled-necks, and the men with flattened-down oiled hair and shirts with silver collar bars. . . .)

"Let's not lie to each other, soldier. We still got the old drive, only we're 1929 Packards and the spark plugs aren't too sparky and the body work isn't what it was, but—" She paused, gave him a skeptical stare. "What did you say you're doing?"

"I've got these two tech sergeants who really know tanks, also a crew to machine-tool parts—"

Souki leaned forward—a wall of bosom—tapped him on a knee with fingers showing thick rheumatic joints, two rings. "Want to talk about it?"

"About what?"

"Marge."

It was his turn to laugh, with a painful tensing of the corners of his mouth. "Lean on your shoulder? Borrow your hankie for a good cry?"

"Well, you haven't any friends, have you? You were always a sort of loner, a half-hick physical austerity, loyal to duty. Now Millhouse has gone, I'm the only one left from our times for you."

"Margerie liked Roger."

"You were always unlucky with women."

"No, Souki. Just I've had two I loved most die."

"Who isn't dying? I count my surviving old friends after every party I give. It's a losing fight, life I mean. Any of the drink left?"

"Plenty."

With refilled glasses they sat and watched some small brown birds scratch under the rosebushes to pick up bits of something twitching with their beaks. Simon sipped slowly. Souki could always make a martini better than most. "Looking back, Simon—hell, it's the only way I *can* look these days, back. Your life, it hasn't been a bad life. Lots of small successes, hatfuls of them—even in the bad times. Close to some big victory. Almost the last great soldier. It's not fashionable today to say you like being a soldier. You liked it, are proud of it."

"You're goddamn right."

Souki tapped his knee again. "Stay for dinner, Simon. Corralled Drew Pearson, State Department folk, a wop cardinal, some nice young nookie—remember when it was called that?"

"I'm flying out tonight to a missile site, then on to a tank-testing installation."

"Going to die in harness?"

"Souki. Keep the garrison flag flying." He rose and bent over to kiss her. He knew now why they had never gone to bed together; he didn't find her odor exciting. Oversweet, like a warm Coke—a body heavy with too healthy, active pores.

"Some young chick you're shacking up with. Don't fool me with missile tests."

"Good-bye, Souki."

She pressed against his chest with her fingers. "Bye, old friend."

After he was gone, she sat in casual thought, close to sadness. The birds were gone, and already, over trees that bowed like penitents in the east, the beginning of a perfect night was being hinted at. A disquieting moment. She would have to bathe, get whopped by her masseuse, be bound in by a girdle and a bra with steel wires. Get combed out, made up, pick the jewels to wear at dinner. Souki sighed and belched gently. She began to recite to herself some Kipling her father had taught her for the Liberty Bond school pageant in 1918. "There's no discharge from the war . . ."

The plane was only half filled and the weather held fine. Simon in uniform—why had he dug up his Légion d'Honneur?—had a window seat and he looked down on the fields and roads of the Republic. General Washington had moved through here on his way to Yorktown. With his French and the needed guns they had brought him. Farther on, Sheridan had ridden hell-for-glory down the Valley. And to the east, bloody business had been done cleverly by Lee, fighting off the Union generals. . . . Nuts! That was the trouble with my fantasies. You take a perfectly good landscape and forget today; the Howard Johnsons, Esso gas stations, and farmer's stands, graft-built highways, roads below loaded with Detroit tin rushing home for dinner, contract bridge afterward, or a Gary Cooper, Bette Davis movie. And what do you do, General Copperwood? *You* make it a historic pageant.

Life is busy going on, behind all those orange-lit windows. Domestic life, children's voices, the smell of cooking, the over-digested evening news flickering TV blue. *Well?* I would have made a lousy civilian, a by-the-fireplace sitter. And a rotten father. (In some murky corner of my mind there is the dim image of a Chinese face—a half-Chinese baby in Shantung Chinese trousers. Perhaps, maybe, my son, and I'm a grandfather now. But most likely, whosoever he was, he's long gone. Dead in the Japanese bombings, tortures, Chiang's dirty games, or Mao's purges. Or just plain dead of starvation, disease. Dead, *dead*. I mustn't think of death, "who had taken down so many."

[349]

The plane rolled and quivered. Simon thought, *now?* But they landed safely, slid with ease into a black, rainy touchdown.

It was good to be back, even in Texas, smelling burned motor fuel, test-ground dust, and the torn pines on the fringe of what the Pentagon maps called TECOM 3. "It's the stinkhole of the Southwest," Major Morris said, as their jeep came to the end of the level ground. "But it's just what we want for testing."

"After two months here, I don't even see it."

Simon got down and walked slowly to the gray canvas-covered shape. It reminded him of a sick elephant he had once seen on a circus back lot when he and his brother Craig went down the main line to Red Willow to see if the circus really had a girl half-woman, half-fish. There had been this elephant under some canvas, just standing there, not swaying. The attendant had told them, "When an elephant gets sick, that's a lot of animal being sick."

Simon motioned to two tech sergeants standing at attention. "Uncover the tank, men. She's not going to get sunburned."

After two months together, they knew the general liked his little jokes.

"Yes, sir," said the tall Negro with the long sideburns. He and the shorter sergeant began to yank off the cover. Simon stood by the major, trying to look impassive as the final shape of the X-4 was revealed. Jesus, that's a tank, he thought, as if seeing it for the first time. Long, wider treads, a turret that suggested a shark, side armor heavy over the treads. Well, I redesigned it and the first tests, unofficial, are over; the engineers from the company that had put this model together had gone back to Detroit.

"This is Sergeant Thomas, major," said Simon. The short sergeant handed him a helmet fit for modern travel with smoked glasses in a band on them. "He's the pilot."

"You have rough terrain up there, sergeant," said the major.

"Roughest, sir."

The black sergeant was holding up a jump suit. "This is Sergeant Wilmot, ammo expert, gunner."

"Wear the suit, sir?"

"No, I'll just take the helmet." Simon turned to the major.

"I'd let you ride shotgun, major, only the test calls for use of a normal battle-action crew of three. You can follow us with the big field glasses set by the radar building."

"That's all right, general. I've got an old back injury I'd just as soon spare. Well, good luck."

Good luck, and hard work, thought Simon as he followed the sergeants into the tank. Two months' work on tests spent on this one tank. And if my ideas don't pan out, it's the junk pile. The AMCTC brass here, which, when you spelled it out, was Army Material Command Technical Committee, hadn't shown any real faith in X-4. Nor the weapons system, by the TECOM, Army Munitions Command servicing new versions of tanks, taking care of their bugs. The X-4 on the boards had been designed to lead the reconnaissance element of an armored division. When Simon took over a year before, it had "more bugs than a Holy Joe mission flophouse."

Simon had improved it so it could now ford a stream, and it carried Shillelagh missiles that homed in on enemy armor by its own system—its main gun could hit a bird's eye at two thousand meters. It had a fire range up to ten thousand meters, and maybe, Simon hoped, beyond that. He picked up the manual. *"Full range, Classified information."*

"How's she been performing?"

"A bitch to work on, sir—you know that. No soft ride."

"That's good—turn her over."

X-4 weighed only twenty-two tons, but Simon liked it better than the M-60 fifty-tonners. The tank roared, went ahead fast into second growth, boulders, and brush. Sergeant Wilmot was testing the guidance system for the Shillelagh missiles, fingering the 152mm gun. Simon was calibrating the sights. "You can pick up a matchstick at two miles in the scope's depth of field."

"Ain't that somethin', general?"

Just the three of them in a buttoned-up steel shell. Simon saw the warning lights blink off to show no malfunctions.

"She fully armed today?"

"Yes, sir," said Sergeant Wilmot as they raced along in a cloud of dust. "Ten Shillelaghs, twenty rounds of 155 artillery shells. No end rounds of 7.62 caliber ammo. Hold on, sir."

"I'm strapped in. Keep her rolling, Thomas."

"Yes, sir."

Simon felt the fillings in his back teeth ache as they crossed a ravine. Wilmot was adjusting the big .50 caliber machine gun mounted on the open cupola, climbing around it like a steeple-jack. Simon checked the artillery rounds that self-destructed inside the breech of the gun, so there were no empty brass shells to discard after firing.

"The XM-4 light for night tests prove out, sergeant?"

"Yes, sir—the electric system moves the light with the gun, we could catch us night raccoons back home with this setup." Sergeant Thomas was carried away by his excitement.

"Raccoons? This tank is a man-meat cooker. It's got a thirty-five mile range, and eighty-five gallons of gas in the belly. Do fifty mph. Bring on them Russian T-54's, T-62 tanks. Zoom! Zap! *Kaput!*"

Simon smiled. "Easy, sergeant."

To himself Simon called the X-4 the "Genghis Khan." Brutal to work on. Gave maintenance troubles. Major equipment failures for six months; circuit failures, weapon misfires, ammo ruptures, engine replacements. Even the 155mm gun out of whack, and alwys fuel spillage and dirt-clogged intakes. It had all made for long work hours—days in the Texas excuse for weather. And if there was field practice soon, under actual battle conditions for some VIP, with the highly flammable 155 ammo, it was time to take out more insurance. He remembered a Korean joke: "Two dollars gets you ten thousand, dead, at the PX machine."

"Test the XM-409 rounds."

"Yes, sir."

"In turn, fire for soft targets against personnel and crowds. Then the canister round."

"The real man-breaker stuff, sir?"

It was a blunt-nosed bullet, sent by TECOM, that exploded

when it hit and had a thousand roofing nails with barbed points, to tear into persons in all directions.

They fired for half an hour at fast-moving speed.

"Now the XM-410, the improved ammo. It's a phosphorus round, that's it—white phosphorus—so, careful."

"It just burns nonstop, sir."

"The new flywheel better?"

"Yes sir, this flywheel develops not a flutter with any heavy pressure. The other flywheel first warped, then failed, like made of cheese."

They were out two hours. Barging through the tough stuff, racing firing up along the ridge, and down. Blasting rock and brush, firing the XM-410 phosphorus shells into solid rock where they couldn't set the landscape on fire. The flare-up, the smoke and flames were impressive. What a change, Simon brooded in the fusty interior of X-4, compared to the stuff we used with Patton.

Simon ordered them to move down toward the camp, leaving behind crushed sagebrush, splintered scrub oak saplings, smoke-disturbed earth and rock, the flattened remains of a desert turtle which had been too slow against advanced armor.

Simon sat in the rocking seat, head down, vibrating to the jolting of the tank, the exhaust sounds and tread-grind drilling into his head. *It would do!* He had created a great destructive machine out of failures. He had made a monster weapon able to perform almost with a delicacy of touch. There was no joy in it for him. When he was young there had been the glory—not laurels and myrtle for honor, but for promotion—and the sense of duty. Later he had thought of himself as a protector. The nation slept, felt secure because he, like so many others, was there to stand between them and enemies who also had the thermonuclear Doomsday bomb.

Simon had to admit he was tired, feeling his years. It was no good for those who didn't handle weapons to say peace was possible without these tools. But still it left grit on his mind to know the weapons would get more and more lethal. Already, someplace, others were working to make X-4 vulnerable, obso-

lete. He had gained only a small technical victory, a little time.
"Thank you, sergeants."

Getting out of the tank, Simon's hip joints seemed to freeze, and his breathing was hard. But two stiff brandies set him up properly before dinner, as he began to write his report for AMCTC.

Epilogue

It is natural to believe in great men. All mythology opens with demigods . . .

—Ralph Waldo Emerson

To understand human beings we must see them in relation to each other, not in isolation. . . .

—Aristotle

(From the notebooks of Simon Copperwood)

Chapter 44

THE Bentley turned majestically at Lafayette Park to head for the White House, and Orderly Sergeant Jake Waitley took his eyes off the tourist buses, the protesters in spasmodic bursts of shouting, gathered under some trees, the fuzz already slapping their mitts against their billy clubs. In the rear-view mirror he caught the old boy sitting there with his aide, Captain Marcus Wystan. You had to hand it to the old hardshell, he sure looked good there today. Feisty as always. Color maybe a bit too high, and chomping hard on his cigar, drawing a good draft on the tobacco. Dressed up as a Mardi Gras parade with all his bars of chest ribbons and medals. His birthday, today, and going to see the President. . . . Tomorrow, maybe, all the "yes-sirring" and yakking I've done will be over with. I been waking him, wiping up after him a long time. I never thought he'd get old, or we'd get old together. Always felt somebody would get a bead on him in a war, or he'd wreck himself—not trusting field reports —flying them choppers over Vietnam, Laos, Cambodia. Tough as a tom mule's mouth. And me dragged along, I felt my tail would be singed for good by them gooks shooting up at us. Gonna retire myself—eat Brunswick stew, guzzle store whisky sitting down.

Jake steered around a group of protesters moving on to the street off the sidewalk, hand-scrawled banners waving among them. Some made a mock curtsy to the four stars on the Bentley's fenders. Tomorrow, Jake thought, he would be putting five-star flags on the car hood, or listening to the old boy's drinking glass clicking as he added ice cubes to his whisky and cursed out everything and everybody, from the statue at the top of the Capitol down to an orderly sergeant. The general's bark was as sharp as his bite and don't ever forget it. Jake chuckled: Heh! Heh!

Simon looked down at the end of the only partially smoked cigar, and banged out its fire in the silver ashtray set in the back of the front seat. He inhaled deeply, twice, and opened his mouth as if in need of more air.

Captain Wystan leaned forward and spoke to the driver.

"Sergeant, right up to the front entrance."

Simon looked at his wristwatch. "We're on time. Let's keep the man waiting, and working up a sweat. Take us around the park again, sergeant."

"Yes, sir."

Simon smiled and winked at Captain Wystan. "Always upset the timetable your enemy is expecting, Marc."

"He's our, he's *your* Commander in Chief."

"Yes. I've had a lot of them. It's been a frustrating game. In the Vietnam snafu I had three Presidents who felt they had my balls clamped in their hands and were pressing." Simon wriggled a bit; the jacket was just a bit too tight. No doubt about it, he was putting on some weight. And an awareness of exacerbated sensibilities he disliked to show.

"They kept me out of the Vietnam fracas at first—as much as they could. The Boston glamor boy didn't like it when I said we had too many soldiers there, faking it as advisers in Saigon. And the killers of CIA were wrong in supporting the killing of Diem, and planning others. And what happened to the Secretary of State? He got hot with talk of 'clear and present danger of Red conquest'! " All those big shots gabbing away that our military task could be completed by the end of 1965. He was aware he was talking too much in keyed-up agitation.

"That," said Captain Wystan softly, "was when they sent you out to survey the truth of the situation."

Simon reached for his cigar case and decided not to light another one. "They didn't like my report. Not just the GYA boys in the Pentagon, but the Texan who liked being C-in-C—at first. The guard-your-ass boys lathered him up with the idea that gives us just a *little* bit more, just a *few* more troops, air power. Oh, they snapped the trap on him, with the Bay of Tonkin stunt."

Captain Wystan wished the old boy would shut up. Too many people knew his opinions already.

"It got you your fourth star, sir, that war."

"Yes, didn't it, and our chicken-fat Bismarck the big prize. So there were a million men, women, and children to bury." Simon patted Captain Wystan's arm. "He's got to give me the fifth star. I saved his predecessor's bacon after the way we poured into Cambodia in a private war; set off those last raids north, and let black-market boys make millions, all the industrial-military pals that got stinking rich on supplies and weapons that didn't always work." Simon grinned. "I suppose you think if I were a good citizen I should have howled long ago?"

"I'm not the general. You think like a chess player—at least four moves ahead. I'd blurt out the truths and then find I've messed up people's faith in the Army, respect for the law, the national safety."

"Stop red-appleing me, Marc. I was a soldier with a soldier's duty. You saw our men dying, grouching. All those poor young bastards we sent to die, or get clobbered, in rice-and-crap paddies, for men playing Napoleon. Kids, kids who didn't have college deferments or uncles on draft boards."

Simon leaned back and felt the Bentley's springs readjust as they took the shock from some rough spot. . . .

His thoughts pushed up a date from his memory. August 2, 1967, no, the third. He was eating from a revolting tin can, some mess of ham and cornmeal, sitting by a wrecked helicopter, there on the Pleiku Plateau. The chopper still burning and two dead, machine-gunned officers looking like busted toys. And Jake opening another can, sniffing it. "Got a dog back home eats better."

"What hit us, Jake?" Simon felt one side of his face rubbed raw, skin sandpapered down—must have hit a tree trunk coming down, and his back felt as if he'd damaged a disk. He was too old for this, and he disliked the idea his body was asking for a rest. Even being so hungry after this disaster. Why hunger now?

"Somebody among the Charlies put up a volley of heavy machine gun slugs into our belly when we came in low to see that village, My Ghon. Our two escort choppers, they got it too. They're down someplace. We're down someplace."

It was beginning to rain. Black, gorged clouds over the dragon

[359]

peaks to the west. Simon took out his map case from the carryall he had had sense enough to grab when the chopper split open as they landed. The case marked SBC ★★★ was nicked by machine-gun slugs, the same burst that had killed the pilot and navigator. Rubbed out from the records, three big Hughy trashers, half a dozen good men. And maybe himself and Jake.

"Radio contact? Set functioning?"

"General, it's all just nothing left in there. We'd better go for a walk before the Vietcong they come to see what they bagged. They never had themselves a general before."

It wasn't good walking in the sloshing pale-green rain. He could feel the blows on his helmet liner, the pelting on his tropical jacket. His back ached and his face hurt even after Jake had rubbed some ointment on it from a first aid kit. Jake, limping, was carrying a grenade bag with some emergency rations, a flare pistol, and over one shoulder a light machine gun. With sobriety and gravity, Simon figured on their survival chances. Behind them a great roar went up, and even in the heavy rain, a white and yellow flash was a spectacle.

"Fuel tank, general. That chopper is hash now."

"We'll head southeast and lay low—wait for the truck convoy going out to bring supplies to firebase Horse-Nose and Bowling Alley."

"No truck convoys, sir. You remember the Vietcong cut the road. We been air supplying the grunts in those fire bases."

Simon said nothing and went stomping through a foot of water, jungle rot, and some strong-smelling flowers that were sickening in their intensity, as if mixed with cat litter. He had never liked cats. He was aware his memory wasn't what it had once been. He had to face it, that often in these jungles a heavy lethargy seemed to set in. He had prided himself on total recall, nearly total recall, in his youth, and in middle age a photo-graphic memory. Now it was a bit out of focus at times. Maybe, maybe it was a growing foreboding and disenchantment with the purpose of this senseless war. He looked at the waterproofed map, measured the scale with a wet thumb.

"I think, Jake, we'd better just sit down someplace."

The sergeant found an uprooted tree, a giant of a tree, lying like a corpse. All around other great hardwood trees were down, splintered, studded with steel bomb fragments. The earth was without grass or vegetation.

In the shelter of the toppled tree, under its spreading roots in the cavity beneath, they lay close together. It was a place that had been heavily bombed again and again for three years.

"Don't get any of the muck in your eyes, Jake. The whole area is one damn noxious miasma—has been powdered with tons of antifoliation chemicals."

"I'll try. I don't want to defoliate any hair I have left." Sergeant Waitley laughed—his black skin turning a shiny gray. Simon patted the sergeant's shoulder. "Kismet, Jake, Kismet."

"Yes, sir," said Jake, and dropped off into some placid state only old soldiers know of; a state that is nearly sleep. (Sheet, thought Sergeant Waitley—been hearing this Kismet line for a long while from the general.)

Simon felt too sodden, too chilled, to sleep. He remembered a prayer some company screwball had thumbtacked on the order board back at base:

"God, our heavenly Father, hear our prayers—these things we need. Give us this day a gun that fires 10,000 rounds a minute, a napalm that will burn for a week. . . . Forget not the least of Thy children as they hide from us in the jungle; bring them under our merciful hand that we may end their suffering. O God, assist us for we do our noble work in the knowledge that only with Thy help can we avoid the catastrophe of peace which threatens us. . . ."

If he had caught the sonofabitch that put it up he'd have fanned his ass—but it was an interesting comment. And so, thinking of a place where nothing would live or grow anymore for a hundred years, Simon, too, slept.

Two days later, a patrol of South Vietnamese soldiers came yelling down the drying-out trail. Some were drunk on rice wine, some had bloody limbs wrapped in damp newspapers. Fine little men, with gold-colored features, looking like twelve-year-old boys, but were older. Two had live chickens strung around their necks and one carried a portable record player and a human head covered with live flies. The men had benign faces showing splendid teeth. They cried, *"Chien hoi!"*

The officer, or NCO, in command was plump and he saluted when he saw the U.S. flag patches on the Americans' shoulders. He made motions of shooting his AH-47, tossing a grenade, and pointing north, bowed and said, "Gee bastha fellas dar Ho Chi Minh, Ho Chi Minh."

That finished his English, but for *yes, sah, no know,* and *fuck.* Simon brought out his map, which puzzled the soldiers, but six hours later they were in contact with a radio post that was heard by a patrol of Cobras. From there it was only three hours before an LOH helicopter with U.S. marking took them to the American base at Bienhoa. Refusing med evacuation, and after a bath, a few drinks, and some decent food, Simon felt his vitality come back. The officers were living, as one captain said, "like in a French court of the great Louis XIV, only without the plumes."

Simon spoke to the man from Washington, a rather sharp-looking White House adviser, named after an American novelist of the 19th century. He was listed as with MOS-Military Occupation Specialty. Simon tried to brief him. "We've peaked at five hundred forty-nine thousand American troops, and it's not going to win any war here."

"Five hundred forty-nine thousand seventy-six are the correct figures, general. Tet was a test and *they* didn't win either. The White House is going on an all-out effort. Going to stop the bombing if they'll listen to reason."

"Bombing just puts their back up."

"Nearly forty-four capitals of the Vietnam provinces have held. We're winning. So we can offer them a fair peace."

"We haven't dented their ability much to replace losses or supplies. Who cares about real estate? Province sharks?"

"The White House is going to stand firm, but fair. I want a meeting of all generals and their available staffs."

"Who's going to mind the war while we meet?"

"Copperwood, I have no sense of humor. Can you give me some idea of what will be said?"

"I could, but I'm not going to. They're mostly CYA career officers. The President will have to do better to get reelected than listen to a wish to expand the troop count. You can quote me."

"He likes you, Copperwood. He likes you a lot. He says you're the only one out here who doesn't bulldust him."

"Tell him I like him too. I like him a lot. Only Washington doesn't know a goddamn thing of the true conditions in a country where you can't run a modern war. His ideas of an offer is no dice for them. They've been fighting for a hundred years."

"General, you're doing a great job—military-wise."

At the end of March the war was still on and the President announced he was not seeking reelection, but that new peace talks would start in Paris, and *all* bombing of the north would stop by November 1.

On November 6, there was a new President in the White House, and General Simon Bolivar Copperwood was relieved of Vietnam duty when his full withdrawal plans were presented and filed away. He was given a medal for his backup plans and tactical use of native troops that had brought the Tet offensive to a halt.

On February 8, 1971, he was again in Vietnam—processing the American support of U.S. air and artillery, aiding the South Vietnamese troops in the forty-four-day attack on the Ho Chi Minh Trail in Laos, against odds. One thousand M-16's, uncounted 50mm tubes, and six tons of ammo had vanished when he took inventory. The natives were selling grenades to the enemy for $30 each. He took to forming mixed U.S.-ARVN patrols so the two allies could watch each other.

Later, everybody was promoted—as if they had actually won a war. Jake Waitley, when they were back, attached the four-star flags to the Army Lincoln assigned to them, and to the Bentley.

Chapter 45

OUTSIDE the White House were cameramen, journalists, and those people seeking individual gratification who usually make up a crowd that has some special privileges not given to another crowd kept outside the tall iron railing that hemmed in the Presidential mansion.

Simon shook his head at questions addressed to him. "Nothing to say, but I've been summoned here for a ceremonial event by the President. . . . That's all. . . . That's all. . . ."

Captain Marcus Wystan, politely but firmly breaking trail for the general, aided by the White House guards in their musical comedy uniforms, got Simon inside. The waxed floors, the walls of old paintings were all familiar to Simon. "This way, sir," said someone who spoke through his sinuses—a man wearing white cotton gloves. Yes, Simon thought, this way he had gone several times to talk to Presidents and Secretaries of Defense. . . .

One warm night not so many years ago people sitting in the city's parks were fanning themselves with copies of the Washington *Post*, lovers locked together on the grass before the Monument, and he had come demanding audience—followed someone else in white gloves—had spoken, not to the C-in-C, but had put the facts in the lowest common denominator:

"Mr. Secretary, we have now—tonight—over a half million men in Vietnam. What you plan will, in the end, add up to a full million Americans fighting a war in Asia. When we do have a million men pinned down in hot jungles and rice paddies, and have killed and napalmed, bombed a couple of million natives dead, someone here had better be aware the Red Chinese and the Russians can, or will, make up their own family battle—their dislike of each other, and come in to *our* war. Will the President listen to me? Tonight?"

"General, the President wants to know why don't the commanders in the field feel this way? They are sure it will not take a

[364]

million men. Maybe a hundred, two hundred thousand more. Perhaps at worst, two hundred thousand, but—"

"We've been committing soldiers by the hundred thousand and more hundred thousands on a dream, a fantasy. At this rate it will be a million soon, a million and a half before we become aware it's a global war."

"The President doesn't agree with you. He feels with more troops, one great decisive blow would end the war."

"Mr. Secretary, I have never gone against any superior officer doing his duty. He is my Commander in Chief. He's not going to see me? Okay. If the number of men we have in Vietnam goes over another hundred thousand, tell him I shall respectfully resign from the Army, and—"

"Respectfully, general?"

"Then go before Congress with facts. Not just mine, but documents I have collected from some commanders in the field—we have a few fine ones. Also the opinions of expert Asian historians who feel there must be a termination to our participation in that war, on the battlefield."

"I'll pass on your—*your* attitude, General Copperwood."

Simon thought, Have I really talked that way, put it that strongly to the sharp-nosed Mr. Secretary? Yes, he had left feeling a bit shaky, but the troops in Vietnam never reached another hundred thousand.

The Oval Room was crowded with TV cameras, journalists used to irrational human behavior, lots of gilt chairs, some public faces. They always, Simon thought, managed to scare up an impressive group of people—on orders—from State and Senate buildings. Also a salting of Congressional wives. The Pentagon was represented by half a dozen uniforms with rows of chest ribbons and chicken-shit braid decor from the War College. A sense of jubilation seemed to be shared by the guests. Simon wondered, Had they been briefed?

It would have been good to have had Roger Millhouse up there as Presidential Military Aide, as in the old days, but Roger, with his flair for ironic gay elegance, shared with his bright young officers, was gone. Buried. Margerie was gone. Who wasn't gone? Simon Bolivar Copperwood wasn't gone, and he felt as if he'd never draw another deep breath again in this overheated opulent room, even with air conditioning purring in the walls.

Somehow, Simon never did know how he got to the raised platform; Marcus Wystan was moving him into place—steering him by his left elbow to a battery of mikes and a mess of wires. Someone was shaking his hand, Woody, Chief of Staff, from the Pentagon.

Captain Wystan rolled his eyes, stiffened as a voice said, "The President of the United States."

Wystan leaned over close to Simon's ear. "Can't get any information as to what's *what*."

"Yes, mouth shut," Simon whispered back, "tight as bull's rear in flytime."

The President shook Simon's hand. It was a face Simon couldn't read, nor get any text from. Eyes like glacé cherries. The voice and the words seemed to come out wet.

"It is my pleasant duty, today, to honor one who has served his country well. Served it in every major war of this century—in honorable conflicts that have helped preserve this great nation. Some may say history has already recorded his deeds, so I shall not do more than outline why we honor him. Not merely as now by me, his Commander in Chief, but my fellow Americans, honors due from our broad land, from every soldier old and young who served every one of us, and who put their trust in General Copperwood, who would serve and command well, lead bravely. . . ."

Christ, that old White House award speech out of J. Walter Thompson. Used by the last three leaders in the White House. Simon tried staring at the journalists and television crews, the guest section solidly planted on the gilt chairs. They seemed to him unreal. Faces staring back, a few smiles, one or two slight nods of agreement as the President talked on. . . . Marcus Wystan standing just behind Simon (with the Secret Service men) touched the general's elbow, calling back his attention to what the President was saying.

" . . . so, my fellow citizens, we come to that moment when the warrior lays down his shield, the patriot, his task done, retires to his fireside, and the good soldier becomes aware younger shoulders will take up his burden of duty and he retires to a well-earned personal life. . . ."

(The bastard! He's giving me the knee in the groin.)

" . . . having served long and well in times of crisis, stood on guard during the crucial times of peace, prepared against any storm that might blow up from any direction, now a grateful nation, a most thanks-filled President on your retirement, general, from the Army. . . ."

(What the devil are they applauding for?)

" . . . this nation's highest honor, this medal given to so few. . . ."

(The Chief of Staff is handing the President that rosewood box and there it is, the kissoff—all gold and the neck noose of red, white, and blue ribbon. He's hanging it around my neck. . . . A half-hug and one step back. He, me, the nation should now be fully bamboozled and mollified. . . .)

" . . . and as you take up the pleasures of the years ahead, the many years, to relive in memory the battle smoke you faced, your deeds not to be forgotten by your nation. . . . So we pay you homage as one who fought and bled so often for the country whose welfare to you comes before any other consideration. . . ."

(Why am I holding his hand in a manly shake, and the cameramen asking to hold it, hold it. . . .)

Captain Wystan was steering General Copperwood to some mikes with a half shove to right turn. Simon heard a voice, and to his surprise it was his own, a controlled, calm tone.

"I thank the nation that sees fit to give me this honor. I have prepared no speech. No—no speech, but as I expected every soldier I commanded to do his duty, I can say I've done no more—I, too, have done what I had to do. Had sworn to do my best when I became first a cadet at West Point, then a soldier and an officer. I leave my military life: There has been over half a century of it. I leave it dry-eyed, I hope not with too much a display of sentimentality. It was the life I picked with the irrational optimism of youth—the life I wanted. I'm making a speech after all. Somehow my talents were enough to serve, and I think serve well. I was never a humble man except when I thought of the American earth I came from, and of late, of being mortal and. . . ." Simon paused, knowing he had to end this charade; there was a diminishing perception of reality. He fingered the medal on his tunic with numb fingers. The President was standing to his right, hands clasped at crotch level, his face a bland dial.

"To end on a better note, I quote the words of a philosopher with which my old instructor at West Point used to dismiss a semester: 'We last as a strain of music lasts. And we go when it goes.' I go. . . ."

All over—his sojourn in Byzantium. Drag out of here. He elbowed Captain Wystan to move. Simon waved off questions as he left the platform; his aide steered him again down halls of oil paintings, past the nearly genuine antique furniture, and out into the warm air. The citizens of the Republic were going about their noontime duties, stopping to watch the Bentley and its fender banners depart with a short crisp sounding of its horn.

"He invited you to stay to lunch, sir."

"Hemlock and soda, Marc?"

"I didn't figure he'd dare, general."

"He dared."

From the sidewalk someone cried out: "The general's car!"

Jake drove on, didn't turn his head. "Was all on the car radio. Live, like they say."

"Live! Yes, live." Simon closed his eyes, settled back.

"Fancy medal," said Jake. "We going home?"

Captain Wystan nodded. "Home."

Simon noticed the four-star banners snapping over the car's hood.

"Take the flags down, Jake."

Captain Wystan looked away toward the river. The old boy took the catastrophic experience cool as an iceberg. "It's customary, general, even official to continue to wear your stars. Also you are entitled to a full staff, cars, all—"

Simon patted his aide's shoulder.

"Captain, I wish I felt like getting falling down drunk. Right now it's all like a bad wound, but the pain hasn't started yet."

The Bentley approached the bridge to Virginia.

Chapter 46

THE night had become oppressive and increasingly humid, as nights could be in the Washington area certain times of the year. Simon had never air-conditioned the old house; to him the Casslins still seemed to be the true owners, with gyrating circles of hovering ancestors. Even if all were dead, including the Senator and brother Ned. Legally, Simon held ownership. But for air conditioning, one would have to install vents in ancient walls through layers of wallpaper, plant ducts through old brick, injure historic rafters.

Simon had once tried a window air conditioner in the bedroom. But the sound of it—like a panting frog, and the kind of air it produced, had annoyed him. Still, even in extreme hot spells, the old house was fairly comfortable; the walls were thick, the great trees that surrounded it not permitting the full searing of the sun to overbake it. Simon had been drinking, not in any fit of lachrymose self-righteousness. Not too much booze. Didn't intend to get drunk. He was certainly eating too much dinner. In his control of his outrage, he automatically ate everything set before him, almost unaware of what he was eating. Jake had produced egg-drop soup (Simon had always favored it in his China days), a roast capon, corn on the cob, and jambalaya. Simon had eaten and coolly cursed. Captain Wystan, opposite him, sipped wine and nibbled on a chicken wing. He did not expect lamentation, but was ready for outrage and complaint.

"Did you see it all on television at six o'clock? The goddamn handing out of the mangy ribbon and medal?"

"I did, sir."

"I felt like I was exposing myself in a circle, in public."

"You certainly looked self-contained and slightly amused."

Simon chewed on capon, removed a small bone from between his teeth.

"A military man always is self-assertive. Fools 'em. In the

morning I want you to take my files out of storage. I'm going to write my memoirs, include my two wars in Asia, and the perverse human impulses that made them—the goddamnest book."

"Those files, general, they contain a—"

"I know damn well what they contain. An atom bomb. The whole nasty truth of our mismanagement of modern wars. The politicians I knew close-up, the disparity between the commanders' deeds . . . and their public statements."

"I suppose, sir, it can be handled with, well, taste?"

"Taste? No taste maybe—but it will be balanced honestly. You'll work with me, Marc. I've had over fifty years of my life given to trying to understand things. Understanding myself, I now admit. Maybe I haven't yet gotten a good picture of myself. I suppose, as a young stud officer, all I was aiming at was pride in self. The polishing of my vanities, and always to look brave in a tight place. Oh, yes, Marc, we all like flattery, the honors, the limelight."

Jake brought in a smoking apple pie. "Will you have it with the Stilton, sir?"

Simon nodded and pointed a finger at Captain Wystan. "Yes, we'll make a bomb of a book. I'll blow them out of the water, all the fat cats, the liars, sellouts." He attacked the pie with his fork. Chewing, nodding.

Captain Wystan sipped his creamless, sugarless, black coffee. "I suppose few men are given the opportunity you have had, sir, of knowing so much and being able to express your views, your mind."

"The mind doesn't act—it conditions action."

Simon sat back and patted his stomach. He had eaten too much in his controlled anger—and it sat heavy, the wrong food for such a warm night. "Captain, don't hope to soften my book when we work on it. Remember, as the years go, the risks cost less."

"General, you're a symbol, look at all the coverage you got today. All the Pentagon praise given out for you."

"There's a term we used in Vietnam, GYA. Protect your rear from friend or foe. We have too many GYA's. . . . Jake, I'll have brandy in my room. The decanter."

"Yes, sir. More pie?"

"Marc, get those files, and don't make any plans for the next few months socially." Simon stood up. "That's if you still want to act as my aide. I'm entitled, retired, to a staff, but. . . ."

Captain Wystan gave out with his ironic, well-bred smile. (Souki called it "Grace with a touch of lasciviousness.") "Wouldn't miss it, working on the general's memoirs. Send up a hell of a dust cloud. All your sins, sir, if you'll admit to them."

"That's right, butter me up. . . . Jake, any bicarb in my cabinet?"

The sergeant wiped his damp face with a paper towel. "Plenty. . . . Don't go blaming my cooking. You been cursing, sir, and pumping rage into yourself all afternoon. That don't set so good, even if you ate with relish everything set down."

Captain Wystan rose and gave a final flick of his lips with a crisp linen napkin. "If my social life is going up in smoke, I'd better collect what I can of it tonight, that is if you don't need me, sir? There's a fancy shindig at the French Embassy."

Simon waved off his aide. "On the double. Just be here bushy-tailed and shiny-eyed in the morning."

Later, Simon, in his shorts, sat by the window, facing west. Just one small lamp by the bed was lit. He had controlled his rages too much, fed too much, talked a great deal more than he should have done to that snotty Southern character. Captain Wystan—a very wise bird—as good a young officer as you'd find, more relaxed than I had been. He doesn't compare with what I was at his age, he's much better adjusted. He hasn't the drive or desires that burned in me. He'll never make general, and doesn't want to, as a patronizing patrician. No, I'm unfair. How the hell does one know? Life is a greedy insucking mouth, Roger Millhouse used to say.

Simon sipped the brandy. His stomach had stopped its protest and seemed willing to accept terms, a truce. Yes, my memoirs will blast off a lot of hides. Maybe, too, discover something vital, new about myself. . . . Something that had always puzzled me (when I admitted I had a problem). What were the true motives of involvements? One doesn't cut off a career like abandoning a love affair.

The whole truth? I have to unwrap layers of vanity and pride, protected from exposure—the inner core. Chinese boxes inside Chinese boxes, inside Chinese boxes. And find what kernel? A core of *what*? The naked self. Me as I am, an untenable military position? Suppose like my recurring dream, *what*? When I'm all unwrapped, unlocked, the last pried-into box open? As usual, I get just a glimpse, and I wake and am back on stage, playing my role again.

Yes, the book will do it, he thought, be like the bull's horns that killed Manolete.

Simon rose from the old, comfortable chair. It had once been Senator Casslin's father's chair, that Assistant Secretary of State who had helped blast Woodrow Wilson's League of Nations plans. Simon tossed off the last of the brandy in the glass, and went to the bed. Jake had pulled back the sheet, no blanket needed tonight.

Why did the bed still seem to give off the odor of Margerie's own personal scent? Some goop she rubbed with her palms into her neck, cheeks, and breasts before joining him, as if in a rendezvous, in an amorous bed. Voluptuous, but never flamboyant. Christ, it is so real, that odor, and it can't be. The years are sure as hell all fallen away. She is reaching for me, running backwards from me, and I'm staring across a ravine. It's a simulacrum, which is fancy for shadow. But I'm feeling a kind of shaking of my head, a body heat. She's there now—standing by the Williamsburg Colonial mirror on the wall. . . .

The mirror was fogged over like a blind man's eye sometimes is—he caught the gesture of her elbow lifted out as she pressed fingers on her hair, shaping it like sculpture. He almost called her name. She turned toward him with a still adolescent doubt. He had the awareness that he could make her real, freeze her here in time, *if* he refused to think of this as a hallucination. Goddamn it, *that* was the true secret of the universe. How simple. Everything could be real at the same time, everything was in one economy package. For the arbitrary conclusion of finality existed only in the will to want it.

She turned, stood there, her arms out in that gesture she used

of dust. "Ten Shillelaghs, twenty rounds of 155 artillery shells. No end rounds of 7.62 caliber ammo. Hold on, sir."

"I'm strapped in. Keep her rolling, Thomas."

"Yes, sir."

Simon felt the fillings in his back teeth ache as they crossed a ravine. Wilmot was adjusting the big .50 caliber machine gun mounted on the open cupola, climbing around it like a steeplejack. Simon checked the artillery rounds that self-destructed inside the breech of the gun, so there were no empty brass shells to discard after firing.

"The XM-4 light for night tests prove out, sergeant?"

"Yes, sir—the electric system moves the light with the gun, we could catch us night raccoons back home with this setup." Sergeant Thomas was carried away by his excitement.

"Raccoons? This tank is a man-meat cooker. It's got a thirty-five mile range, and eighty-five gallons of gas in the belly. Do fifty mph. Bring on them Russian T-54's, T-62 tanks. Zoom! Zap! *Kaput!*"

Simon smiled. "Easy, sergeant."

To himself Simon called the X-4 the "Genghis Khan." Brutal to work on. Gave maintenance troubles. Major equipment failures for six months; circuit failures, weapon misfires, ammo ruptures, engine replacements. Even the 155mm gun out of whack, and alwys fuel spillage and dirt-clogged intakes. It had all made for long work hours—days in the Texas excuse for weather. And if there was field practice soon, under actual battle conditions for some VIP, with the highly flammable 155 ammo, it was time to take out more insurance. He remembered a Korean joke: "Two dollars gets you ten thousand, dead, at the PX machine."

"Test the XM-409 rounds."

"Yes, sir."

"In turn, fire for soft targets against personnel and crowds. Then the canister round."

"The real man-breaker stuff, sir?"

It was a blunt-nosed bullet, sent by TECOM, that exploded